THE LOST BOY
OF SANTA CHIONIA

THE LOST BOY

OF SANTA CHIONIA

Juliet Grames

ALFRED A. KNOPF

NEW YORK

2024

THIS IS A BORZOI BOOK PUBLISHED BY ALFRED A. KNOPF

Copyright © 2024 by Juliet Grames

All rights reserved. Published in the United States by Alfred A. Knopf, a division of
Penguin Random House LLC, New York, and distributed in Canada by
Penguin Random House Canada Limited, Toronto.

www.aaknopf.com

Knopf, Borzoi Books, and the colophon are registered trademarks of
Penguin Random House LLC.

Sappho's "Fragment 84" from *Sappho: A New Translation,* translated by Mary Barnard,
used with permission from Literary Executor of the Estate of Mary Barnard and from the
University of California Books Division.

LIBRARY OF CONGRESS CATALOGING-IN-PUBLICATION DATA
Names: Grames, Juliet, author.
Title: The lost boy of Santa Chionia / Juliet Grames.
Description: New York : Alfred A. Knopf, 2024.
Identifiers: LCCN 2023048798 (print) | LCCN 2023048799 (ebook) |
ISBN 9780593536179 (hardcover) | ISBN 9780593536186 (ebook)
Subjects: LCGFT: Novels.
Classification: LCC PS3607.R356 L67 2024 (print) | LCC PS3607.R356 (ebook) |
DDC 813/.6—dc23/eng/20231019
LC record available at https://lccn.loc.gov/2023048798
LC ebook record available at https://lccn.loc.gov/2023048799

Jacket image: *Palizzi, Calabria* by M. C. Escher © 2023 The M. C. Escher Company—
The Netherlands. All rights reserved.
Jacket design by Jenny Carrow
Map illustration by Katherine Grames

Manufactured in the United States of America
FIRST EDITION

This book is dedicated to its grandparents
Nancy L. & Paul V. Oliver
Linda D. C. & Michael F. Grames
who among them gave me the blood and breath to write it.

La disperazione più grave che possa impadronirsi d'una società
è il dubbio che vivere rettamente sia inutile.

The deepest despair that can take hold of a society
is the fear that living honestly is futile.

—CORRADO ALVARO

CONTENTS

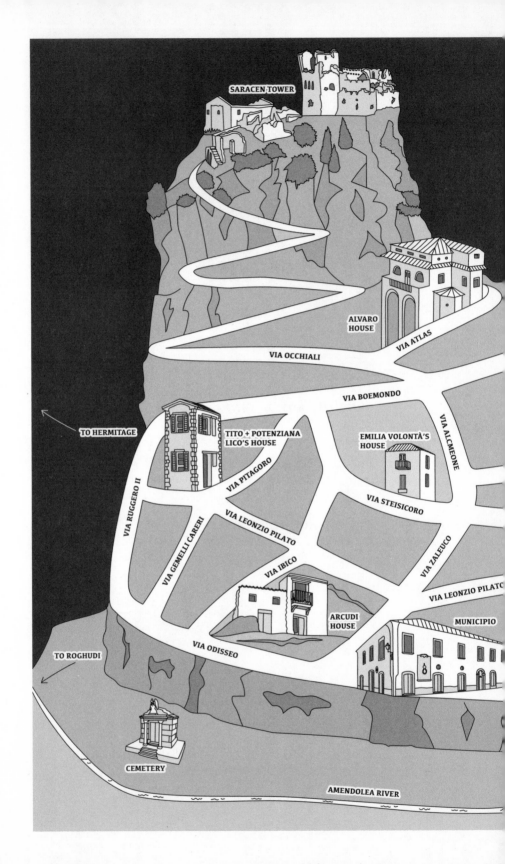

WHERE
IS
LEO
ROMEO?

1

MY FATHER USED TO TELL ME THAT GROWING UP MEANT UNDERstanding who was at fault wasn't what mattered; what mattered was who had to pay the consequences. "Some people never grow up, Francesca," he'd say, and when I remember his words I still hear his voice—a nasal baritone one might not expect from such a large man. "Some people grow old still pointing their fingers, or waiting for justice to bring down its hammer. But finding a culpable party doesn't fix a problem. A grownup is someone who knows when to take action, and who knows how to manage consequences."

I inherited my father's fondness for aphorisms; I scrutinize myself through their lenses even if I don't entirely subscribe to the aphorisms themselves. I've often wondered, for example, if my father's brand of grown-up ever puts away the guilt they accrue for those consequences they somehow know how to "manage."

I've been plagued of late with the urge to tell the story of the year I grew up—the story of what happened in Santa Chionia that winter of 1960–1961, when I was twenty-seven years old. I was a bluestocking with big dreams for building a better world, one needy child at a time; my training had prepared me to weather many forms of calamity, but not, it turned out, evidence of cold-blooded murder. When the time came for that, I had to wing it.

I've waited almost too long to make a record of these events, in part because I have been haunted by my role in them. I could have taken the true story of the Lost Boy of Santa Chionia to the grave, the way so many good Calabrian women have taken their dirty secrets: women like Cicca Casile, like Emilia Volontà, like Donna Adelina Alvaro.

But I am not a good Calabrian woman. I'm an American, and we Americans, culturally denatured as we are accused of being, sometimes struggle with concepts like honor and tradition. I've decided I'd rather dishonor myself and come clean, now that the price of the truth is mine alone to pay.

Back in the autumn of 1960, there was a village named Santa Chionia nestled in the remote heart of the Aspromonte massif in southern Calabria. The catastrophic flood that would exhume an unidentified skeleton and rewrite the village's fate began on October 11, six weeks after I arrived with my nursery school charter and my relentless idealism.

The village flooded every year, my landlady told me, ever since the Saracens and the Greeks had battled each other for the fertile valleys below. October would come and the rain would slalom through the streets for a few soggy, burbling days, topping up the summer-empty cistern and causing the mountain to bloom with mushrooms. For nine hundred years, this battle-hardened people had battened down for the ordeal and then cleaned up when the storm had passed. Life went on, as life always did, unless it didn't.

But something had changed after the war. The weather patterns—like a few other things—had taken a turn for the worse. The autumn rains no longer glided harmlessly through the village but boiled into landslides, sluicing through stone walls, rocking foundations in their mortar sockets like teeth in a geriatric shepherd's loose gums.

The day the rain began, I had been impressed by its volume; it became annoying on the second day, as it settled into unbailable puddles and the smell of unemptyable chamber pots permeated the kitchen. It had taken me, daughter of privilege, three days to understand that the rain was terrifying. That help was not coming—that help could not get here.

"You see what it's like now," my landlady, Cicca, said as the flood roared down the packed-dirt alley, ricocheting off residences before bursting through the city wall and plunging into the ravine. "It's because of your American bombs," she explained. "You knocked down one of the cliffs that used to hold back the floodwaters."

Cicca Casile was a somewhat insane, generally disagreeable woman of approximately five feet in height who wore her steel-gray hair in a short, masculine pompadour. No one else remembered the Americans bombing this part of the Aspromonte. But Cicca relished being offended by me and my large-footed, immodest Yankee ways, and I recognized it was within my power to bestow a small joy on her dingy, combative little life by letting her.

After four days of being locked together in a fug of increasingly personal aromas, Cicca and I had managed to suppress our mutual antipathy and to pass the time together. Night and day had been suspended in the interminable pounding and the howling half dark, and I felt I might be going mad. We sat with a pine sap lamp burning between us in her second-floor salon, redolent with the wet-dog smell of rennet. Even over that I caught the oily scent of Cicca's scalp, peachily visible in the space between her rather far-flung follicles. We stared perversely out her house's single glass window as if we were watching the evening news— not that Cicca had ever imagined such an object as a television. The glass creaked in the window frame. The roof of old Gerasimo's house below us, only forty feet away, was invisible except when the wind blew through so fiercely that it cut open the wall of water.

"What if roofs collapse?" I was picturing the decrepitude of Santa Chionia's lower alleys. "If this goes on much longer people will die."

"Of course they will die, how could they not?" Cicca shouted over the clobbering of the rain. "Maybe we will all die this time."

Technically it was the second time in my twenty-seven years that death had breathed down my neck, but I'd been unconscious the first time, and so had lacked the interval for end-of-life introspection that being caught in an ongoing natural disaster afforded me. I found myself disappointingly unphilosophical about the whole thing. This might be the end of my story, a Barnard grad from Pennsylvania, washed away by a flood that everyone should have been able to predict was coming. I thought of the thousands of hours I'd apparently wasted on personal refinement so that I could go out into the world and make something of myself—on my doctoral studies in Oxford and Venice; on language study and posture training and calisthenics, in hopes that a more elegant package might make me likable. I had never felt less elegant, or less liked, than I did sitting in that cheese larder with Cicca, my skin rashing against undergarments stiff with four days' imprisonment. I tried hard to convince myself that I didn't regret leaving behind my embassy job in Rome—cushy Rome, with its aqueducts, just one of which would have been pretty useful up in the Aspromonte right then. In the face of my incipient demise, my rationale for devoting my life to charity work looked pretty flimsy.

I thought angrily about how I had never had a chance to be a mom. Well, that was out of my control. But I wished I hadn't dropped out of my history doctorate—I might have been an underpaid but much less irrigated junior professor by now. At the very least, I wished I'd had a chance to make some kind of impact here in Santa Chionia, if this whole adventure was going to cost me my life—to not die ingloriously and without struggle, as the Poet would have said, but to have managed to do some great thing.

I had to be brave—for my elderly landlady's sake if nothing else. I smiled at Cicca, doing my best to keep my terror out of my teeth. "I'm grateful to be sheltering with you here."

Cicca scowled at me. "It wasn't my idea," she said, and I laughed as if I thought she was kidding.

When the sky cleared, the flood of 1960 only left behind one corpse, and it had already been dead a long time. An enigma: nothing but bones, beginning with a femur I watched two boys pull from the rubble of the destroyed post office on Monday, October 17. It was not uncommon to find a femur among the shrubs, for the feral white cows that clambered over the mountain footpaths were clumsy and often plummeted to their deaths in the ravine. But this was not a cow femur—even I, city girl, knew by some atavistic instinct, my blood spooking through my veins as the boy climbed out of the tumbled stonework, brandishing his find like a pine resin torch. His shouts carried brightly through the windless mountain morning.

The men who would be called upon to solve big problems in the village were all within earshot, and they began to trickle into the piazza to see what the commotion was. I shall enumerate them so that you may decide which you consider suspect once we learn there had indeed been a murder—I hope you do better than I did:

First to arrive, dapper in his burgundy jacket, was the proprietor of the tavern-cum-general-store; he had only to cross the piazza. Then the sallow, black-coated municipal secretary, followed by the mayor, who was in the last weeks of his reelection campaign and was very much about town. So was the communist challenger, who canvassed in the piazza every morning. The one traffic cop probably *should* have been there but was not; however, there were two aging roustabouts I recognized because they were always in front of the tavern, as if they never had anywhere else to be, no goats to tend or gardens to till—the taller was easily spotted in any crowd because of his ears, which stuck out like the handlebars of a bicycle. And of course there was Don Tito "the Wolf" Lico, who had always been there, and always would be, long after Santa Chionia had seen its last of me.

Hanging back in the alley was the village's tawny stray dog, who watched with his black eyes bulging and his too-long tongue hanging out of his port-side jaw, where it had dried into a stiff and cracking black fossil.

The gathering included no females—not even the dog. Meanwhile the curtains on every balcony window trembled in the fervent breath of invisible spectators.

"Santa Chionia is a matriarchy," Don Pantaleone Bianco, the village priest, had told me. "Do not be confused by our machismo. It is women who have all the power in the family, and the family is everything here."

Don Pantaleone himself appeared at the wreckage of the post office only moments later. He must have come running all the way from the rectory but he bore no sign of exertion—one more of his suspicious charismas.

I watched from my shutter-shadow as the scene played out like a silent film. There was deliberation; then Mayor Stelitano and the priest followed the secretary back to the town hall, where, I could only assume, he placed a phone call to the *carabinieri* station three hours away. Saverio Legato, the *puticha* proprietor, reluctantly returned to his shop, but the other men stood guard until the remains were collected by the proper authorities.

At that moment in my sheltered and orderly life, the idea that the "proper authorities" might not be the police did not cross my mind. I went back to work with my usual single-mindedness, never imagining that the only person who would ever investigate the skeleton's circumstances would be me.

2

HOW HAD I, AN AMERICAN COLLEGE GIRL, ARRIVED AT A MOUN-tain precipice in the remotest hinterlands of Italy, in this village "forgotten by God and by man"? Well, on foot, for there was no other way to get there (technically I had declined the offer of a donkey).

On Tuesday, August 30, 1960, I had first made the three-hour mountain-cresting journey from the village of Bova, where the nearest drivable road ended. I was escorted by Dr. Teodoro Iiriti, the kind, bluff-faced cardiologist who had first petitioned my employer, the charity fund Child Rescue, to assign an agent to his indigent hometown; accompanying us were two nuns from the Bova convent. Chaperones. It was 1960 across the rest of the world, or at least some parts of it. But in the Aspromonte it was the Aspromonte.

I was not prepared for Santa Chionia—but what could have prepared me? Nothing anyone had told me turned out to be untrue, not even the things that contradicted each other. Santa Chionia tolerated no discomfort with paradox.

She emerged from the valley as her virgin martyr namesake must have emerged from a bath, springing up abrupt and dripping behind the mountain dewlaps that shielded her from the lascivious view of the sea. The rising sun glinted off her façades. The suddenness—where there had been only the thick silence of the mountains, now there was an ancient civilization.

The *paese* was an island cut from the mountainside, its medieval stone houses tessellated directly into the cliffs. The habitable area for eighteen hundred souls, if souls one believes in, was delimited by the eight-hundred-meter drop to the ravine. The Attinà waterfall, which separated Santa Chionia from the Bova road, had once crashed into the silver bed of the Amendolea River below. These days the Amendolea was a damp thread persevering through a rocky wash gorge whose immediate appeal must have been most obvious to aspiring suicides.

That anyone had chosen to try to live there—it was insane.

In my capacity as a nursery school teacher whose main purview here in Santa Chionia was to reduce its abysmal child mortality rate, my bleak first thought was that geography might play an irreversible role in those statistics. How the devil did mothers teach their toddlers not to tumble over the side?

I have always lived for the feeling of being overmatched by circumstance.

Our party had come to a standstill when we rounded the bend and Santa Chionia hove into view. I was aware that my native companions were no less awestruck.

"I—I almost can't see it," I managed. "It's so—it's so bright it disappears."

"That's the light of the Aspromonte," the doctor said, and the nuns murmured in agreement, *"La luce dell'Aspromonte."*

Three hours earlier, when we had set out from the doctor's house in Bova, I had watched this double-chinned and soft-fingered intellectual strap a rifle over his shoulder.

"There are wolves in the mountains," he'd explained, blasé. "You must never go out walking except in broad daylight, and never alone."

I had spent the plodding hours as we'd crested the foothills pondering whether the wolves had been a metaphor.

The wind cut past my ears so that all I could hear was its echo, like listening to the sea in a conch shell, but when it dropped away I caught the keen of women's voices, a lament in a minor key.

"That singing. Is it a funeral?"

"The beating of the broom plants," Sister Grazia replied. "Down in the riverbed—it is difficult labor. The women sing to make the day go faster."

I could see no women, only hear their eerie chant, and I had no idea what broom plants were. My mouth was dry of words.

I had to swallow my vertigo as we entered the *paese*. A concrete bridge broached the plummeting Attinà waterfall, connecting the donkey path from Bova to the escarpment of Santa Chionia's southeast wall.

"Built by an architect from Rome," the doctor told me. "Until 1955 there was no bridge here."

Sister Grazia added, "Just a plank of wood for the shepherds to get their goats across."

"A plank of wood?" Even the concrete beneath my feet seemed too flimsy to fight the gravity. "Did no one ever fall?"

The doctor and the nuns laughed out loud this time. "Of course they fell," chirped Sister Maria. "How could they not?"

Six weeks and five days later, when the October rains had finally stopped, the first person to visit our dreary prison was Cicca's evil neighbor, Mela, with the news that the Bova bridge had been destroyed by the flooded cataract. Now that single access point that had once connected Santa Chionia to the rest of the human world was an eight-foot stretch of watery head-smashing death.

Desperate to stretch my legs, or perhaps to relish the absurdity of my new challenges, I skidded down the muddied marble of via Sant'Orsola, the village's main "street," an accordion of steps that fanned through the center of town down to the destruction of the piazza. I followed the city wall east, past the gap the landslide had blasted through the stonework. I stopped to stare at the void in respectful alarm—from a safe distance, behind the surviving northwest corner of what had once been the post office. Under that pile of mortar not ten feet from my saddle shoes, unbeknownst to me, lay the skeleton that would haunt me for the rest of my tenure in Santa Chionia—really, for the rest of my life. At the time, in my innocence, I thought the worst thing I had to worry about was whether the damage to the piazza would prevent me from opening my nursery school on time.

My nursery school building, directly across from the post office, was untouched—a miracle for which I was grateful. The same could not be said for many of the buildings in the stooping cavelike slums of the lower alleys. I followed via Odisseo toward the exploded masonry that had once been the Bova bridge and gawped at the empty space over which I had so recently, so hubristically, walked.

There was no way in or out of Santa Chionia anymore, thanks to the flood. Or, more accurately, thanks to a century of state neglect. It was 1960, and in Rome the Italian Space Research Council was developing a satellite to launch into orbit; meanwhile the Chionoti had no plumbing, no school, no road to connect them to opportunity.

I stared at the rushing waterfall, thinking of civilization so impossibly far away.

I was trapped in Santa Chionia, but there was nowhere in the world I was more needed. So I concluded without a self-preserving modicum of irony. After all, what is altruism but egotism?

It is hard, writing this, to resist sugarcoating my youthful self's naivete. But it does neither you nor me any good to pretend that I was prepared for that skeleton.

3

"THE BRIDGE TO BOVA IS OUT, YOU KNOW," DOTTOR TEODORO Iiriti said when he arrived at the rectory for our weekly lunch. "A damned inconvenience. I had to drive all the way to Roccaforte and walk."

That would have been two hours of climbing through the gorge. The doctor's portliness didn't suggest an athletic constitution, but everyone I ever met in the Aspromonte was a "walker," to use their terminology. An American might have said "mountaineer."

"And then the mayor dragged me down to look at that skeleton so I can write up a medical certificate for the police report."

"Lucky you were here." Don Pantaleone Bianco, the parish priest, gestured to a chair and the doctor settled his bulk into it. "Otherwise who would have done it?"

The doctor and the priest were the two men responsible for my being in Santa Chionia. In September 1959, Dottor Iiriti had attended a benefit gala in Rome, where he met my boss, Sabrina Mento. One of those fateful rapturous conversations of mutual assurances had ensued. The doctor pressed his friend Don Pantaleone to put together the formal petition requesting the installation of a Child Rescue nursery school. One year later, here I was.

At the priest's urging, I took my usual seat. "Cicca told me it floods like this every year?"

"Well, this year was worse than most," Don Pantaleone said.

"Not the worst!"

"Not the worst," the priest conceded. "Nineteen fifty-four was very bad, and of course 1951. That was the year Africo and Casalinuovo were destroyed."

Dottor Iiriti held up a warning finger. "Excuse me. The towns were *not* destroyed. That is propaganda. They were *abandoned*."

"The government calls it transferment," the priest explained to me. "The Italian state is always pushing us to transfer from our mountain villages down to the coast for our safety and convenience."

"Ha!" the doctor barked. "Safety and convenience! Those poor Africo people are living like refugees in roadside camps a decade later, waiting for the state to find them a new home!"

"Wait." I was thinking of how much of Child Rescue's precious funding I had already spent on my nursery school. "Are you saying there is a chance the population is going to be removed from Santa Chionia?"

The priest must have seen the alarm on my face. "Don't worry, *maestra,* Santa Chionia will *never* agree to transferment."

"One hopes," the doctor said. "But who can say? We can't control the weather. Our summers never used to be this long or this hot. Look at this!" He gestured to the priest's centerpiece, a fruit arrangement, as Don Pantaleone's ancient housekeeper placed a bowl of soup in front of him. "Figs in October?" He lifted a spoonful to his mouth immediately, behavior which my mother, had she been there, would not have allowed to pass without a corrective tongue cluck. "In any case, foolish to hide a body under the post office."

Dottor Iiriti's turn of phrase—*hide a body*—gave me the opening to ask the question that had been preoccupying me all morning. "So was someone murdered?"

"Of course not." The men spoke in such emphatic unity they might have been a church choir. "Things like that don't happen here," the doctor declared, waving his chubby fingers, as the priest was shaking his gray-streaked curls, saying, "In a town this size?"

"I've never seen the two of you agree on something before," I teased. My curiosity, however, was privately turning in darker directions.

"We are a tight-knit community of simple Christians, *maestra,*" Don Pantaleone said. "We are goatherds and farmers. All over Italy they think we Calabresi are criminals and lunatics, when you have seen for yourself we are peace-loving family men."

The aged housekeeper was standing at my side with a bowl of soup. As she set it down, she caught my eye in a way that felt meaningful. *"Cheràmine,"* I said proudly—*thank you* in Greco, the local language, which I had been practicing—and she gave me a grave nod before retiring to stand by the wall.

"This is the safest village in the world." The doctor dropped his spoon with a clatter so that he could mesh his fingers together. "We are like *this,*" he said, shaking his tangled hands at me. "One family with endless ties of blood and marriage. We all protect one another."

"All right, Teo." The priest chuckled gently. "*Maestra,* eat before your lunch gets cold."

"So, then, but—" I tried. "If someone wasn't murdered, why would there be a body under the post office?"

"Any number of reasons," Don Pantaleone said. "There have been priests who have been uncompassionate about who they allow to be buried in consecrated ground. It can be a real tragedy for a family, a draconian village priest." Don Pantaleone Bianco had not chosen that fire-and-brimstone role for himself. He opted instead to cut more of a handsome-favorite-uncle figure, with none of the eggplant silhouette one becomes accustomed to in priests. I'd thought since I first saw him that there was something a bit too sexy about him. He was trim, "a mountain man" is how he described himself, and the tightness of his arm muscles shifted discernibly—just short of obscenely—under the black silk of his cassock when he orated. Despite his appearance, though, I had found no evidence that he was taking sexual advantage of his flock, as small-town priests in his position sometimes did. Don Pantaleone didn't even seem to be embezzling tithe money for private use; the tithing basket wasn't passed during mass, since almost no one in Santa Chionia had any money to put in it. What was a good-looking man with no dark secrets doing devoting his celibate life to God in such a forsaken place? I had not yet concluded my inquiry.

"The body might have been buried during the war," the doctor said. "When so many Christians die in such a short time, funerary traditions fall apart." His thick black eyebrows lifted together like the beat of a butterfly's wings as he sank a crust of bread into his bowl. "In 1943 there was a cholera epidemic here. A quarter of the village died. A medical tragedy, cholera in the mountains—unheard of. It was a terrible time."

I knew about the cholera epidemic. The village's sanitary history had been a large part of Child Rescue's decision to send me here. "No one knows who the skeleton is?"

"No one has come forward." Don Pantaleone gestured to my bowl. "Eat, Franca. Don't be polite."

The soup revealed itself to be bean and borage—I was new to many of the mountain herbs the Chionesi ate, but this one was spiky and pock-marked in a way I recognized from my landlady Cicca's cooking. "So that will be the end of it? No investigation?"

"The *carabinieri* will investigate, when they get around to it," Dottor Iiriti replied, then said to the priest, "I have a medical evaluation you must give the police. I can't deliver it myself, as Ippolita and I are headed back to Rome tomorrow." The doctor was a cardiac specialist who spent most of the year at the Sapienza University research clinic.

"Tomorrow!" The priest refilled the doctor's wineglass. "And then you're not back until Christmas?"

"Unless I am unlucky and dragged into an inquest." The doctor laughed dourly and wiped his mouth. "You must do what you can to spare me that annoyance, Pandalemu."

"Will it affect me, the skeleton?" I asked. "I mean, will it affect the nursery? Will the police need to investigate my building, too? Or—"

"No, no, no," both men spoke again in their uncanny unison.

"You'll have no problems," Don Pantaleone assured me, and the doctor echoed, "No problems at all."

4

LEAVING THE RECTORY, I LINGERED IN THE CHURCH PIAZZA. I extracted my student application file from my briefcase and leaned against the stone baluster that capped via Sant'Orsola. As I flipped through my notes, reminding myself of my to-do list, the warm mortar was grainy against my tweed jacket. The swarming hills glowed green with last week's rain and the afternoon sun twinkled on their tree-lined flanks. My heart stung with melancholy.

The best nepenthe for a broken heart is hard work—no possibility of overdose.

The only clock in town, on the modest bell tower above me, said it was almost three. Instead of going back to my desk this gorgeous afternoon, I would drop by some of the addresses I had culled from the housing register and see if I couldn't solicit a few more student applications for the nursery school I would be opening in January. Just down via Ruggero II was a *MAFRICI, SALVINO,* three years old, a prime candidate. I had not yet spoken about my project to his mother, *DOMENICA,* or her husband, *CORRADO,* employment listed as *SHEPHERD.*

Today was their day.

I experienced the usual challenges in locating no. 24 via Ruggero II— civic addresses were not held in high esteem; few houses displayed their number, and plenty of people willfully denied knowing their own address. I navigated around a roadblock of three wild white cows, chewing menacingly on a shining acanthus. After some aimless blundering up the tilting dirt alley, I resorted to the age-old fail-safe: calling out to an old woman propped in a doorway spinning hemp.

"Good afternoon, *gnura!*" I tried, first in Calabrese, then in my beginner's Greco.

The woman gave me a deep nod. Her eyes were a snowy blue two shades lighter than the cloudless sky.

"I'm looking for the Mafrici family."

"You've found us." A thirty-something woman appeared in the doorway, a baby in the crook of her elbow. This, I knew from the register, would be ten-month-old *VINCENZO.* He was a gorgeous baby, impish and dark. "You're Maestra Francesca. Come in, teacher, come in."

Encouraged by the warm welcome, I followed her into her house, a single all-purpose room with a dirt floor. The shutters were open to the southwest, letting in the bright mountain light, but even so the room felt like a cave, the eight-foot ceiling black with soot from the floor hearth, on which a lentily-looking pot was cooking. Two black-haired girls— *MARIA,* eleven, and *ANTONELLA,* ten—whispered polite greetings from their textiling stations against the stone wall. One was stitching a shirtsleeve; the other was shuttle-picking at a linen loom. Two chickens bathed in the dirt under the treadle, which her feet barely reached. I would have wished the girls were in school if there had been a school for them to go to. Three-year-old Salvino sat cross-legged on the pallet bed. One child was missing: *DOMENICO,* six; if I had to put money on his whereabouts, I'd guess down in the lower piazza, where there was an ongoing game of Brigand King.

"Sit, *maestra.*" The woman's torso was encased in an inexpertly crocheted yellow sweater, which underserved her dainty face. "What can I offer you? Coffee?" She pressed her left wrist, the one not holding the baby, against her forehead, shoving a black curl behind her ear. "Maria, go fetch some cheese from the loft. Antonella, hold this baby so I can cut up some bread."

"No, please, Gnura Domenica, the coffee is more than enough," I said hastily, before the obedient daughters upset their work on my behalf.

"Mica, *maestra*. Please call me Mica."

"Then call me Franca." To put her at ease, I smiled a goofy, cheek-lifting American smile—the kind no one in the Aspromonte but a baby would return. The baby in her arms, for example, did. "Will that baby come to me? I love babies."

"I think so. He's not so picky, the little monkey."

I set my briefcase on the uneven floor and hooked my thumbs under the little guy's armpits. He tolerated my swinging him through the air, then rewarded me with a giggle after I'd settled him against my ribs. My whole torso was hot with his gentle trust.

"Speaking of monkeys . . ." With my free hand, I undid the clasps on my briefcase and pulled out the stuffed monkey I'd hidden inside. "Look what I have." I turned toward the bed, where the three-year-old was watching me with too-large eyes. "Are you Salvino?"

He said, barely audibly, "Yes."

"Salvino, come meet my friend Zuzu." I held out the monkey, a knock-off of Zippy from *The Ed Sullivan Show;* where the official toy had black letters spelling "ZIP" across its yellow T-shirt, mine only had the letter Z. A box of fake Zippys had arrived in the donations at the Cosenza clinic right as I was packing to come to Santa Chionia. "Don't be shy."

Salvino was playing cautiously with the monkey when his skinny mother set a barley coffee in front of me. On the saucer was a tiny wooden spoon intricately carved with geometric patterns.

"You're very good with children, Maestra Franca."

I stifled the pride the compliment caused to bubble up in my belly. "I've had lots of practice in my job. Do you know why I'm here, Mica?"

"To open a school?"

"A nursery school, actually. And your Salvino is the right age to attend."

I explained Child Rescue's mission, to reduce child mortality through the disbursal of medical and educational services in the townships where children were most vulnerable. I described what the nursery school would offer its pupils: nutritious lunches; pedagogically directed playtime; hygienic education for both students and parents, that they might help their village rise above its atrocious circumstances. Though I didn't put it that way to Mica.

"What do you think? I hope you'll apply."

"Apply—what do you mean?"

"There's a simple form. I have one here right now." As the baby tugged curiously at my hair, I took one of the typed questionnaires out of my briefcase. "I'd be happy to help you fill it out. You can bring it down to the nursery any weekday between eight and five."

There should have been no written application, of course, especially in a village like Santa Chionia, with a high level of illiteracy. Why did we risk shutting out some of the neediest with gatekeeping deterrents? But back in 1960 we didn't yet understand how humanitarianism could be a form of colonial violence—or at least we weren't admitting it. Sabrina insisted on protocol, in this as in all things. She believed every parent needed to demonstrate they were willing to work for the services we were bestowing on them. It was the ineradicable streak of patrician in her. And I always did what Sabrina said. Usually.

Mica studied the form. "I can do this." Her fingernails were clean. It required pathological fastidiousness to keep one's fingernails clean in a waterless village. This Mica was going to be a soldier in my war against infant mortality in Santa Chionia.

"That's wonderful. But, Mica, we do have some hygienic requirements."

"Hygienic requirements?" she said nervously.

I had to be careful not to embarrass her in front of her children. "We need to know parents are reinforcing the child's education at home." I gave her my big smile again. "You're almost there. It'll be just a few changes."

Mica's bulging goiter, a product of her iodine-deficient mountain diet, bobbed in her slender neck as she swallowed. "Changes? Like what?"

"Well, we have to get the animals out of your living space."

"Out of the house?" Her face contracted in dismay. "Even the chickens?"

"You'll see the results right away. You won't have to delouse the children anymore, and the fleas will disappear. You'll all get fewer colds in the winter. Everything will smell better. Your cooking will taste better."

"But *maestra,* we have no land. Where will I put them?"

I stood up, jouncing the squirming baby. He placed his warm little palm flat on my chest, and I felt my heart right under it tighten. "Let's step outside. I bet we can figure out a solution."

The garden was small, terraced against a retaining wall that plummeted a vertiginous twenty feet into the backyard of the neighbors on the street below. Salvino trotted along behind us, Zuzu clutched to his chest.

Mica's face wrinkled in worried exhaustion as we discussed where she could build a coop for the chickens, how she would keep them from destroying her grass peas. She was only three or four years older than I but it felt like a generation gap—my modernity and her life experience a chasm between us.

I took her hand in my free one. "Listen, Mica, you have a beautiful family and an exemplary home. Together we can make huge changes here in Santa Chionia."

"Maestra Franca, can I ask—you're American?"

"I am. From Philadelphia."

"But you sound like a Calabrese." Mica gave me a searching little smile. "You don't look Calabrese, but you sound like us."

I felt my ears redden with pleasure. I owed my linguistic facility to my mother, who had brought me up speaking her native dialect in no small part so she could complain about my father (not that he listened, which was the heart of the problem). The affirmation that my accent wasn't as bad as my aunts claimed it was warmed my heart.

"Look Calabrese," I scoffed. "What does that mean? Calabresi look like everything."

"They don't look like you, *maestra.*"

"Well, my mother is Calabrese, and everyone says I am just like her." Technically people said I *acted* just like her; in fact, I had a lot of my Nor-

wegian father's physicality back then, his ash-wood coloring, his broad
shoulders and heavy bones. It was a body type that had suited me well
when I had rowed competitively at Oxford, though it had never helped
me fit in with a crowd, particularly not in southern Italy.

"Well," Mica said, "if your mother is Calabrese, you are Calabrese just
the same."

There was a tugging on my jacket sleeve, and I looked down to see
Salvino's upturned face. "Here is your friend Zuzu, *maestra*." His words
were clear and precise for a three-year-old's.

I resisted reaching out to stroke his worried little brow. "No, Salvino,
he's your friend Zuzu now." I looked forward to being his teacher.

5

WHEN I LOCKED UP THE NURSERY AT FIVE P.M., TURI LAGANÀ, THE
lanky gray-haired tavern-loiterer with the absurd ears, was standing in
front of the rubble of the post office, his arms crossed over his chest and
his feet spread, a militant guarding stance—still waiting for the *carabinieri* to come collect the skeleton. With the bridge to Bova destroyed, I
realized, the law might not respond with the usual alacrity, modest as it
was.

I climbed up via Sant'Orsola, pausing, winded, in front of the church
to watch the sun set beyond the gorge, then persevered up Cicca's alley.
My neurotic little landlady was out, perhaps collecting acorns for the
pig or gossip-trading with her nemesis, the evil neighbor Mela. In the
wine-dark kitchen, I scrutinized the shadows to see what I might eat.
Although this house, unlike many, was outfitted with electricity, I knew
better than to turn on the light. The thought of wasted electricity terrorized Cicca, and no emergency was sufficient to warrant its use. A single
bare bulb hung over the gas stove like a mysterious reliquary for a wire
saint; Cicca stood at the stove in front of it worshipfully for many hours
every day but never turned it on.

I located the black lentil bread under the discretion of a kitchen linen,
sawed myself off a piece, and tucked into my room. I had done little to
personalize it, since Cicca snuck in when I wasn't there and rearranged
all my things anyway. My one addition was a potted euphorbia—an elec-

tric green and yellow splash of color I had successfully transplanted from the sunbaked mountainside.

I fumbled with my Zippo in the dimness and lit the sap lamp on my desk, then lined up my evening tasks: my journal, which you can thank, ironically or not, for the bones of this text; next, a clean page of stationery already addressed to *Dearest Sabrina,* on which I would record a slightly sanitized version of what had transpired during the previous week; and the birthday card for my mother, to be crammed with strictly joyful-sounding adventures lest her incendiary fatalism set in.

As I opened my journal I relived Mica's compliment, which I had let burn like a campfire coal in my drafty heart. *You're very good with children, Maestra Franca.*

It was a bittersweet distinction, and hard-won. Not even three years ago, children had terrified me. They symbolized weakness and subjection, a triumph of base biology over discipline and accomplishment. Until I was twenty-five, I had never even held a baby—a byproduct of being a spoiled only child. I was a narrow-minded silver-spoon twit.

My very first day at work at the baby clinic in Campobasso, Sabrina Mento had cracked open my personal taboos. The movie reel of that moment still reruns so clearly in my mind: the role of Francesca Loftfield played by a dirty-blond giantess with an incredulously sagging mouth; placid, stout Sabrina, her glossy black hair in a businesslike ponytail, levering a three-month-old into the arms of the former much as one would transfer a watermelon at a picnic.

"You won't break her," Sabrina had assured me. "They're sturdy things, babies."

Stock-still with fear, I held the swaddled baby, hot as a manicotti, while Sabrina examined her mother for a milk duct infection. Every nerve in my upper body was pinched with stress, every muscle about to cramp. I felt abandoned, armless, and also like god.

At the end of the mother's appointment, Sabrina came to collect the baby and wrinkled her squat nose. "There is a soiled diaper in that bundle, Teresa. Franca will change her for you." She'd given me a reassuring smile. "We'll do it together."

I watched in a state of high anxiety as Sabrina untucked the cloth-bound mess, held up the now-crying baby's ankles to show me how to wipe. "Nothing that comes out of a baby's innocent little body should scare you," she chided. "As long as you wash your hands."

I held those little ankles bracketed between my fingers, just as Sabrina showed me, and wiped that innocent bottom clean. I have thought of Sabrina every time I've changed a diaper, because she was the one who taught me how. I believe that would have made her happy, to know that I think of her every time I see a baby's naked bum.

Two years and hundreds of diapers later, I was a different person. I was wonderstruck by children, by their quick and secretive minds, by their heart-turning resilience and the gift of their trust. They were a field of study more fascinating than any obscure texts over which I had once labored during my doctoral research.

By the time I arrived in Santa Chionia, I knew already that I would never have my own—not given my marital status and the price of my past mistakes. But women like Mica privileged me with the sacred task of educating theirs.

Sabrina Mento had found me in Rome in September 1958, at a fund-raising soirée at a senator's house. Back then I was answering phones at the US embassy by day, and by night stumping around the slums in the shadow of the Vatican helping my fellow receptionist Maria Luisa evangelize vaginal suppository contraceptives, quasi-illegally. I was twenty-five years old and nursing a specific kind of broken heart. The night of that party, I approached Sabrina because she was standing so humbly against the floral wallpaper that I thought I was being compassionate.

Sabrina Mento was not like other Italian gentility. The well-heeled ladies I'd met had been largely of one impressive piece: austere, decisive, any one of them ready to go head-to-head with Babe Paley and emerge from combat unruffled, unless strictly theatrically. Sabrina was different—soft-spoken, diffident, chubby as an American. If I were to be honest I would use the chauvinist word "dowdy" to describe her, but I cannot, in good conscience, be honest. It would be, besides, like applying that adjective to a Brazilian wandering spider, fuzzy and patient in a blush of bananas—technically precise but fatally misguided.

By the time we left the party I had fallen in love with Sabrina's world-view: dazzling, compassion-soaked, mule-headed optimism. Ten hours later I'd packed two suitcases—abandoning all my other impedimenta in our Trastevere apartment—quit my coveted embassy job, and followed Sabrina to the Mezzogiorno as her assistant.

What Sabrina had accomplished for Child Rescue was nothing short of miraculous. Since 1947, she had opened twenty nursery schools and infant clinics, plowing through the meridional war wreckage in a second-hand car, huffing unfitly up bombed-out hillsides to carry powdered milk and medical supplies to derelict orphanages.

The condition of the Italian south after the war was grim—I am prone to hyperbole, but I feel subdued as I try to think of an adjective that comes closer to capturing the truth. Specific to Child Rescue's eponymous mission: the streets were full of children sporting kwashiorkor potbellies and spackled with impetigo, burrowed by worms and empearled by lice. They squatted pantsless in the streets and reeked poignantly of stowaway diarrhea; their pathogenically rich diets caused constant inflammation in their runny tummies.

At the baby clinic, Sabrina and I treated children with basic nonpharmaceutical remedies, organized vaccinations with visiting doctors, glad-handed with Cadbury Dairy Milk and bars of soap. We campaigned for funding, taught nighttime alphabet classes, looked women in the eye and outlined the mechanics of contraceptive methods that could be undertaken with or without the cooperation of one's husband.

We could not Rescue every Child, of course. Between the high price of antibiotics and the scarcity of medical professionals, some victims of fate—the tuberculars, the typhoids—were beyond our help. But the ones who died during our acquaintance—I still remember their names, sixty-five years later.

All our work was complicated by circumstance: No water, no electricity. One disgruntled doctor assigned to every third township. There was the mind-numbing arbitrariness of Italian bureaucracy, which I feel too tired to even go into here; the constant undermining of all progressive efforts by politicians and priests; the whimsical extortionists, who ranged from petty syndicates to the telephone company. And fatally, the indefinite delay on the receipt of any international funds. My heart muscle never recovered from the vicissitudes of waiting for a vacationing government official to approve the release of monies while a human life hung in the balance.

"You cannot let yourself fall into bad habits," Sabrina admonished me. "You will be frustrated by the limitations of what you can offer, but everything has to follow procedure. Their need is a bottomless well that you can't fill. If you dump your whole self into it you'll use yourself up. Then you're no good to anyone."

A more egregious pot-and-kettle tableau Michelangelo himself could not have painted. "I am only trying to keep up with you!" I retorted.

She patted her round belly. "Keep up with me! Silly Francesca." Sabrina was asthmatic, but she tackled tasks with the mettle of a Marine, wheezing into the wind as she trooped up steep hillsides, hairline turning chili pepper red when she squatted to be eye level with her favorite scamps. "Listen. If you want to lead a life of true activism on behalf of others, you must think of yourself not as an engine of change but a conduit. You are not a battery; you are a wire. The energy for change flows *through* you, not from you. You are there to complete the circuit."

In July 1960, Child Rescue approved a petition to open a nursery school in the province of Reggio, in the heart of the Area Grecanica, only a hundred miles from the village where my mother had been born. "It will be two years of discomfort for you, Francesca," Sabrina told me when I accepted the transfer. "I don't think there are many agents who could take this assignment." A transparent and effective appeal to my ego. "These people have suffered. The child mortality rate has been over forty percent."

I swallowed to loosen the seizure in my own throat. "The ones who have suffered most are the ones who need us most," I replied. There was no bravery about it; it was a Pavlovian call-and-response.

I stuffed my bags with bars of Camay and toy monkeys. I knew the kinds of obstacles I would face. I would be distrusted, demoralized, and discomfited. But if I succeeded in Santa Chionia—if I won the respect of the people, if they let me and my sponsors bring a bit of modernity to their difficult existence—I could reroute the future for a whole generation. I would save children's lives.

"Nothing will go as you plan" were Sabrina's last words to me when we parted ways. She'd smiled her closed-eyed smile. "Stick to your protocols and make no exceptions. *No exceptions.*"

6

IT WAS ON TUESDAY, OCTOBER 18, THAT I MADE MY FIRST EXCEPtion to one of Sabrina's rules with respect to the skeleton of Santa Chionia. The rule in question was *Do not provide assistance with anything that is not directly related to your mission,* and I had seen Sabrina herself break it about twice a day. I made my first exception casually, arrogantly unmindful of possible consequences.

That damn skeleton.

The day started out inauspiciously, with one of Cicca's prophetic dreams. "Peppinedda came to me last night," she said as she presented me with my coffee—ersatz, of course, made of barley. "It's going to rain all day, Peppinedda warned me. 'Make sure Maestra Franca carries her umbrella!' Peppinedda told me."

Peppinedda, Cicca's long-dead sister, took a curiously prescriptive interest in me from whatever apparently permeable afterlife Cicca imagined she had gone to.

"Thank you for the warning," I said. The strip of alley visible through the kitchen window was cheerfully bright with autumn sun. "I will bring my umbrella."

The deal between us went like this: I paid Cicca five thousand lire each week, more or less ten dollars at that moment in Italy's dizzying currency-exchange history. Cicca provided room and board, as long as I never, ever touched any of her pots, knives, or cleaning supplies. On the one hand it was an awkward arrangement for me, a grown woman, to have to turn over my dirty laundry for washing. On the other, I had my own room; Cicca Casile lived alone, for reasons I did not yet understand, in a two-bedroom house of postwar construction, one of few in all of Santa Chionia. Whatever the challenges of living with Cicca, they were more tolerable than sleeping in a one-room hut with a whole family.

Dropping onto the other stool, Cicca rubbed at the side of her cubeshaped head with the heel of her hand for a minute, then inquired, "Are you seeing the mayor today?" She wasn't impressed with me, but she was smug about my affiliation with the mayor.

"No, *cummàri.*" I swallowed with some difficulty—the black lentil bread was dense and particulate. "Not today. Limitri Palermiti is coming to tile the floors."

"No!" Even Cicca's short hair seemed to be standing at attention. "You can't!"

"What?" I asked, alarmed. "Why?"

"You can't tile in the rain!" Cicca clutched her face in both hands. "The mortar will never set! This must be why Peppinedda warned me!"

There was nothing to be won by engaging with Cicca. Instead I said, "Oh no, I guess I better figure out what's to be done." I stuffed the rest of the bread in my mouth as a conversational prophylactic and headed out, umbrella ostentatiously in tow.

The October morning was clean and green, the quiet dirt streets already sunbaked. At my footsteps, sunning brown lizards scattered into clumps of dill-feathery yellow ferule. I turned down via Sant'Orsola, where barefoot children watched me from doorways. I called out *"Ciao!"* and they ducked their heads. Old women sat spinning on stoops; young women undulated up via Sant'Orsola in the opposite direction with barrels on their heads, coming back from the cataract on yet another water run. They were slender, Chionote women, one and all—they lived on mountain grasses and lentil bread, they walked miles just to have water to boil their barley coffee or wash their babies' bottoms.

"Good morning, *gnura!*" I called out to each of them, if I didn't know her name.

"Good morning, *maestra!*" they called back.

I met few men. Some Chionoti men did farmwork in the olive and bergamot groves, but the vast majority were shepherds, away with their flocks for months at a time in the massif interior, where they slept in moss-covered paddock huts and crossed the treacherous forest paths to sell ricotta at the markets in Locri or Oppido.

At the bottom of Sant'Orsola, the stray dog with the too-long tongue was standing by the nursery door, his head cocked as if he was waiting for me. "You," I said, mournful that I hadn't saved any of the bread, and scratched his forehead.

I let myself into the nursery, a Fascist-era brick block that had been built as a *carabinieri* barracks. For nine years, two gendarmes had been stationed in Santa Chionia, protecting or oppressing the local population, depending on your viewpoint. They had both died in the cholera epidemic of 1943, and no replacements had been sent; Santa Chionia's only approximation of law enforcement these days was Officer Vadalà, the traffic cop. That was a no-show job if ever I heard of one: there was no traffic in Santa Chionia, as there was no street wide enough to accommodate a vehicle of any kind, or even the umbrella Cicca had made me carry if I tried to open it fully.

My first task in Santa Chionia had been to arrange the purchase, with Child Rescue funds, of this abandoned *carabinieri* building to repurpose as my nursery school. It was the one structurally sound modern building adaptable for my needs, but it wasn't the ideal space for nurturing tiny spirits, what with its martial feel and the mythic whiff of plague. I'd had my work cut out for me—work that had started with war against nature, hacking down brambles that had grown in the dirt floor and were bursting out the windows. I'd dislodged the resident bats, painted the walls, sourced a hodgepodge of furniture. I had far to go, but the floor tiling would be a big accomplishment.

Limitri Palermiti, the village shingle maker, did not arrive at eight as promised, which unfortunately was not a complete surprise. I gave him a grace period of one hour, then went out on the hunt.

Across the piazza at the *putìcha* the usual quorum of middle-aged men in black and brown caps was playing cards. Not one of them looked up.

"Have you seen Limitri Palermiti?" I asked Saverio, the proprietor.

"He was here. Gone now."

My next stop was Limitri's house. By the time I got to the top of via Sant'Orsola I was cross and sweaty. The church was empty, the rectory door closed—Don Pantaleone's diploma academy, the Association for the Future, was in session.

Limitri's wife, "the Palermita," was sweeping chicken feathers out onto the flood-rutted street. "He's doing Don Tito's roof," she told me.

Fool me once, I thought grimly. "Remind me where Don Tito lives."

She gave me the sidelong glance of a vindictively long-married wife. "Via Pitagoro. The big yellow house."

I'd never been introduced to the Licos, but I knew Don Tito and his wife, Potenziana, were Very Important Chionoti. Don Pantaleone Bianco had explained that Tito Lico was known as "the Wolf," a pun on his last name, since "*licu*" in Greco meant "wolf." The priest had been amused to tell me Don Tito's wife was better known as the Lichena, "the Wolfess."

At the yellow house on via Pitagoro, the lone freestanding building on a street of pocked row houses, I spotted Limitri Palermiti squatting by a tumble of terra-cotta shingles. "Good morning, *maestra*!" he called jovially, that squirrely bastard.

"You promised to tile my nursery."

"Not today, *maestra*. Next week."

"Yes, today! I saw you yesterday and you confirmed." I sounded like my mother.

"Don't shout, *maestra*! You misunderstood, I confirmed for next week."

"I did not misunderstand, and you know it."

Limitri Palermiti lifted his arms helplessly. "What am I supposed to do? Don Tito—"

"Maestra Francesca, isn't it?" Tito Lico's wife, the Wolfess herself, had emerged from the house. She wore a blue linen dress that made for a picturesque contrast against the yellow stucco, as if she lived in one of the few painted houses in the village just so she might be seen even more attractively when she stood in front of it. "The American?"

"I am." I wished the put-together woman had not first seen me shouting at devilish Limitri. "I'm sorry to disturb you."

Donna Lico reached out to clasp my forearm. The contact felt shockingly intimate until I realized she was checking the quality of my blouse. "This is nice. Who is your tailor?"

"I got this in Rome," I said apologetically. "Now, Donna Lico, I—"

"You can go back to your nursery." She was studying my scalloped collar now. "I'll send Palermito down when he's done."

"If you don't mind, I'll stay right here."

"Suit yourself." The Wolfess stood silently for a moment, then took out an embroidered handkerchief, which she used to dab her upper lip. "Tell me more about your nursery. My niece has a four-year-old daughter. Would she attend?"

"She should certainly apply."

She appraised me with wide, unsympathetic black eyes. "How do you teach a classroom of toddlers?"

"Well, it's not like the babies are sitting at desks. They are playing, napping, getting healthy exercise, learning hygiene and manners." I adopted a pleasant, wide-eyed expression. Potenziana was a well-off woman. She was a potential valuable ally. "Studies show children who attend this kind of nursery are more likely to continue education past third grade, then to get high-paying jobs that benefit their families."

The Wolfess's unsmiling face tightened. "There is no middle or high school here. Only the Association. But that's private, poor children will never go there."

"Well, maybe there *will* be, once children start to require it."

"Maybe." Her eyes flicked critically to my bust, my waist, my briefcase. "Who exactly is paying for all this?"

"Child Rescue is an international charity. Donors' funds have covered all the building-related expenses, and the salary of two teachers." I didn't mention that I hoped to hire two local teachers, and that every conversation I had with a Chionese woman was a vetting for these positions. "But we need the involvement of the Chionoti to make it work."

For a moment we watched Limitri crab-walking along the roof. "Well," the Lichena said at last. "I wish you the best of luck. Palermito! Don't keep the teacher waiting all day." She nodded at me and retreated into her house.

It was significant that the woman did not, after all this, invite me in for a beverage.

"Go on, *maestra,*" Limitri begged on his next journey to the ground. "I'll come meet you after lunch. Actually Monday morning is better—"

"Absolutely not. I am waiting right here until you're done."

For the next hour, I leaned stubbornly against the rock wall opposite, my skin itching as the white morning sun caramelized on the back of my neck. So much for Cicca's prophetic dreams—I wished just this one time Peppinedda had been right. I undid my bun and arranged my hair in a protective hedge, passing the interminable minutes quizzing myself on Greco vocabulary. At least this hour in the sun would streak a little more blond in; I relied on the exoticism of my Nordic phenotype to inspire people to forgive me for the cultural faux pas I had to commit in order to get the more uncomfortable parts of my job done.

When Limitri was finally cleaned up, the broken tiles collected into a burlap sack, I marched him back to his house to pick up his supplies.

Together we hauled them down via Sant'Orsola. I was fumbling for the nursery key when a man shouted across the piazza.

"Palermito! *Maestra!*" It was Sebastiano Massara, the communist who was running for mayor against the Democratic Christian incumbent. "Have you decided how you're voting on November seventh?"

Limitri set his crunching sacks of tiles down and crossed his arms. "I'm a Christian."

Massara pulled his brick-red cap off his cheerfully bald head. "That doesn't mean you have to vote for the neo-fascism of the Christian Democrats! Communists are Christians too, you know."

Jiggling the door handle open, I envisioned Lenin rolling over in his grave.

"*Maestra?*" The communist had stepped inside the dark nursery after me, hefting a tile bag helpfully. "What are your thoughts on the mayoral election?"

"You know I can't vote," I reminded him. "I'm here in a strictly apolitical capacity. To open a nursery school."

"There is no such thing as apolitical, *maestra,*" the communist said. "You *are* political. You are a tool of the bourgeoisie, who use cultural institutions as a means of maintaining capitalist hegemony."

I'd endured my fair share of dogma during my starry-eyed Student Labor Union days and I wasn't about to sit through a lecture. "Child Rescue sent me here to improve the lives of children, not promote capitalist hegemony. Surely *all* potential voters want to improve the lives of children?"

"Well, *maestra*—"

"We're short on time. Would you like to help us tile the floor?"

Massara took the cue, but offered over his shoulder as a parting volley, "Don't forget! Communists are Christians, too!"

Crouching to uncover a bucket, Limitri said bitterly, "He'll never win."

"You don't think he has a chance?"

"He's a convicted criminal! That's where he turned communist, in prison."

I tried to picture the voluble, friendly zealot behind bars. "Convicted? For what?"

"Attempted murder," Limitri answered loftily.

"Are you serious?" I peered through the unelectrified shafts of sun and shadow. "Who did he try to kill?"

Limitri rubbed his neck. "It was a long time ago. I don't know the details."

Yeah, right. Because there was such thing as a secret in a village.

I passed the increasingly hungry hours of the afternoon in truculent focus, my skirt straining over my thighs as I attacked the packed dirt with Limitri's spare trowel. My sleeves were caked in mortar. Under the laundering terms of our agreement I'd have to trust Cicca to do her best to save them with her olive oil and herbs, or whatever purgatory hocus-pocus she insisted on destroying my clothes with.

At half past four I paid Limitri and locked up the nursery, fantasizing about taking dinner straight to bed. But any such peaceful plans for the evening came to naught. As I removed the brass key from the tumbler I felt a hand on my elbow.

7

I WAS SO SURPRISED TO SEE HER OUT OF HER USUAL CONTEXT THAT I struggled to place her. It was Don Pantaleone's housekeeper, I realized when she spoke to me in Greco, simple words I felt lucky to understand.

"Teacher, can you help me?"

"Help," I repeated, stunned. I had tried to use Greco phrases around town—*kalimèra*, "good morning," *cheràmine*, "thank you"—but no one had engaged me in a real Greco conversation before. All my preparation failed me, as it always does in these situations, leaving me bobbing for absent words, like an inchworm waggling its desperate little neck into the breeze. I resorted to my mother's Calabrese. "How can I help you, *gnura?*"

"We can go inside?" She tipped her pointed chin toward the door I'd just locked.

"Certainly."

We sat by the window in the soft slanting light. She was dressed head to toe in black, with a black wool sweater pulled over a high-waisted black linen skirt. She had an ancient face, one that might have been peeled off a black-figure painting on a 2,500-year-old pot, or pried from a Byzantine mosaic: as narrow as the leaf of a sweet potato vine, her nose like the blade of a spear. It was a face many Americans might have mistaken for Chinese or Cherokee, although I have never in my long life met anyone of any race who looked like Emilia Volontà.

I did not know her name in that moment, though—and was finally conscious of my mortification on that point, that I didn't know her name though she had cooked for me and served me with her own hands.

"Tell me your name." This was something I knew how to say in Greco.

"My name?" she echoed, her expression one of mild surprise. "I'm Emilia Volontà. My married name is Romeo."

"I should call you Gnura Romeo?"

"Me? You can call me Emilia, teacher."

When she said nothing else, I tested the limits of my Greco with, "I help you, Gnura Emilia? How?"

The woman was obviously nervous; I watched her tangle her fingers in her skirt. "My son is lost," she said at last. Her voice was high and nasal. "I want to know the truth."

"Lost?" I blurted in Calabrese. "What do you mean 'lost,' *gnura*?"

I shall transcribe her Greco side of this conversation as I imagine it might have happened, based on what I inferred from the fragments I understood. You will have to decide for yourself how thoroughly you believe me, in the same way I have had to decide how thoroughly I believe myself.

She tilted her bird chin up and met my eye. "My boy, my Leo, he disappeared. They told me he emigrated to America, but he never came home again. He never sent money, like the other emigrants. He never sent a message for his mamma."

I felt a pang for Emilia Volontà. She was not the first woman to approach me to help her track down a missing immigrant relative. I knew this story as well as my own grandparents'—the families ruptured by the ocean, and by the poison-laced capitalist incentives that kept them from reuniting. "He went to America? Where, what part?"

She shrugged, her thin shoulders rising as high as her ears.

"You don't know."

"I don't know."

The persimmon light of the setting sun settled on her sharp face, planing its angles like a Picasso portrait—although Emilia Volontà had surely never heard of Picasso. My stomach growled, audibly.

"You said—a boy?" She must have been in her late seventies; any son of hers would be a full-grown man.

"Fifteen years old." After a long pause, during which I wondered if I was misunderstanding her entirely, she added, "That was forty years ago."

"Forty years." I swallowed. "You—you haven't heard from your son in forty years?"

"I never knew if he was alive or dead. His own mamma never knew to pray for his soul."

I felt the pressure in my chest rising. To lose a child, flesh of one's flesh, when he was only fifteen years old, when his journey should have been just beginning—my eyes had begun to tear. *Stop it, Francesca.* I swallowed again. It was nothing but indulgence to appropriate other women's pain. "It will be hard to find him," I managed eventually. "Not without more information about where he went. America is a huge country—many countries. And forty years is a long time."

Emilia Volontà turned her shimmering eyes up to meet mine. "No, teacher, I don't think he's in America. I think he's here, in Santa Chionia."

In the silence stretching over our abortive bilingual conversation, I understood the words she had not said. "You think Leo is the skeleton under the post office."

I did not imagine that her glance slid toward the door, which I had left standing open. There was another dreadful silence, then her shoulders rose again in that dramatic shrug. "When they dug up those bones— I think that was my Leo telling me the truth."

The hairs on my arm were standing on end. I wasn't sure exactly what she was asking me to help her with, but I was fairly certain it would fall outside my purview as hygienic advisor. "If you think there has been a murder, you must call the police."

"Police?" Her black eyes widened in alarm. "Not murder! No, teacher, an accident."

"I don't understand, *gnura.*"

"I think my Leo died, and they didn't want to break my heart, so they told me he emigrated." She tapped her breastbone twice with the middle finger of her left hand. "At first we didn't worry. I was so busy with the other babies. Then we wrote him a letter, and a year later it came back, return to sender." Her glance slid toward the door yet again. Who could she think was listening? "They told us to wait. What else could we do? We were still waiting when my husband died."

I imagined what it must have been like to never know whether to grieve, that long limbo, normalcy flowering into fear into helplessness— to have been betrayed by fate at some point, but to never be sure when.

"So what do you want from me, *gnura*?"

She leaned forward abruptly and wrapped her cold, silky fingers around mine. "I know Pino Pangallo at the *municipio* has let you look through the family registers. You can ask Pino to check for Leo's, his what's-it-called. Emigration paper."

"Visa?"

"Visa. If they have a visa for Leo, it means he went to America after all, and I am wrong."

"Gnura Emilia, surely you can go and ask Pino yourself."

"I can't. I'm just a *paddeki*." My heart clenched to hear her call herself by the racial slur Italians used for the Greci. "I don't know my letters, I wouldn't understand the paper. But you—they have to respect you."

I wondered who "They" were—she had now mentioned "Them" several times.

Sabrina would have reminded me I wasn't supposed to get involved in personal problems, although during my two years working for Child Rescue I'd been asked to assist with everything from a real estate purchase to delivering baby goat triplets. There is something appealing about seeking the aid of an outsider, who could offer intercession as conflict-free as a saint's. At least, that's what I told myself, to validate my meddling.

The fact is, I was a sucker for a sweet old lady.

I tried one more deflection. "What about Don Pandalemu?"

"Don Pandalemu?" She studied the floor—Limitri the shingle maker's craftsmanship, maybe, or something more metaphysical. "No, no, teacher, it would be better if you did it. Men are—they don't take these things seriously."

Emilia Volontà was old, she was lonely, she was illiterate. What harm could it possibly do to scare up her son's visa? I turned to a mostly empty page in my datebook. "Tell me the details, *gnura*. Leo Romeo, son of Emilia Volontà and . . ."

"Natale Romeo. Born in 1904."

"All right. And he left when?"

"On the feast of San Sebastiano, 1920." I watched her brow tighten and I felt the pain in my chest again.

"I will see what I can find, Gnura Emilia," I promised, peering at her through the dusk. "I have to get home to Cummàri Cicca now—she's expecting me."

The woman let me escort her to the door, where she laid her cold hand on my arm again. "Please, don't tell Don Pandalemu." She raised her slanted eyes to me in entreaty. "He already thinks I am a simpleton. Please, no one has to know."

She tapped her nose with the tip of her index finger, then turned and clambered up via Sant'Orsola.

8

AT SUNSET, WHEN I RETURNED TO CICCA'S HOUSE, I WAS GREETED by a hitherto unprecedented sight: guests. Two forty-something men, one sitting at my cranky hostess's table, the other standing by the hemp scutcher, brandishing the livid red and muscle-white carcass of a slaughtered goat. I hoped they hadn't been waiting for me long; his arm must have been tired.

"*Maestra.*" Bestiano Massara, the communist, sprang to his feet and flourished his already doffed cap. I tried to take him seriously as an attempted murderer. "We have come to welcome you to Santa Chionia, on behalf of the Communist Collective. We brought you this goat." He beamed, showing me cheeks as burnt orange as winter tomatoes.

"That's generous of you, *masciu*. But I cannot accept a present from any political group." I felt Cicca's baneful eyes on me. She did not want them to take the goat away.

The standing man said, "It is my wether. Consider it a gift from my family."

"Thank you, *masciu* . . . What is your name?"

"Maviglia." With his mole-brown free hand he pointed to his companion. "You know Massara."

"This is so generous of you," I said, and before I could endanger the present any further, Cicca snatched it by its striated legs and declared, "I'll roast it!"

While Cicca took her carving knife to this exciting project, Maviglia the goat-bringer ushered me to a stool. Wary of recruitment attempts, I folded my hands under the table where I couldn't fidget.

"We are here to assure you we have the same goals for this beautiful city, *maestra,*" Bestiano Massara said. "It is the Democratic Christian mayor who has brought you here, but that is no reason we cannot all work together for the sake of the people of Santa Chionia!"

"I agree absolutely." I turned my American dentistry on each of the men. "I hope your families will be involved in the nursery school."

"Here, *maestra,* try this." Massara pulled a handkerchief bundle out of his ill-fitting jacket and untied it, revealing a pile of almonds. "The end of this year's harvest."

I obeyed. The flavor was so intense it tasted like the bottled extract my aunt Dolly used in her pound cake, so powerful I'd assumed it was fake. Disbelieving, I cracked a second shell.

"I see in your face, *maestra.*" Maviglia the goat-bringer lowered himself onto the last stool and tugged his leather vest straight. "You have tasted the secret of the Aspromonte."

"We have the most ancient varietals—walnuts, cherries, pears, brought here in Homer's time," Massara said. "You could not have come at a more pivotal moment, *maestra,* when the Italian government wants us to abandon that heritage to relocate to the coast."

The mention of relocation summoned up sour unease in my belly, and I shelled another almond to suck on. "I very much hope the *paese* is not going to be transferred elsewhere. But my goal here is to reduce the infant mortality rate. Infrastructural changes have to be made if this is going to be a village safe for children to grow up in."

"You are here because our village has become an outrage platform," Bestiano Massara said. "The poorest, the most miserable city in Calabria, the journalists call us. But the poverty you see—none of this is native to our character. Calabria was once wealthy, covered in factories and farms, with world-famous centers of learning like Cosenza and Seminara. The delinquency, the amorality—these conditions have been forced upon us by the Italian government."

I was surprised by his words: "delinquency," "amorality," code words for organized crime and prostitution—these were accusations made by activists and travel writers but which no Calabrian ever discussed in relation to his or her own village.

I studied these scarred men, thinking of my own Italian grandfather. "How can I help you, my friends?" I said at last.

"Be aware of the election, *maestra,*" Maviglia said. He spoke with an insistent softness that polished his advice into a warning. "It doesn't not involve you."

Bestiano Massara, the politician, spread his hands. "The election will be our chance to turn everything around. *You, maestra,* can remind people they have the power to choose a different destiny. A better world where our hard work is rewarded with dignity."

I was moved by his optimism. "I am sympathetic. But a Child Rescue agent is nonpartisan. She must be available to whoever needs her," I said, quoting Sabrina's precious protocol, "with clear eyes and unbiased heart."

"Be careful of that unbiased heart." Maviglia, abruptly playful, waggled his eyebrows. "We have lots of good-looking men up here in the mountains. If you don't watch it you might fall in love with one of them."

"Now that would be a conflict of interest I must prevent at all cost," I said as charmingly as I could. I was freshly, hideously aware of Sandro's ring against my sternum, the cold lump of gold hanging from a chain where no Chionoti would ever, ever see it.

Cicca elbowed between the communists to set a platter of olives and pickled stuffed eggplant on the table. "Good-looking men like you? I don't think she has anything to worry about."

"Don't listen to her." Maviglia winked at me. "If she were thirty years younger she'd marry me in a heartbeat."

The communists stayed past the last chiming of the church bells. I struggled to fall asleep, stimulated by the woodland autodidacts, unsettled by the prospect of transferment they had raised. A second thing was bothering me, too: the conversation with Emilia Volontà. At the time, I'd been distracted by the exertion of impressing her with my fledgling Greco; now, as I digested its contents, they troubled me more and more.

I fumbled in the chilly dark to light my desk lamp, then opened my datebook to the notes I had taken.

Leo Romeo
ma—Emilia Volontà, dad—Natale
b. 1904, left 1920
"They"

My mind's eye was stuck on the image of the woman's slanting gaze as she tapped her nose—informing me the conversation was strictly between us. In the Aspromonte, even the most frivolous scalawag would never disrespect such a request. I was honor-bound now.

Did she suspect violence? But the scenario she described was so far-fetched. If Leo had been killed in an accident, why would he not have received a Christian burial? Why would his body have been dumped in an unmarked grave?

But *someone* had been. A *human skeleton* had been hidden in the foundation of the post office. I remembered the brandished femur gleaming in the morning sun, and again my skin rippled with warning.

If there was any chance Emilia Volontà was right, that her son was dead and some "They" had been involved in covering that fact up—the sweet old lady could be dragging me into a problem I shouldn't be a part of.

I closed the datebook, pretending I was going to have any discipline at all about not getting involved in other people's business.

9

"NO ONE SPEAKS GREEK IN THE ASPROMONTE ANYMORE," SABRINA had told me as she helped me pack for Santa Chionia. "It's only the grandparents who even understand it."

When I'd received this assignment, I'd had the idea of impressing my new hosts by learning their obscure minority language and was crestfallen to hear there would be no point. But that couldn't stop me. I read what I could about this endangered piece of cultural heritage. There had been a relatively recent time when all of Calabria spoke Greek; now it survived in the remote pockets of Area Grecanica in an Italian-Greek mélange called Greco. Some considered Greco the living child of the classical language of Homer and Herodotus, a remnant of Magna Grae-cia, when the Calabrian city of Sybaris was one of the largest in Europe. It was a Greco speaker, the fourteenth-century monk Leontius Pilatus, a correspondent of Petrarch and Boccaccio, who first translated the hith-ertofore lost works of Homer from classical Greek into Latin. So you could say it was a Calabrian Greek who kicked off the Renaissance, if you were a Calabrian apologist, which you should be.

But how was I to learn any Greco, in light of its obscurity? Shame-lessness helps in language acquisition more than any other single skill, and with that natural gift I had been richly endowed. However, a gram-mar book is also helpful, and the only actual linguistic manual I could find about the Greco dialects of the Aspromonte, a study from the 1920s by Gerhard Rohlfs, was written in German—not one of the languages I already spoke. Learning German in order to learn a possibly extinct dia-lect of classical/Byzantine Greek was a bridge too far, even for me.

Then I arrived in Santa Chionia to find that my infallible Sabrina had been quite wrong. The village was so remote, so isolated, not only had the Greco language survived, there were people like Emilia Volontà who spoke nothing else.

Toolless, I had been trying to teach myself Greco by making word lists and memorizing phrases. Cicca helped me, sometimes, when she wasn't being a total pill.

Cicca and I were in the middle of one of those Greco lessons over break-fast on Wednesday morning when Oddo, the postman from Bova, inter-rupted with a telegram.

"You didn't come all this way for me?" I asked guiltily.

"It's my job, *maestra,* isn't it?" Oddo took the barley coffee Cicca had poured him and grinned at me. He was not a young man, but he had the affect of one. "And no, not only for you. There's always something for Don Pandalemu."

Even before the flood, when Santa Chionia had had a post office, Oddo had only worked out of it on Wednesdays, unlocking the defunct building for the *carabinieri* who would arrive with the weekly pension money for distribution. Now, Oddo explained, the pensions could not be delivered, because the requisite armed guard was unable to access the *paese*—unmitigated tragedy for the old men who counted on that money. (There was no state concession at all for elderly women. Back then we were still fighting to have child-rearing and housework recognized as real labor. What a bitter privilege to see my comrades' granddaughters on that same damn front line sixty years later.)

While Oddo bartered Bova gossip for Cicca's Chionese news items, I retrieved the letters I'd been stockpiling: the aerograms for my parents and for Alexis Kelly, my best friend in Philadelphia; the formal reports and informal letters for Sabrina. The birthday card for my mother would only be three or four weeks late.

"How did you get here, with the bridge out?" I asked as I handed Oddo the stack.

He drank the coffee down, wincing. "They've put the old bridge back up."

"You mean the plank? You didn't cross the ravine on a plank of wood!"

"I was too lazy to go the long way." He chucked his chin in the direction of my notebook. "What Greco words are you learning today? *Destroy, fix, skeleton, investigation, urgent.* Hm, your list seems to be missing *handsome postman.*"

"I already know how to say that." I grinned back. "Those are the first words I learn in any language."

"Off I go, ladies," Oddo said, lifting his cap off his knee. "Letters to deliver and waterfalls to cross."

"Oddo, you're not really going to cross that plank bridge," Cicca said.

Oddo patted his carrier bag. "This helps me balance."

We laughed and waved him off, most likely to his death. There is something about living your daily life in a language to which you are not native; it provides a reality buffer that blunts absurdity.

More dangerously, when you're distracted by the excitement of an unfamiliar cultural environment, the distinction between "something I would never do" and "something people just do here" becomes blurred. Your subconscious becomes resistant to categoricals.

The telegram was from Sabrina, and it was more than a week old:

PRAYING YOU ARE SAFE FROM FLOOD STOP SEND
NOTICE ASAP STOP ASSISTANCE AVAILABLE IF NEEDED
STOP BACI SM

"Oh no!" I stood, tugging down my skirt. "I have to catch Oddo before he leaves!" The last thing I wanted was my boss to think I was dead, or to send embarrassing help.

"We didn't finish studying Greco!" Cicca called after me, wronged and resigned. She didn't like when I was in her house bothering her, but she didn't like me to be anywhere else, either.

I caught up with the postman at the *puticha,* where he was chewing the fat with the male patrons. Elsewhere a tavern like this would have been cloudy with cigarette smoke, but here in Santa Chionia no one cared much for tobacco. Maybe because there was no legal way to buy it, although legality was an inchoate concept up here in the mountains.

Saverio Legato, the proprietor, greeted me with his usual sidelong glance. Either he didn't take me seriously as a customer or his capitalistic strategy was to increase the perceived value of his wares by playing hard to get. No one else acknowledged me at all.

I tore out a page of my datebook, which was suffering various misuses lately, and scratched out a return message for Oddo to send via the Bova telegram office. I wrote in English to increase my mystique.

BRIDGE OUT BUT ALL ELSE WELL STOP NURSERY
PROCEEDING SMOOTHLY STOP LETTER FOLLOWS STOP
BACI FL

"Thank you again, Oddo," I told the postman. I handed him five hundred lire, which he pocketed without checking how much I'd given him so neither of us had to acknowledge the service fee I'd included.

As Oddo tucked my message into his sack, I caught the eye of Don Tito Lico, Tito the Wolf. He was tall even when seated, with smooth golden-brown cheeks emerging from a black beard lush enough for Polyphemus the Cyclops. The patch of sunlight coming from the east-facing window fell short of his face, disguising his expression, but it did catch on the gleaming facets of his carved chestnut walking stick.

Child Rescue ethos encouraged agents to befriend village power brokers. I could make an effort here. I spoke across the morning shadows. "Don Tito, I met your wife. She was kind and let me steal Limitri the shingle maker away to tile the nursery school."

The big man shrugged, his sprawling black eyebrows conveying that he didn't know anything about that. Saverio Legato crossed his arms over his chest. Turi Laganà, the ever-present loafer with the protuberant ears, squinted at me, disbelieving, and tilted his head in a way that drew my attention to a shining ham-colored scar running down his neck. The montage made me realize why the quiet Don Tito was always so noticeable: all the other men were clean-shaven; all the other men had set their caps on the table.

"I was overjoyed by Donna Potenziana's interest in my nursery school," I tried again. A little exaggeration never hurt anyone, did it? "I hope she might have some advice for me. Perhaps suggestions for Chionote women who might make good teachers."

Finally Don Tito spoke, his voice soft as a willow branch and inflected by the singsong Greco accent. "My wife is not an educated woman. She cannot help you, *maestra*."

That was the opposite of what I might have hoped he'd say. "I meant—a woman of her status are, can . . ." I heard myself mistaking my Italian like a clumsy child. "The education of *bambini* is so important. When well-respected women like your wife support nursery schools, they inspire humble people in the community to follow their lead."

"*We* are humble people, *maestra*." Don Tito the Wolf corrected me gently, as he might speak to a wayward granddaughter. "We are shepherds, the sons and daughters of shepherds. We mind our own business." I felt the other men's eyes on me. As if to soften the blow, he offered, "I am sure she wishes you well in your work."

"Thank you, Don Tito," I managed, and without letting my voice crack. "We appreciate that." I used "we" so he might think that I was bigger than just myself, spitting into the wind. "Thank you, Oddo. See you next week."

As I turned into the piazza the wind cutting down via Odisseo sluiced a few ruinous tears out of my eye. I had misstepped by trying to speak to the man. The don's nonengagement would diffuse over these other men, who would diffuse it over their wives. I had done much damage in two poorly planned minutes.

I buried myself in paperwork. I had plenty: most time-sensitively, I had the village land register to finish annotating—Pino Pangallo, the *municipio* clerk, had lent it to me, in compliance with a written request from Child Rescue approved by Mayor Fortunato Stelitano. The register, first compiled in 1955 so Santa Chionia could receive housing development funds, contained data on every household, including the inhabitants, their employment, and their estimated income. The last was the most problematic notation, in a village where people were proud—I was reminded painfully—of their humbleness, their *umiltà,* and where craftiness in taking advantage of the abusive state was a highly admired trait. At least the register gave me some idea of who lived closest to the desperate verge, where my nursery's taking one toddler off the mother's apron strings might mean the difference between life and death for a struggling family.

Realistically I could not build the pupil list of thirty-six until I had solicited applications from all the families with strong candidates and interviewed every family to understand their true level of need.

In other words, I needed to get to know everyone in town.

Would this be more difficult, after my social failure with Don Tito? All the book-learning in the world had not helped me anticipate the subtlety and sophistication of a group of illiterate goatherds.

For this kind of lack of judgment, I fear there is no cure—so quoth the driving instructor at the Radnor Township Department of Motor Vehicles who had failed me the one time I attempted to obtain a driver's license. I never bothered to try again, because the prognosis sounded convincingly fatal, and because back then I'd had Alexis Kelly to drive me around.

With the retrospective balm of second-wave wisdom, I can dismiss that driving instructor as a misogynistic pig. But I can't say he was entirely wrong about my judgment.

10

ON FRIDAY MORNING I STOPPED BY THE *MUNICIPIO* TO RETURN THE housing register. Pino Pangallo, the clerk, was sitting behind his desk, his jaundiced pate shining under the electric lamp. I wondered, not for the first time, what he did all day when he was not specifically looking something up for me.

"Maestra Franca." His brown eyes were round as beads in his thin face. I guessed he was in his midforties, although his bushy mustache made him appear a generation older.

"Your register." I passed him the borrowed record book. "Thank you again."

"It was nothing. Is there anything else I can do for you?"

"I need to place a phone call, to the electrician in Melito." I set the fee on the counter and read him the digits. On the first and second attempts there was no ringing, and I began to worry that the line was cut again. The third try went through. I listened to the ringing on the other end for a long time, feeling the phone thrum in my hand.

"It's still early," Pino said. "You can try again in half an hour."

What would I do if the call would not go through? I might have to make the six-hour trip to Melito to schedule an appointment in person. I opened my datebook to see when such a journey might be slotted in, turning past the notes about Leo Romeo. My hand paused of its own accord.

A woman's teenage son had disappeared without a trace forty years ago.

A human skeleton had been brazenly stashed in the village's central piazza.

On impulse more than by any other, wiser guiding principle, I asked, "Pino, would you be able to look up an emigration record for me?"

Pino looked at me rabbit-eyed, waiting for more information.

"Leo Romeo," I said. "Born in 1904 and left Santa Chionia in 1920. Do your records go back that far?"

"Certainly. Why do you need this, *maestra*?"

What was I to say here? A stranger's emigration papers were none of my business. Were they a matter of public record?

"You know his mother, Gnura Emilia Volontà," I started. But Emilia had been adamant I not tell anyone I was checking. It was too late to backpedal entirely. "She asked me to write a letter for her. She hasn't known Leo's address since her husband passed."

It was my first lie. A thin one, almost the truth, and I felt satisfied with myself at the compromise between my own ethics and a promise I hadn't exactly made.

"Leo Romeo," Pino repeated, pushing back his chair. I watched him slip through the door to his archive room, counted along with the clock's noisy minute hand until he returned with a bark-brown binder labeled *ROMEO*.

"You are looking for an address for a Leo Romeo?"

As Pino turned the diverse pages—which ranged from time-stained brown to quite fresh looking—I realized the binder contained civic documentation for three generations of Romeos: marriage banns and property deeds; visas for emigrants bound for Calgary, Canberra, Cologne; letters of endorsement; copies of naturalization records in foreign languages. What had once been the Romeo family was scattered all over the world. I wondered if every Chionese family had a binder as fat as this one, and what Santa Chionia would have looked like if those young men had been able to find opportunity here at home, instead.

Pino had turned the last piece of yellowed paper. "I have no visas for any Leo Romeo. Are you sure you have the name right?"

"Could we check the birth register? To make sure?"

Pino took punctilious minutes to close the album, delicately neatening the edges of the papers. Then he disappeared into the archive room and returned with a vellum-bound volume. On the spine was a label that read *Cert. di Nascita, 1898–1941.*

"You don't know the month?"

"I'm sorry, Pino."

Pino produced a ruler, which he placed on the birth registry to make it easier to read. He checked every line, starting in January 1904 and coming to an end in October, where we found an entry for ROMEO, LEO on the twenty-first.

The same birthday as my own mother's, fifty-six years ago that very day. For some reason the coincidence made me feel queasy.

Well, Leo wasn't imaginary. So where was his visa?

I noticed three of the five names listed above Leo's on the page had asterisks to their left, obviously not made with the initial entry—the pen strokes were thicker.

"What does this star mean?" I asked.

"The registrar would mark the birth record like this for anyone who died unmarried." Pino pressed the tip of one spider-leg finger against the inky marks. "To indicate there would be no further progeny from that line," he explained. "Usually it means the deceased was a child. Look, *maestra*." He opened to a new folio, whose top line was dated 1938. "Look."

My gaze dragged down the column of stars even without his emphatic index finger to guide it.

"Look," Pino said again, and turned another page.

The column of stars marched on, unbroken, until two lines from the bottom, a 1939 date.

"We call it the year of the pagans," he said. "When every baby born died before it could be baptized."

"But—" My eye was still traveling the column, the information not yet making sense. "Every single baby?"

"Those were dark years," Pino said. "There was a terrible famine. You would salute elders sitting in their doorways and they wouldn't return your greeting because they were dead of hunger. You know how it is; when things start to go wrong, more and more things go wrong. Christians were still homeless from the earthquake, or living in rubble."

"The earthquake? You mean . . . the earthquake of 1908?" The 7.1-magnitude quake had resulted in fifty thousand Calabresi dead. My mother had been only four years old but vividly remembered the tremors all the way up in Catanzaro.

Pino gave me an arch little frown. "Yes, 1908, what other earthquake?"

"There were still homeless people thirty years later?" I knew better than to let it beggar belief, but.

"The government was late sending us the relief funds." Then Pino said, very softly, "Thirty-three little lost souls."

My nausea surged, that patient parasite of grief that waited for these opportunities. All those babies—all their mothers—

"But not Leo Romeo," Pino said, breaking the hush. "He did not die unmarried, or there would have been a star by his name."

"Who did he marry?"

Pino shook his head. "You saw the Romeo record, *maestra*. There was no documentation for him. No marriage certificate."

I suppressed my impatience. "So Leo Romeo was born here in Santa Chionia, and he didn't die or leave. But he hasn't been seen since 1920."

Pino's eyes narrowed. I was impugning his encyclopedic knowledge. "These old records, *maestra*—they are not complete. Some papers were lost in the floods."

Nonsense—I had just seen the thoroughly maintained volumes of records. But never mind. "That's right, the floods. You mean in 1951?"

"And then another in 1954. But it was the first that destroyed the town hall. Such a mess. It washed away the whole hillside here." Pino nodded in the direction of the piazza. "Houses gone, mud everywhere."

There was a critical detail—how could a suspicious skeleton have stayed buried through all that? There was no way the body under the post office could be Leo, disappeared in 1920—he would have reappeared in 1951, what was left of him, or been swept away forever.

"So this whole *centro* was built afterward," I said. "The town hall, and also . . . the post office?"

"The post office, the oven, *tutto questo*." Pino made a curving gesture with his right hand, visually describing the neighboring stretch of city wall.

Whoever the dead man actually was, his body must have been stashed during the rebuilding in 1952. That was unsettlingly recent. "What used to be where the post office is?"

"The post office."

"Before the post office," I repeated, thinking Pino had misheard me. I realized I was wrong only as he pulled the registry toward him, his movements as jerky as a doll's.

"The *old* post office." The atmosphere in the room had changed, as if the air itself had thickened. I swear I could hear him putting together the pieces of my inquiry. "There was another post office in the same place."

Damn it. Pino Pangallo knew I was fishing about the skeleton.

"Shame to have to rebuild again so soon," I said as lightly as I could. "Should we try the electrician again?"

11

AT DINNER THAT NIGHT, POTATOES AND BROCCOLI RABE, CICCA seemed sullen. I wasn't sure if she was annoyed with me or if maybe the situation with evil Mela next door had escalated.

"I saw the emigrant records in the *municipio* today," I mentioned to distract her. "So many visas. There are Chionoti all over the world."

"Switzerland, Germany," Cicca said. "Australia. Argentina." She halved a potato somewhat savagely with her spoon. "What were the men supposed to do? There was no money here. The first time I ever saw money in my life I was thirty years old."

After a moment of distracted silence, during which I struggled to imagine a young adulthood so devoid of capitalism, I asked, "What about you, Cummàri Cicca? Do you have family abroad?"

"My mother had three brothers who went to Philadelphia."

"Philadelphia—where I am from? Were there others? Chionoti who went to Philadelphia?"

Cicca shrugged. "Sure."

As any Italian-American would have done, I immediately began imagining the scenarios in which Cicca's uncles might have crossed paths with my own mother. Angelina Loftfield, née Spadafora, had been born in a Calabrian hamlet of shepherds and weavers and agrarian laborers, not so different from Santa Chionia. But my mother's emigration story had been gentled by cash—her passage had been paid by my grandmother's brother Joseph, a tailor who had come to South Philly in 1908. By 1920 Great-Uncle Joe was a middle-class artisan, flush enough to help his siblings bring their families across the Atlantic to pursue the American dream. Angelina had lived in her uncle's house in the belly button of Philly's Calabrese enclave until she was eighteen, long enough for her to determine she didn't want to settle herself down in *that* particular faux-village. My mother had always warned me against dating Italian men; Cicca's American cousins might well have been some of the chaps who'd helped Angelina decide to marry "out."

"Where are they now?" I asked. "Those uncles who went to Philadelphia?"

"Dead, *certo*. Eat."

"But their families?"

"I don't know." She pushed another heap of potato onto my plate, as if I were not an adult woman. "I never saw those uncles again."

The cold finality of her statement rankled with subtext, but it was not in one of the languages I had studied. "They couldn't read or write," I guessed. "They couldn't keep in touch."

"They couldn't write, we couldn't write! Who could go to school, *allora*! No one. Those boys," Cicca said. "The ones who went away in that generation—they are lost."

Lost. I thought again of Leo Romeo, the boy who had gone missing in 1920; of his mother, Gnura Emilia, trembling in patient fear for forty years, waiting for news that never arrived about that precious little person she had bloomed in her body, exhausted herself to nurture and protect. I felt the familiar pressure on that tender patch on the underside of my heart.

As if to underscore the melancholy, a mouse-gray moth that had been warming its thorax by the sap lamp dropped to the table and sat on the edge of the plate, beating its wings once.

"What's the matter?" Cicca was eyeing me suspiciously. "The potato's no good?"

In the interval required to pop a piece of potato into my mouth, chew, and swallow, I wrestled my self-indulgent empathy back into its cage. "The potato is perfect."

"Then why are you sad?"

I was hardly going to tell Cicca the truth. Not the whole of it, anyway. "I was thinking about your lost uncles," I said. "Cummàri Cicca, how did your uncles pay for their tickets back then, if there was no money?"

"You had to borrow the money and pay it back."

"Borrow from whom?"

"The don. He would arrange a ticket."

"Don who? Not Don Tito Lico?" I didn't think the man could be older than sixty.

Cicca's face contorted in disgust. "Don Roccuzzu Alvaro," she said.

"The old don." Her face resettled into its usual half scowl; I wondered which man her contempt had been for. "He died in the cholera."

"He was a rich man?"

"Yes, very rich. He built the big Alvaro house up the mountain. He built the post office for the *paese*."

"The first post office?" I felt my heartbeat accelerate. "When was that?"

"The year we had the fish feast," Cicca said inscrutably, then mercifully added, "Maybe around the time Il Duce was elected."

Sometime in the early 1920s. So it *wasn't* out of the realm of possibility that the skeleton was in fact Emilia's son Leo, hidden in the foundation of the first post office.

But why? What could a fifteen-year-old boy have done to get himself murdered?

I shifted my stool closer to Cicca's floor hearth.

"Don Alvaro—was he a baron?"

"What baron. He was a goatherd, like the rest of us. We never had nobility here in Santa Chionia. We're free people."

I had questions about the historicity of this—surely Santa Chionia must once have been a vassal of someone; some ruling body had built the Saracen Tower, the Norman ruin that hulked on the peak above the village—but I kept my foot on the gas. "How did Don Alvaro get rich, then?"

"From the immigrants," Cicca said. "He would loan them money at thirty percent interest."

Sounded like a nice guy. "No wonder people didn't come back. They probably couldn't afford to."

The moth had begun a curving trek across the oily plate. I raised my hand to shoo it away and Cicca's arm shot out, blocking me. "Don't you know better?"

"No!" I yelped, shaken. "What?"

"You never kill a moth!" Cicca snatched up the plate. The moth stubbornly refused to take wing, even with the movement. "That is the soul of a family member that has come back to see you."

"I wouldn't have killed it," I protested. "I never kill anything."

"I hope not."

I decided this was my cue to go to bed. "Here, *cummàri,* my rent." I pulled my briefcase up into my lap and took out the bills I had prepared for her.

Cicca took the money and counted. Later, I knew, she would call over evil Mela and have her check that the foreigner wasn't taking advantage. "Where did you get the cash?"

"From the post office," I said. "Why?"

"The post office hasn't been open since before the flood."

"I had it from before."

"What, you've been carrying it around with you? For weeks?! What are you thinking? You will be robbed!"

I was shocked by the violence of her reaction. "Relax, *cummàri,* who is going to rob me in Santa Chionia?"

"There are no-good bums everywhere!" Cicca's square cheeks were red with energy. "Peppinedda told me you were in big trouble. Now I understand! Do you have *more?*" She pressed a hand to her face. "You *cannot* have money in my house!"

"I don't even know if you're joking." I stood up to leave and was suddenly towering over her. "How do you expect me to pay for all the things I need to buy? Be reasonable."

"You *cannot!*" Cicca's neck was so short that when her jaw dropped, her chin fell all the way to her chest. "O *Dio!* Peppinedda knew, Peppinedda knew!"

"Come on." All I had to do was not say what I was thinking. And yet: "I don't believe your dead sister warned you about anything, and neither do you. If it makes you uncomfortable to have money in the house, I'll lock it up at the nursery. But please," I said, righteously rational, "if you don't like something I'm doing, tell me. Don't pretend your dead sister speaks to you. We're not children."

I was not expecting what came next: the yellowed whites of her eyes turned pink in her frozen face, and tears started to slide down her cheeks. Spluttering obstinacy, transparently backhanded compliments, sneaky revenge—these were all things I had learned to anticipate from Cicca. Tears—no, I was not prepared.

"*Cummàri,* I'm sorry—" I tried, but she turned and stomped up the stairs.

· · ·

I went to my own room and tried to read the new Sappho translation my father had sent me while I listened to Cicca sobbing through the concrete walls. The reading proceeded poorly; my sap lamp was smoky and my soul was a three-days-dead jellyfish carcass. I lingered on fragment eighty-four:

If you are squeamish
don't prod the
beach rubble.

My job in Santa Chionia was to help women. Today I'd made an old woman cry.

I'd lost patience with Cicca for her histrionics. Meanwhile I knew perfectly well that women like Cicca, raised in a hereditary patriarchy with no legal or social protection, resorted to histrionics because they had no other power. If you make a big scene about something, you don't always get what you want. But if you're disciplined about escalating everything up to a crisis, you train everyone around you to dread what's coming, and then you get your way some of the time preventatively. I understood these behavior patterns—not only from years of fieldwork with the humblest and angriest of women, but also I was my mother's daughter. Angelina Loftfield had been schooled to fight dirty to live to fight another day, even if there wasn't necessarily a fight to be had. The conditioning was hard to break down.

Miserably I unbarred the wood shutter to let out some of the sooty smoke. Bats dipped past my window, the haunch of Montalampi brilliant gray in the starlight. The moon was new, and in her silvery absence the stars were so splendorous and abundant that the constellations I had memorized for my Barnard astronomy course were unrecognizable. *La luce dell'Aspromonte.* The same amount of light makes a dramatic difference in darkness this dark.

I couldn't hear Cicca's crying anymore; perhaps she had fallen asleep. I was about to attempt the same when I spotted the moth on my wall. There was no way it was the same moth Cicca had rescued in her kitchen, but the poetic logic of that idea appealed to me. Cicca claimed a moth was a ghost come to visit, and I certainly felt visited by ghosts tonight.

I approached the moth slowly, presenting it with the edge of an envelope, nudging gently at its feet until it stepped on board. As I walked it toward the false safety of the rushing ocean of night, where it would most likely contribute metabolically to the cycle of life, I noticed the faint brown pattern on its beige wings—two faded circles, like hollow eyes that disappeared into the dark as the creature flapped away.

Hollow eyes, like those of a hungry child. The image stuck in my head and I could not blink it away. With an eerie regret I closed the shutter, snuffed the lamp, and lay down on my broom mattress. I thought of Emilia Volontà's missing son—imagined his thin adolescent face, its hollow eyes like the moth wings in the dark.

I had to find him. I had to find Leo Romeo.

12

THE REST OF THE WEEK WAS DRIZZLY, THE GRAY FOG LYING LOW. The streets were silent; looking back now, I realize the Chionoti must have been as apprehensive as I was that the floods would return. Cicca was not speaking to me, and I had no spare moment to figure out how to earn her forgiveness. I spent much of Saturday and Sunday trying to eradicate a roundworm infestation that had taken hold in several houses at the slum end of via Leonzio Pilato, where I ended up using the last of the piperazine tablets I'd filched from the Cosenza baby clinic. The children would need second doses, and I fretted away the weekend over how I could possibly arrange a replacement shipment.

On Monday afternoon when I arrived at Don Pantaleone's rectory for our weekly lunch, Emilia Volontà was not there. I was disappointed and relieved. I hadn't been confident in my ability to pretend I wasn't dying to talk to her. Now I would have to sit on my questions about her son Leo, conspicuously absent from the town's visa records, and what she thought he'd done to get himself mashed into the mortar under the post office.

"I must apologize in advance, my dear *maestra*," the priest said as he served me a bowl of red-flecked *pappaluni* beans with broccoli and potato. "I will need to turn you out early this afternoon, as I have to make a trip to Roghudi. I've been deputized to pick up the pensions for the old folks."

Santa Chionia's neighbor to the southwest, Roghudi, was two hours away via the Amendolea gorge. *You must never go out walking except in broad daylight,* Dottor Iiriti had warned me—this was the Aspromonte, after all, the brigand capital of Italy, or perhaps the whole world. Now that it was beginning to sink in that at least one person might have been murdered here in recent memory, I was alarmed by the priest's perfunctory derring-do. "You'll be coming back alone at dusk with all that money?"

"I trust the Lord to protect me and my good intentions." Don Pantaleone chuckled. "It's so little money it would hardly be worth stabbing a priest over." He set down a bowl for himself, then took his seat.

Doing my best to sound casual, I asked, "Where is Gnura Emilia today?"

"She had to go to Roccaforte to the pharmacist," he said. "But it's good for me to cook for my guests from time to time."

I murmured apologetic compliments. The soup really was tasty. I thought for the eighty-ninth time what a waste of a husband the priest was.

Don Pantaleone was a Santa Chionia native, reassigned to this parish after high-flying years in the archbishopric at Reggio and then the Vatican, and he was thus uniquely capable of explaining local particularities. His bead on the mayoral election was that Stelitano was sure to win; no one took the communist Bestiano Massara seriously. He was also certain the bridge to Bova would be rebuilt immediately—except no construction could be undertaken until spring, naturally. We discussed the science course the priest was introducing at his academy, the Association for the Future.

This seemed like the opening I had been waiting for. "Don Pantaleone, I was wondering—is there going to be a funeral for the person whose skeleton they found under the post office last week?" I was concentrating so hard on trying to appear innocent and uninvested, on the correct mode of voice and deployment of eye contact, that I lost track of where my hands were and banged my spoon hard against my bowl.

"Are you all right, Francesca?" Don Pantaleone examined the bowl with amused concern. "I hope my flatware doesn't offend you. That's ceramic from Seminara, the best I have to offer."

"Just my boundless grace." I tried my best to sound lighthearted. *Damn it, Frank!*

The priest mercifully moved on. "Ah, the post office skeleton. No, alas, no funeral yet. That good soul must wait until the coroner's inquest has been concluded and the remains are returned to us."

"Returned? Where are they now?"

"In Reggio." Don Pantaleone dabbed his mouth with a linen napkin. "There is no coroner in Bova, so for postmortem examinations the *carabinieri* there must rely on the state police facilities in the capital."

I had somehow missed the *carabinieri*'s coming to collect the bones. I was annoyed to learn this but wasn't sure why—had I somehow thought the law would have more information than I already had, or that they would share any of it?

Well, maybe they would have something about the corpse's identity to share after the inquest. I wondered how much could actually be determined from a set of dry bones. "How long will that whole process take?"

"Weeks. Months." Don Pantaleone raised his eyes and palms to the ceiling in a pantomime of supplication. "God prevent that it's years. But I doubt our little *paese*'s long-dead corpse is going to be the forensic priority of those hardheads down in Reggio. Santa Chionia is never first in line."

So I was on my own in figuring out if the skeleton was Leo Romeo. I had been sitting all weekend on an idea, and Emilia Volontà's absence made it possible for me to act on it. "Don Pantaleone, so sorry to change the subject here, but I've been going through the housing assessment compiled for the 1957 lottery. I'm using that data to build a need-based pupil list, as you know." He nodded. "Well, it's not always complete. It would be really helpful if I could corroborate some of the entries." My second lie relating to the skeleton, and this one patently more duplicitous than the first. I knew from experience that parochial records contained information that municipal records did not, especially about property transfers, marriages, and baptisms. What I was really looking for, of course, was anything at all related to Leo Romeo. "Are your records kept here in the rectory?"

"Right over there." He nodded to a shelf against the far wall, the area of the rectory where he taught his Association classes. "Dating back to 1950, when I took this placement."

"Where are the rest? In the church?"

"There are no others."

I tried to hide my dismay. "What happened to your predecessor's?"

"I had no predecessor, Franca." The priest put down his spoon, folding his hands on the arm of his chair. My eye was drawn to the thick gold band he wore on his right hand. "Before I arrived here, there had been no priest in Santa Chionia since 1921."

"No priest? How can that be?"

"Haven't you heard that Santa Chionia has been forgotten 'by God and man'?" Don Pantaleone said wryly. "That's the God part."

I'd never heard of a town this size, eighteen hundred people, without its own priest. Santa Chionia was geographically isolated, too far from any other *paese* for the citizens to rely on another parish for their spiritual and civil needs, like weddings and funerals.

"I don't understand," I said at last.

Don Pantaleone's eyebrows lifted in disbelief. "You really haven't heard the story."

I felt a preemptive chill. "I haven't."

"Well, *maestra,* I apologize in advance for what I am about to tell you." He shook his head, and the sunlight slid off his steel-gray curls. "My predecessor was one of the bad apples, as it were. He felt that his vow of celibacy didn't apply out here in the wilderlands, and he was found to have taken advantage of local girls. Some fellows decided that a man with such hot-blooded desires needed to be settled down with a wife." He hadn't broken eye contact. "They carried him up to the Saracen Tower on the back of a donkey. When they got to the top, they performed a sort of wedding ceremony, marrying the priest to the donkey. They celebrated, emptying a barrel of wine while the priest wept like a widow at her husband's funeral. His cries could be heard echoing through the valley all night long. Then the wedding guests packed the new husband into the wine barrel and dropped it off the side of the Saracen Tower."

As I pictured the embarreled fornicator, I remembered, grotesquely, the formula for acceleration due to gravity, which I had not used since physics class in high school.

"They killed their priest." I had never heard of a *paese* retaliating against an exploiting priest before. Usually people were so afraid of losing access to their sacraments that they watched one another suffer on in silence. A clever crowd-control tool, the immortal soul.

"The church never sent a replacement. Or no one would accept the assignment."

The cleric had had it coming—his type made me sick; the predators who installed themselves like ticks in the infallible armpit of the pontificate, earning themselves transfers to increasingly remote and unpoliceable villages, harvest after delicious human harvest. But I was also philosophically opposed to trial without jury and summary justice.

More to the point—what Don Pantaleone was describing was gleefully premeditated murder. Here, at the hands of people I had almost certainly met.

"Who did it?" I asked before I could stop myself.

"I don't know." The priest's smooth, sloping brow gave no hint that he was lying. "I could guess, but what would be the point? They are all dead."

I'm sure they are, I thought. "You must remember, though." Don Pantaleone would have been about fifteen at the time.

"I was away at seminary when it happened."

I heard myself emit a nervous laugh. "One week ago we were sitting right here and you said to me no one had ever been murdered in Santa Chionia. And today you're telling me about a murder!"

Don Pantaleone held up a finger. "That was not murder. That was Aspromonte justice."

"Aspromonte justice," I repeated.

"It's a moral system cultivated over a thousand years of mountain independence. When the government and church do nothing to protect people, a man must be able to protect his own family. We are an autochthonous culture. The only hope we have of regaining our former glory is through autochthonous justice."

The executed priest's cries could be heard all night long, Don Pantaleone had said, which meant no one had stepped in to stop them.

What else, I wondered, would be considered not murder?

"What did Santa Chionia do without a priest for thirty years?"

Don Pantaleone Bianco gave a humble shrug. "Made do. The priest from Roghudi would come and perform weddings. All the babies would be baptized at once."

Pino Pangallo's "year of the pagans" made even more sad sense now, if there had been no priest to baptize the babies. "What about mass? Or last rites?"

He took a pear from the bowl and began to peel it with a long knife he pulled from his belt. "The Chionoti are devoutly faithful, as you've seen for yourself. But we do things our own way. For some aspects of faith we are willing to martyr ourselves. But then some others, well—we don't feel as strongly."

"Like killing a priest. No one was afraid for their souls?"

"What does your soul matter when you have no control over your life here on earth?" The priest met my gaze again as the single coil of peel fell from his denuded pear. "Finally the church did something good for Santa Chionia when they sent me back here. I understand how the Chionoti think. Maybe the diocese wouldn't approve of the way I run my mass. But if I'm bringing a distrustful stray flock back into the fold of the church, I believe God approves of whatever methods I employ."

It was total heresy. The Fourth Lateran Council would have had Don Pantaleone boiled alive in his own holy water. I struggled with my grudging admiration. My father, an atheist humanist, had raised me to see religious structures as nothing but tools for controlling the laboring class; my years working for Child Rescue—working around the Catholic Church, and the hypocrisies and cruelties of some of its officials—had only reinforced Dad's doctrines. But was it possible that, for the impoverished people of Santa Chionia, who lived, literally and metaphorically, on the edge of the abyss, a compassionate religious leader might actually be a gift? That he might bring enough quotidian comfort that it would outweigh the fact that he was dragging them into the clientelist exploitation and sexual slavery that was organized religion?

"Did you want any fruit, Franca?"

"No, thank you." The story had turned my stomach.

"Well, I hate to put you out, but it must be nearly two—" As he said this, the bells of San Silvestro began to clang, and I wondered briefly if the priest was a demon. "I am supposed to be in Roghudi by four."

"Of course." I hurried to stand. "Thank you for lunch, Don Panda-lemu, and travel safely."

"You do the same, dear *maestra*."

13

I SPENT MONDAY AFTERNOON AT MY DESK, TRYING NOT TO LOOK out the window too often. Across the street, the rubble of the post office stood somewhat sinister against the dreary sky. A little flicker of dread about that skeleton burned constantly in the back of my mind. Meanwhile, Bestiano Massara, undeterred by the chilly damp, had set up his bench right in front of the ruins, an ad hoc Communist Party clubhouse he would hardly leave for the next two weeks leading up to the election. Don Pantaleone Bianco might have been surprised to learn how much custom the communist had.

At four o'clock, I crossed the piazza to Fortunato Stelitano's office, where I laid out my plan for nursery school recruitment for the next eight weeks. The mayor wished to accompany me on the applicant interviews, beginning the next morning. I warmly accepted his offer, even as I balked on the inside. If Sabrina were here she would have reminded me that the mayor's participation helped guarantee the longevity of the nursery. The third of the four goals of activism: create effective political alliances. But the implication of Stelitano's attention annoyed me. He was using me as an excuse to visit constituents on the eve of the election. As I left his office, I hoped I personally was not going to be the kiss of death to the mayoral campaign of the teary-eyed, cap-clutching communist.

As I was crossing the piazza, preparing my ever-disappointing cardio-vascular system for the climb up Sant'Orsola, I saw the slender, crooked figure of Emilia Volontà coming westward down via Odisseo with an oblong water barrel balanced on her head. Recalling that she'd had some medical need in Roccaforte earlier, I hurried to intercept her.

"*Kalispèra, cummàri,* can I help you?" I said in Greco, pleased with myself.

The wrinkled woman tipped her pointed chin up to appraise me with her black eyes. "Help me?"

"Let me take your water."

"No, teacher," she said, turning her face to the mosaic of flagstones. "I have far to go."

"It would be no trouble," I said, but I wasn't confident that was true. I could hardly balance a barrel on my head like mountain-bred Chionote women. "But also, *cummàri,* I have news for you. About your son Leo."

She didn't say anything, and was still looking at the ground. Remembering her style of physical communication, I stepped closer to her and wrapped my fingers around her cold left hand, which dangled free by her side.

"Listen, *cummàri,* you were right, there is no visa for Leo." I watched the grid of her wrinkled forehead contract like a fishnet and I felt my heart begin to ache for her again. "I have a few ideas about where we could look next. You mentioned you'd sent him a letter?"

"I don't remember," she said, extracting her hand from mine to balance the barrel on her head. She took a step back and I felt the wind whistle between us. "I'm sorry, teacher."

"I was thinking that I could—"

She took another step back. "Excuse me, teacher." Her face was shadowed by the setting sun, but I saw her black eyes slide past me. "Good night."

As she hurried away up via Sant'Orsola, I stood in the naked piazza, feeling stupid—rejected, rather, like a wallflower passed over at a dance. The wind battered at my skirt and a chill crawled up my neck. I turned to look over my left shoulder. Outside the *puticha,* Saverio the proprietor stood in the doorway, and three men sat on the bench in front of the window. Turi Laganà, with his familiar stockpot ears, was staring at me with an expression of abject hatred; next to him was a forty-something man with rather professorial glasses. The third was Don Tito Lico, who gave me a little bow.

"Good evening, *maestra,* " he said. His voice was soft as ever but somehow carried over the windy distance between us.

"Good evening," I shouted into the wind. I stood awkwardly for several seconds too long, trying to figure out what to say next, then gave up and headed home, my skin rigid with goose bumps as the men's eyes followed me up via Sant'Orsola.

14

THE DONKEY WHO LIVED ON VIA PIRIA WENT OFF LIKE AN ALARM clock at five thirty the next day. I woke up lying on my belly, the weight of my torso bearing down pleasantly on my hip bones. I rolled over onto my back and tested the surprising flatness of my stomach. Just when I'd put my old self up on a shelf, Santa Chionia with her punishing verticality and her subsistence diet was going to make me svelte again.

I opened the shutters and let the cool morning swarm into my bedroom. For today's home visits, I decided on my favorite cornflower-blue dress. I opened the drawer where I kept my underwear and stockings.

It was empty.

The room was so dimly lit that my subconscious assumed it was an optical illusion. I reached in too quickly, expecting my fingers to meet fabric, and knocked my knuckles hard against the wooden bottom of the drawer.

As pain radiated through my hand, my incredulousness gave way to anger. Cicca must have come into my room—while I was asleep?—and taken every stitch of underwear.

With the lubricious morning air circulating between my bare legs, I padded barefoot across the cold tiled foyer. Cicca was scrubbing out her soup pot with ash in the garden behind the kitchen.

"Good morning," she said pleasantly. It was the first time she had spoken to me since our fight. "Give me a few minutes and I'll fix you some coffee."

I stared at her, an old woman crouching in the rosy-fingered dawn to do knuckle-grinding housework, and I collected my compassion enough to say, "Cicca, where is my underwear?"

"Soaking over there." She lifted a sandy hand to point at a basin sitting in the dirt by her cabbage. "Mela gave me a new special soap that makes clothing soft."

We looked each other in the eye for a moment. I tried to guess what this was—a power play, so Cicca could remind me of my place, or perhaps she genuinely wanted me to have softer underwear. Or maybe both; her moral scheme was mystical.

"Don't worry. They will be dry by tomorrow morning."

"What am I supposed to wear today?"

"Wear the ones you have on now."

I felt my face heating up. I should not have had to say that I had worn no underwear to bed—not to my burgling landlady, out in the garden for all the neighbors to hear!

Maybe Cicca guessed the truth, because she said snidely, "You know, I never had any underwear at all when I was a girl."

My neck hot with fury, I went back to my room and put on my dress and shoes. In the half dark I used my hand mirror to try to evaluate the full-body presentation: Would anyone guess my secret? The dress came down to midcalf, with a cowl skirt that clung politely to my legs.

No klutzing today, I promised myself. I made myself walk back to the kitchen and sit at the table while Cicca, singing a Greco ditty to herself, boiled my coffee. Supreme excellence, I reminded myself, consists of breaking the enemy's will without fighting.

No slipping, I coached myself as I headed down the slick flagstones of Sant'Orsola. *No ankle-twisting.* Most days I wore my plain brown pumps to go traipsing up and down the village, but today I had vengefully chosen my blue leather Bruno Maglis with the decorative studs. I was going to make an elegant first impression, goddamn it.

Speaking of elegance, it is difficult to walk down a long flight of shallow stone steps with your thighs pressed together, in case you are wondering.

I preferred to make my first visit, potentially a sensitive one, before I was encumbered by the mayor's company. According to the registrar, there was only one woman in Santa Chionia who had earned a middle school certificate. Until eight years ago, when Don Pantaleone had opened his private academy, there had been no middle school option for Chionoti children. The boys whose parents managed to scrounge the money for tuition attended seminary in far-off Reggio or Gerace. But sending away a girl—not to put too fine of a point on it, but I might as well express the concept of "girl" as "nubile mountain virgin"—to live with strangers in the pursuit of something as morally ambiguous as an education was, let us just say, not done.

This one woman had, somehow, done it. Her name was Isodiana

Legato and she was twenty-seven years old, just like me; she was married to a man named Santo Arcudi, and the couple had four children, one of whom was the right age to attend the nursery school. She was my top candidate to be my head teacher.

The Arcudi address was toward the western end of town, on via Zaleuco. The street, whose northeastern side was simply cliff face, narrowed into an enchanted-feeling alley, the rock wall blanketed in moss that glowed in the deflected morning sun. High above me, someone had driven cast-iron dowels in a geometric pattern into the sheer schist, and from them hung vibrantly green geraniums. Children's voices gurgled from the shallow balcony, whose persimmon-orange doors were cracked open.

The Signora Arcudi who answered my knock was a delicate dark woman with a sagittate Greco nose but a round face. She was wearing a close-fitting housedress that buttoned up to her chin. This was my quarry.

"Yes?" Her eyes and eyebrows both were a lustrous black.

"I'm Francesca Loftfield, the nursery school teacher." The stakes felt high; I was glad I'd worn my fancy shoes. "You are Signora Arcudi?"

"I am."

"My records indicate you have a daughter, Lucia, who is eligible to attend." After some detective work I was patting myself on the back for, I had figured out Isodiana Legato was probably the niece Potenziana the Wolfess, Tito Lico's wife, had mentioned; she was also the sister of the *puticha* owner, Saverio Legato. "May I talk to you about the school and the application?"

"Oh." The dark-haired woman hesitated. "My husband isn't here, *maestra*."

"That's all right. I can talk through the information with you. Or I could come back another day," I hastened to add, gambling that offering her the option to turn me away would make her less likely to do so.

For an anxious moment I thought I had failed, but she finally said, "Come in."

I mounted the concrete stoop and stepped into the moist stone stairwell. As she bolted the door behind me, I caught a noseful of jasmine oil. I opened my mouth to remark on it but forgot what I was going to say when the housewife turned and locked me in her dark gaze. The frozen moment felt jarringly intimate.

"Come with me, *maestra*." She spoke to me in textbook Italian, with a soughing Calabrese lilt.

I followed her slender calves and bare brown feet up the stairs into the salon, where an equally round-faced baby was sitting on a rug, grasping a well-slimed potato. An incongruous glass chandelier hung rather low above us.

"This is Antonino," my hostess said, following my gaze to her fat, perfect child. She bent over to scoop up the baby, who rested his potato on his mother's shoulder and twisted to observe me with bat-black eyes. "Please." She gestured to the sofa, an upholstered piece the Arcudis must have commissioned from a shop in Bova or even Reggio.

Absolutely no tearing your skirt, I reminded myself as I settled on the green cushion.

"I am so glad to have the chance to talk, *signora*," I enthused as she took a diffident seat beside me. "Your aunt mentioned you might be interested in getting involved."

"My aunt?"

"Donna Lico?" Had I made a mistake? I'd been so pleased with myself for ferreting out their matching maiden names. "She's your aunt, isn't she?"

"Oh!" Isodiana said, and the baby raised his potato and mimicked, "Ooh!" She wrapped a hand around the bare leg protruding from his linen tunic, causing a little flare of jealousy in my evil heart. "Yes, Zia Potenziana."

She was more receptive now that I had alluded to her formidable aunt. I had to hope that when they talked about me behind my back they would decide they liked me.

Propping my briefcase on my lap, I removed one of the typed-up forms I had brought from Cosenza. "Let me give you an overview of my organization and our mission."

Mother and baby watched me from under matching thatches of curling black hair as I described the nursery school. *If I had had a baby*—I couldn't plug up the thought—*if I had had a baby, would it have looked as much like me?*

"It sounds very good," Isodiana said.

"Oh good! You think you'll apply for Lucia?"

"Yes." She gave me the beginnings of a smile—small, but it brought me joy and hope. Later I would remember this feeling, find myself returning to it, and I would marvel at the power of this luminously ordinary woman. "*Maestra,* would you like a coffee?"

"I would love one." That bought me more time to tackle my next challenge: to plant the idea that she might make a good teacher. "Here, let me take the baby."

She hesitated, her upturned lips tensing.

"If it won't upset him to be away from his mamma."

"I don't know." She passed Antonino to me by his armpits. He gazed into my eyes with some consternation as I sat him on my own hip, absorbing the bittersweet warmth of his meaty little torso. He smelled vaguely of his damp potato.

Antonino and I trailed the pretty housewife to the kitchen, and I tried to collect data surreptitiously. The walls were bare except for a carved wooden crucifix, but the Arcudis were obviously not poor. Near the kitchen was a shelf covered with a crocheted doily runner—the Arcudis' votive altar, where a candle burned in a tiny dish in memory of the beloved deceased. I brought the baby closer to look at the three silver picture frames. On the left was a photo of a forty-something man, clean-shaven, sitting on the bench in front of the *puticha,* a walking stick braced against his spread knees as he whittled. He was looking up at the camera with a smile in his eyes, if not on his lips, his knife frozen in time against the bulge of his thumb. To the right of this photo was a much older seated studio portrait of a lissome young woman in a waistless silk dress; her Peter Pan collar made me think the photo was taken in the early 1930s, despite her Victorian hairstyle. Isodiana's deceased parents, I assumed, or her husband's, or one of each. The third was of a teenage boy, his stance impatient and newsboy cap diving toward his nose. I thought it was Saverio, the *puticha* proprietor, at first glance, but the nose was too paltry. Another brother who must have died. I was struck by the journalistic photos—unusual for a remembrance nook, which in most houses featured formal studio portraits or brutalist passport photos. Isodiana must have a photographer in her family, I thought.

Even more interesting was the shelf the photos sat on—it was a book-
case. More books than the priest had in his school; more than I'd seen at
the doctor's house in Bova. The bindings were mostly old and I struggled
to make out titles. There was a *Geografia* of something, and *The Adventures of Pinocchio*.

"What a collection," I remarked, forgetting about my undergarment
issue as I squatted to see better. The baby's thigh against my forearm was
as soft as yogurt.

"They were my father's." Isodiana was decanting water from the jug
on the counter into a Napoletana, but her eyes flitted up to meet mine.
There was an unmistakable nugget of pride there. "I've read them all," she
added, almost too quietly to hear.

I rose and joined her. "I saw you have a middle school certificate.
The only woman in Santa Chionia. Did you go all the way to Reggio to
study?"

"Gerace. My brother was going to seminary at the same time. We
lived with my mother's sister."

"What a wonderful example for your daughters."

"I thought maybe I wanted to be a teacher." She laughed, self-
effacing, and placed the pot on her gas stove—the first I had seen in
Santa Chionia—then collected the baby from me. I missed him at once.
"It was silly to go that far."

"Not silly at all," I protested. "You know, studies have shown that
when a woman is educated the benefit ripples out into the whole community."

"My parents indulged me." She looked up at me and smiled again.

"Mine, too," I said.

The little smile spread, and I was locked in the intensity of her strange
charisma. How neatly her curves pressed against the fitted housedress.
Her husband had married a perfect wife, in shape and voice and manner. Here we stood, the same age, the same interests, so many loci lining
up. Her lot could have been mine: loving mother who spent her free
time caring for her appearance and her family so she might be quietly
adored—a "good woman." *I* wanted to quietly adore her. I wanted her to
want to be my friend.

We were not the same, though. She had settled down into this wifely life at an age when I'd been running off to distant lands, adventures, degrees, careers, liaisons—

Would my life look more like Isodiana Legato's if my mother had never left Calabria?

I recovered my voice. "It is not too late for you to be a teacher. I hope you'll consider teaching at the nursery school when we open in January."

"Oh." Her smile dropped away. "Not me, *maestra*."

"It will pay a salary." I could feel the energy of her interest, tried to guess her objections. "We could figure out childcare for the baby."

We both watched the percolator start to fizz with heat.

"You'd be perfect for the job," I tried. She would not actually have been Sabrina's preferred candidate—Sabrina believed women with no professional qualifications were best, that they would be the least precious about getting grubby with toddlers. But Sabrina wasn't here, was she? "It would be a gift to the children of Santa Chionia."

Isodiana looked shyly sideways at me through her dark eyelashes. "No, I couldn't."

"Think about it," I said, and then, to perpetuate the myth that I cared at all about his opinion, I added, "Talk it over with your husband."

As I was finishing my coffee, three children filed into the room. *GIOVANNI, 6; LUCIA, 4; OLIMPIA, 7.* The little boy wore cuffed pants and suspenders, the girls knee-length dresses with puffed sleeves.

"All dressed. Good job, Olimpia," Isodiana said. "Look who's here, the American *maestra*. Say hello."

The children complied in shy voices. Their mother's genes were strong in all of them—whip-thin limbs; dark eyes; glossy black hair, thick with a slight curl.

"Nice to meet you all." I crouched on the floor, mindful of my skirt, so I could be eye level with Lucia, my future pupil. "This is my friend Zuzu." I showed her the stuffed monkey I had surreptitiously pulled out of my case. "Do you know what Zuzu is?"

Lucia stared at me sullenly, her bottom lip poking out in suspicion. Olimpia extended fingers as soft as pine needles and gave her sister an encouraging push. Another few beats of silence, then Lucia shrieked, "MONKEY!"

"That's right!" I presented Lucia with the doll. "Would you like to play with Zuzu?"

Lucia would—very much. Meanwhile the church bells were ringing the half hour.

"You better get going," Isodiana said to her older children. She kissed Giovanni on the cheek, then Olimpia, to whom she handed a burlap sack. "Give this to Don Pandalemu. See you at lunch. Be careful."

I needed to go, too—my interviews with the mayor started in half an hour. I followed Isodiana down the stairs, hoping I had made the right impression. She was so hypnotic, so calm, so polished. I wanted her to be the solution to one of my problems.

As she let us out, it took her a long moment to unlock the door, so I was forced to notice something I had missed earlier: when she'd let me into the house, she had double-bolted the door behind me, with an iron sliding lock as well as an oak beam. An unexpected amount of security between that beautiful family and the wicked outside world.

By five o'clock, when I parted ways with Mayor Stelitano after eight hours of student-parent interviews, the balls of my feet hurt so much that I had forgotten I wasn't wearing any underwear. Damn the Bruno Maglis, source of my power and my oppression. As I started to ache my way up Sant'Orsola, my spirit basking in the day's professional successes, it occurred to me that I could squeeze in one more good deed.

Dreading every additional step, I wobbled back down to the *puticha,* where Saverio, the proprietor, was tucking boxes of table salt into neat stacks under the liquor counter.

"*Maestra,*" he said, unfriendly as ever.

"Good evening."

The shop was empty except for Tito the Wolf, who sat with a pack of cards on the table in front of him, as if an opponent would appear at any moment. The glass tumbler by his hand was filled with what looked like milk.

"Good evening, Don Lico," I added pointedly.

The man nodded to me but did not remove his cap.

"Did you want something, *maestra*?" Saverio asked, not exactly solicitously.

"A *salame.*"

"What kind?"

I searched his face for a resemblance to Isodiana, his sister. It was there, now that I was looking for it. The sleeves of his well-tailored shirt were rolled up past his elbows and I saw the strength in his arms and his tapered waist. "The best one. You pick."

"You have to tell me spicy or not spicy. You Americans can't eat spicy, right?"

"Yes, we can," I said defensively, but then remembered my mission. "But this isn't for me, it's for Gnura Cicca."

"The spicy one." Tito Lico's voice startled me. When I turned around to look at him, he was sorting through the playing cards as if he hadn't spoken.

As Saverio cut down a *salame* from the rafter, it finally dawned on me—there should have been no salt for sale. He did not have a salt and tobacco license. I knew, because Cicca had made the six-hour round-trip walk to Bova in September to buy salt from the licensed *tabacchi* there. I couldn't help being amused by this quite literal manifestation of the concept "under the counter."

"How much?" I asked as Saverio placed my sausage on the counter.

"Nothing." His dark eyes on me were both searching and sullen. "It's a gift from Don Tito."

"Oh no, there's no need." I had meant for the sausage for Cicca to be an act of contrition; it felt like a moral shortcoming if I didn't pay for it.

"It's his pleasure," Saverio said.

I turned again to look at Tito Lico, but the man was staring down at his cards, any expression concealed by that huge black beard.

"Well, thank you, Don Tito." I took the *salame* and tucked it into my briefcase, where I hoped it wouldn't secrete sausage oil on my notes. "That is generous of you."

The older man looked up long enough to nod in my direction.

I never got around to telling Cicca that Tito Lico had paid for the sausage. I watched her slicing coins off and chewing on them with such joy—spicy had been the correct choice. She was speaking to me again, finally, and I thought, *What's the harm in letting her be happy with me?* The more indecisive time that passed, the greater the damage if I were to come clean. So I went to bed with my secret.

In the treacherous privacy of my lonely room, I could not sleep.

What were in fact the odds that Cicca would not find out I had misrepresented the provenance of the sausage? Everyone found out everything here. Then I would look truly terrible, taking credit for a gift paid for by someone else.

I was so troubled by this, and by my cramping calf, that I believe I had only just fallen asleep when the damn donkey went off an hour before sunrise.

These are the kinds of things you lose sleep over in a village like Santa Chionia.

These kinds of things, and others.

15

WEDNESDAY WAS A FRUSTRATING DAY WITH ORLANDO THE ELEC-trician. I was barely able to keep myself awake. At least I had on underwear.

At five o'clock, I sent the poor man home—he had a long walk. The setting sun cast my shadow against the nursery door as I locked up. I should have noticed the other shadow merging with mine before I did. The hairs on my arm were rising in alarm when a strong hand seized my wrist.

Marinating as I had been in Don Pantaleone's stories of Aspromonte justice, I felt my heart cramp in panic. I must have been expecting a brigand kidnapper or angry mafioso. It turned out to be someone far more dangerous.

"Maestra Franca." A statuesque woman of about forty was staring at me fiercely, her fingers still tight on my wrist. I had never seen eyes like hers, the color of shucked hazelnuts, clear as stained glass. The black lashes vibrated with nervous energy.

"Can I help you?"

"You're helping that senile old cabbage Emilia Volontà, aren't you." When the woman opened her mouth to speak, I glimpsed a dark cavern of gums. "She's trying to convince you the man under the post office is her son, but she's wrong. It's my husband."

My heart sped up again. So much for discretion. "What do you mean?"

"Come now." The woman flashed a sly smile. Her toothlessness, no doubt a product of inadequate nutrition during pregnancy, was a shame in her otherwise arresting face. "Why don't you let me in? So we don't have to talk about it in the street." She gestured casually to the *putìcha,* in front of which Saverio Legato and the mayor were chatting.

I took her point, although not especially sanguinely.

Sitting across my desk from her, just as I had sat across from Emilia Volontà last week, I took slow, thin breaths, trying to calm my pulse as I studied this fearsome woman. Her hair was wild, natural curls blown into the beginnings of a rat's nest, a sort of beggar's bouffant. Somehow the mess only called attention to her face, to her eerie and glittering sand-colored eyes. For anyone not impressed, there was an even more arresting quantity of sloping bosom shadowboxed by the sagging collar of her wool sweater.

"Please, *gnura,* tell me your name and why you wanted to see me."

"Vannina Favasuli." She never seemed to blink. "I'm the widow of Mico Scordo, although no one will admit that my husband was murdered, his body thrown under that shit-pile of bricks." She flung an accusatory hand toward the ruins of the post office, and I saw the black grime grouting the creases in her palm. "That lying hag Emilia is using you. Every Christian in this Godforsaken hellhole knows it's my husband."

I was struck dumb by the oration.

"I know in my heart he's dead." Vannina Favasuli made a fist and thumped it displacingly against her left breast, maybe to indicate where the aforementioned heart was. "For eight years they've lied to me, told me my Mico went to America. Then why hasn't he sent me a penny to support his children?"

Was there an epidemic in Santa Chionia of men who went missing to America? I waited to see if there was more of Vannina's speech still to come, and when there wasn't, I said cautiously, "I don't know anything about this, Gnura Scordo. I can't help you."

"Yes, you can! You can help me prove that the bones are Mico's, and then his killers will have to give me widow's rights, something to support his children."

My mind's eye was commandeered by the image of a wine barrel plummeting off the Saracen Tower. "If you believe there has been a murder, you must go directly to the police," I heard myself saying for the second time in my life.

"Go to the police! Like a rat!" Vannina Favasuli mock-spat over her shoulder and then crossed herself; I watched in alarmed fascination. "The police protect whoever pays, and widows have no money. Can't you see?" She plucked at her burlap skirt, ragged enough to reveal a substantial spread of bare flesh.

"But what good would it do to find out your husband was murdered if you won't go to the police?"

"I need you to help me find proof," Vannina pleaded. I smelled her desperation in the dirty sweat on her winter-bare feet. "Otherwise the *carabinieri* will never listen to me."

My heart was pounding so hard that the muscle around it felt sore. That damn skeleton. Why had identifying the corpse become my problem?

And how many missing men were going to be put forward as candidates?

"I operate strictly within the purview of my employer's mission," I said. "I can't get involved with anything else."

"You're helping old Emilia."

Give them one finger, my mother would have said, and they take your whole goddamn arm. "All I did was check the emigration records for her, since she can't read."

"All *I'm* asking you is to do the same for me," Vannina retorted. "I need your help as much as she does. You think Pino Pangallo at the *municipio* will even let me into his office?"

"Vannina! No. I cannot be associated with any kind of covered-up crime."

Her manner changed drastically; she was piteous, tears rushing down her face. "Madonna, I can't sleep at night, I dream of his restless soul, begging for rest, a Christian burial." She stretched herself nearly prostrate across the desk to clutch my hand, palpating the palm. "Please help me, kind *maestra*." She lifted her soot-smeared skirt to wipe her face, baring even more leg in the process. "My children are starving, six children, my daughters with no father to protect them, they shall be victims of the wolves!"

I rode out a wave of revulsion, thinking of the beggars I'd seen crying out their miseries on street corners in New York and Rome, performances they hoped to trade for a few coins. The most wretched ones cannot be helped, Sabrina would have reminded me. If you try, you squander the opportunity to change lives that might actually be changed. You must know when to walk away from that which cannot be redeemed.

That's the trouble, though. Walking away when you might be someone's last hope at redemption.

"Why don't you go back to the beginning," I said when the drama had wrung itself out. "Tell me your whole story." I could spare the woman half an hour, let her feel like she had been listened to; it was an inexpensive gift that might be of greater help to her twisted psyche than anything else.

Vannina Favasuli had fallen in love with Mico Scordo when they were children. They were apart for many years, because he left to go to America when he was fifteen to work for his uncle, but they'd gotten married when he returned at twenty-one.

"Mico worshipped me like a Madonna. He went out every day to pick me flowers on the hill. He was an angel, a perfect creature from heaven."

". . . And then?"

Vannina hiccupped. "And then I had the twins. Carmela and Niceforo."

"Twins! Without a doctor?"

"Twins run in my family." Vannina waved her feat away, insensible to the spike of horror she had caused me. "Mico went back to America so he could send us money. But that was bad timing—no one was allowed to come or go during the war. I thought I was never going to see him again," she said. "I thought we were all going to die."

"It was a hard time."

Mico had finally been able to come home after all the fighting was over. From then on, he emigrated every year, coming home in the summers and sending a packet of money every month. The last time Vannina saw Mico was in August 1952, when he supposedly got on a boat and was never heard from again.

"But you don't think he went to America?"

"I know he didn't. He never said goodbye." Vannina's hazelnut irises rolled before she fixed them on me again. "I wrote him a letter, I was so angry, but then the landlord in America returned the letter to me— wrote that Mico never came back."

"And no one in Santa Chionia has any forwarding address?"

"His brother won't give me a straight answer. Who knows what he's mixed up in."

I stared hard at her, analyzing her face until she looked away. Did she really think her husband had been killed, or was this some kind of performance? I felt pity and distrust. "Why did you call Gnura Emilia a lying hag earlier?"

Vannina lifted her face to show her bright, hypnotic eyes. "I shouldn't have said that," she said appealingly. "I didn't mean it."

The seed of doubt had been planted, though. Why had Emilia been so cold to me in the piazza? Why had she insisted I be secretive about her inquiry about her son Leo?

"I'll tell you what," I said. "I'll do for you exactly as I did for Gnura Emilia, and I will check the emigration registry for evidence that Mico left." I couldn't do something for one woman and refuse to do it for another. "But that is all I can do for you."

The woman allowed me to lead her to the door. "I am humiliated," she said, her left hand clinging to mine. "I don't know if I'm a proper widow or an abandoned woman, I'm a pariah, I have no pride, I have only shame . . ."

"Go home, eat some dinner," I said, my mother's prescription for most spiritual ailments. "And think hard about what I said, about going to the *carabinieri*."

On my climb up the steps of via Sant'Orsola, I reflected that I could do a better job of listening to my own advice. As I sat at Cicca's table waiting for a bowl of the concoction she was stewing, I thought hard about whether *I* should be going to the *carabinieri*. Two women had now made me aware of missing persons in this isolated village; one had specifically alluded to violent crime. I didn't exactly believe there had been a murder in Santa Chionia; if there *had* been, it wouldn't have been a secret for very long. Not unless the entire town was conspiring to keep it so.

It was difficult, however, to imagine a reason besides murder that an unidentified skeleton would have been dumped in the foundation stones of a civic structure.

What I knew so far amounted to hearsay. What was I going to do, make a six-hour round-trip hike over the plank bridge to Bova to tell some police officers that a secretive old lady and an indigent drama queen were involving me in a proxy tussle over some unidentified bones?

"You're quiet tonight," Cicca accused as she set a wooden bowl in front of me.

"I was thinking, *cummàri.*"

"About what?" She squinted down at me, ready to be offended.

I labored over my word choice. "The skeleton they found under the post office. I was . . . I was wondering when the police are going to finish their investigation."

"The police don't come up here." Cicca sat across from me and passed me a carved wooden spoon.

"Police don't come to Santa Chionia? Ever?"

"Only sometimes to arrest Christians for no reason and take them away to the jail in Bova." She made it sound like a pheasant hunt.

"Who investigates crimes?"

"What crimes?" Cicca scowled—not an angry scowl, just one of the habitual settings of her face. "Do you know about a crime?"

"No," I said, cowering.

Cicca snorted. "Well, eat before it gets cold."

I looked down at the brown bowl in front of me. "This—this smells *so* good," I said, and I wasn't even kissing up. It wasn't always easy to enjoy Cicca's cooking. Some of the mountain grasses the Chionoti were accustomed to were extraordinarily strong-flavored, or tough to chew; Cicca had amazing stamina for chicory and bitter lettuce. My molly-coddled spirits wilted every time I encountered yet another dish of lentils. But tonight's cuisine was stupendous, something I would have been impressed to be served at a restaurant: soft, finger-length semolina noodles in a soupy sauce of fresh porcini mushroom and parsley. "Cicca, this is delicious. What do you call it?"

"Pasta with mushrooms," she replied with charming modesty. "Do you like it?"

"I love it." I lifted a porcini on my spoon. "This kind of mushroom is so, so hard to find in America. My mother can never buy them because they are so expensive."

"In the Aspromonte they're free," Cicca said. "Once the October rains come, the forest is bursting with them."

Cicca seemed pleased with me tonight, so after a few minutes of silent partaking I ventured, "May I ask your opinion about something?"

"My opinion?"

"Who—who do you think that skeleton under the post office belongs to?"

I watched the skin around her eyes tighten. After a moment she said, "Someone we should pray for."

I didn't give up. "But—do, do you know who it is?"

"Do I know?" Cicca shook her head in reproachful disbelief. "I don't know anything."

I tried one more time. "If the *carabinieri* never come up to Santa Chionia, how are they going to figure out what happened?"

Cicca fixed me with her level gaze. "All these years have passed and no one was worried about it before. It seems like the best thing would be if we went on not worrying about it now."

16

CICCA'S FAVOR WAS A SINE CURVE THAT EBBED AND PEAKED according to how freshly she had reminded herself of my outrages. On Sunday morning she was friendly enough. "You have to come to mass today," she told me as she fired up the Napoletana percolator.

Mass was not generally part of my plans. Sabrina's policy on church-going was that it wasn't required of her agents. My mixed-faith parents had not troubled to instill in me any notion of a higher power, and it had always felt like a discourtesy to sit among religionists and try to keep a deadpan while thinking vicious thoughts about their collective self-opiations and their unscrupulous slave masters.

I could not forfeit the opportunity to kiss up to Cicca, is the thing. "All right, *cummàri*. But why?"

"We celebrate All Souls, it's very important."

It was October 30, and this turned out not to be true.

The church was sparsely adorned—the only art was the Byzantine-style altar fresco of San Silvestro with his gray challah of beard—so there was nowhere to look but at the winsome priest. Don Pandalemu interrupted the Latin liturgy to deliver a stirring admonishment about the civic duty of voting, reminding congregants that Deuteronomy requires us to make our wise men the rulers of our tribes. Other than that demonstration of the lack of separation between church and state, there was nothing remarkable about mass. There was, for example, no mention of the post office corpse, or any entreaty to keep its unknown loved ones in our prayers.

Cicca was twitching with energy throughout the homily. We hadn't quite been dismissed yet when she grabbed my hand and tugged me to my feet. We were the first out the door, where the upper piazza was milling with men of all ages, many leaning on hand-carved walking sticks. It was a confusing sight in the fresh harshness of high morning—were they all waiting for their churchgoing wives?

We did not head home—instead Cicca drew me toward the stone wall that marked the top of via Sant'Orsola. Next to us was an adolescent olive tree planted in a weather-whitened wine barrel that called to mind images of plummeting priests; at its base was seated a teenage boy priming a three-drone bagpipe. The bladder winched under his elbow had discernibly once belonged to a sheep.

Not waiting for a wife, I guessed.

Finally catching on, I tucked myself behind Cicca and waited for whatever was going to happen to happen.

The piazza filled quickly, women in calf-length broom skirts and white kerchiefs disappearing behind men in white button-downs that varied in levels of shabbiness. Some were barefoot; others wore leather-strap bindings instead of shoes. Above us, a chorus line of four pigeons whirred from the church roof, while a fifth, the soloist, strutted back and forth under the crucifix, which was smaller than him.

I had never seen so many Chionoti together at once.

The last to swagger out of the church door—certainly by design; the piazza had fallen silent—was a short, skinny man of middle years. He wore a tan newsboy cap and carried a piece of firewood. The swagger was not native to this man's personality; I saw shame or nerves or some other kind of stage fright on his face before he raised the log over his head and shouted, "Whose wood is this?"

The pullulating silence extended as a black-haired young man stepped into the ring of spectators. He had the lithe brawn of a not-yet-fully-adult male and towered over his opponent. "It's my wood, Masciu Petrulli. I left it at your door."

"Niceforo Scordo. You wish to marry my daughter?"

"I wish to marry your daughter Agathi, Masciu Petrulli." The boy's words were respectful but his tone was defiant.

Terrifying suspense hung in the silence.

Agathi's father thrust the cordwood into the younger man's chest. "Marriage is not for you, boy."

Niceforo Scordo—he must have been Vannina's son; I saw her wild beauty in his dark face—accepted the wood with both his broad hands. His shoulders were quivering.

Agathi Petrulli's father did not leave any room for debate or rapprochement; he walked, glassy-eyed, into the crowd, which shuffled to let him escape down via Sant'Orsola.

Young Niceforo, meanwhile, turned slowly to confront the spectators. His face was blank of any emotion, the wood cradled in his left arm rather like a Madonna's infant Jesus.

I scanned the crowd for Vannina Favasuli. Had she just watched her son's public humiliation? I didn't see her, but there were so many people.

Startled, I yelped when the bagpiper at my side roared into action. Pumping out an incongruously upbeat refrain, he puffed over to the spurned suitor and stood at his elbow. As the crowd began to disperse, the men tipped their caps to Niceforo. He did not nod back but I watched him meet all their gazes.

The hexatonic keening of the bagpipe chased us home down via Boemondo.

"How dreadful," I said to Cicca. "To be cut down like that in front of the whole town."

"No, you are wrong. It is his *honor*." Cicca was triumphant, as if she had been part of the battle herself.

"Poor kid," I said. "Well, he certainly hid his disappointment like a man. So stoic—he didn't even look surprised."

"No surprise," Cicca said, removing her huge iron door key from her bosom as we turned into our alley. "He knew the offer was no good."

"Someone warned him?" Everyone in town had known to show up for mass to see the proposal play out. "Or was it a hopeless cause the whole time?"

"No," Cicca said sadly. "I was hoping it would be a good marriage.

Niceforo is a good boy—you saw, *che bravo.* It's not his fault." She jimmied the lock on her door and knocked it open with her blocky hip.
"In Santa Chionia, when a boy proposes, he leaves the wood outside the
girl's house. If the girl's father accepts the proposal, he brings the wood
in the house. If he does not accept, he brings the wood to church and
returns it to the boy."

"Wait." I followed Cicca into the kitchen, sure I was misunderstanding. "So Mr.—what was his name? Petrulli?"

"Giuseppe Petrulli," Cicca said. "He's my cousin."

"So Masciu Petrulli never brought the wood into his house, so that
meant everyone knew he was not going to accept the proposal?"

"Exactly."

"And everyone came to mass to see the rejection?" I was even more
horrified than before. "Why would Niceforo even show up?"

"To show he is a man," Cicca said. "To show he has honor."

"That's—that's horrible."

"It's beautiful," Cicca said. "Don't you see? By showing his face he has
told everyone in Santa Chionia that he has chosen honor over his own
pride or, you know. Manly desire." She took her pot down from its hook
on the wall. "That's why we have no *fuitina* here in Santa Chionia. Our
men are honorable. I'm going to make pasta for lunch."

"*Fuitina*" was a word my Italian mother never taught me, although there
was never a time when it didn't shadow the edge of my consciousness
about what it means to be a woman. The first time I remember hearing
it I was ten years old, sitting dumpy and aghast at my aunt Phyllis's doi-
lied dining room table as Phyllis described for my aunt Dolly what had
happened to my pretty older cousin Gigi, whose father had caught her
engaging in an unencouraged behavior with an American GI and who
was now in the process of having a marriage arranged for her.

Fuitina means "the escape," literally, or by implication "elopement,"
in dialects of Calabria and Sicily. The founding concept of *fuitina* is that
once a man has taken sexual possession of a woman, there is no option
except a "reparative marriage" to restore the woman's honor. All *fuitina*s
have one element in common: premarital sex, or, to put a fine point on
it, loss of virginity by the woman involved. In terms of narrative arc,
though, there are two different kinds of *fuitina*. In the happier itera-

tion, a "decorous" *fuitina,* a pair of young lovers finds that their commitment to each other is not approved of by their families. Together they find a respectable place to spend the night together—the house of a sympathetic aunt, for example. Once the hymen has presumably been breached, none of the parties who stood in the way of the union can object to a marriage anymore. It can also be a way to save money on an expensive wedding.

But the "bride" herself cannot object to marriage after a *fuitina* in the case that the loss of virginity occurred without her consensual participation. This is where the second kind of narrative arc must be introduced. Say, for example, a man desires a young woman who is in love with someone else, or who simply doesn't desire *him.* The aspiring "groom," sometimes with the help of loyal buddies, kidnaps the recalcitrant wife-to-be and restrains her until he has physically ensured she will never be able to marry anyone else.

Whether or not the men of Santa Chionia were "honorable," as Cicca maintained, I wasn't convinced there was no such thing as *fuitina* here. After all, Cicca wouldn't have had a word for the problem if the problem didn't exist.

17

MONDAY MORNING A SHADOW DARKENED THE NURSERY'S OPEN door. A diminutive shadow—a woman.

"Teacher." It was Emilia Volontà, respectfully waiting to be invited in.

I wondered if the scene of my snubbing in front of the *puticha* last week was as dramatic in her memory as in mine. But I was not supposed to act like a petty child.

"Come in, *gnura,*" I said in my dumb Greco.

It was an important part of my work, the willingness to be snubbed, although one I was never pure enough of heart to master. You must be willing to have people be embarrassed to be seen with you if you are going to be effective at, say, distributing illegal contraceptives.

"How can I help you, *gnura?*"

"You asked me to bring you the letter?" The envelope she showed me was as age-spotted as the hands that held them.

I stood and took it from her. The addressee, an Annunziato Volontà in Chicago, c/o Vittorio Olivieri, had been slashed through with blue ink, the English words *NOT AT THIS ADDRESS* running in neat block letters underneath. The return address read:

R. Alvaro
Santa Chionia (RC)
Italia

We stood together by the window as I opened the flap. The paper had been crisply folded for decades and the crease buckled in resistance.

Signori:
 The debt of 300 lire for the passage of Leo Romeo remains to be repaid. A year has passed since this money was loaned to you. There is now due 30% interest. This amount shall compound until we have been repaid in full.
 Cordial Salutations,
 Rocco Alvaro

"Do you know what this says?"

Emilia Volontà's docile expression didn't change. "That we were looking for Leo and could he please write home."

My hurt feelings had faded away entirely into pity. This awful letter was the only memento she had of her lost son. Don Alvaro had thought so little of Emilia he had lied to her about the contents, hadn't even respected her enough not to let her keep this evidence of his heartlessness.

On the other hand, this was a clue—I could now trace Leo Romeo to Chicago. Documents like this one would be case-breakers for my burgeoning nonbusiness of tracking down missing immigrant men. Half of me was rolling my eyes at myself, but only half.

If I was going to be an immigrant detective, I was going to need a better-organized dragnet. I went to my desk; opened my datebook to the Leo Romeo page, as I now thought of it; and readied my pen. "*Gnura*, who is Annunziato Volontà?"

"My brother. He was the one who took Leo to America."

"What happened to him?"

Emilia Volontà's shoulders rose all the way to her ears in one of her slow, bony shrugs, a gesture I now recognized as an expression of anguish. "I don't know, teacher." The low brown knob of her goiter retracted into her slender neck, and I waited for her to find her voice. "They told us he had been killed by a train in America."

They.

"But we didn't hear about that until many years later. Not until after my husband was gone."

Yet another man who had disappeared to America. "I'm sorry, *gnura,*" I said. She nodded at the floor, the morning sun combing streaks of silver into her white hair.

My imagination, always a liability, had begun to spin sinister scenarios that might explain why both Emilia's son and her brother had vanished. Instead, I tried to concentrate on where I could go next for more information.

"This sender," I asked. "Is this Don Roccuzzu Alvaro?" I remembered what Cicca had told me about "the old don," the goatherd who'd made himself rich off of extortionate lending to emigrants. In 1920, a common laborer might have earned a lira for a day's work, as my grandfather had been fond of reminding me. The debt described in this letter was a year of a man's life. "He paid for Leo's passage?"

Emilia nodded. I turned the letter over again, hoping I had missed some data that could point me toward a next step. The dead don was a dead end. Would his widow keep records of his forty-year-old correspondence?

Emilia Volontà was watching me think, her lips compressed. I realized I was nibbling on the end of my pen and pulled it out of my mouth. That was it—a secretary. Rackets like this always involved a middleman, didn't they? I could hardly imagine the self-appointed town boss taking dictation from a humble housemaid like Gnura Emilia.

"Was Don Roccuzzu the one who wrote letters to Leo for you?"

"No," Emilia said. "That was someone else."

Bingo. "Who?"

She hesitated—attempting, one might innocently assume, to recall a name from forty years earlier. "Ceciu Legato."

Another Legato. I wondered how this Ceciu was related to Poten-ziana, Saverio, and Isodiana.

"Is Ceciu Legato still around? I can ask him if he remembers any other information."

"Ceciu? No, he emigrated, too."

At least I had another name—another lead to chase. I copied down the names and Chicago address and handed the brittle letter back to its victim. "Okay, *gnura*. Let me think what I can try next." The bells of San Silvestro sounded the hour. "You must excuse me, I have an appointment with the mayor. I will see you at Don Pandalemu's later?"

"Yes, yes," Emilia Volontà said. "I will see you later, teacher."

When she turned to leave, I saw her hair was pinned into two spiral-ing braids, thin and tight on her head. I thought of a lonely old woman sitting in her empty house and taking the care to pin up her hair like that. For whom?

I hoped the pins didn't make her scalp sore.

I did not see her later. Mayor Stelitano and I passed Don Pandalemu on via Steisicoro between interviews. The priest and the mayor engaged in a lengthy conversation about a number of fallen trees on the priest's property up the mountain; the mayor had promised to arrange a permit for their sale as timber but had apparently forgotten to get the clearance. They argued in heated Calabrese as though I were not there. As we were parting ways, Don Pandalemu switched from musical dialect to school-house Italian and said, "Oh, Francesca, we must lunch some other time. I have to go to the diocese."

Just as well—we had so many interviews to do. As Cicca had told me judgmentally, lunch never need be more than two chestnuts and two figs, which I should keep in my pocket at all times.

In the late afternoon, I sat at Cicca's kitchen table to write up my daily notes while she blanched fava beans. We both made an effort, chatting and snacking on carefully rationed slices of the spicy *salame*.

"Do you know Emilia Volontà?" I asked her.

Cicca turned around to examine me for my sanity. "Do I know her?"

"Of course you know her," I ventured. "Is she a relative?"

"Is she a relative," Cicca repeated disbelievingly, but then she admitted, "Not especially. We didn't grow up together; her family lived in the countryside."

I sought the right question to ask, the one that would draw out the gossipy Cicca. "Did something bad happen to her son?"

"Her daughter," Cicca corrected. "Rosa."

"Her son Leo," I said before I could think better of it. *Follow the lead, Frank.* "What happened to her daughter Rosa?"

Cicca didn't say anything for a long interval. I was certain I had slammed the door on whatever splendid bird had been about to fly out of that cage. I watched her lift the favas out of the pot with a slotted spoon, then begin rubbing off their skins with her industrial-strength fingertips.

But she did reply, at long last. "She died during the war. Her fiancé got drafted and she died of a broken heart."

Before I had a chance to learn more, *"Allo?"* came a man's voice from the foyer, someone's attempt at English. I braced myself as Cicca went to receive the visitor.

I knew it was a special occasion, because when she returned to the kitchen Cicca pulled the cord on the lightbulb.

"Maestra Franca, Officer Vadalà is here to see you." Cicca clasped her hands imploringly in front of her low-hanging bosom; she was clutching a fistful of empty fava pods like a tussie-mussie. I wondered mootly about fava floriography.

"Officer," I said, standing. Santa Chionia's lone municipal cop had a square, weathered face and pale blue eyes. Perhaps I was in breach of some obscure town ordinance, behind on a residency permit processing fee or something like that.

"Sit down!" Cicca cheeped. "Officer, let me get you some *salame.*"

"Don't go to any trouble," the traffic cop said, but he was already pulling out the stool, and in short order he accepted a glass of wine.

The least awkward choice I had was to sit back down. "How is your family?" I said stupidly.

"My wife is sad. We lost the goat in the flood. All the firewood for the winter ruined."

"Terrible!" Cicca had lost her own woodpile but apparently preferred to keep the spotlight on the officer. "Poor goat! Your poor wife!" Her eye flicked up and caught mine and I realized she was as uncomfortable as I was to have this man in her house.

Halfway through Cicca's precious sausage, Officer Vadalà got around to his point. "The Lichena was telling me about your school, Maestra Franca."

"It's a nursery," I said, cautiously optimistic. "For three- and four-year-olds."

"It sounds like an intelligent project." He took a bite out of the lentil bread Cicca had set by his hand. "The Lichena mentioned there are a limited number of places."

"Yes, thirty-six." My optimism was acidifying in my throat. "I'm in the process of collecting applications."

"Then I'm coming at the right time." The cop wiped his oily mouth with the palm of his hand. His face was thin, but when he retracted his neck a double chin appeared for long enough that I registered it as a warning. "I want to make sure that you have included my sister's son. Gianni Lentini. He's a rascal, but he's bright. You'll be glad to have him."

"We'll be glad to have him if we end up selecting him out of the pool of candidates," I corrected. By then, I had identified the attempted shakedown, and my nerves had evaporated into annoyance. Annoyance not, I confess, untinged by a glimmer of triumph; enrollment in my nursery was a prize worth attempting to extort. "I haven't seen an application from your sister." I reached for my briefcase, which was resting by the officer's feet. "I can give you the form right now."

"Is that really necessary?" Vadalà regarded me mildly. "I've put in a good word; what other information do you need?"

Under the table, I pressed my fingernails into my palm. "My organization requires everything to be regulated. Have your sister fill out the application."

"All right, I understand." He sighed but took the paper, then pushed back his stool and stood. "Thank you for taking care of it, Maestra Franca. I'll let my sister know."

I had not yet learned, when I was twenty-seven, to let men like Officer Vadalà go drifting by. My blood was boiling with the idea that he might leave pretending there was an agreement between us. I leapt up and darted to block his passage. "Nothing is taken care of, officer. Your sister can fill out the paperwork, like everyone else."

"Now now, there's no need for theatrics," he chastised. "This is simple, *signorina*. I am telling you that my sister's son should be in your nursery, and you are going to listen to the good advice of local law enforcement." He touched his hat, as if politely, but it only underscored the fact that he had never bothered to take it off. "After all, who could give you better advice?"

The threat in his words was clear, but my hot head was aflame. "You'll find I cannot be bought or coerced."

Officer Vadalà's mild expression was gone, replaced by sleepy-looking critical appraisal. He turned to Cicca and said, "Your tenant isn't clever about making friends."

Cicca was wringing her hands, and before she could burst into tears, I replied, "I'm not here to make friends, Officer Vadalà. I am here to *save children*."

"Everyone needs friends," he said warningly to my back, but I was gone, slamming the door to my bedroom and pressing myself against the seam.

On the other side, I heard Cicca imploring the officer. "Please don't be angry with her. She's American, she doesn't understand."

"Pigheaded." His voice was loud enough that I was certain I was intended to hear, as were curious neighbors. "No one can help her if she won't help anyone else."

"Everything will work out!" Cicca shrilled. "I'll take care of it."

I waited until the end of Cicca's effusive goodbyes. By then, the pounding of my heart had diminished and all that was left was rage. I confronted her in the kitchen.

"How dare you make promises on my behalf," were the first words out of my mouth. "You have nothing to do with my nursery. Nothing!"

"I was protecting you, stupid girl!" Cicca's wiry brown eyebrows rose in a wide diagonal, like bug antennae. "You must do as the officer says, Franca. He can take away my house! He can burn it down! He can kill my goat, or steal it and give it to his wife!"

"No one is going to steal your goat! Don't you see he has no power at all? He is a tiny-town traffic cop! You give him power with your fear!"

My resistance bon mots were white noise to Cicca. "Just put the boy in the school! There doesn't have to be any trouble."

"There's not going to be any trouble." I was so angry my voice was cracking. "There never is trouble when everyone follows the rules."

Cicca turned her square face up at me, showing me the brown circles under her eyes. In the unaccustomed electric light, she looked old. "What if he hurts you?"

"That's absurd," I said. "I'm here to open a school. Who would want to hurt me? I'm protected not just by my charitable organization but by the Italian government."

"What does that matter if you're dead?!"

It was so ludicrous I had to fight back laughter, which only made me angrier. I stared at Cicca's anguished face, then gave up on having the last word and stepped outside, slamming the door pointedly behind me.

18

IT WAS ONLY FIVE P.M.—THE LOUD BELLS OF SAN SILVESTRO STARtled me when they clanged behind me as I stomped down via Sant'Orsola—but the sun was burning among a neon-orange bed of clouds. It would not linger; in the bowl of the mountains, sunrise and sunset are abrupt, as is the temperature change of twilight. I had no jacket, but I was burning with fury and fear—at what the cop's threat meant, at whether I had made an enemy with real power today.

Before Santa Chionia, I had never feared anything except failure.

These were some of my thoughts, in their various gradations of blasphemy, as my stony steps jolted my bones:

That woman!

Cicca was a victim in this. She had been raised to fear authority. She was stupid because she had never had the opportunity to be otherwise. She was not the problem.

But seriously.

Why couldn't I be more like Sabrina? She would have gracefully dispatched the sleazy cop with no hard feelings or promises.

That insipid weasel of a supposed officer of the law was a cancer on this struggling town. If he tried to extort something so inane from me, what else had he felt entitled to from much more helpless people?

How can I go on living in Cicca's house? With a new firefight every week?

At home in Pennsylvania the maple leaves would be passing their peak—the foliage tourists would be motoring out to the dainty villages of the Main Line and admiring my dad's chrysanthemum garden. I could be sitting with Dad in my parents' solarium, drinking his favorite Chinese tea among his ship-in-bottle collection while we irritated each other by distractingly raising exciting points in our respective reading materials.

I missed my dad. And my mom. And having friends.

You have no right to a solarium and imported Chinese tea when the poor women of Santa Chionia have no walls and no food.

An outsider, even if she was reviled, was required to shake things up. As long as their parents lived in the hereditary thrall of people like Vadalà, the children of Santa Chionia had no one with the tools to fight for them.

Be the wire.

The year of the pagans—all those lost babies—

By then, my anger was gone, and the dusky boulders and draping succulents lining Sant'Orsola were gauzy in the swirl of my tears.

You must never go out walking except in broad daylight, Dottor Iiriti had warned me, *and never alone.*

But don't let me mislead you—that thought never crossed my mind as I dribbled down the crooking flagstones toward the lower piazza.

19

SOMEONE HAD HUNG A BURNING SAP LAMP IN FRONT OF THE locked town hall, and it cut a slice of homey diorama out of the darkening piazza. The air, usually prickling with carbonized pine, was tonight rich with some aromatic herb, not quite lavender, not quite mint. The *puticha* was glowing from within, a Grandma Moses kind of small-town glow, the supple murmur of men's laughter easing out of the open shutters. An invitation to forgiveness: I would buy something luxurious, even more expensive than the sausage I hadn't paid for, and bring it home to Cicca as another apology present.

The *putìca* was packed, men in newsboy caps leaning against the wine barrels, tables patchworked by mustard-colored playing cards. The stinging smoke of a single cigarette, clenched like a mussel beard between the gray lips of a man I had never seen before, was barely discernible over the herdsmen's musk: sweat and oily sheep's wool.

Saverio, the proprietor, was not behind the counter. I scanned the faces; so many strange men—*pastori* come down from their mountain paddocks? I stepped gingerly through the too-close gentlemen, who made no effort to let me pass. Their unwelcome was not oblique. I would buy something and get out.

At last I located Saverio Legato—I *swear* I caught his eye—but his conversation stretched on. I stood at the counter, shifting awkwardly in my black bunnies, sinking deeper into a frumpy crisis of self-loathing while all those men pretended they didn't see me. I cannot tell you how long these minutes felt—you would think I was exaggerating.

The stranger who saved me must have come in behind me, and when he called over my shoulder, "O! Saverio!" I yelped in shock.

I whirled around and found him right at my elbow.

"*Scusate, signorina,*" he said, removing his cap. "Saverio," he called again. "You have customers."

I assume Saverio made some cynically apologetic reply, but I don't recall because I was completely, adolescently distracted by the specimen beside me. He was enormous, the breadth of his shoulders testing the humble wool of his brown jacket. He was only a few inches taller than I, but my other half is Norwegian. He was politely holding his cap in both hands, so a glorious bloom of chestnut curls was on full display.

"Ugo," Saverio said, restored behind the counter. "What can I get you?"

"The *signorina* was ahead of me." The specimen nodded at me.

Saverio's eyes slid to me facetiously. "How can I help you, *maestra*?"

When I tried to speak, there was a cough in my throat, which could in theory have made me feel even dumber than it did. "Sweets," I managed. "Do you have any candies or chocolates?"

"Only this." Saverio pulled a white box from under the counter. "Chocolate-covered chestnuts. They are expensive."

I needed to buy something to justify this pageant. "How much?"

Saverio was a savvy man; he certainly sensed he could have named any price. There was a long pause while he gauged his gouge, during which I exercised great discipline and did not perform any further examination of the specimen. "Five hundred."

"Thank you," I said. Maybe it was outrageous; surely no one in Santa Chionia would have been able to afford five-hundred-lire chocolates. Or maybe it was the right price for a fragile delicacy. I would never know. Or care—it was something like fifty American cents.

"I got it," the specimen said. Of course I could not come ill-advisedly into the *puticha* and be allowed to purchase my own luxury items.

"No, *grazie*," I said to him. "You're kind but that's not necessary."

"Don't take this away from me, *signorina*." He never looked at me, just deposited a heap of coins on the counter. Saverio took the money without counting it. "If a man cannot even buy a woman a box of chocolates, what is left for him in this world?"

I'd heard some version of that classic line at coffee bars all over Italy. Somehow, on the unlikely lips of this soft-spoken young man, it sounded not at all like he was making a pass—it was anesthetized, even ironic.

"Thank you," I said again, and took the chocolates. *Ugo.* I thought of Victor Hugo, of Eponine and Marius. "It is too kind of you."

As the specimen followed me through the crowd to the door, I heard men murmuring his name in greeting. I was grateful to whichever of them blocked his passage. My reputation in Santa Chionia needed rehabilitation, not further savaging.

I hurried across the now-dark piazza in the whistling cold, but he caught up with me before I had turned up Sant'Orsola. "Let me walk you home, *signorina*."

I had already made a mistake in accepting the chocolates. "No, thank you. My hostess is expecting me." My heart was pounding. I did not need this on an evening like this one, when I already had no friends.

"You misunderstand," he said in my ear. "It is best not to walk alone. There are many strangers in Santa Chionia tonight."

I knew he was not incorrect, and yet I heard in his words the exact kind of gentleman's offer that was inextricable from the threat itself. How had I been so stupid as to get myself into this?

"I'm fine." I tried to speed up, but there was no faster way to walk than I already was. I succeeded only in introducing a jiggle in my backside, which I regretted as soon as I felt it.

"All right," the specimen Ugo said. "But I am heading up to visit Cummàri Cicca anyway, so I hope you don't mind if I walk with you."

Via Sant'Orsola was a cascade of shadows. The houses seemed especially dreary, shutters drawn earlier than usual. Should I turn around and go back to the bar?

His expression was so mild, the set of his enormous shoulders so relaxed. My gut instinct told me he was not a sex pest.

My gut instinct had led me astray many times before.

When my mush of emotions had been tamped down by the physical activity, I asked, "What's going on today? Who are all the men, I mean."

"It's a reunion of old friends," Ugo said. "Friends and cousins."

The autumn evening was cold on my legs. Finally it sank in that this Ugo had known who I was and where I lived. "You know Cummàri Cicca," I said when I'd caught my breath.

"She's my father's aunt," Ugo replied. "I haven't been to visit her since I got back."

"Back from where?"

"Milan." He paused long enough for me to sense, when he did speak again, that he was volunteering more information than he needed to. "I've been living there for the last ten years. I work in a steel factory."

We were passing the mayor's house, where new geranium pots had replaced the ones that had been smashed by the flood. "What brings you back to Santa Chionia?" The emigrants usually came back only for August and Christmas.

"My father is dying," he said in the same even, unanimated voice. "I quit my job to come help my mother."

"I'm so sorry." I now felt guilty for having distrusted him.

"It's all right, I can get my job back whenever I want it," he said.

"I meant—"

"I know what you meant," he said with rueful good humor. "What are you going to do." I was still trying to think of how to respond when he spoke up again. "See that?" He was pointing to the moss-skirted obelisk at the corner of via Erodoto.

"The stone?" I passed it at least two times a day. "Is it some kind of shrine?"

"Not exactly. It's a saint stone." Ugo had stopped walking, kissed his index finger, and extended his hand to rub the smooth patch on top. "To show respect to Santa Chionia. It's lucky. Go ahead."

I imitated his obeisance. The smoothness was familiar under my fingertip.

"The others are in the forest," Ugo said, and resumed walking. "The goatherds know where all of them are. This one used to be in the woods, too, but then they had to cut the road through here, so they dug around it."

"So they must be ancient."

"More than a thousand years."

"What are they for, exactly?"

As we rounded the bend, Ugo took off his cap, spilling a quiver of curls, and rubbed the back of his neck. "You know the story of Santa Chionia?"

"She was a virgin martyr, one of three sisters," I said. "Killed by the emperor because they wouldn't forsake Christ?" The last part was a guess, but all the virgin martyrs were essentially the same, except for which specific body parts were desecrated by which lurid method. I had looked Chionia up before arriving in the village, but the precious little about her was lumped together with her sisters, Agape and Irene.

"She was burned to death, but when the fire died down her body was untouched by flame, her skin as white as snow. That's what 'Chionia' means in Greek—'snow.'"

When Ugo said "Chionia," he pronounced it "*hYON-ya*," and hearing his native Greco accent tip into his clean schoolhouse Italian I felt my heart skip a nonproverbial beat. He was a character straight out of a goddamned Jean MacLeod novel, minus the kilt and the bagpipes. Then again, the Aspromonte was lousy with bagpipe players—he might well be one of them.

"Before she was arrested," Ugo was saying, "the saint fled into the mountains to hide sacred texts. She buried them in the forest where they'd never be found by the emperor's men. She left these saint stones to mark the true path to Christ, but only the forest dwellers would recognize them because to the men from the city they looked like regular rocks."

"How could she have left stones here?" I said, compensating in hostility for the flare of attraction that had just flickered in my belly. "Santa Chionia surely lived thousands of miles away in Anatolia or somewhere like that."

"We can't know she wasn't here." He nodded toward the ridge above us where the ruined tower sat. "We had Saracens."

"Oh come on. No one believes Santa Chionia came here, do they?"

"No," Ugo admitted. I heard amusement in his voice. "But she was a mountain person, and she protects mountain people. If you believe those kinds of things."

His manner was too subtle—I couldn't tell if he was flirting.

We did not speak for the length of via Boemondo, where windows were open and anyone might note our passing. At Cicca's alley I spotted Mela, the evil neighbor, peering around her door before drawing her head back like a lizard. I halted in my tracks.

Ugo had stopped with me. "What's wrong?"

I would look like a fool, and probably also a bad person, no matter how this all unfolded. "The truth is, I got in a disagreement with your aunt. I . . . I lost my temper and went storming out of the house. She's probably still angry with me."

Even in the gray-black twilight I saw the corners of his eyes lift in mirth. "I'll cheer her up. She's always liked me."

"You must give her this." Embracing my cowardice, I thrust the chocolates toward him; his careful hand did not touch mine as he took the box. "They were meant for her."

He doffed his cap, certainly making fun of me. "Good evening, *maestra.*"

"And to you," I replied, mortified, and ducked behind the concrete staircase in the foyer, hoping Cicca wouldn't catch me on my way to my room.

On the other side of my closed door I heard Cicca burst out of the kitchen and smother Ugo with accusatory affection.

· · ·

I stretched out across the bed, listening to garbled sounds of reunion. At the horizon of my vision the linen bust of my dress flicked up and down, the too-fast ticking of a poorly built clock. Ugo stayed for about twenty minutes. I assumed Cicca was telling him the most grotesque imaginable things about me. Which did not, I reminded myself, matter one tiny bit. I heard her walk him to the door and kiss him a recriminatory goodbye.

How bad were the things that had happened today, truly? Vadalà had threatened me, yes, but in the greasy, effete way of lazy cops—would he actually sabotage me? That seemed unrealistically savage.

I thought of the strange, unfriendly men in the tavern tonight.

The best thing I could do for myself was to try to feel less alone. I sat up, momentarily dizzy. I rearranged my wrinkled blouse, headed over to my desk, and wrote out a letter, crisp and impersonal, so Sabrina would feel free to share it if necessary:

Dearest Sabrina,
  Matters move forward smoothly here in Santa Chionia. The facility is almost ready for children. The application review process is being assisted by Mayor Fortunato Stelitano.

Vadalà had most likely been appointed by the mayor. I wondered whether Mayor Stelitano, who had been so cordial and helpful up until now, would continue to be so.

I was, however, dismayed today by the arrival at my personal residence of the municipal policeman, an Officer Vadalà, who used threatening language to attempt to secure a promise that his sister's son would be admitted to the school outside of the application process. I iterated our policies and provided him with an application form.

I wished I could spell out how sinister the awful man had been. Instead I concluded by trying to strike a balanced chord of professional confidence:

I am certain this threat will amount to nothing, but thought it best to inform you since it has been issued by an officer of the law.
  Warmest wishes from the Aspromonte.
  Francesca Loftfield

By the time I had addressed the envelope, my hands were not quivering anymore. I wasn't convinced that bringing Sabrina into my problems was the best thing to do—if the Child Rescue board became concerned about my well-being or my competence, the Santa Chionia operation might be folded entirely. Vadalà might have ruined everything for everyone because he couldn't envision a world in which he didn't get his own way.

I did not want to think about Vadalà anymore tonight. My effort to switch mental tracks resulted in a vision of Ugo, the *puticha* lamplight bending around the curves of his—

NO.

To stop myself, I pulled another sheet of paper out and wrote the words *Dear Sandro.*

They were head clearing indeed.

I stared at them, my mind freshly blank, the pain spreading in my chest as if a small animal had clamped its teeth into my heart. Intellectually, I was amazed every time by the ache, that after all these months it had not dissipated. Surely someone else would have left it behind by now. Surely *he* had.

But I had started the letter and Sandro would have wanted me to finish it. Sandro would always want the letter, even if some other woman was lying in his bed as he read it.

> *Dear Sandro,*
>   *I hope you are well. Since I last saw you Child Rescue has sent me to the Aspromonte. I am building a nursery school in*

I could not write "Santa Chionia," because this way when he did not show up out of the blue, I would be able to pretend it was because I had withheld the information.

> *. . . a tiny village so high up that it is warmed by a pocket of wind they say comes all the way from Africa. It is wild here, feral boar-pigs wandering freely through the forests and silky goats clogging the street when everyone is trying to get to church. I think you would like it—it would reinforce your wrongheaded ideas about the secretive, romantic knifewielding south,* cavalleria rusticana *and all that.*

I had almost come to the bottom of the page. Should I risk spilling myself onto a whole new sheet of paper? That seemed self-indulgent. Instead I concluded:

Just wanted to let you know I am well. A kiss for your father.

I addressed the envelope to Sandro's father's house in Lonato, where Sandro would be visiting for Christmas. I did not need to consult my datebook for the address.

When I had sealed the envelope, it was only eight thirty, but I felt like a child who had cried itself out, so exhausted I went straight to sleep without any dinner.

20

ON TUESDAY, NOVEMBER 1, I WOKE UP BRACED FOR BATTLE AGAINST my tiny oppressor. Cicca, though, had an entirely new stratagem.

The kitchen's east wall was effulgent with the late dawn, the rear window standing open to the popcorn cheeping of the goldfinches that infested the hillsides. Cicca poured us each a cup of barley coffee and sat gravely across from me.

"Peppinedda came to me," she said without preamble. "She explained you are in great danger." She was staring me in the eye so unblinkingly that I became self-conscious. "She said, 'Cicchedda, that innocent girl is all alone here and God will send her many trials, she is as pure as Santa Chionia, blessed virgin burned at the stake.'"

The purity thing was definitely sticky. "I—I am grateful she is concerned for me?"

"Peppinedda told me, 'Cicchedda, from now on, you must be like her mother, who is not here to protect her.'" Her small black eyes appeared to be swimming with sincere tears. "You must forgive me for not understanding."

The declaration was so plainspoken I wasn't sure what to say. "*You* must forgive *me* for being such a disruptive tenant."

"My house is your house." Cicca's soft square face quivered with emotion. "When your job is over, it will still be your house."

Who could guess what was behind this, but my heart filled with gratitude at this one de-escalation. "That is very generous, *cummàri*." Deciding to press my luck, I added, "Does that mean I can do my own laundry now?"

Cicca waved dismissively. "After breakfast, after breakfast. Look what I've made you." She pulled a linen off of a plate of brownish lumps, like oddly colored peeled tomatoes. "These are the last of the summer."

The fruit menaced me enigmatically. "What is this, *cummàri*?"

"Indian fig. Very tasty." She wedged her most recent loaf of bread, a waning gibbous with the diameter of a bicycle tire, against her bosoms and began to saw lustily toward herself with her murderous carving knife. "Go, eat."

The fruit was a slick glob more fibrous than could easily be cut through with a fork. At last I managed to separate a piece. It was slightly sweet, quite starchy—not an item I looked forward to eating in the quantity that had been presented. "It's good," I said dutifully, and stuffed the other half into my mouth. The faster I ate it, the faster it would be over with.

"It's good, right?"

The second chunk of tepid prickly pear sat upon its predecessor in a mischievous pile in my belly. In Professor Mead's undergraduate seminar, we'd read about the Tohono O'odham of the Sonoran Desert, who had subsisted on these blobs of cellulose. I wondered balefully what conquistador cretin had stolen it from those colonially oppressed people and brought it here to oppress another.

The morning's bonding was not yet over. "My dear girl," Cicca said, putting down the knife, "if you are going to be on my side now, you need to know why everyone hates me."

I let the "on my side" go by with helpless alarm. "Hates you? That's not true at all."

"It is," she said sternly. "And you must know the truth if you live in this house."

"I was thirteen when my father died, and then came all the bad luck," the story started.

I had met none of Cicca's six siblings because there were none left; they had all died young. Meleddu fell into the ravine when he was eleven.

Pietro died in the first war—they assumed. He'd gone away and never came back. Pepe, the last hope for the Casile name, was killed in a tavern brawl in 1928.

"Right here, at the *puticha*?" I asked.

"It was a misunderstanding. They were drunk and took offense."

The *They* paddled unnervingly through the muddy canals of my brain. "Who?"

"I don't know who," Cicca said, and then, "Someone who died later."

I would say the tragic circumstances beggared belief, except I knew Cicca's family history was nothing extraordinary here in this forgotten republic. *Nasty, brutish, short.*

The grimmest story of all was that of Peppinedda, my celestial intercessor. Peppinedda went into labor with what would have been her first child. Two days of agony passed; the midwife was helpless with her cat's-foot and her bowl of smoke. Peppinedda was tied to a stretcher and eight men were recruited to carry her seven hours through the gorge to the closest doctor, in Melito. Peppinedda was in such terrible pain that halfway down she was screaming at the men to toss the pallet off the cliff and let her die on the rocks.

"And then she went silent." Cicca had held my gaze the entire time.

My throat was filled with bile. I felt the empty spasm in my abdomen where my phantom fetus often kicked.

The frightened men continued on to Melito, where the doctor removed the too-late baby from its squandered mother. On the miserable return journey, Peppinedda began to burn with fever. She arrived home in Santa Chionia in time to die in Cicca's arms.

"That was fifty years ago. She has been gone twice as long as I had her, sweet girl." Cicca's voice was bright with pain, and her math was almost good. "I miss her every day."

The altitude makes a person more emotional. I felt the cold hand of sweet dead Peppinedda pressed against my heart.

"I was afraid if I got pregnant God would put me through what he put Peppinedda through." Cicca brought me a linen towel to wipe my snot. "But I never did."

At thirty, Cicca had taken it for granted that she would never marry, especially with the shortage of men after the Great War. Then Pietro

Tripodi was widowed and needed a wife to take care of him and his four children. He wasn't much of a catch: he was forty-five and a wino. But Cicca's mother convinced her to marry, as she'd never have another chance.

Pietro could not work, since he had a bad back and liver disease. It was up to Cicca to keep them all fed. At night, when her stepfamily was sleeping, Cicca toiled down the mountain to work in the jasmine groves, harvesting the unblossomed buds that would be wasted by the dawn; by day she took in washing and needlework. All the money went to pay for Pietro's liver serum.

Pietro's physical ailments made him impotent, so they only had sex a few times during their marriage; Cicca wasn't embarrassed to describe those times in illustrative detail so I could understand why they hadn't been successful. She would have liked a baby of her own, but not Pietro's, so her regret was ambivalent.

His children, a boy and three girls, were in their teens when Cicca married Pietro. They missed their mother, and had been abused by their father, and in return they abused Cicca, who they decided was a simpleton. The oldest sometimes hit her.

"They didn't like my cooking." Cicca blew an airy raspberry.

Pietro died in 1940, and Cicca was free to move in with her mother and last living sister, Caterinuzza. Caterinuzza had a "head problem," as Cicca described it. "When she was little, everything was normal, smart, but she never grew up." At forty-two, Caterinuzza was like a big baby. "But that was why we loved her so much. You have to love a baby, right? Even when they make messes and hurt you."

After Cicca's mother died in the cholera, Cicca juggled breadwinning and babysitting her adult sister. Then fate smiled on them for one brief moment: the housing lottery of 1957. There were twenty new houses: concrete construction, earthquake-proof, outfitted for electricity. Cicca, who qualified to enter as a caretaker, won herself a house.

People were angry that childless old women were taking up a modern dwelling that should have accommodated a whole family. "You should hear the things they said, to my face!" Then less than a year later Caterinuzza's eternal childhood ended quietly in her sleep.

For seventy years Cicca had been worked like a mule by every person who should have loved her. Now she was all alone.

. . .

"That's why I have a room to rent to you," she concluded. "And that is why everyone in Santa Chionia hates me."

"No one hates you, *cummàri*."

"They do."

"I don't believe it! Name one person."

"Vannina Favasuli," she replied immediately. "And everyone else. I am a stupid old woman who would make the world better by dying off."

How many times had I wished I hadn't moved in with Cicca? Or wished she could just be a different person?

I knew this, about difficult people—that they were difficult for a reason. And yet I needed the reminder every day.

I reached past the pile of bread and gripped Cicca's palm so I could feel her pulse. "*Cummàri*, you have told me your secrets, so I should tell you mine."

"Secrets?" Her eyes glowed brighter than two sap lamps.

I shouldn't, I shouldn't do it. What if it backfired and she kicked me out?

"First, you should probably know I'll never be a virgin martyr." I retracted my hand to pull the gold chain with Sandro's ring out from under my dress.

21

THE PROBLEM WITH SANDRO PREDATED SANDRO, OF COURSE—IT wasn't his fault I'd needed him as much as I had, or pursued him so indefatigably, or been so crushed by our severance—although he was a man who rejected these kinds of teleologies. Sandro would have had you believe we found each other with blank and capable hearts, that we chose each other and that was that, nothing else to unpack, no one to blame for the byproducts of this union. I was nothing at all like Sandro in this one way; I have always been a hoarder of human emotional experience and knot my scars together like a fisherman's net, the molting crab caught inside of which is my own damn self. My heart has never been blank, or capable of anything besides angrily clicking its crabby claws and offering my unprotected carapace for mercy or for frying.

I was twenty-two years old when I married Sandro Cenedella. It was

1955, and twenty-two didn't seem young to us back then; my fiery convictions about the modern thinking female's duty to subvert patriarchal institutions seemed, in the dreamy halo of our love affair, like commitments I'd still be able to get back to later.

I met Sandro in 1954, when I left my Oxford doctoral program at St. Hugh's College for a research exchange at Ca' Foscari in Venice. I was at that time pursuing a DPhil in the history of the Crusades, and my quest was to unearth a missing Venetian primary source that would finally reveal who was at fault for what had happened in 1204. (I did *not* solve that timeless mystery, because I never finished my degree.)

It was twenty-nine days into my Venetian deployment, a Wednesday—October thirteenth; let me not pretend I do not remember the date. I'd just left the library, where I'd been retranslating passages of *The Chronicle of Morea,* when the hand of fate, which I don't believe in, intervened, and a rainstorm roared across the canal. I had no umbrella— Peppinedda would have been peeved. Not wanting to make a run for home over the slick bridges in my worn boots, I retreated to the shelter of the student hall.

As I stood, mousy and wet, in the vestibule, the beautiful Italians flickered past me with their long noses and leather derbies. Engrossed in their ever-vivid conversations, they stepped around me, ignoring me in a way that made clear they had seen me taking up space. I remember painfully my feeling of isolation that all my hard work had done nothing to cure. I was a lonely person then, as now, if for different-feeling reasons—lonely despite a loving circle of friends and family, whom I had left behind in Pennsylvania on my quest to figure out what the purpose of my life was. I had been a misfit in Barnard, a Main Line finishing-school girl with some rather unfinished rough edges and an "ethnic" décolletage; I'd been too young when I matriculated, only sixteen, and finished in two years. I'd gotten much done there, and at Oxford, in very short time, in large part because I had no sex; sex was for women who were going to nestle willingly into the patriarchy. But there were moments like this one when the social cost of my ambition daunted me— which is to say, in the melodrama of my Italian-American lexicon, drove me into soul-crushing despair.

As I had learned to do from my mother, another Italian-American woman with big feelings, I lanced the boil of this sadness in the most sensational way possible: by upending everything. It took me a total of twenty moody minutes to decide how.

Halfway down the corridor, the dingy gray of the afternoon was broken by a patch of light—an open classroom door. A meeting of the Student Labor Union was in session, but I'm not sure how much that mattered; it was a room I could linger at the back of in my damp brown suit. That was how the fire of the Revolution was lit in my heart. In my yearning to connect with anyone at all, I suppose I could have just as easily joined the Jehovah's Witnesses or become a pyramid scheme beauty product saleswoman; I have always been soft of psyche.

Then Sandro Cenedella stood in front of the forty or so assembled students to speak.

The lecture was a refresher about the core goals of activism, "which you should repeat to yourself every morning," he instructed the attendees as he sought an eraser in the chalk tray. He was thin as a spindle, with an academic's disregard for his wavy chocolate-colored hair. "It doesn't matter how well you know the rules; catechism must be repeated to be internalized."

I wrote them down, right into *The Chronicle of Morea*.

CORE GOALS OF ACTIVISM
1. *Win meaningful victories*
2. *Build movements that don't recapitulate the power structures we seek to challenge*
3. *Create effective political alliances*
4. *Inspire hope and action*

Contemplating his scholar-chic nonchalance and the trouser tapering around his derriere, I, for one, felt inspired to take action.

In retrospect I think how silly I was to fall in love with the workers' politics of a skinny college boy who had never worked a day in his life, but I forgive other hot-blooded students the same. If young people didn't go around falling in love with this or that, willing to throw their bodies before the cannon, the whole world would have burned down long ago.

When the meeting broke up, I loitered hopefully. I didn't need to think of what to say because Sandro came right up to me. "You're new," he said.

I stared at his beautiful hands—violinist's hands—with their spidery articulation and muscular knuckles, and I noticed that his shirt had come untucked in back. I felt like someone had pulled taut a wire stretched between us: this was a person I wanted to get, and that tiny inelegance, that untucked shirt, made me think there was some chance I *could*.

"I would like to learn more about meaningful victories," I said, because I have never succeeded at subtlety, and had given up trying for it. "Maybe you could teach me?"

Sandro Cenedella was a fourth-year undergraduate, a polymath with competence in an astounding diversity of disciplines. A budding journalist, he'd already published several articles in *Il Gazzettino,* the northeastern Italian daily, about things like American business influence and the necessity of government regulation. This byline was a big deal among the fawning Union boys and a catalyst for lust among the entirety of the female student body, to my jealous eye. Sandro was affectionate and clear-spoken and he listened well, then inevitably devastated you with an argument better than any you had ever heard before, regardless of his familiarity with the topic at hand. He was interested in literature and not poorly read; I was nearly cataleptic with joy to learn he had read *The Sound and the Fury* (in translation).

I was besotted on first sight, but the thing that reduced me to helplessly obsessed was the music. Sandro's journalistic aspirations meant his family's sixth-generation violin-making business would die with his father. Sandro had turned his back on his legacy, but he never quite left it behind. He wouldn't play for any size audience—there lingered some hang-ups, certainly, about having betrayed his father—but when he was anxious or angry, he would take out his hundred-year-old violin, which he modestly described as one of his great-grandfather's cast-offs, and lock himself in his study to play segments from Tartini's G minor sonata. There were many days during the dissolution of our marriage when I hated him with every fiber of my being; still, when I hear the plaintive chorus of the Devil's Trill my heart is tender.

It was a torrid love affair, one I can't help but feel deserves better than the paltry recapitulation I could possibly give it here. Every hour with him felt like the most extreme hour of my life, until the next hour came. I was willing to give it all up for him.

And I did. I dropped out of my Oxford doctoral program to stay in Venice. We were married in the church of San Stae—I nominally converted to Catholicism so we could. My parents sailed to Italy for the wedding. My poor dad must have had his doubts; Ma, meanwhile, was caught up in the romance: my mother, who had cautioned me my whole life against ever getting involved with an Italian man—"They're all the same," and by "the same" she meant "unfaithful." "Why do you think I married your father?"

Sandro was not "the same." But infidelity isn't the only thing that can ruin a marriage.

On paper, it should have worked. We had everything important in common, I thought—notions about money, politics, religion. We agreed we did not want children, maybe ever, but certainly not until we were thirty at the earliest. Who knew every single one of those stress points would be pressured by reconsideration within the first years of our marriage? We were so young, twenty-two and twenty-four, and we were both individuals of such vociferous convictions I think neither of us had quite realized we didn't actually know yet what those convictions should be. I was absolutely crazy in love with Sandro, chemically and psychologically intoxicated by him, desperate to keep earning his sweet attention. But every other aspect of our relationship shifted beneath my feet, floodbattered pilings much less sturdy than the rotting eight-hundred-yearold ones that just about held up our leaky Santa Croce *pensione*.

The first big surprise, to me, at least: when Sandro graduated from Ca' Foscari, instead of applying for bottom-rung copy desk jobs, he accepted a contract from Banca d'Italia, where his uncle secured him a cushy asset management position. I thought he was joking when he told me at dinner one night that he was going to Rome for an interview at a bank—I literally bit my tongue, after which every fork of polenta I swallowed was tinged with the taste of my blood.

"To get us started," he said. "So we don't have to live on a reporter's salary. I'll write in the evenings." I sucked my tongue and stared at him; we both knew better. "When I've built up my byline, I'll quit."

I loathed the idea of our deriving our livelihood from a financial institution—that went against everything I thought I stood for. But it was hard to loathe the prospect of steady income, especially when Sandro seemed to feel so much pressure to step up and provide for us. Besides, I would have followed him anywhere.

Our first year in Rome was like a long honeymoon, redolent with red sauce and history. Sandro was making enough money that every day was accented with delightful little luxuries—a flush toilet in our apartment, new wardrobes to wear to dinner parties hosted by his blueblood colleagues. But while he spent ten hours a day at the office, I was listless at home. Being a housewife didn't suit me. A lifetime of indoctrination aside, I was a mediocre cook and I abhorred cleaning—I would never have imagined the cosmic joke of my future as a hygienic advisor. After a disheartening attempt to get my doctorate transferred to Sapienza, I landed a job at the American embassy, where my Ivy League education and multilingualism qualified me to answer phones.

As our Roman honeymoon stretched on, two years of sun-soaked *aperitivi* and strolls in Trastevere, I chafed against my status quo. What was I accomplishing as Signora Cenedella? My job was fancy but monotonous; now that it was too late to resume my studies where I'd left off, I felt remorse about the years of academic investment I'd squandered by getting married. My personal projects, language lessons and dabbling translations, felt trifling and ineffective.

My fellow receptionist, Maria Luisa, was the first person to involve me in women's advocacy. At five o'clock, when the embassy closed, she brought me to rallies, and eventually, when she knew she could trust me, on contraceptive counseling missions in the *borgate* slums. I finally understood the horrific struggle of the Italian proletariat—the struggle my mother's family had been lucky enough to flee. The conditions in the slums were staggering. Children starving, children dying, children being sold, a world of Gelsominas. I met women who'd had more than thirty pregnancies—*thirty*. Women endured botched abortions and the assumed resulting damnation so they wouldn't have to watch another child die—all because they were denied, by law and by their spiritual leaders, the right to choose not to get pregnant. Witnessing this brutality was enough to change the course of my life. On this one point I have never looked back with regret.

. . .

Three years into my marriage, at a juncture when Sandro and I were experiencing a disheartening amount of marital friction over my "risky" extracurricular activities, I was myself a victim of contraceptive failure—pregnant despite my medical knowledge and my precautions. I was flabbergasted. The psychological stutter, if I'm honest, was almost as traumatic as what followed. The night I told Sandro I was pregnant, I was already at least four months along but had been either subconsciously or willfully ignoring the signs. He was overjoyed, and I accused him of sabotaging me. Thus unfolded the worst fight we had ever had. He told me there was something abnormal about me for not wanting to be a mother, about the fact that I hadn't "outgrown" that quality by now; I told him I was disgusted by the notion of his baby in my body. I cannot write more— I am sick afresh sixty years later remembering what we said to each other that night. I shut myself up in our library and slept on the hard wood floor, feeling my heartbeat twanging under the awakening discomfort of the new pressure in my abdomen.

The next day, despite the framework of his character, Sandro came to me and apologized. He told me he would help me terminate the pregnancy if that's what I felt I needed to do. He could ask his uncle for a referral for one of those relaxing spa weekends in a lushly appointed villa in the Lazio hills where all the well-to-do Roman ladies went to take a load off their minds.

Why did I say no? I railed at myself for being brainwashed by the same social constructs I'd vowed to overturn. I'd always wanted other things out of life than to be a mother, and simultaneously wanted better for an unborn baby than the lackluster mothering I could possibly offer it.

But—no. I couldn't do it. I wasn't willing.

As the months ticked by, I became more and more attached to the little thing inside me. She won me over. I can't help but believe we would have been the best of friends.

The pregnancy did not make it to term. I woke up on August 8, 1958, to learn I had been in a coma for a kidney infection. The two days before I was admitted to the hospital are completely missing from my memory. The thirty-week-old preterm baby had struggled against the overwhelming odds for four days in an incubator.

. . .

These days, they say that nine out of ten marriages do not survive the death of a child. I am sure the statistics were different back then, especially in Italy, where divorce was simply not an option. But Sandro and I were not one of the exceptions. Everything he said seemed to have been intended to make me furious or miserable. The worst, somehow, was "Give it time—you'll feel normal again." He couldn't see—or refused to see—that normal was Heraclitus's river, that there was no stepping into it a second time.

Further to that topic of Italian divorce: it's not like I didn't seek one. It's that they didn't exist. This was an investigation that consumed me starting in September, in the nadir of my despair, my body a junkyard of collapsed core muscles and unrequited hormones, when every single word Sandro said to me—innocently, retaliatorily—was a further defacement of the corpse of our intimacy. He had lost his daughter, too. Half a century later, when I have learned, after long practice, to compartmentalize that bedeviling grief, I look back on that young man he was with compassion. He could have done better, but he tried, he did. He didn't mean to be cruel—at least, not at first. At first he tried hard to comfort me. I could offer him no reciprocity. The merest sight of his face made me sick with rage and disgust. The only way I would survive this hopelessness was to leave.

My prospects of obtaining an annulment of my Catholic marriage, however, were extremely poor. The only possible route to approach the ecclesiastical tribunal would be to claim the marriage had never been consummated—absurd, given the origin of our grief—and in order for us to convincingly maintain the argument that we couldn't go back and try again, Sandro would have had to be willing to declare he was impotent under cross-examination by a jury of priests of the faith that, it turned out, he believed in rather devoutly. We were not the only couple pursuing paths around Italy's immutable divorce laws, and so the tribunals were notoriously harsh on these petitions, requiring invasive supporting medical examinations—in other words, much false evidence and third-party dishonesty. Even if Sandro hadn't felt like his manly pride and the purity of his immortal soul were being compromised, he had never wanted to end our marriage.

Next, I considered marriage contract loopholes I might be eligible for as an American citizen. I had not made the mistake of confiding in my parents about my marital unhappiness—I didn't want my dad to be disappointed in me, and my mother was already, constantly. (She had, on their August visit a year prior, sniffed out the tension between me and Sandro and had cautioned me not to annoy him too much, because, quote, "I just don't know if anyone else would be willing to put up with you.") But I had written to my high school best friend, Alexis Kelly, who had just started her second year at UPenn Law, to see if she had any practical advice. Her findings dashed my hopes further. When Sandro and I had oh-so-romantically married in Venice, I had submitted to Italian law. Even if I abandoned Sandro and fled the country, we would never be legally divorced, which would mean neither of us could legally remarry, either. Not that I desired such a thing—I spent many hours during this period fantasizing about the spinster scholar lifestyles of so many of my mentors—but Sandro would never let go of the hope of a family, and the fact of me meant I was his only choice.

Also, he loved me. I understand that now. At the time, I never wholly believed it—the ghost of the chubby bookworm I'd been had followed me into, through, and out of my marriage, casting a pall of insecurity and desperation over my every interaction with Sandro. But Sandro had never let that ghost get to him. He had loved me, for whatever his own reasons were, from the beginning.

In any case, I couldn't live with him anymore, not even long enough to figure out how we could live apart. So I ran away.

I met Sabrina three weeks after I was discharged from the hospital. I needed somewhere to go to escape myself. So I followed Sabrina to the Abruzzi. I was no longer a historian, nor a government factotum; I was not a mother. I would be something else. Someone better than myself.

Sandro, however, would not put me behind him. He wrote to me often, daily. My mind was trying to heal itself, walling off any thought of him or the baby or the other life I had been imagining for the three of us. In fits of pique I would write back, punish him with feverish catalogs of my daily activities without him, the weight of my yearning—for him; for some *version* of him; for what we had lost together—pulsing in the empty space between the details. I would miss him acutely for the amount of time it took me to drop the letter in a mailbox.

In May 1959, eight months after I'd left him, Sandro came to the Abruzzi with a hamper full of gifts and prevailed upon Sabrina to let him spend a few nights in the unfinished guest bedroom of the town house where we were living. I ended up spending those same nights in the guest bedroom with him. In this changed setting, the bad thoughts were smashed down. But little things niggled: casual mentions of our future family, the traditionalist vision of his own life he was marching toward. By the end of his stay, I had a cool lump in my heart. But he departed with a notion that I would be coming home soon.

Alone in the dark after he left, I thought of the Tartini sonata and of the fierce little life we had created together, and I sobbed. He wore me out, he broke me down. I loved him as fiercely as I ever had, even in the beginning, but for the same reasons he made me angrier with the world than any other human being I'd met.

I never went back to Rome.

In November 1960, I had not seen him for eighteen months, and at that moment I was certain I would never see him again. Almost.

22

I DIDN'T TELL CICCA ALL OF THIS, OF COURSE. IT IS SO HARD TO know how to share our private truths, or if we actually have. It is so hard to know how much someone else already infers.

As the milky morning light crept over Cicca's kitchen, the squat wrinkled woman pulled her stool around the table and took both of my wrists in her hands.

"Fate has brought us together," she said. "We are family now."

Her grip around my wrists was a manacle. I was a prisoner of this agreement; I understood it was forever binding. I was glad.

As she released my arms, Cicca said, "It's not too late for you to be happy."

"Maybe it's not too late for you, either, *cummàri.*"

"Too late, what? I *am* happy." She spread her hands like a beneficent Jesu. "Look at my beautiful house!"

I laughed. I felt giddy despite the existential weight of eleven cactus fruits dragging me down by my belly. "You know what would make me truly happy?"

"What?"

"If you would let me do my own laundry."

After this miraculous rapprochement, I spent the morning at the stone basin behind Cicca's house gloriously washing every piece of dirty clothing I had been setting aside to wear yet again. It was only that night, at dinner, that I noticed that my hand hurt—a nonsense little irk. As I listened to Cicca's report on evil Mela's latest outrage, which involved a brazen appropriative maneuver in the contested strip between their respective bean patches, I rubbed absently at my left palm. It felt like a pinch in a nerve, getting worse. I rubbed and rubbed and then—

"Ouch!" The stabbing sensation was so sudden the word popped out in English.

"What?!" Cicca cried.

"My hand, *cummàri*." In the scant light I made out no broken skin, no visible bruise. I went to stand directly under the bulb, which had been turned on for the special occasion of our new friendship. There, the culprit: a tiny dot, from which issued the slenderest of brown fibers. I probed it with my fingers, outsized and clumsy, and was finally able to pull it free. I tested the sore spot again, and the pain was gone.

"What?" Cicca cried, demonstrating an excessive level of abject fear. "What is it?!"

"Wouldn't you know, I think it was a pricker of some kind."

"A pricker?"

I recalled with regrettable vividness my breakfast. "Maybe from the Indian fig."

"That's impossible. I scrubbed the prickers off every one with my own hands." The umbrage Cicca had taken was almost unimpeachable.

Almost.

When I had control over my voice, I said, "*Cummàri,* tell me, where did you scrub them? In the basin outside?"

"Exactly," Cicca said, mollified, but I saw a flicker of shrewd satisfaction in her eyes.

In case you were looking for an efficient method for weaving thousands of tiny cactus spines into fabric, may I suggest rubbing them aggressively against a stone washboard? Also consider using very cold water so you lose feeling in your hands and never notice the spines pricking you.

As I peered in dismay at my underwear in the dusk, I remembered what Don Pantaleone had told me about Aspromonte justice.

After all this, Cicca conned me into going to All Saints mass—the actual All Saints mass, not the one she'd lied about on Sunday. Who should be there—just what I needed—but wild-eyed Vannina Favasuli, sitting five pews ahead of us, her drooping neckline baring a greater proportion of her bosom than was conventionally anticipated at a November evening church service. She had not brought any of the six children she'd mentioned to mass with her. She rotated in her seat and stared at me for the duration. When we exited, she was lurking behind the olive tree barrel at the border of the church piazza. I wonder if she was disappointed that I didn't shriek when she jumped out.

"Are you avoiding me? What have you found about my Mico?"

"I haven't—I haven't had a chance to look," I said, angry at myself for stammering.

"You haven't looked!" The woman's eyes were as wild as her ratty hair.

"I've had a busy week—"

"You said you cared about helpless women and children," Vannina said with what sounded like heartfelt disappointment.

Some congregants were lingering to watch how the encounter would play out. It was a good week for churchside spectacles.

I stepped toward her. "Vannina, you are making a scene." Out of the corner of my eye I saw Cicca cross her arms over her chest, my tiny body-guard. "How can I or anyone help you when you undermine yourself like this?"

She strategically quieted down. "But you'll look, Maestra Franca?"

"I gave you my word, didn't I?" I said severely—overcompensating. "You've waited eight years and done nothing. I don't see why you're in a rush to find out the truth now."

Cicca harrumphed and started off toward home, and I strode after her, my relief growing as I became more certain Vannina was not going to follow.

"You really don't like her," I said when I caught up. I remembered Vannina's was the one name Cicca had mentioned specifically when she'd been listing her enemies. Vannina had not even acknowledged Cicca's presence on the street just now. Such behavior to an elder was so rude it was impossible, unless it was a feud, in which case rules were different. I unfortunately had a congenital knowledge of Calabrian silent treatment.

"Vannina? She's nothing but a stray dog."

This seemed to contain less vitriol. Cicca loved stray dogs.

In her kitchen, Cicca pulled the cord on the lightbulb—O brave new world!—and gestured for me to take a seat at the table. "You should stay away from Vannina, *pedimmu*. She's cuckoo. No wonder her husband left her for another woman."

Aha. "Her husband left her?"

"That's what they say." With reverence she might have reserved for a fragment of the True Cross, Cicca lifted the lid from the box of chocolate-covered chestnuts. "My nephew Ugo from Milano brought me these. They are very expensive."

I wondered if pretending she didn't know I'd walked home with Ugo was her way of giving me a pass on yesterday's bad behavior. "They look very fancy."

"Have one!"

"Me?" I tried to appear overwhelmed. "I've never had anything like this." I took a performative bite. "This is—wow, this is one of the most delicious things I've ever tasted." It was hard to get the words out; I felt like I was laying it on too thick.

Cicca didn't care about sincerity, only ritual. I could see in her fatuous smirk that I had said the right thing.

I'd try my luck.

"So about Mico Scordo. You said he left Santa Chionia for another woman?"

Cicca selected a chestnut for herself. "Vannina used to be very beautiful. She had all the men chasing her. But she is so crazy, always nagging, always jealous. So her husband ran off with some other woman who wouldn't scream at him."

Vannina seemed like a handful, but the man hadn't minded that when she'd been young and beautiful. "He just left his children behind?"

"Some men don't care about that." Cicca took a groundhog-toothed bite of chocolate.

"Who was she, the other woman Mico Scordo ran away with?"

"I don't know. That's just what people say."

"And no one has seen or heard from him at all since 1952?"

Cicca's façade of hapless, dull older woman dropped away, as if she had pulled the cord on her own bare bulb. "You think Mico Scordo is the skeleton under the post office!"

I was caught so off guard my mouth went dry. "I don't think anything." I tried to laugh it off. "There's way too much village history for an outsider to ever catch up on."

"You stick with me," Cicca said, tapping her forehead as she pushed herself up from the table. "I know everything there is to know. By the way," she said, thrusting the paper-wrapped remnant of the spicy *salame* at my chest, "here's your sausage. I can't eat anything that Tito the Wolf paid for."

23

WHEN I LEFT FOR THE NURSERY ON WEDNESDAY MORNING, I DID so with the increasingly desperate desire to scratch at my prickling arms or rearrange my intolerable panties. I had examined the pair I was wearing before I put them on, but the damn prickers were everywhere, embroidered into the fabric.

The sky was thickly overcast, but the *municipio*'s door was propped open. I took it as a sign that it was time to get Vannina Favasuli out of my hair. I passed through the musty front corridor and found Pino Pangallo sitting behind the registrar's desk. "How can I help you today, Maestra Franca?"

"I'm hoping you can look up another immigration record for me. Domenico Scordo."

"Mico Scordo, eh? You sure are interested in these old-timers." Pino spoke mildly, but I detected an alertness in his manner.

"It's for his wife, Vannina. She heard I helped Gnura Emilia look for an address, and now . . ." I rolled my eyes. "Apparently this is my new side business. I must not be much of a businesswoman, though, because no one is paying me."

"You're generous with your time, *maestra*." Pino was eyeing me in a way I couldn't read. "Vannina could have come here herself."

Thanks, buddy. "You know Vannina," I said, hoping that would be enough. I assumed everyone knew Vannina.

"Give me a moment."

Pino disappeared into his sanctum of sensitive and boring information. I waited at the window, scratching at my itchy rib cage with my elbow as I watched a white cat pose artfully in the doorway of the *puticha*. The bells of San Silvestro rang nine o'clock. It was taking Pino much longer to locate the record today.

To distract myself, I moved to the opposite wall, on which hung black-and-white photos of Chionoti at work and play: a young shepherd crouching to bind his leather-strap shoes; a woman weaving on a waist-high loom. Two bushy-haired barefoot girls in black dresses looking down from a balcony; two overexposed bare-legged boys filling jugs of water from the sunny Attinà cataract.

My eye caught on one photo in particular: six men in tailored jackets standing in front of this very *municipio* building. On the far right of the photo was a boy giving a cheek-bulging blow into a bagpipe. A date in the corner: August 1952.

The same month Vannina's husband, Mico, had disappeared. A coincidence, and barely even that, but I found I was very interested in the photo.

Everyone was eight years younger, but some men never changed. Don Tito the Wolf, for example, might have stepped from this photograph on his way down to the tavern this morning. His shaggy head rose above the other men's like the highest peak in a mountain range. I recognized Turi Laganà by his German shepherd ears; next to him was the professorish man in glasses I'd seen at the *puticha* last week. Finally my eyes fixed on a man whose face was vividly familiar but whom I couldn't place. Why did I recognize him?

I was still staring when Pino Pangallo emerged from his lair, moving across the linoleum floor on silent feet to join me.

"The *festa* to celebrate the opening of the new town hall," Pino said.

"That's you," I realized out loud, pointing to a callow-looking version of the man beside me, his baby face devoid of the signature mustache.

"Yes." We studied the photo together, a companionable warmth filling the space between us. "I was glad they rebuilt so quickly after the flood—I was worried I'd have no job. That was all Don Tito." He tapped the glass with a manicured fingernail, *click-click* right over the boss's face. "He funded the rebuilding out of his own pocket. Otherwise we would have had to wait for the relief funds, and we'd still be waiting now."

"Don Tito built the town hall himself?" Plus that fancy yellow house of his. Exceptionally deep pockets for a guy who spent all day in the *putìcha* drinking goat milk.

"And the post office," Pino said. "And the communal oven."

Tito the Wolf had commissioned the building of the post office. What were the odds he did not know whose body had been dumped in its foundation? I felt my heart clench in—what, excitement? Fear?

"And he paid for a bridge over the Attinà," Pino was saying. "We thought if we built the bridge the province would finally lay a road to connect us to Bova." Pino grimaced at me sheepishly. *"Purtroppo."*

"That must have cost Don Tito a fortune."

"He didn't want it to be like after the earthquake. You know, *maestra,* what good government promises are." There was real anger in his voice; it was not the typical resigned despair of a civil servant. "For them the flood was an excuse to get us to leave. The state tried to remove us in 1951, did you know? At the same time they transferred Africo and Casalinuovo down to the marina. They tried to remove us all—Gallicianò, Condofuri, Roghudi, and Chorio—all the Greco towns. The Chionoti wouldn't go."

I hadn't heard this before. "Why did the government want to remove you? Because it was more expensive to rebuild than to just shut down the whole town?"

"Because they are afraid of us. They want us where they can keep an eye on us." Pino nodded in the direction of the *putìcha*. "Isn't it interesting that they were able to figure out how to install a telegraph cable up here in 1901 when the *carabinieri* were trying to track down the brigand Musolino, but in the sixty years since they haven't been able to figure out how to build us a simple road?" He tapped his temple with one delicate finger.

"Why did the Chionoti stay, when the Africoti left?"

"Transferment is the mayor's choice. The Africo mayor chose to leave." Pino cleared his throat, a disgusted grunt. "Their old folks couldn't take the heartbreak of losing their mountain home. A fifth of their population has died since they moved."

I swallowed the lump in my throat. I wanted to ask him more. But I had already dragged out the chitchat too far for the context of my errand. I indicated the leather-bound volume he was holding. "You found it. I was worried—you were gone a long time."

"It was not in the right volume," Pino said, somewhat defensively. He balanced the top edge on the windowsill so he could turn pages. "Here you are. Domenico Scordo, departed Santa Chionia on August twenty-eighth, 1951."

I stared hungrily at the passport photo. Mico was the perfect physical match for Vannina, strikingly handsome, with curling black hair and big, round nostrils like a bull's.

"Here, I copied down the mailing address for you," Pino was saying, but my eyes had fixed on the problem.

"I'm actually looking for his 1952 visa."

"He left for the last time in 1951. See?" Pino sanctimoniously paged through the leaves to show me four consecutive visas, starting in 1934.

"I must have made a mistake," I said, knowing I had not. I took the stationery on which he'd printed an American address in block capitals. It was a South Philly address: *817 SOUTH 8TH STREET, APARTMENT 9.* Old Mico had been living a few blocks from where I was born.

"You can write to him there. But you'll never hear back."

My heart was already thumping. "What do you mean?"

Pino shrugged. "He's not a nice man, Mico Scordo. He runs off, doesn't take care of his family . . ." He held my gaze for a long moment. "I don't know him well. But he was very bad to my wife's older brother."

I was dying for more information. But that was my prurient curiosity, and I wasn't getting myself in extra trouble today. "Thank you, Pino. I better go now—I have a meeting with the mayor."

I took my leave, no closer to solving my Vannina Favasuli problem.

As unsettling as Mico Scordo's missing visa was, what bugged me for the rest of the day, hanging weirdly like a poorly chosen piece of art in the front room of my mind, was the photo of the six men and the bagpiping boy.

Part Two

—

WHERE IS MICO SCORDO?

24

IN FORTUNATO STELITANO'S PLUSHLY APPOINTED OFFICE, I STARED at the mayor's thinning curls while he reviewed my list of applicants. I knew I had to speak up about Officer Vadalà's visit on Monday night. It would be awkward; I had to be careful not to insult Stelitano's personal friend. I forced the words out. "Mayor, I had an unfortunate encounter with Officer Vadalà."

Mayor Stelitano looked up from the list curiously. "What do you mean, 'unfortunate'?"

"Well. He stopped by Cicca Casile's house." The heat rising in my chest made my skin itch even more under my pricker-lined bra. "When he was there, he . . . he suggested that I admit his sister's child outside of the standard application process."

The mayor handed the list back. "A misunderstanding, I'm sure."

"I'm sure. But I . . . I didn't want there to be any confusion."

The mayor was watching me knowingly, and I averted my gaze to his chickpea-brown silk tie. "He's a good guy, Vadalà," Stelitano said, and I realized he had already heard about the confrontation from the cop. "Just cares about his family. Let's get going with the interviews." The mayor stood up, adjusting his jacket. "The more Christians we see together, the more misunderstandings we avoid."

That day, we visited four families. I wish I had room here to share the details of their various struggles, ingenuities, and hopes. These are the beautiful lives folded away in the crinkled pages of my notebook, their legacies imprisoned in my inadequate handwriting. They have always been more interesting than their chroniclers. The people who have the time, training, and self-obsession to write things down are rarely the ones with the stories most worth telling.

It was three o'clock when the mayor and I parted. There was time to shoehorn in one more task—the opportunity to make this a gold-star day.

My heart buoyant in anticipation, I took a right down spooky, mossy via Zaleuco, where the Arcudi family lived, the aloofly immaculate oasis at the crumbling heart of Santa Chionia. Above me, the green leaves of the hanging plants glowed with blocked sunlight. I felt like I was spelunking, or daffily traipsing into a fairy grotto.

Isodiana Legato answered her door, black eyes glistening in the shadows. *"Maestra."*

"Kalispèra," I replied, smiling my dumb American smile. "May I come in?" I didn't want to be a dumb smiling American, was the thing; I wanted to be her subtle friend.

Isodiana dipped her head. "The baby's sleeping," she warned me as I stepped into her invisible drift of jasmine. She reset her door locks, her almond-brown fingers slightly hyperextended, elegant as Penelope's must have been as she unwove her loom each night.

In the salon, her two daughters were sitting on her fancy green divan, the older one, Olimpia, embroidering, and the four-year-old, Lucia, with her hands suspiciously folded in her lap, one devil-may-care hank of black hair swooping out over her brow like a fascinator.

As their mother filled the coffeemaker, I squished in next to the little girl. *"Ciao,* Olimpia. Lucia, how is Zuzu the monkey?"

"I don't know." Lucia regarded me with the clear-eyed sociopathy of a four-year-old. "Ask her yourself."

"I will," I said, chastised.

I searched the room for any sign of the monkey until Isodiana returned with a tray of biscotti. "The coffee will be just a moment," she said, her willow-whip of waist bending so she could offer me a cookie. How had that delicate figure borne four children?

"No cookie for me, thank you, *signora,"* I said. My itchy thighs felt especially flabby against the pricker weave of my skirt.

"You have to take one," Lucia said. "Otherwise I can't have one because guests must take first."

"Lucia!" Isodiana's eyes widened in horror. "I'm sorry. There is no excuse for her."

"No, she's quite right." I took a cookie. "I know the rules as well as she does."

"Well, she won't have one now at all," Isodiana said, and whisked the plate out of Lucia's reach. Silent Olimpia stopped stitching long enough to rest a restraining hand on her sister's knee. "We filled out the nursery application for Lucia. Shall I go get it?"

"Yes, marvelous," I said. "I'm so glad, *signora*."

"Please, you must call me Isodiana."

As I basked in the radiant gift of her familiarity, I watched her gracefully set the tray on her table and disappear into the hallway. I broke the cookie I'd taken in half and handed a piece to each sister. Lucia accepted hers stoically as her due, but Olimpia gave me a tentative smile. We had destroyed all evidence of the crime before their mother returned with the form.

"Here you are."

I admired the neat handwriting before sliding it into my briefcase. "Isodiana, have you thought any more about taking a nursery teacher position?"

The genial expression on her face faltered. "Oh no, not me, *maestra*."

This was not the answer I was expecting. "Why not?" In my mind I had already contracted her; we were already developing curricula together like Sabrina and I had, sharing wine in the evening after the students had gone home. "You have so much to offer the children of Santa Chionia," I said. Her face was hardening before my eyes. I tried again. "You'd enjoy it so much, getting out of the house, bringing home some spending money—"

"I have my own children and a husband to take care of. It's really impossible."

I wanted to say more, but watching her slip away from me was immobilizing.

After a few beats of awkward silence, which I failed to fix, Isodiana said, "Oh! The coffee must be ready."

Abandoning the little girls, I followed her toward the kitchen. I felt like I was in free fall. Why did I care so much? Counted chickens, I suppose. Had I read her all wrong? Projected my own desires onto her, ascribing my quintessentially American careerism to quite an un-American creature? But she'd told me she'd dreamed of being a teacher.

"Was it your husband?" I remembered, too late, her daughters a few feet away. "He didn't care for the idea, did he?"

"No, *maestra,* I didn't mention it to him. I knew I wasn't interested."

Abashed, I watched her take out a sugar bowl and put two profligate spoonfuls into each cup without asking my preference. The world felt ruined until she looked up at me and revealed the smile on her girlish face.

"I love sugar," she confided.

"Me too," I said. The world was unruined. We could still be friends.

As I drank my coffee I asked her about safe things like what she was making for dinner (grass peas—Santo's favorite); how was Santo (very well, although he had broken his glasses); where did one get new glasses (Reggio; there was no optometrist closer). She asked me nothing at all about myself. Either she felt it was rude to pry as I was prying, or she didn't care to know more than she already did.

The sound of San Silvestro ringing the half hour reminded me to get going before I wore out my welcome. "Thank you for the coffee," I said, "and for the application. You'll let me know if you change your mind about the teaching position, right?"

Isodiana laughed sweetly. "I won't, *maestra.*"

I turned toward the door, and boom! There was Zuzu, staring at me cheekily from the top of the bookshelf, where she slumped next to the silver picture frame. "Aha!" I said. "Lucia, I can ask Zuzu how she is now." I walked over to the bookshelf and picked up the monkey, rearranging her miniature vest. "How are you, Signora Zuzu?"

Lucia galloped across the room. "She had the cholera this morning." She took the monkey from my hands. "She's better now."

"I'm glad to hear that," I replied gravely.

It was surely Zuzu's intention the entire time, to get me in trouble. If only I had kept walking out the door. But—

My eye caught on the pictures in the silver frame again. There he was: the man in the *municipio* photo whose face had been nagging me all day. It wasn't someone I knew—I just recognized him from a picture I had seen before: this picture, right here.

"Is this your father, Isodiana?"

"Yes," she said.

"Was his name—" I searched my memory of the conversation I'd had with Emilia Volontà, flipping through my mental notebook for the name of the Legato man who had written the debt letter to her brother in Chicago on behalf of the dead Don Alvaro. "Ceciu?"

"Yes," she said. She was standing at my elbow. "Vincenzo. They call him Ceciu. He lives in Philadelphia now."

"Philadelphia?" I repeated. For once I was smart enough to not say what I was thinking, which was, *Why would you have a prayer shrine for him if he is not dead?* Instead I said, "I'm from Philadelphia."

Isodiana took no interest in that coincidence. She was still staring at the picture. "He's a wonderful man," she said softly.

"Maybe you'd know," I realized out loud. "Did your father happen to keep an address log of Chionoti emigrants abroad?"

"Excuse me?" The ice in her voice made me look up from the photo. Her black eyes were as wide as if I'd spat on her floor.

I was caught off guard by her reaction. "I think—" I fumbled for the right entry point. "Your father had a job as a secretary for Don Roccuzzu Alvaro, right?" She stared at me in stony silence. "He wrote letters for emigrants and their families, didn't he?"

"I don't know anything about that."

"I'm asking for Emilia Volontà," I blurted. It was more important to repair this moment with Isodiana than to protect the meaningless anonymity of my inquiry. "Your father once wrote a letter on her behalf and sent it to her son Leo in America. I'm trying to find any other Chionoti in America who might know where Leo is living now."

Isodiana shook her head, her brow drawn over her small, pointy nose.

"I know it's almost certainly a lost cause, but I thought I'd check. Perhaps your father kept an address book?"

"I have never seen anything like that."

"Oh well," I said, trying to sound glib. "Like I said, it was a shot in the dark."

Isodiana's gaze had dropped to the silver-framed photo, her scowl crimping her tawny forehead in anger, or pain. Something I had said had upset her. What?

"I was wondering," I said, searching for a Band-Aid, "could I borrow one of your books? I've run out of all my own reading material."

After a discernible moment's hesitation, Isodiana said, "If you'd like." She removed a paperback from the top shelf and handed it to me. "This one is my favorite."

Rattled by the vicissitudes of the last half an hour, I bid the Arcudi family goodbye and hurried up the mountain in the dwindling light, the book clutched against my belly.

Cicca and I shared one big bowl of polenta garnished with fried whole cloves of garlic. Sabrina wasn't here to comment on the hygiene of shared plates or on *no exceptions*.

"I have some questions for you, *cummàri*."

"For me? Why not."

I figured I'd get her blood pumping. "Pino Pangallo at the records office told me that after the flood in 1951, Don Tito Lico rebuilt the town hall out of his own pocket."

I could already see red coming up in her cheeks. "Tito the Wolf! See, that's his whole game, he tricks Christians into saying good things about him."

"But it's true? He paid himself?"

Cicca sniffed elaborately but didn't answer.

"Where does he get all his money? Isn't he a goatherd?"

"*That* money he got from the government," Cicca said angrily. She scooped a clove of garlic into her mouth and chewed unnecessarily.

"I don't follow," I said.

She looked down at the polenta, deciding how much to regret telling me.

I waited. I won.

"The earthquake," she said finally. "The government was supposed to send us money to rebuild our houses. But they didn't send it for a long time. Twenty years. Then when they finally sent it, it . . . got lost. The mayor back then . . . there were some problems."

"Problems?" I prompted delicately when she hesitated.

Cicca lifted her shifty dark eyes to meet mine. "The money disappeared." She was angry, but she still wasn't naming names. "But then the

Wolf, he . . . he got all the money back. It took a long time. *That* was the money he used to build the *municipio*. It wasn't *his*. It was supposed to be for the whole *paese*."

"Where did it go?" I asked.

She shook her head. "I don't know."

My imagination was running wild. "How did he get it back?"

"Little by little," she said, opaquely. "Little by little."

I could not fall asleep that night. For the first time that day I was free of the pricking torment of the cactus needles, as I'd made the controversial decision to climb between my bedsheets entirely in the nude. I hoped Cicca would not choose tonight to sneak into my room and engage in purported tidying.

It was hard not to think about all the things I had been told not to believe about Calabria: about brigand kings and vigilante assassins. Reticent, unexcitable Don Tito the Wolf didn't seem like a murderous gangster, but what were the odds he wasn't somehow the one responsible for the post office skeleton?

I'd been born in South Philly. I was smart enough to know the difference between intimidating men and dangerous ones.

Or at least, I *should* have been smart enough.

Was there some kind of bumpkin mafia in Santa Chionia? A hinterland militia of self-styled honorable men who kept the villages under their own extrajudicial control—something more organized than a handful of temperamental ditchdiggers with the traditional stilettos and grudges? I didn't enjoy the thought, but it also didn't feel completely foreign— a theory I had, on some level, already absorbed into my daily life.

Sleepless, I listened to the whickering admonishments from the chicken hutch. By the light of my sap lamp I examined the book Isodiana had given me: *È stato così,* by Natalia Ginzburg, published in 1947. I wondered where this copy had been purchased, what complex journey it must have made to find its way to Santa Chionia, so far from any bookstore. Right there on the first page, though, was mention of a dead baby. My stomach seizing, I snapped the book closed. Was I going to have to read a whole book about a dead baby just to impress an incurious housewife?

I put out the lamp and lay in the dark thinking—about the diaphanous Isodiana Legato, who should have been my friend but who made me feel like a rejected suitor; about her father, Ceciu, who kept coming up in conversation but who was not here.

25

ON THURSDAY MORNING I WENT STRAIGHT TO THE *MUNICIPIO*. I wanted to see the photo collection again, particularly the photo of Ceciu Legato with Don Tito the Wolf. In my naivete, I did not consider I might need a pretext for this errand.

Pino Pangallo was wearing his usual meticulous cotton jacket. "How can I help you today, Maestra Franca?"

"*Buongiorno,* Pino. I just came to see—" But I turned around to find a bare expanse of butter-yellow paint. "Oh! I was coming to take another look at—" My tongue thickened in my mouth as I noticed his expression, small black eyes as wide and round as I could imagine them. "What happened to the photos?" I asked finally.

"They've been taken down for cleaning." There was no trace of yesterday's friendliness in Pino's mien.

"Cleaning?"

"Cleaning."

What did that even mean? "Can you show me the one photo again? I wanted to—"

"I'm afraid they're not here," Pino interrupted.

"Where are they?"

His gaze was boring into me. "They were taken away."

"Well, who took them?" As if that mattered; I was hardly going to knock on some stranger's door in order to chase down the photo I'd only wanted to see out of curiosity.

Pino's shoulders rose. "I can't say."

"Fine." I knew my face only concealed half my opinions. "Would you at least be able to tell me who the men in that one picture were? In front of the new *municipio*?"

Pino's drilling gaze became unfocused and wandered toward the window, as if he were lost in reflection. "I'm sorry, I don't know which photo you're talking about."

"You remember!" That was too much. "The one with—you're in it! It's you and five other men, and a boy playing the bagpipes?"

Pino shook his head vacantly. "You'll have to come back when they've been cleaned."

I stared at him, incredulous, but he showed no sign that it bothered him to look me in the eye and lie.

What had made Pino Pangallo completely change his personality overnight?

"Fine," I said again, and then, unloading all the sarcasm I had been biting back, "Have a *great day.*"

As I stomped across the piazza, I caught myself clawing like a monkey at the itchy fabric under my armpit.

Possible criminal conspiracies aside, I had plenty of things to worry about. I had less than two months to get the nursery into suitable shape to welcome children, and year-end paperwork and donor solicitations to complete. I had minor but time-consuming side concerns, like the fact that I had gotten my damn period—I'm not going to get into details here; suffice it to say that Italy in 1960 had no tolerance for American sanitary napkins (how would one dispose of them in a village that spoke a language with no word for "garbage"?), and the work-around solutions were medievally inconvenient.

Plus there was the mayoral election. As I sat at my desk with the above-noted correspondences, I watched Mayor Fortunato Stelitano and communist challenger Bestiano Massara cross and recross the piazza on their respective campaigns. Shepherds had come down from the mountains and congregated on the stoops, whittling cheese molds for their sweethearts, playing *mora* or throwing a rag ball. Had they all come into town to vote? What about the twelve nuns who'd arrived to spend a week "in contemplation" at the rectory, where they slept on the floor? The *centro* was bustling, barefoot women running back and forth with buckets or huge wooden trays balanced on their heads—to the cataract to fetch water, or to the communal oven to bake extra bread—and the hopeless dog with his dry hanging tongue trotted after all of them.

On the day of the election, I watched from the nursery window the parade of *paesani* undertaking their civic duty. Turi Laganà, of the German shepherd ears, and his buddy Pascali Morabito sat on either side of the *municipio* door for the full nine hours the polls were open—proctors, I guessed.

Do you know it never occurred to me to wonder on whose behalf they sat there? I just assumed they were legitimate authorities. Who knows, maybe they even were.

Mayor Stelitano rewon his seat, as Don Pantaleone had declared a foregone conclusion, and the Democratic Christian center-right renewed their dominance in Santa Chionia for another five years. And that, I foolishly thought, was the end of that.

26

I WAITED TWO DAYS FOR THE FRESHLY REELECTED MAYOR STELI-tano to resume candidate interviews, but he was very busy and, frankly, had decreased incentive to bother visiting poor villagers now that their votes were faits accomplis. I had already lost much time in the name of cooperation. On Wednesday, November 9, I set out on my own to tick some names off my list.

FOLLIA, PAOLO, 3, lived on via Teano, where drying laundry hung across the alley and one immodest pomegranate tree bulged with so much fruit its branches drooped convexly under its own bounty; I took a moment to admire its pruning. I found both husband and wife at home; little Paolo's father had been injured in an agricultural accident. The Follias were a family on the precipice; the father's infirmity could cost his six children their future if he had one more stroke of bad luck. Paolo's selection for the nursery school might be the break they needed. I slotted his application into my top-priority group.

After I bid the Follias goodbye, I sat under the pomegranate tree and flipped through my notes looking for other children who lived on via Teano. A few weeks ago I had been concerned I wouldn't be able to excite the community about my project; now I felt a new anxiety settling in my chest, the anticipatory remorse I would feel for the applicants I would have to exclude. Maybe if I did well this year Sabrina would be able to find me a budget for an expansion—

Horse, then cart, Frank.

There, a via Teano address: *SCORDO, ANTONIO, 3.* His parents were *GREGORIO* and *TERESEDDA.*

Was Gregorio related to Mico Scordo, Vannina's missing husband?

I remembered what Vannina had said about her brother-in-law, that he had stonewalled her when she'd asked him about Mico's whereabouts. *Who knows what he's mixed up in,* she'd said.

The house was only two doors down.

Teresedda, the mother of little Antonio "Ninuzzu," offered me the standard barley coffee. She had large hands and hair the light color of rushes; it was hard to tell if it was starting to gray. I stuck to Child Rescue business, sensing no suitable moment to ask about Mico Scordo. After upsetting Isodiana Legato last week I was wary of overt snooping.

I was making my goodbyes at the doorway when a hatless man came striding down via Teano. He was cross-looking, at least ten years older than Teresedda, gray hair shorn and glinting over his scalp. He was much bonier than the dark-haired man in Mico Scordo's visa photo, but I still recognized Mico's face in his.

I found I wanted to talk to him very much.

"Your husband?" I asked Teresedda.

"That's him," she said, then called, "Huu, Ligòri! What are you doing here?"

"There's a hole in the fucking hutch roof. Fucking Enzu didn't say a thing, so who knows how long it's been there."

"Oh, the language," Teresedda said hopelessly.

Gregorio "Ligòri" Scordo stopped to scoop Ninuzzu off the ground and sit him on his shoulders. "Who are you?" I watched his suspicious brown eye travel down my skirt suit and land with some distaste on my pumps.

"Act like a Christian," Teresedda chided. "This is Maestra Franca, the American nursery school teacher."

Ligòri's expression melted with chagrin. "*Scusate,* Maestra Franca. Invite her in, Teresedda, what's the matter with you? Offer her a coffee. Or something else. An *anisetta*?"

"Ligòri! She already—"

"A coffee," I interrupted. "If you don't mind," I said apologetically to Teresedda, who looked confused, having only just cleaned up my first coffee.

Back at the table, I listened to voluble Ligòri's rather sophisticated opinions about the importance of early education, which he'd read a magazine article about. I was always spiritually restored to meet a man like Ligòri Scordo—someone I didn't have to convert.

"I had to teach myself to read, *maestra*," he told me. "By the light of the moon while I was out in the mountains with a bunch of bleating sheep. There's no reason for our children to have to live like we do. Every child should have access to public schooling. And I don't mean a diploma factory."

"Diploma factory?" I had never heard the term before.

"A pay-to-play." Ligòri waved angrily at the north wall—the direction of the church. "You know how much the Association charges for one of Don Pantaleone's meaningless diplomas?"

"Watch your tongue," Teresedda said to Ligòri in Greco. My eye caught hers before I remembered I should pretend I didn't understand.

I felt my pulse pick up. "How much?"

"A lot." Ligòri shot his wife a baleful look. Then, rebellious, he added, "I don't have any need for a priest who keeps a gun under his cassock."

"Don't listen to him, *maestra*," Teresedda said, setting down another coffee in front of me. She ruined her reassurance by adding, "The priest only carries a gun for his own protection because he has to walk alone through the mountains."

Distracted by the vision of the dashing priest with a telltale bulge at his hip, I reminded myself why I'd wanted to talk to Ligòri Scordo in the first place. "I was wondering, *masciu,* do you know Vannina Favasuli?"

"Vannina? She's my sister-in-law."

Teresedda, standing with false deference behind her husband, began enjoining Ligòri in mumbled Greco not to let "the poor girl" get mixed up with "that crazy nanny goat who comes to church with her chest hanging out." "Look at her, Ligòri, the last thing she needs is a problem like your sister-in-law."

I tried to look perplexed by the tirade, which I was clearly not intended to understand. I would have to figure out a way to ask Cicca if the Greco word "nanny goat" had any sexual connotations.

"All right," Ligòri said to his wife, then glanced at me and switched to Calabrese. "What does Vannina want from you? Her kids are too old for the nursery school. Her son's getting married."

"He is?" Did he mean Niceforo, whose rejected marriage proposal I had seen in the church piazza two weeks earlier? The boy rebounded from heartbreak quickly. "Vannina is trying to track down Mico, your brother. I was wondering if you'd heard from him."

"Never." Ligòri looked away and his mouth twitched. "He might as well be dead in a ditch, it's all the same to me."

"Ligòri!" Teresedda remonstrated, and Ligòri, sheepish, reached up to rub his prickling scalp with the palm of one hand.

"Sorry," he said, and then added, "That bastard doesn't keep in touch with anyone, not even his own wife. Why would he write to me?"

"Brotherly love?"

He ran a finger along the coffee foam line inside his empty cup. "You want to hear a tragedy, *maestra*? I had three beautiful brothers, every one of them killed in the war. Good men. Just torn apart like sausages." He squeezed the bridge of his nose for a moment—fifteen years later, and this man still missed his brothers enough to cry in front of a stranger.

"Ligòri." Teresedda put a hand on his shoulder. Her wrists and forearms were dappled with soot.

"Then I have one scoundrel brother," Ligòri said, looking up. There was a smear of coffee, like war paint, under one eye. "*He's* the one who survives, the pig, excuse my language. He abandons his family and runs away to America. The last time I saw him was when he came home to pay off his debt to Tito Lico. I doubt we'll ever hear from him again."

My mind tumbled through four thoughts at once. "Debt?"

Ligòri didn't respond; he was just watching me. Teresedda had drifted back to the stove and I had the feeling she was avoiding being part of the conversation.

"What debt did Mico have to Tito Lico?" I asked plainly, then waited, meeting his eye, until he shifted on his stool and sighed in resignation.

"I don't know the details. I just know he was paying it back for years, and then got in trouble and had to borrow more." Ligòri Scordo threw up his sun-dark hands. "Who knows. He was always rushing from one thing to another."

I spent a moment crafting the right question to ask. "If Mico was just going to disappear anyway, never look back, what was the point in paying off his debt first?"

Ligòri looked at me like I was simple. "Even a man like Mico wants to make sure his family doesn't have *that* kind of trouble."

Teresedda was very still, her face turned away as if she were trying to erase herself from the room.

It was time for me to leave. "Well. Thank you for letting me meet Ninuzzu, and for the coffee."

"Oh, no, thank *you*," husband and wife said in unison.

"Listen, *maestra*," Ligòri said as Teresedda was about to let me out a second time. "I don't think there's any reason to track down Mico. He's never coming back here. But . . ."

"But what?"

Ligòri was still sitting at the table, and shrugged in the shadow. "But you can try my sister Francesca. She's a servant up at the Alvaro house. If anyone keeps in touch it would be her."

It was almost noon, so I stopped home for lunch. Cicca was so excited to see me she made us pasta with potato.

"Can you tell me about the Alvaros?" I asked as Cicca drizzled olive oil over my plate. Between my searches for Leo Romeo and Mico Scordo, I had plenty of excuses for indulging my curiosity about Santa Chionia's self-appointed aristocracy. "I've never met any."

"Oh, there are no Alvaros anymore," Cicca said. "Just Rocco. Don Roccuzzu's grandson. He's your age. He's not married yet." It wasn't clear if this was a warning or an advertisement. "Don Roccuzzu and Donna Adelina only had one boy, Gianni, and six girls. Gianni only had Rocco, no other children; no one but Rocco to carry on the Alvaro name now."

"Don Roccuzzu died during the 1943 cholera epidemic, right?" I asked, and Cicca grunted assent. I wondered who'd stepped in to pick up the pieces of his extortion business, or whatever other disreputable sidelines he'd had going. "What happened to his son—Gianni?"

"Gone," Cicca said with some venom. She plunked herself on her stool.

"You didn't like him?" I took a less-than-wild guess. "The son?"

"Gianni?" Cicca snorted like one of those creepy white cows that despotized the city limits. "I like everybody."

I let that one go whizzing by. "Tell me about him."

After a hesitation, during which Cicca was transparently regretting her words, she said, "Some Christians cause problems that other people have to fix."

My heart was thumping with the suspicious interest it had been exercised by so often since that skeleton was uncovered. "What kinds of problems?" I asked, but Cicca didn't answer, busying herself with a piece of potato. Was she telling me Gianni Alvaro was the kind of guy who left open a window someone else had to close when it rained, or the kind who left a body someone else had to figure out how to bury under the post office? Was she telling me Gianni himself was the problem someone else had had to take care of?

"Cummàri?"

I watched for a minute as she stonewalled me.

"Rich people get away with murder, don't they?" I tried.

Cicca looked up and scowled. "I never said anything about murder!"

I'd have to come back to this line of inquiry later. "So the one grandson, Rocco, he's inherited the house?"

"That's right. Don Roccuzzu has one other living grandson, Santo Arcudi, but he's not an Alvaro."

Aha. Isodiana was married to the grandson of the old don. This made aesthetic sense—the expensive furnishings in the Arcudi house, the paranoid number of locks on the door. "I met Santo's wife," I said, oh so cool. "Isodiana Legato?"

"Isodiana's a good girl. Don Roccuzzu was her grandpa, too."

"What? Really?" It shouldn't have surprised me; first-cousin marriage was more common than not in the Aspromonte, especially if a family had any money at all to protect.

"Isodiana's mamma was Donna Richelina, the youngest. Donna Richelina and Santo's mamma, Donna Olimpia, they were sisters. We called them the princesses of Santa Chionia." With one olive-oily hand, Cicca slicked down the feathery spiral of hair that poked up out of her head like a radio antenna. "Beautiful girls, all of them, but especially Donna Richelina. Just like Isodiana, with that shiny black hair. So gentle."

Gentle—was that the word for Isodiana? I was embarrassed to feel my pulse had picked up at the thought of the woman, of her elegant, muted movements and unbreachable walls.

"Don Roccuzzu's other daughters, they were married away to different *paesi*," Cicca was saying. "Rich, rich men. Those girls took their big dowries and now they live in castles all over Calabria. Platì, San Luca, Gerace, Rosarno."

Another thought was twinkling at the periphery of my mind, an idea about tracking down a lead to Leo Romeo. "Isodiana's mother—what did you say her name was?"

"Donna Richelina." A morose nostalgia overcame Cicca then. "The princess of Santa Chionia," she said again, quite sadly, and I marveled at the poignancy, that this battered old woman should reminisce without resentment about some rich girl whose dad seemed to have kept the entire town under his crushing thumb for forty years.

"Is she still here in Santa Chionia? Or is she in Philadelphia with her husband?"

Cicca tipped herself off the stool and collected the wooden spoons from the table. "She's gone," she said, then added after a viscid moment, "What a lovely lady, Donna Richelina."

That didn't help me get closer to Ceciu Legato or the correspondence work he'd done for Don Roccuzzu. Somewhere, someone must have preserved the records of Chionoti immigrant debts—otherwise it would have been a pretty feeble extortion business. What I knew about the dead don suggested he'd been anything but a feeble businessman.

Ligòri Scordo had pointed me toward the Alvaro house on my mission to track down Mico—maybe while I was up there I could finagle a peek into the late don's papers.

"I'd like to see that fancy Alvaro house," I said out loud.

"To talk to Francesca Scordo," Cicca said.

I was taken aback. "What?"

"You want to ask her about Mico?"

I was so surprised I laughed. "How did you guess?"

Cicca shrugged modestly.

"*Cummàri,* I don't know what your secret is, but you should be a spy!"

27

ON FRIDAY, NOVEMBER 11, CICCA MADE ME PROMISE I WOULD BE home early to celebrate Saint Martin's Day.

"Which one is Saint Martin? I can't remember."

"San Martino is when we drink wine and eat *zzippuli*."

Whatever poor old Saint Martin got himself canonized for, I assumed he couldn't object to wine and doughnuts in his name.

But first, my two-pronged Alvaro house operation: today would be the day that I would finally get Vannina Favasuli off my back, but if I was lucky in my information-gathering maybe I would rustle up some shred of hope about Leo Romeo for Gnura Emilia.

Off I went up via Occhiali, where I had never ventured. The sun was boisterous and the wind inconsistent. I passed the deserted cistern, and an unintimidated tribe of bees feasting on a scrub blanket of pink flowering succulent; their thrumming was so loud and the wild mint bursting from the rocks so fragrant it felt like a May morning. As I climbed higher, Mount Etna in her shawl of snow emerged on the horizon, rising above a cloud bank over Sicily.

There was no mystery which was the Alvaro house. The "road" had apparently been laid with pink-gray flagstones for the Alvaros' exclusive enjoyment. The façade was two tall stories and contained six pairs of windows—like a castle, or a prison.

The broad-shouldered, dark woman who answered the iron-braced door was clearly Mico Scordo's sister; she could have been Mico himself had she been slightly less feminine.

"Signorina Scordo," I said. Cicca had apprised me of the woman's marital status, and of a number of other details that were probably not central to my mission. "My name is Franca Loftfield. May I speak to you?"

"Me? Why?"

"Your brother Ligòri sent me." This was not a lie.

"Oh, Ligòri." She rubbed her tawny neck with one floury hand. "I have a lot to do."

"I won't take too much of your time," I said, but she had already stepped aside to let me in.

I followed the other Francesca through a tiled foyer and past a double set of balconied staircases that would have struck even Norma Desmond as a bit too majestic. Down the hallway in the brightly lit kitchen, a fire roared in the oven—no need for the Alvaro help to schlep bread dough all the way down to the communal oven in the piazza.

The woman didn't bother with pleasantries like offering me a beverage, just returned to the flour well she'd poured on the table. "What is it you want?"

"Your sister-in-law Vannina is trying to track down your brother Mico."

The woman gave me an incredulous scowl. "What does that have to do with you?"

She had a point. I needed the woman's sympathy if I was going to learn anything from this visit. "Vannina got it in her head that I could help her find him and she won't stop badgering me." By now I had a good idea of how the Chionoti talked about Vannina behind her back, and I only felt a little bad doing the same.

"I haven't spoken to Mico in years." Francesca Scordo had made quick work of her dough, which was no longer a flour well but a sticky glob matted to her fingers. "He's a selfish prick. He never helped Mamma during the bad years, not one lira. He sat out the war getting fat on American beefsteak, spending money right and left on hats and shoes."

Bitterness had collected in the furrow over her brow. Cicca had told me enough about what had happened to Francesca Scordo during the war for me to infer particular resentment there.

The winter sunlight streaming through the open windows was gray and smoky with floating flour. "Do you know where he's living these days?"

"America, I guess. If he's dead in a ditch I don't care."

Mico's brother Ligòri and his sister Francesca had worded their antipathy identically. A coincidence?

I watched her muscular palms press the bread dough into the wooden tabletop. "Do you think he's dead in a ditch?"

Francesca Scordo looked up long enough to meet my eye. "*Purtroppo,* no, he'll never pay for any of his sins."

A slender dark-haired man had stepped into the frame of the open back door and was kicking mud off his boots against the jamb. "Who is this?" he said, his eyes passing over my bosom. He was about my age and was wearing a tailored waistcoat under his jacket—Rocco Alvaro, the heir to the Alvaro kingdom, the only son of Don Roccuzzu's only son.

"It's the American teacher," Francesca Scordo said, giving the dough ball one final whack. "She's looking for my brother Mico. Trying to figure out if he's dead in a ditch."

I could have done without this unfortunately accurate specificity. I made myself meet Rocco's heavy-lidded gaze. "His wife is looking for him," I said.

"Why?" Rocco picked through a bowl of winter pears on the counter. His efforts to clean his boots had been less than assiduous. "So he can give her a good beating for whoring herself out to any man who catches her eye?"

"Actually, his son is about to get married." I was privately pleased with myself for my quick thinking.

"Well, Mico Scordo ain't up here. Fix me a sandwich, Francesca." Two pears in one hand, he grabbed her face and kissed her cheek like a bratty beloved nephew might. I saw no affection register in the woman's expression. Rocco exited the kitchen, his footsteps scuffing along the tiled hallway. I imagined the crust of mud he was leaving in his wake.

"He's not all bad," Francesca Scordo said, draping a linen towel over the dough ball. "I tell my Maria she can never let herself be alone with him. But his father was a good man and maybe someday he'll grow up."

I was fairly sure Rocco Alvaro hadn't been out of earshot during this pronouncement. "Does your Maria work here, too?"

"She helps with the cleaning and looking after the old lady. My back isn't so good." The other Francesca pulled aside another linen cloth to reveal a haunch of prosciutto crudo, and I watched with envy as she took a long knife to the striated fat. "I keep telling her she has to try to find herself another job, but what is there in town? Nothing."

"Does she like children? I'm looking for two teachers for my school."

"She couldn't teach. She has no schooling." Francesca Scordo covered the prosciutto again. I don't think anyone would have minded if she had offered me a tiny piece.

"It's a nursery, though—babies. Perhaps she'd be just right for it."

"I don't know."

The occlusion of the prosciutto had dampened my spirits. I made no headway with this woman. I'd never talk her into letting me into the dead don's old papers, if they even existed. My climb up the mountain had been for naught. "I better be getting back, but listen, why don't you send Maria down to the nursery to talk about the job?"

Francesca Scordo shrugged. I had no idea whether she would relay the message.

She led me back across the tiled foyer, but while she was still unlocking the grand front door Rocco Alvaro appeared at the balcony on the right-wing staircase and called down, "Hey! Teacher lady. You leaving already?"

"I am."

He came bobbing down the stairs, a jaunty syncopated descent. "You come all this way up the mountain and you don't even look around the house? That's what you really wanted, right? To see how the rich folks live?"

I stared back at Rocco Alvaro as unabashedly as he stared at me. Was this his idea of flirting? Or was he belittling me? It didn't really matter. "Are you offering me a tour?"

"If you want one." He gave me a toothy smile and I noticed the shining white points of his incisors. *Nice teeth,* I thought, despite myself.

Francesca Scordo, holding the heavy door open, was giving me a sad sneer. What was I going to do, follow a questionably mannered young man through the huge deserted house? I felt a knot of nerves, or maybe better judgment, in my stomach.

"I do want one," I said.

"Go make her a sandwich, Francesca," Rocco said, dismissing the chaperone. "Let's start with the dining room, *signorina.*"

My heart began racing as soon as we were alone, but Rocco seemed more interested in keeping me on my toes than in testing my ability to fend off sexual advances. He turned a dial on the wall and the reflective surfaces flared like a firecracker, bright with electric light cast from a crystal chandelier similar to the Arcudis'.

"Voilà," Rocco said, the French word sounding like a joke in his mouth.

The light bounced off stacks of gilt-edged china, enough to host a dinner party for twenty-five, arrayed in a glass and chestnut cabinet that ran the full length of the wall. I had never seen anything like it before, not in the palazzos of my wealthiest Roman friends.

"Don Roccuzzu must have really liked dining."

"He did. You can see for yourself when you get to the portrait room."

I couldn't begin to tally up a price tag for this ostentation. Don Roccuzzu Alvaro had been one hell of a goatherd.

Next, the library, with an alarmingly grand mahogany desk. My heartbeat accelerated in hope, but the single bookshelf contained only cloth-bound books, nothing that looked like it could be a diary or record book. I would have loved to know what the dead don bothered to read, but I had already lingered too long craning my neck when Rocco sniggered behind me. "That's what we use for killing rats."

"What?" Startled, I followed his gaze back to the bookshelf. "Rats?" It was only then, unnerved, that I saw the glass liter bottle of muriatic acid sitting on the shelf next to the books I had been staring at. Its factory-printed label was such an anachronism in this nineteenth-century diorama that my brain had blotted it from the tableau.

"Rats, *signorina*." Rocco Alvaro crossed his arms over his waistcoat. "We can't tolerate even one in a town like this. They breed and overrun us."

I found my voice. "I've never seen a rat in Santa Chionia."

"Exactly." After a long beat of sizing each other up, he said, "You know, it's rude not to acknowledge the lady of the house."

"I'm sorry?" I searched the salon for a clue as to what he meant.

"The lady of the house," Rocco repeated, excruciatingly slowly. One eyebrow flicked with amusement. "My sainted grandmother, Donna Adelina. Excuse yourself, *signorina*."

I wondered battily if he was making a joke, if a dead grandmother was sitting in an urn among the gaudy ceramics. But no—as my eyes traveled the room again, they latched on to the velvet armchair by the window, and the gray figure sitting in a bleaching bar of sunlight. She was a shred of humanity, her right hand tangled in a rosary, her age-blued eyes fixed, unimpressed, on her grandson. I would have walked right past her.

"Excuse me." I bumbled ridiculously into the semblance of a curtain-call bow. "Thank you for allowing me into your beautiful home."

The old woman's eyes moved from Rocco to me. She lifted her left hand, like a saint in a Byzantine mosaic, then swatted it downward and turned away. We were dismissed.

I contemplated that unpleasantness as we continued through rooms outfitted so luxuriously I couldn't decide if they were splendid or tacky. When we reached the grand staircase again, Rocco gave me a sly smile. "Did you want to see my bedroom, or should we save that for next time?"

"I think one floor is enough for today." I wished I'd thought of a better rejoinder, since I should have guessed he would say something like that.

His smirk stretched into the now-familiar toothy grin. "After all that exertion you must be hungry. We better go get you that sandwich."

Clomping back down the mountain none the wiser about Mico Scordo's or Leo Romeo's whereabouts, I was so focused on placing my feet that I shrieked when a man's deep voice called out "Signorina Franca!" from only a few feet away.

I skidded and threw out my hands for balance, my panicked gaze finally fixing on Officer Vadalà, who had been crouching in front of a large rock by the side of the road. A saint stone, I now recognized.

The officer was coming toward me and my heart began to pound, the memory of our last encounter flooding my faculties.

"What are you doing up here, *signorina*?" he said in a tone the high school hall monitors used to use to reprimand us for torn stockings.

"I am coming from the Alvaro house. Rocco invited me for lunch." I wondered if I'd regret implying a personal relationship later, but for the moment was pleased with the way Vadalà's face tightened. "And now I'm on my way to my next appointment," I added, hoping he'd assume someone was expecting me. "Have a nice afternoon, officer."

"Travel safely," he called to my back.

I turned to smile and wave at him, pretending I thought we had each forgiven the other. I hurried all the way back to the *centro* with my heart in my throat.

28

IT WAS TIME TO TIE THINGS UP WITH VANNINA—DUE DILIGENCE had been done.

I had a notion of where she lived because I'd seen her sitting on a stool at the mouth of an alley of run-down row houses, not far from the public latrines. I passed a building with a crumbled front wall that yielded a coquettish view of blackness below the collapsed ground floor. Next door, a fig tree burst through the lichen-encrusted pine skeleton of an abandoned roof. It was impossible to say when anyone had last lived in these buildings; they were thicketed in ivy, their stoops slick with green moss, but ground cover grows fast.

The alley was empty except for a one-eyed, one-eared orange cat, who regarded me from his roost on a truncated stone wall, and a single elderly woman, stone-gray hair in a gnarled chignon. She was carding wool in front of a curtained doorway.

"Vannina Favasuli," I said, answering the woman's unspoken question, and the woman pointed to her right.

Vannina's head emerged from one window down. "Here," she called, then disappeared from the pane, and in an act of dark transportive magic was immediately pulling me into her house.

I had been in many almost unbearably shabby homes in my time working for Child Rescue, and Vannina's was another. A single room, dank, dark, and dirty: the humid, nose-clogging smell of mildewed clothes, cooking ash, and animal cohabitation thickened the air.

"Sit," Vannina commanded. Her curling hair was hanging down over her breasts today, partially obscuring the trench of cleavage. "You want some soup?"

"I've already eaten, thank you." My stomach rebelled at the strong smell of barley and scalded goat milk overlaying the ammonia animal stench.

"You'll try my wine."

"No, that's—" I had to accept something. "All right, a little wine."

Vannina brought a jug to the table. "Tell me, you must have news."

I took a wooden cup from her and sipped politely. Through the wine I could taste the ash Vannina had used to clean her dishware. "There is no visa on file for Mico. At least, not from 1952."

Satisfaction settled on her features. "I knew it!"

"But there is a mailing address." I took Pino Pangallo's paper from my datebook to show her, but Vannina was already shaking her head.

"That's the same address I wrote to. Look." She leapt onto her bed like a child, kneeling as her fingers worked over a patch of the wall.

I took the opportunity to pour my wine into Vannina's cup, then followed her to take a look. Affixed to the stone wall was a shrine to her missing husband. In the center was his passport photo, and a photo of Vannina as a bride, her stunning beauty humorously suppressed by her stodgy wedding dress. Next to her was a mountain gorilla of a man; his mighty left hand, with the tendoned knuckles of athletic youth, reached across his own body to close around his bride's upper arm. I couldn't help but think many women besides Vannina must have been curious about what those giant hands might have felt like wrapped around their own arms.

There was other memorabilia, but my eyes had fixed on one photo: a copy of the one that had disappeared from the *municipio,* of six men and a bagpipe-playing boy.

Why did Vannina have this photo?

"What a handsome man," I murmured, conscious that I'd been tongue-tied too long.

"An angel," Vannina replied, but the words were rote. She had pulled a piece of damp-stained paper from the wall. "Here you go, see?"

I took the paper, afraid it would disintegrate. It had two different Philadelphia addresses on it. The top address, on Marvine Street, had been X-ed out, and the second address matched the one from the visa in Pino's album: *817 South 8th St., Apt. 9.*

"Why is this one crossed out?"

"This was where he lived when he first arrived in America. Then a few years later he moved to this one. I wrote there so many times. Finally I got a letter from the roommate, who told me Mico didn't live there anymore."

"And that man didn't send you a forwarding address?"

The crease in Vannina's forehead deepened. "*Maestra,* you are ignoring the most important part. Why did *he* not write to *me*? The letters just stopped, no explanation."

Perhaps because, as Cicca had told me, Mico Scordo had run off with another woman. Meanwhile, I had already done a considerable amount of extracurricular snooping in the service of Vannina's denialism, stacking up warnings and irritating once-helpful civil servants along the way. I did not want to alienate any more people in Santa Chionia by getting caught up in this detested woman's attention-mongering.

But Vannina was watching me, her unblinking hazelnut eyes aglow in the afternoon light. What would get her off my case?

"The last letter you sent here"—I tapped the South Eighth Street address—"someone wrote back to you?"

"Yes. His name was . . ." Vannina, thinking, absently rubbed at a bare patch of eggshell-smooth skin to the left of her breastbone. My eyes reflexively followed her hand. How much the woman constantly had on display, and how casually she drew attention to it, without even noticing. Maybe. "Louis. The roommate he was living with in Philadelphia." Whistling between her missing teeth, my hometown's name sounded like *Peel-a-del-PEE-a.*

"But the letter was in English."

"Pino from the *municipio* translated for me."

Suspect. "Do you have the letter still?"

I sat stoically as we went through every carefully folded piece of paper in the box in which Vannina kept Mico's letters. Before he disappeared, Mico had in fact been a faithful correspondent.

"You see what a good husband he was." Vannina pulled a letter out of the pile and tilted it toward the light. I caught the words *always in my heart* and *I cannot wait until I see you* without even focusing my eyes on the page. I felt a cold prickling of uncertainty.

"How hard that must have been for you to be away from him so much."

"There was no choice." Vannina rubbed her trenched forehead with the palm of her free hand. "What work was there here? This Godforsaken hellhole. Santa Chionia is Satan's chamber pot."

This unexpected turn of phrase startled my attention away from my task. "Do you really hate your *paese* that much? Would you vote for transferment?"

"Would I vote for transferment." She widened her eyes at me, like *I* was the crazy one, and I could see white all the way around the irises. "No one's asking my opinion."

"I'm asking. Is that a yes or a no?"

"*Yes.* Are you blind, *maestra*?" Her snarl was all the more vicious for its toothlessness. "Look how I live! Mud seeping from my walls. Begging for scraps to eat." Suddenly subdued, she added, "If we transfer we'll have modern houses and—what do you call it, water that comes through a pipe."

"Plumbing."

"Plumbing, and a train station so we can take the train far away from here."

Nervously, I wondered how many exhausted Chionote homemakers might secretly feel the same way. "The people of Africo are still waiting for their promised houses nine years after they transferred. Aren't you worried you'll just end up living in barracks?"

She swept her chin in a circle, indicating the whole of her squalor. "Barracks would not be worse than this."

Her point was vividly and effectively made. Despair for her—for the hopelessness of my work—tightened around my heart like a swaddle.

I rallied. "Did you find the letter from Louis in Philadelphia?"

It was still in its envelope, and I knew almost everything I needed to from the return address. The name of the sender was not Louis but Lois—Lois Blake. Pino Pangallo's English might not have been sophisticated enough to know the difference.

Mrs. Favasuli:

The man you are looking for, Dominic Scordo, who you say is your husband, has not lived at this address for months. I will not pretend I understood your letters but I took one to a friend who speaks Italian and boy was I shocked and humiliated to have my friend see what it said. Dominic certainly never told me he had a wife and a family. I realize this is not your fault any more than it is mine but I felt I owed you a letter so you at least know what kind of man your husband is. I have made mistakes but I am a Christian and I will pray for us both. But please do not send any further letters here.

Lois Blake

Even after I handed the letter back to Vannina, I could feel this stranger Lois Blake's faraway pain throbbing in my fingers. Maybe Pino Pangallo *had* understood the English—maybe that's what he'd been referring to when he'd said Mico wouldn't write back.

"It says he doesn't know where Mico lives now, right?"

"Right." What else could I say?

Vannina was stroking the riffled tops of the letters with her index finger, but abruptly she pulled the cover over the box. "He was murdered. I've known it all along." She leapt off the bed; her chest was heaving. "Eight years of lies. *Liars!*" she shrieked, and clawed at her hair, at her face. "*Liars. They slaughtered him* like a *pig*!"

"Vannina!" I caught the tall woman by the forearms so she couldn't strike out. "I need you to calm down, or I'm going to leave." It was what I would have said to a three-year-old child.

She fell silent, regarding me with red-stained eyes. Her skin under my hands was feverishly hot. She repulsed me, I who might be her only friend. She had nothing, no respect, no husband, no answers. I felt a renewed rush of compassion.

"All right, Vannina. Tell me—plainly, in order. What do you think happened to Mico?"

We sat together on the bed, and I tried not to worry about fleas. I had to rewash all my clothes anyway to get the damn cactus prickers out.

"The night before he was supposed to go to Napoli, there was a feast down at Pascali Morabito's," Vannina said. "I waited up for Mico all night. I was worried. And then"—she wiped her nose—"Turi came over the next day and told me they had drunk too much and fallen asleep, and Mico had to rush to catch the train." She concluded listlessly, "He never came home for his things."

That was legitimately alarming. "He left for America without his belongings?"

Vannina nodded toward the far corner of the room. "That trunk over there."

There it was, still waiting for him eight years later, gray with muddy dust. Feeling a cold fingernail scratching at my heart, I said, "What about his passport? He would have needed that to get on the boat."

"Someone broke into my house." Vannina was picking at a bleeding cuticle, and I watched a pink patch of surfacing blood appear as she flicked the shred of skin to the chicken-trodden floor. "They stole his passport and purse."

"That same night? You said you waited up—you would have heard someone, surely." I gestured across the airless space.

"Do you know what they do to you if you cross them?" Vannina's lovely face folded into a toothless sneer. "They wait for you in the forest—maybe when you're collecting wood. Then one of them trusses you like a goat and the other slits your throat. They leave you for the wolves, but first they sprinkle salt over your new smiling mouth." She dragged a finger across her neck.

Ick. Enough theatrics. "Vannina, what you've told me so far doesn't make sense." I followed a hunch. "Tell me the truth. You don't really think he's dead, do you?"

Vannina pressed her full lips together, then released them in a glistening pout. When she finally spoke, it was with thoughtful coherence. "This is why I think he's dead, Franca. We had a terrible fight that night, because I didn't want him to go out. He was getting mixed up with bad men. But he went out anyway, he said he had a job to do, and then he never came home." Vannina twisted her wedding ring off her finger and studied it as she kept talking. "There was a big problem that summer. You know Ninedda Lico?"

"I don't." My ears had perked up.

"She's Tito's daughter. You know Tito the Wolf." This last was not a question. "She had fallen cuckoo in love with Mico. She was a teenager, dumb as a sheep. She wanted to give him her virtue. It was embarrassing to see, how she would follow him around. But it scared me, too. You know what happens when a girl like that gets her feelings hurt." She drew her finger across her neck again.

"What happens?" I said anyway.

"She is in love with him, he tells her no, she is spurned and wants him dead, so in revenge she tells her father he disrespected her, and then they find his corpse in the ravine." Staring through the crack in the shutter at the street, she added philosophically, "He would have gotten it for fucking her, just the same."

Vannina made it sound like Santa Chionia was a nineteenth-century opera, full of vengeful virgins and forest vigilantes. She was also the only person in Santa Chionia who refused to believe Mico had run off on her. I thought, uncharitably, I might not blame him.

It was true, the fact that Mico's visa was missing from the *municipio* records was weird. But Leo Romeo's visa was missing, too.

"What exactly are you asking me to do, Vannina?"

"Prove Mico's dead!" Her eyes bulged at me in vexation, her sandy irises rolling like a stallion's. "Make them pay! Help me feed my children!"

Guilt stole over me like a chafing wool shawl. I had done nothing to make life better for this pathetic, annoying woman. Vannina's problems had nothing to do with me, I reminded myself. But Vannina's problems had nothing to do with anyone, and her circumstances indicated she was unable to shoulder them alone. My purpose in life was to oppose the notion that people could only help one another when there was something to be gained for themselves.

The trouble was, not only was there nothing to be gained from helping Vannina, being associated with her in any way might alienate me from the rest of the town, especially if she was insisting on accusing some of the wealthiest power brokers of possibly nonexistent crimes.

I would stall. "Let me think about this." I peered at her shrine, my eye drawn uncontrollably to the photo of the six men and the bagpiper, to the uncanny familiarity of Isodiana's father, Ceciu Legato. "Can you tell me why you have this picture?"

Vannina pried the photo off its backing. "These are the men who killed Mico," she said softly. "Tito the Wolf. Turi Laganà, the goat-fucking swine. And Pascali Morabito."

"What about the other three?"

Vannina narrowed her eyes at me, reminding me of an ornery house-cat about to sink his teeth into your hand. "No, not them."

I wasn't sure why I cared about the photo so much. Partly, I realized, because Pino Pangallo had been so obstructive. Hereditary obstinacy, for which I must both blame and thank my Calabrian mother. In any case, I wanted to show the photo to Cicca and ask for her dossiers on each of the men in it. "Can I borrow this photo?"

Vannina looked unhappy about the request. "You'll have to bring it back."

"Of course." I closed the photo in the pages of my datebook. "Now I must go—"

Vannina seized my forearm. "But what are you going to do about Mico?"

What was there to do? "I'm going to write a letter," I lied, then backed myself up by taking out my datebook again. "Here, let me copy down the other address you have. I'll try writing in English. Maybe whoever is there will be able to forward it to the right place."

"There is no right place," Vannina said darkly. "Since he's dead." But she proffered the yellowed sheet of paper for me to copy.

29

I LOCKED UP THE NURSERY AT THREE, SELF-SATISFIED WITH A day's meddling and looking forward to a Friday evening of wine and doughnuts. I hauled myself up via Sant'Orsola and bounded into Cicca's kitchen, winded and buoyantly disheveled. "*Cummàri!* I'm home!" I called in my most obnoxious imitation of Desi Arnaz, because it made Cicca laugh even though she had never heard of *I Love Lucy*.

It was only after I had made this graceless entrance that I realized there were two extra people at Cicca's table: a round-faced middle-aged woman, who was smiling at me in a most forgiving way, and—who else—the specimen, Ugo, leaning on the table with one unrealistically large elbow, smooth chin cupped in his unrealistically large hand. He was real, though—no, I had not invented him the other night. My gut spasmed with knowledge that I must not, for many reasons, feel attracted to him. As was to be expected of the wardrobe of a forbidden mountain-man love interest, *his* was rather letting me down. His shirt seemed barely able to contain the physiological product of his steel-working, and his cap had been politely removed to unleash the glory of his curls.

"Franca," Cicca said smugly, "this is my niece Tuzza and her son Ugo. He's your age and he's not married yet."

No way, Cicca. She wasn't seriously going to try to—

"Francesca is very smart," Cicca bragged, patting Ugo on the head. "She speaks ten languages." That wasn't true. "And she's very good with children."

Tuzza benevolently interrupted, exclaiming, "Finally, we meet the American teacher!" as she pushed herself up to greet me.

I forced myself out of my stupor, noticing the dark circles under her eyes, and I remembered that her husband was dying. I kissed her cheeks with all the compassion a cheek-kiss can communicate. "Gnura Tuzza, it is a great pleasure to meet you."

Ugo had risen, too, and stood diffidently by the window. "A pleasure, *maestra*," he said, deadpan.

"A pleasure," I echoed, as stiff and awkward as I'd warned myself not to be. I could feel Cicca glaring at me. "Please, call me Francesca," I mumbled.

"All right!" Cicca cried. "Now the wine!"

"It's our Aspromonte tradition to try this year's wine for the first time on San Martino," Ugo said as Cicca scuttled to her pantry under the stairs.

"Oh," I replied stupidly. Now I regretted receiving Vannina's sour wine with so little gratitude or ceremony this afternoon.

Tuzza gestured to the plate sitting in the middle of the table. "Why don't you try this, Maestra Francesca? It's a Santa Chionia specialty." The item in question looked like a bagel, shining with a baked-on egg wash and speckled with sesame seeds.

"Ooh, are these *zzippuli*?" I asked as Cicca returned with a decanter. "They are very different from doughnuts in my mother's *paese*."

Cicca and Tuzza laughed gently at me, humorous foreigner, doesn't know what a doughnut is. "No, no, no," Cicca was saying as Tuzza explained, "This is called *scaddatèdda*. It's made with cumin seeds."

"*Scaddatèdda*," I repeated. That would be dialect for "little scalded thing."

"Yes, because you boil them before you bake them."

I imagined round-faced Tuzza fetching water from the cataract to boil the cumin cakes by her dying husband's sickbed, then running them all the way down the mountain again to the communal oven to bake them. "How special," I said admiringly.

"Yes, very special," Ugo agreed. "We only eat them for someone's birthday." He caught my gaze and cut his eyes toward Cicca.

"What!" I pointed an accusing finger at her. "What a stooge you are, *cummàri*! I can't believe you didn't tell me."

"Birthdays are nonsense," Cicca grunted, pleased with the attention, and thumped the decanter onto the table. "Ugo, you pour."

Cicca's wine was as fizzy as a cream soda and zipped through the blood vessels of my brain. I sipped nervously, hoping its witchcraft didn't loosen my tongue.

As Cicca fried doughnuts, Tuzza quizzed me solicitously about my life and work. I expended twenty percent of my energy on trying to sound coherent, the other eighty percent on not looking at her son, who apparently felt no self-consciousness about not returning the favor.

Tuzza especially wanted to hear about America. "It must be magnificent," she said. "We have so many problems here."

"America has many problems, too."

Tuzza's brow contracted in distress. "Not like us! It cannot be."

I hesitated, conscious of the mythology, of the fact that Tuzza most likely had relatives who had gone to America and never come back. I didn't want to disparage something she looked up to any more than I wanted to let her feel disparagement at her own homeland.

"Honestly, the problems look different on the surface," I said finally. "But really they are exactly the same: rich people who are so jealous about protecting their wealth that they have no respect for human life."

"But in America at least everyone has a chance to succeed," Tuzza said, and her manner was so innocent and appealing that I hated to argue with her.

"I wish that were true, *cummàri*," I said.

Tuzza nodded toward her son. "I tell Ugo he should go to America."

Ugo gave his mother a half smile that made me want very badly to see the other half. "Only if you came with me, Ma."

Tuzza squeezed her son's enormous forearm with one broad, affectionate hand. "What do you think, Francesca? Would you show us around?"

Doing my best to ignore Cicca, whose motives were about as opaque as a stained glass window, I put my hand to my breast and said, "It would be my pleasure."

30

NOVEMBER 21 WAS THE FIRST MONDAY LUNCH I HAD WITH DON Pantaleone Bianco in almost a month. I admit I scanned his silhouette for a sign that he was packing, as it were, but his cassock appeared altogether too venially trim-fitted to accommodate a firearm.

Emilia Volontà greeted me at the rectory door, and her colorless affect reminded me I'd promised her I'd think of a next step in tracking down Leo. As she served us roasted wild fennel, the priest described his natural science course for his diploma students. I half listened—Don Pantaleone wondered if the Fund might be able to make a donation for some rudimentary lab equipment—while I pretended to take notes, flipping through my datebook to recall what Emilia and I had talked about.

Seeing it in the datebook brought it back with discomfiting vividness— it had been the same day Officer Vadalà came over to Cicca's and threatened me. I had been so emotionally discombobulated that when I went to bed I must have turned the page in my planner without completing my to-do list. Most of the items were moot at this point, but not all of them:

piperazine replacement
Annunziato Volontà, Ceciu Legato

Ceciu Legato had turned out to be a dead end, and following that lead had alienated his daughter, Isodiana, on whom I'd pinned so many hopes.

"Damned if I do, damned if I don't," I muttered in English. Don Pantaleone raised an eyebrow. "I forgot to write to the Fund to request a medical supply shipment," I told him. "I was supposed to have sent a letter weeks ago."

"You shouldn't make yourself feel too bad, Franca. No shipment could have arrived with the bridge out."

That was weak consolation. "When will the bridge be rebuilt?" I asked. "Can Mayor Stelitano make it happen now that the election is over?"

"Oh, *maestra,* if only. We have to wait for the state to authorize a work detail, and then it has to be run through their approved contractors."

"That's . . . maddening," I said, though I wasn't surprised. "You've had a natural disaster, and daily life is supposed to wait patiently until bureaucracy can run its course?"

"There it is," the priest said. His musical voice was matter-of-fact. "The problem with centralized government. When the elected officials are all from the north, why would they expedite an outlay of funds down south?" He offered me the bowl of bread. "The Italians loathe us. We have neither their respect nor their affection. If they wait long enough, maybe we'll starve to death and solve their problem for them."

"Better to let them die and decrease the surplus population," I murmured, trying to translate the Dickens on the fly.

"*Brava.*" Don Pantaleone tapped the table resonantly with one vigorous finger.

"That is a very dark view of the state."

"It is a realistic view, my dear."

I remembered Pino Pangallo's theory about the nondelivery of disaster relief. "Do you think the state would withhold rebuilding funds to force transferment?"

I was expecting the priest to pooh-pooh the idea as he had last time, but instead he ate some bread. I waited, feeling a growing sense of anxiety.

"It is exactly the kind of thing they would do," he said finally. "We just have to do our best to get by in the meantime."

"But . . . Stelitano ran on an anti-transferment platform."

"Unfortunately he has other things to worry about. Have you heard Massara is challenging the election results?" But our conversation went no further, as two teenage boys arrived for an afternoon diploma lecture.

I took my leave. As I passed the saint stone on via Sant'Orsola, I stopped superstitiously and kissed my finger to rub on her bald patch.

31

AROUND THREE P.M. I LOOKED UP TO SEE A CURLY-HAIRED SILHOU-ette at the nursery's open door. I identified Cicca's nephew Ugo by wishful thinking alone.

"Hello," I said, trying not to sound excited to see him. "Come in."

He drifted across the room to stare out the window, then said very casually, "I was thinking maybe you'd like to go out for a bit." He was a murmillo in a shepherd's tuxedo: a white button-down with a loose open collar and a linen-wool jacket the color of weak tea. There was a leather satchel strapped across his chest in a way that made me avert my eyes.

"Go out?" I repeated, traitorous heart a-pounding. "There's nowhere to go."

"You know. For a walk." He could not have looked more nonchalant if he had been trying, which made me wonder if he was trying. "We'll look at some beautiful countryside."

I should assume I was misreading the signs. "I don't go out for walks," I said. *Pound pound pound.*

Ugo sat in front of my desk, lithe as a panther, which made no sense given his size; his clothing didn't even rasp against the unfinished wood. "I've seen you walk."

"I can't spend time alone with any man." Mostly to remind myself, I added, "For the sake of my job, there can be no question about my virtue or personal loyalties."

"My father's dying." His expression was somehow both grieving and mischievous—*Yes, I am playing this card.* "Distract me for the afternoon."

A useful arguing technique—ignoring your interlocutor entirely and pressing your case. I'd have to remember that one.

"I have work to do still." I felt my modest resolution slipping.

"If you really cared about that you would have said so first."

What *did* I care about? My job, my reputation, my conscience. Sandro. Time and distance hadn't made me stop caring about him. Thinking his name caused the pain in my chest to gyre.

Focusing instead on Ugo's ruddy face, boyish but for the single trench cut crookedly over his eyebrows, was like pulling a doily right over that gyre and setting a delightful vase of flowers on top.

Hands stuffed into his trouser pockets, he nodded toward the door. "Come, *maestra,* you're overthinking this."

I was not overthinking it. Just—for the record.

Shutters were flung open to the afternoon sunshine and the alleys echoed with the noises of invisible housewives starting their evening cooking.

Ugo touched his cap and said *"Kalispèra"* to every person who passed us, which was four women of various ages, each with a water bucket on her head. Four women, four separate gossip networks, all of them surely leading to Cicca.

Spending time with this man could only cause me grief. And yet. *Pound pound pound.*

At the top of via Sant'Orsola, where the domino stairs opened up onto the church piazza, we headed west down via Boemondo. We passed the cistern, then Ugo turned right onto a barely discernible dirt track.

Thick silence settled on me, as if we had stepped into a different realm, maybe ascended to a higher altitudinal plane too rarefied for the prosaic noises of the village. As we climbed the increasingly steep switchbacks, Ugo half turned to give me an endearing look of concern. "The road here is no good," he said. One curly side-lock lifted in the warm November breeze. "Are you all right?"

"I'm great." *Pound pound pound.*

"I'm taking you up to the Saracen Tower. You haven't been, have you?"

I had caught up to him, relished a lungful of lavender-scented air. "No."

"No one comes up here, except sometimes shepherds." He started up the trail again. "Watch out for goat presents."

As I followed Ugo's broad back up the scabrous path, my gaze traveled down to his trim thighs, and I hurriedly looked down at the flaking schist beneath my shoes. Absent now, in the moment of this writing, the self-consciousness of my youth, I feel obliged to add that his posterior was flattered by the melding drape of his trousers. There was no way he was unattached—that would truly be a travesty I couldn't imagine the Chionese Union of Future Mothers-in-Law sanctioning.

Whether he was single or not, according to local mores, by climbing the mountain alone with him I might as well have slept with him. If I didn't it would basically be a waste of my forfeited reputation. Something for me to keep in mind.

At the last turn the path spilled out onto a surprisingly large plateau. A warren of crumbled stone foundations was all that was left of the tower.

What lay before us was too much for words. From our precipice, the Aspromonte rolled into the invisible Ionian Sea. The forested cliff tops appeared furry at this distance, the late-afternoon sun laying an ashy orange film over the glowing dark green. Below us, the scimitar of the wash sliced through four million years of geology.

Ugo was pulling the strap of his shoulder bag over his head. "You're a good walker for a city girl."

This had been a test. I smiled, pressing my teeth together to try to control my breathing. He came to stand by my side, and we were both silent for a perfect long moment.

"The river used to be navigable," he said at last. He lifted a hand as brown and flat as a bread peel and used it to trace the gorge below us. "The water was so high that Roman ships could sail all the way in here for our timber."

"No way."

"Truly."

"How could the topography have changed so much in only two thousand years?"

"It happened after the big earthquake in 1783. Up there is where the water comes from." Ugo pointed behind me to the northeast, where the pine-blanketed slopes of the upper massif filled the sky, even more savagely altitudinous than our wild little foothill. "There was a lake in the middle of the forest—an enormous lake. The earthquake cracked the mountain and the lake drained away, so now the *fiumara's* source only puts out this trickle." Shielding his eyes with his shelf of a hand, he squinted into the sparkling sun.

I didn't say anything. I was overwhelmed by the too-muchness.

"Are you afraid of heights?"

"Only that I'm going to jump." As soon as I said it, I heard how it sounded and felt myself burning. "I mean—not that I want to kill myself. Only that—"

"Like a bird," he interrupted, generous. "*Capito.* There's a temptation to try to fly."

My heart—my stupid heart. *Pound pound pound.*

"Didn't they—" The ravine was so far below us that the dry wash bed appeared to be tumbling full of actual water. "Didn't they throw a priest off in a wine barrel?" I could now vividly imagine which point of impact had ended his troubled spiritual journey.

"Someone told you about that, eh?" Ugo was threading through the muqarna of broken stone walls. "Come sit over here."

I picked through the nettles to join him on a stony stoop. We were at least ten feet from the edge of the cliff but my throat was tight with fear.

Ugo sat decorously away from me, removing items from his bag and lining them up on the wall: a cheese wrapped in linen, dried figs, and pears. He'd planned ahead.

I let myself examine the clean, healthy lines of his jaw and his bulging arms. His nose had a crook in it and his eyebrows were disorganized. He wasn't a handsome man, just an extremely sexy one. It was hard to tell how well he knew that about himself.

"Worth coming for a walk, eh?" He was slicing wedges out of the cheese with a tiny knife. "Try this. Our specialty."

I took a piece of cheese from his broad thumb. I'm sorry to tell you this because it will do you no good, but it was the best cheese I have ever eaten. "What is this called?"

"*Caprino.*"

Goat cheese. "It doesn't have a specific name?"

"It doesn't need one. There's nowhere else in the world they make it."

I held it on my tongue, feeling the creaminess as the salt crystals loosened. The friendly wind combed through the curling hairs at the nape of my neck. I had no idea of the time; I hadn't heard the church bells ring once since we'd ascended. Could there be an actual rift in reality that separated us from the world?

"Ugo," I said, and felt myself flush at saying his name out loud.

He turned his amaro-clear eyes on me. Who was he?—this ostensibly simple man, a blue-collar bruiser with shepherd parents and no formal education, a steelworker who looked like he belonged on the Eagles' offensive line.

"May I ask—how is your father?"

"He's been asleep for four days now."

"I'm sorry," I said. For a long moment we watched the mountains, the dusk discoloring the illuminated horizon. "Should you be there?"

"It's too late. He'll never wake up." His thick neck pulsed over his Adam's apple.

Should I ask him more? Carefully, I said, "I'm so sorry. I am close to my own father, and imagining going through what you are right now is very hard." This way, he could choose to talk more about his father or change the subject by asking about mine.

After a short pause, during which he regarded me unbrokenly, he decided on the latter. "What is your father like?"

"He's a sweetie. But very distracted. He's a professor—your stereotypical academic. He would absolutely love this," I said as I accepted another piece of *caprino*. "He's crazy about cheese."

"A professor. That's very fancy." He was separating us by class in his mind. "You're his favorite, aren't you."

"Well. I am his only child. But yeah, I've always been his buddy. He would drag me along with him everywhere when I was a little girl. He brought me to his lectures, and the numismatic club, and the symphony—he'd be so disappointed in me when I'd fall asleep."

"You can tell," he said. "We have a saying, '*Caprone dolce, capretta tenace.*' Do you understand? Kind father, strong daughter—'*capretta,*' it means a female baby goat."

I laughed. It was so perfect. "Thanks. I'm not so good at the goat terms."

"Stick around here. You'll pick them up real quick." He gave me a smile then—a real smile that lit his deep-set eyes.

If the intention of the smile was to plant the idea that Ugo would be a kind father to tenacious daughters, well . . . it was a success, and stimulated biological repercussions.

I sort of debated the words, but not enough. "Are you?"

"Am I what?"

"Sticking around?" My throat and ears were hot again from my forwardness.

Ugo made me wait a beat too long for his answer. "It's impossible." He was rubbing a fig between his thumb and two thick fingers. "I have to go back north after Christmas."

There was no reason to feel any dismay. "Why?" I bleated, *capretta.*

The slow lift of his big shoulders conveyed helplessness. "That's where my life is."

What was in that life—a fiancée, a string of lovelorn girlfriends? "Are you happy there?"

Ugo took his time replying, eating the fig in two careful bites. "In Milan, an emigrant man is nothing more than a pair of arms." He thumped his right biceps with the heel of his left hand. "People realize you're from the south and say, 'Oh, you're one of *them*.' Or worse, they think they're complimenting you when they say, 'Oh, you're nothing like *them*.'" After a long silence, Ugo said, "You miss your homeland like you miss your mother. It's the thing that made you. But it is too late to correct Santa Chionia's course." He tipped his swarthy jaw toward the ravine. "It's like the river that's never going to run again."

His matter-of-factness chilled me. "The whole reason they sent me to Santa Chionia was to prove you wrong," I said. "Small changes can have far-ranging results."

"An optimist," he accused.

"What is so wrong with Santa Chionia that it can't be fixed?"

"The people who control everything don't want anything to change," he said. "They must make sure no one has the power to oppose the system, right? So the rich must do everything they can to block new opportunities. And the poor people are too afraid that they'll lose the little they have if they step up."

"That's just the human condition."

The sun was speeding up in its descent, doing its best to appear a victim of gravity, like us all. I swear I saw the moment it happened—the shift from a yellow ball suspended in the sky to an orange ball sliding into the sea. The drama of the streaks of red lying above the Ionian horizon was exaggerated further by the maroon pall blanketing the backlit mountains. I remember it so perfectly and yet cannot believe my own memory—the extremity of the color was such that it has called into question for me every other memory I've carried throughout my life.

"We've been living by our own laws for a thousand years," Ugo said. "The problem is that when you are so isolated, to defend against the monsters outside, you have no defense from the monsters within."

A cold pebble of unease slid down my sternum. "What kind of monsters?"

Ugo gave me a leveling look. "Listen. You can never trust anyone but yourself. Remember that. You can never show any fear. A completely dry response—no capitulation, no accepting favors. Otherwise they have you snared."

They.

I thought of the *salame* Don Tito the Wolf had bought me. Had I—would Ugo classify that as accepting a favor?

A cool twilight wind nickered among the ruins of the tower, the dry grasses knocking noisily against the ancient stonework. I caught the scent of pine smoke and shivered with fresh nerves.

"You mean Mayor Stelitano?"

Ugo grimaced. "He's not the worst of them."

"Who is?" I knew, though, that he wasn't going to give me a straight answer.

"Don't you see?" he said after a moment. "It's no one person—it's the system. Everyone is implicated."

I sucked my bottom lip, trying to think of missed signs of corruption. What industries were there to corrupt? "So appropriation of government funds," I guessed. "Grafting from earthquake and flood recovery projects?" He didn't say anything, but Cicca had already given me enough to think about there. I stretched my imagination. "Construction," I tried. That's where things would have started in Philadelphia—with the contracts. The fact that there was no road to Santa Chionia, no public school—were those entirely the fault of state negligence, or were there also inhibiting factors on the receiving end? Would greedy men really stop children from getting an education in order to pocket some illegal coin? I wished I was more surprised by human beings' capacity to take advantage of one another. I thought of Don Alvaro and his thirty percent interest. "Extortion?"

Ugo moved his head in what might have been agreement. "The problem is, we're so proud of our brigand history. We have a mythology about it, that it was a resistance movement. The truth is, there is no romance in these men; they're nothing but predators. You've heard of Giuseppe Musolino?"

"The Brigand Musolino. King of the Aspromonte. Of course," I said, indignant.

"Gentleman-thief, robbing the rich to help impoverished orphans, avenging the dishonored." He laughed humorlessly. "In reality, that man was nothing but a hit man from a criminal family. His sister managed all the real business, the extortion and armed robbery networks. When anyone stood in her way, she sicced her brother on them."

My mouth had dried, leaving only the cloy of fig. I was hearing Vannina's voice in my head—*they sprinkle salt over your new smiling mouth*—picturing the wild-eyed woman drawing her finger across her throat.

"We take a bloodthirsty madman and turn him into a folk hero," Ugo said. "That's how we end up living in a brigand world, where bad deeds might be good and no one in power can be trusted. Where men like Giuseppe Musolino are crowned king." He rubbed the side of his neck. "Men like me, well. Our choices are to work for them or to leave."

We talked until it was dark—about Milan, Ugo's job, his brother who lived with him. I managed a few diverting reciprocal stories, deceitfully avoiding the subjects of Venice and Rome and Sandro. I would have sat with him all night, but if I let our "walk" drag on into the falling darkness, I might literally stumble off the mountain and die, or at the very least be murdered by Cicca when I got home.

"It's late," I said, hating myself.

"We'll be fine," Ugo replied, but he packed his picnic into his bag.

I turned my back on the magnificence and the vertigo and we picked through the ruins in the thickening night. We were not too soon—the ground was obscure, the loose stones treacherous. The whistling wind shot up the canyon and across the plateau, a terrifying reminder of the potential fatality of a misplaced step or a weak ankle.

If this were a movie, Ugo would have reached back and offered me his hand.

We trooped through the gloom until the path arrived at via Boemondo—we were back in Santa Chionia.

"I go this way." Ugo's dusky silhouette was childish—his left arm hanging dissolutely, his shoulders hunched. "Give my regards to Cummàri Cicca."

"I—" *Pound pound pound.* "Yes, of course."

He touched his brow as if he were tipping an imaginary hat and I watched him disappear down the slope.

I didn't know what I had done wrong—said something offensive, revealed too much of my fundamental unattractiveness. Maybe just read the situation incorrectly. For crying out loud, I was a married woman. Sort of.

That night after dinner, I lay in the gray moonlight and reminded myself that it was a bullet dodged, not having to confront what would have happened if my stupid hormonal hopes had borne fruit. I made myself replay my first date with Sandro, the twelve hours we spent wandering the canals of Cannaregio in the October rain until the last *bacaro* had closed. I had been hurt and furious when he'd dropped me off at my leaky apartment without making any attempt to come inside, or even to kiss me.

I had not been able to sleep that night, obviously. The next day, with nothing left to lose, I had grilled his disloyal friends at the Union until they gave up his address and I'd tracked him down to his bachelor pad near the Frari.

"Why didn't you make a move on me?" I had shouted at him as he stood, mildly alarmed, his arm propping open his door. "What is it? Is there something wrong with me? Do you have a girlfriend? Is that why you aren't inviting me in?" He would have to decide in that moment if a voluble, buxom American-Calabrese was in fact what he wanted.

"No girlfriend."

"Why, then? Why would you spend so much time with me if you don't like me?"

"I do like you. I like you very much." He was smiling, like he couldn't help himself. "I didn't want to take advantage of—"

"That's horseshit. No man has ever felt bad about taking advantage."

"I never said I would feel bad," he had said.

I didn't need to close my eyes to remember the curl of his hand cupping the back of my neck, the bright warmth of his broad violinist palm against my vertebrae as he pulled me toward him. I remembered the swarming of fresh physical contact as vividly as if that new love were the only love we ever had.

Six years and hundreds of miles away from that moment, I listened to the sound of my tears sliding into the broom pillowcase. I had had such a passionate love affair in my life—a reciprocated one. So many lives never have a love story in them. I had no right to regret that I couldn't have two.

32

I HAD TO GET MY HEAD BACK IN THE GAME HERE.

On Tuesday morning my first stop was the *puticha*. I had Saverio the proprietor's nursery application for his son, *VINCENZO,* on top of my pile. I weathered the anticipated interval during which the man did not look up from his newspaper. The end of the interval never came, though, so I was forced to say, "Good morning, Saverio. I wanted to see when would be a good time for me to make a home visit to you and your wife to go over your nursery school application."

"Discuss it right now," he said, dropping the *Corriere della Sera* on the polished chestnut counter. I knew better than to look at its date.

"Certainly, if you like. But I'll still need to pay a home visit. My organization requires a salutary inspection of a child's abode."

His eyelids slid thickly down as he studied me—he was either incredulous at the demand or rudely half-napping.

"My wife is home right now," Saverio said finally. His gaze drifted over my shoulder. "But this afternoon would be best. Why don't you go over at one o'clock."

"One o'clock is perfect." The skin on the underside of my arms was prickling. I turned and—in the most unsurprising of possible outcomes—found Tito Lico sitting by the window, the blackness of his eyebrows cutting through the shadow.

I felt my smile stretch into a toothy fear-smile like a chimpanzee's. "Don Lico."

He gave a slow, deferential nod. *"Maestra."*

Covered in gooseflesh, I took my leave.

When I arrived at Saverio Legato's house at one o'clock, the door was answered not by Saverio's wife, Sinedda, but by Potenziana the Wolfess, looking stately in a dour black velvet dress. The woman's hair was pinned in the kind of French twist I had never once been able to get my hair to make.

"Come in," the Wolfess said, with no illusion of welcome. "Sinedda's just washing up from lunch."

Tito Lico had sent his wife to supervise my visit. I thought of Saverio's drifting gaze, of the way he had corrected himself to make sure I went over in the afternoon.

"Good to see you, Donna Lico," I forced myself to say as I followed the woman into the sitting room. "I owe you thanks for spreading the word about my project."

"I thought only to help my busy nieces." Potenziana took a seat on a green velvet-backed chair and turned her dark, warmthless stare on me. "So far my recommendation has only made hassle for them. You upset poor Isodiana."

My tongue sat numb against my teeth. Isodiana had complained about me to her aunt. "I'm sorry to hear that."

"Isodiana is a timid creature." Potenziana held my gaze. "She's like a child, she becomes very nervous. You really should have visited her when her husband was home."

The velvet fibers shrieked against my bottom as I shifted on the over-stuffed cushion. "She seemed competent and smart to me."

"You've only just met her, my dear," the Wolfess said, not kindly. "Apparently you must learn to have less confidence in your own instincts."

Sticks and stones, I told myself, fighting to keep my shock off my face.

Potenziana was watching me like a hawk—or, I suppose, like a wolf. "Listen to good advice, *maestra,* or Christians will ask themselves how they could possibly trust you with their children."

At that threat, my hurt runneled into anger. "Excuse me, Donna Lico—"

But that was when Sinedda came out to the sitting room with the coffee. Shaken, quaking under the antipathy of Potenziana's scrutiny, I conducted the inspection as sterilely as possible, then hurried on to my next interview.

Somehow I had made an enemy of Potenziana the Wolfess, perhaps the most powerful woman in Santa Chionia.

33

IT WAS NOT GERASIMO'S DONKEY BUT THE TOLLING OF THE BELLS of San Silvestro that woke me up on the morning of Friday, November 25.

I found Cicca sitting cross-legged on the kitchen floor, her back curled like a child's, crusty dried tears flaking from her cheeks.

"Filippo is dead," she told me. "Forty-six. Only forty-six."

Ugo's father. His agony had finally ended.

"What do we do?"

"We offer *paramithia*." Cicca held out her hands and I pulled her up.

"Paramithia?" I had not heard the Greco word before.

"Comfort," Cicca translated. "It means we cook."

We brought chickpea casserole down to Ugo's mother's dark house on via Erodoto that afternoon. The Squillacis would light no lamps and burn no fires within these walls as long as they were in deepest mourning.

I had been nervous about what to say to Ugo, but there were so many black-clad neighbors swarming the house that I needn't have worried. The family sat in vigil by the corpse, whose widow, mother, and sister would take turns weeping for the next three days, whether they felt like weeping or not. I was exhausted for them by the end of our visit.

"How long does mourning last?" I'd asked Cicca as I helped her toast the bread for the casserole.

"It depends, on the age of the good soul, on your relationship to the good soul. For a husband or a child, maybe months, or years. Every case is different."

"Who is expected to go into mourning? The immediate family?"

"Expected, what! No one expects anything. You go into mourning because you are in pain."

"No, I meant . . ." I was blushing, embarrassed by my poorly chosen words. "Who generally mourns?"

She blinked, mystified by the question. "Everyone. Everyone feels the pain."

"Everyone?"

"The *paese.*"

A small consolation for the bereft widow and children, but a real one: to see every person in the town, almost every person you had ever met, grieve with you and for you. This was the power of a village: a family binding that extended past wife, husband, child.

In the cemetery procession, I tried to control my tears as I thought of my own father, already twenty years older than Ugo's father would ever be.

Back home in America, it was Thanksgiving. I imagined my nerdy Nordic father sitting among the twenty-eight shouting Italians squashed into my aunt's apartment on Catharine Street, the meatballs and red sauce they'd be eating alongside the thirty-pound turkey from Esposito's, the argument they'd have over whether Isgro's cannoli were worth the cost. My dad would be quietly eating a second cannoli, biding his time until my uncle had come to the end of his invective about the outcome of the presidential election.

I missed him so much I cried again when we got home to Cicca's.

I spent the afternoon writing him a very long letter.

"Is there any chance you could place an international call?" I asked Pino Pangallo on Monday morning.

"No, *maestra*." Pino was cold with me—again, or still. "The phone line is out."

Of course it was. "So I'd have to try the *municipio* at Roghudi?" I wanted to hear my dad's voice, but I wasn't sure I wanted to hear it badly enough to go trekking up and down the chilly gorge to drop twice my rent on a three-minute phone call.

"You can try in Roghudi," Pino said with faint disapproval. "Better luck in Melito."

Six hours each way, on foot and by bus—that was over my limit. A little bit dejected, I left Pino behind his registrar desk and went to work.

34

AT LUNCHTIME, DON PANTALEONE ANSWERED THE RECTORY DOOR himself, and I decided Emilia Volontà's absence was a sign that I should take this unchaperoned opportunity to ask the priest for some help on my personal quests.

"Do you know a man named Ceciu Legato?"

The priest gestured for me to serve myself from the platter of salami and olives. "Of course. He's my cousin."

Naturally. "I'm trying to find out about some business he did."

"When he was mayor?"

"What? He was mayor? Of Santa Chionia?"

"Before Stelitano."

"I had no idea." Isodiana, granddaughter of the late Don Alvaro, had also grown up as the mayor's daughter. Legatos owned the one shop in town, the *puticha*—they were Santa Chionia elite, politically as well as fiscally. My suspicion about Isodiana's votive altar flared anew. "But wait, Don Pandalemu, why did the mayor abandon his *paese* and emigrate to Philadelphia?"

The priest absolved me of my irony by pretending he didn't hear it. "It was a tragedy. Ceciu gave up his seat when his son Francesco was killed. A road accident. Only twenty-one." His face solemn, Don Pantaleone braced a loaf of bread against his cassock and began to slice off slabs, his technique not unlike Cicca's. "It was a very hard time. Fortunato Stelitano was the head of the council then and stepped in as interim mayor until he was formally reelected in 1955."

"I had no idea," I said again.

"What was it you wanted to ask Ceciu about? Fortunato will know about all his mayoral activities."

My mind, which had been hatching and crosshatching its infatuated private portrait of Isodiana Legato with these new details of family tragedy, pivoted back to Leo Romeo and the paperwork trail I was trying to trace in Chicago. "Actually, this was about business Ceciu did for Don Roccuzzu Alvaro in the 1920s. Immigration stuff. Apparently Ceciu used to maintain correspondence between Don Alvaro and *emigrati* abroad?"

Don Pantaleone gave me a curious frown. "I don't know anything about that. If Ceciu comes home for Christmas you can ask him then. But maybe I can help you in the meantime. What exactly are you looking for?"

I fumbled for words as the priest calmly overturned my theories. I must not mention Emilia Volontà. "Mico Scordo. Do you know him?"

"Of course," the priest said again. "My mother was his mother's aunt."

"Oh." Why hadn't I just come to the priest for information in the first place?

"What about Mico?" Don Pantaleone prompted.

"His wife is looking for him to tell him about their son's wedding." I'd been proud of inventing that excuse at the Alvaro house, but now it sounded flimsy. "Mico stopped sending money home after this last trip," I said, trying to strike a tone that implied wry commiseration about deadbeat dads rather than suspicion of murder. "Vannina's last letter to him came back, and Mico's visa is missing from the *municipio*."

"Hmm." Don Pantaleone ate a slice of cured sausage in lacertilian silence, then said thoughtfully, "How about Dante Nazzareno?"

"I don't know who that is."

"The *padrone* in Melito. He arranged all the Chionesi visas for Don Roccuzzu. He would be quite old now, but if he's still around maybe he can help you. His office was down by the covered market."

"Oh!" I said again, but this time I felt hope. "Dante . . . ?"

"Nazzareno. Like Jesus the Nazarene."

"And Dante like the *Inferno*. Okay, I won't forget it. Thank you, Don Pandalemu."

The priest's anachronistically smooth forehead rippled. "But, Franca, one thing."

"Yes?"

"You said you had questions about emigrant correspondence from the 1920s? Mico Scordo didn't emigrate in the twenties. He's a much younger man than that."

"Oh." Damn it, I'd said 1920s because I'd been thinking of Leo Romeo. I was not cut out for sneaking around. "Right. Thank you."

"I'd like to go to Melito tomorrow," I told Cicca at dinner. It wasn't just pursuing an unlikely lead on my ill-advised quests. It was also high time I checked back in with civilization—I needed to visit the bank and shop for some amenities. "Do you want to come?"

"You can't go," Cicca said. She looked genuinely astonished by the suggestion.

"Why not?"

"You're in mourning for Cousin Filippo!"

"I am?" I said, confused.

"The whole village! For one week! We stay home out of respect."

"Got it. I'm sorry, I didn't know." My private train of thought was racing away down a dangerous Ugo-related track, and I sought to derail it quickly. "So we can go on . . . Friday?"

Cicca clucked her tongue as if I were still offending, but she said, "Friday is good."

Fortune smiled on me for observing the mourning period, because on Wednesday Oddo the postman brought me a letter from Alexis Kelly, my best friend in Philly. It was postmarked November 4, so it had not been in transit too terribly long.

> *Frank—*
>
> *To yours of Sept. 9—crikey, I can't believe it's been two months. I'm so busy I don't know what day it is. Not complaining. It keeps me from getting too cranked up over all the election coverage. I've got a terrific new gig and actually I'm typing this while I'm supposed to be prepping for a hearing, so if the letter ends real abruptly it means I got caught and fired. Anyway just needed to say before any more time elapses WHAT DO YOU MEAN about Sandro? Nothing you wrote makes any sense and you need to send me an update.*
>
> *Are you coming home for Christmas? It'll be worth it, I've got so much news for you. Let's just say there's an issue with a man, which is to say I have met one, and that's a big problem because I don't have time to be an attorney and a girlfriend.*
>
> *Dammit, I've got to get to court. Send me news about your wild Italian life. You know what news I mean!*
>
> *Love,*
> *AK*

The letter was typed on watermarked letterhead, the Law Offices of Sadie Alexander, with a West Philadelphia address. Alexis must have been patting herself on the back for sticking out law school.

An idea was forming. I folded the letter and tucked it into my datebook.

On Friday morning, Cicca and I set out for Melito in the coolness of dawn. It was two hours to the closest bus stop, in Roccaforte. We descended via the footpath the women used to fetch water from the *fiumara*, laddering down sloping dried mud and the occasional treacherously worn flagstone.

"Peppinedda came to me in a dream last night," Cicca told me as I skidded after her. "She told me we're going to have good luck in Melito."

"Oh good." Thanks a bunch, Peppinedda.

The late-autumn sun caught up with us by the time we'd reached the rocky riverbed. Cicca's sturdy old legs were always two paces too quick for me. As we ascended from the wash bed up to Roccaforte, we passed densely fruiting orange trees. My stomach and mouth were both pinched in dehydration and I wished we could steal one to suck on.

In Roccaforte's central piazza, Cicca cagily slipped me a dried chestnut as we waited for the bus among strangers. My saddle shoes, which had been my best bet at the beginning of the day, were pressing ominously on my swollen toes. I scoured the panorama for any evidence that due north, behind an undisclosable number of gullies and glens, was Santa Chionia.

The bus was packed—the route from the mountain villages to the commercial center at Melito ran only twice a day. For two and a half hours we bumped down the switchbacks, my life flashing resignedly in front of my eyes at every turn. The sun glared ever more vertically down on us, baking the wheezing Fiat pullman in sandy haze. Cicca sat rigidly beside me, scowling at anyone who made eye contact, her hand squeezing my thigh.

At last the switchbacks ended and we were following the flat progress of the *fiumara* through groves of waxy-leaved trees.

"Jasmine," Cicca said, pointing past my nose. "When it's in bloom the air smells like a bottle of perfume."

Cicca had probably never owned a bottle of perfume herself. "And those are bergamot," I guessed. The interstitial citrus trees, genus obvious from their shiny foliage, were slouching with tennis ball–sized puckered fruit, the adolescent green ripening into a mustard yellow.

"Yes, bergamot," Cicca said. "Prunella—this hamlet—is famous all over the world for bergamot."

As a citizen of the world myself, I suspected this was an overstatement, but I wished it to be true.

The bus left us in the Melito piazza, where the church clock read

11:20. I felt my blood pressure rising—businesses would close for lunch soon, and many wouldn't reopen.

"We find the old man first," Cicca declared, reading my mind. "When you're that old, every minute counts."

"Words to live by, *cummàri*."

"Where is he?"

"All Don Pandalemu told me is that his office was near the market."

Cicca nodded across the road. "That's the market right there."

"Okay. Then . . . I guess we ask around."

We started at the *tabacchi* directly across from the market.

"We're looking for Dante Nazzareno," I said.

The youngish man behind the counter shook his head wordlessly.

We tried the butcher two doors down, then the produce stand, where neither of the men guarding the tables nor any of the three shoppers had heard of a Dante Nazzareno. Neither had any of the men drinking coffee and smoking at the bar on the corner.

"Or any Nazzarenos," I tried.

No Nazzarenos were known.

"Dante Nazzareno, who used to arrange visas for immigrants in an office near here."

No such offices were known.

We persevered, heading down the alleys stemming away from the thoroughfare. We tried a shoemaker, but the shop was empty, although the door was open. We spoke to two women seated in front of their respective houses, turned the corner, and found another bar, where no one had ever met anyone named Nazzareno.

"I must have the wrong information," I said, feeling bad for having dragged Cicca on this goose chase. Also hungry. "All right, there's nothing more we can do. Let's go get some lunch, what do you say?"

"No!" Cicca shouted, surprising me.

"My treat," I said. "We can—"

"No! No eating until we find him!"

"But, Cicca, how can we possibly find him when no one here has ever heard of him?"

"You ask." Cicca brandished her pointer finger and peered up at me cunningly. "You ask until they remember."

. . .

Back on the boulevard, there was now a hook-nosed woman behind the counter at the shoemaker.

"Dante Nazzareno," Cicca announced without any other fanfare.

"Alighieri," the woman corrected.

"Not the writer—" I started to say, but Cicca spoke over me.

"You say Alighieri?"

"That's what everyone calls him," the woman said to Cicca. I might as well not have been there. "He comes down to buy vegetables every day before lunch." She pointed a scarred brown finger at the produce stand we had already visited.

"Thank you, *signora,*" I called over my shoulder; Cicca had already taken off.

At the produce stand, Cicca declared, "We're looking for Alighieri."

One of the shoppers, a thirty-something woman, had been there the whole time, or perhaps she'd gone away and come back. "Oh, you meant Alighieri. Dante Nazzareno, his real name is," she scolded me, as if that were not the name I had given her the first time I asked, the name she had never in her life heard before half an hour ago. She pointed across the street at the bar, where an eighty-something man in a gray wool jacket was negotiating the door with a cane. "That's him right there, with the blue cap."

Ask until they remember, Cicca had said. *Ask until they remember.*

35

DANTE NAZZARENO HAD CLOSED HIS AGENCY IN 1950, BUT HE still owned the building. "My nephew, the accountant," he said, nodding to the name plaque as he unlocked the outer door for us. "I let him use the ground floor."

After a grueling journey up a flight of stairs, Dante Nazzareno unlocked a second door and led us into a dark office. The old man shook open the blinds, then sat behind the dusty desk as if he were ready to resume his business exactly where he'd left it.

"So tell me what you want."

"We're trying to track down two men from Santa Chionia."

"Up the Attinà," he said thoughtfully. "I arranged visas for many men from Santa Chionia in the hard years." In the dim light coming through the vertical blinds, his thick brows cast such dark shadows that his eyes looked like holes in a skull. "Many for Don Rocco Alvaro."

"Yes, these would probably both be . . . under his aegis."

I wrote down names and birth dates for Leo Romeo and Mico Scordo on a piece of paper Dante Nazzareno handed me, then Cicca and I stole silent glances at each other for an endless ten minutes while the old man rooted through the contents of his filing cabinets. It was stressful to watch, and I worried he would do himself physical harm on my account. Eventually he lurched back to his desk with a pile of folders and opened the one on top.

"Here, Leo Romeo, sailed from Napoli to New York on January twenty-sixth, 1920. Arrived at Ellis Island, cleared immigration, received by American agent on February fifth."

There he was, Leo Romeo, Emilia Volontà's lost son. The boy who disappeared forty years ago, the good boy who never came home to visit his mother. The passport photo took my breath away. Leo Romeo, off to make a living doing hard labor in a foreign country, was a skinny boy with scared black eyes and a slightly blurred open mouth, as if he had not properly understood the instructions not to move for the photo shoot.

This terrified lost boy, this black-eyed helpless child—there was no way he was alive. I imagined his quivering ghost in the chair I was sitting in right then—this was the closest I would ever come to him. The dreary dust on the shelves around me pulsed in the darkening of my tears, and suddenly I saw a whole host of the lost, the men who had come to this office to stake their life on a hope and who had never been heard from again, victims of exploitation or accident or criminality or their own weaknesses, their stories never finished because there was no one to write them.

I turned my face down toward my skirt, trying to get hold of myself. The urge to cry only increased.

"What's the matter, *signorina*?" I heard Dante Nazzareno say curiously. "Surely you don't know this man?"

I shook my head, regaining control. "It's just . . . Seeing his face is very strange." I cleared my throat and scanned Leo's visa until I found an address—the same defunct Chicago one for Annunziato Volontà, care of Vittorio Olivieri. Another dead end.

Maybe Dante Nazzareno could at least point me toward my next quest. "*Masciu,* who is Vittorio Olivieri?"

"A labor agent I worked with in Chicago. When Christians like"—he peered at the folder—"Leo Romeo bought a visa package, it included the job contract, the ocean liner ticket from Napoli to New York, and all the requisite paperwork. Arranging the passport, the medical clearances. After 1924, I also applied for all the entry visas."

When the United States tightened their immigration restrictions. "Would Vittorio Olivieri have a record of where Leo lived or worked?"

"Olivieri is gone." Dante Nazzareno raised his hooded eyes, silencing me with the weight of what he left unsaid. "It will be very difficult to follow that further, *signorina.*"

Cicca watched me expectantly as I marshaled my fervid thoughts. The American quota system had always seemed ripe for exploitation. The man in front of me didn't look heinous or conniving, or like a kingpin who had harvested the souls of thousands of innocent men. Maybe he was just a professional who had spent his life helping other men realize their dream of prosperity abroad.

Maybe I was just a terrible judge of character.

"What about Mico Scordo?" Cicca asked. She'd sat in silence for most of the interview, and her alacrity now made me wonder what she knew and had not told me.

The agent's eyes darted to Cicca and then back to me. "I'm afraid I cannot help you there." He fanned the folders, showing us eight different Domenico Scordos, from Bova, Palizzi, and Staiti. None were from Santa Chionia. I examined each visa just in case, but none resembled the brooding hulk in Vannina Favasuli's wedding photo.

"I'm sorry to disappoint you, *signorina,*" the agent said.

I felt many things, but none of them was disappointment. "But I know that he emigrated. He came back and forth many times after the war."

"I wouldn't have a record of anyone who emigrated after 1950," Dante Nazzareno reminded me.

"It was much earlier than that," Cicca declared. "He emigrated in 1934." She nodded critically at the file cabinets. "You should have a record in there."

"Nineteen thirty-four?" the retired *padrone* said doubtfully.

"She's right," I said, surprised at Cicca's memory. "So why wouldn't you have a file? Was there another immigration agent?"

The old man turned his cloudy eyes on me. "Not who did business with Don Alvaro." His jacket resettled into new crags over the cave of his torso as he shrugged. "But who knows."

Don Alvaro wouldn't have spread his chips around. Clientelism was religion as much as religion was clientelism.

The only explanation that made sense was that someone had removed Mico's file, or paid or coerced Dante Nazzareno to do so. The old man and I stared at each other, both of us wondering how far I would push.

A gust of wind squealed by the window, rattling it in its trenches. It was as if Peppinedda was giving us a sign that it was time to leave.

"How can we thank you for your trouble?" I wished I could read Cicca's mind; would she want me to offer him money or some other kind of gift? I never developed a knack for Italian transactionalism.

"You can't," the old man said, waving us toward the door. "It was nothing."

36

THE SALT OF THE MARINA THICKENED THE MIDDAY AIR. I WAS hungry.

The bank wouldn't reopen until two. I talked Cicca into letting me buy her lunch, but not before taking a turn through the market. Her glee was focused and shrewd; she did not come to town often. Whenever Cicca expressed enthusiasm for some item, I would buy some "for myself." In this way I accumulated twenty pounds of alimentary bonanza. I tried not to worry about things like whether I would survive the climb home through the gorge, or whether Mico Scordo had been murdered and a vast conspiracy invoked to erase any public record of him.

Cicca had never in her life eaten in any kind of restaurant, not even a café like the one by the train station. The air was murky with cigarette smoke. I realized how accustomed I had become to the pure, tobacco-free air of Santa Chionia. She was simultaneously outraged by the café's prices and incredulous at the offerings, a mind-boggling four different kinds of panino. She wouldn't admit to wanting anything, so I ordered one of each, and two coffee sodas.

"You were suspicious because Mico had no file," Cicca whispered when I took my seat next to her. At least she was making some effort to keep her voice down. "I could tell."

I struggled to pull the legs of my stool out from the tangle of bur-lapped groceries. "Don't you think it's strange?"

"Mico Scordo isn't dead. He just ran away because his wife is so crazy."

"Oh, Cicca." I rubbed the bridge of my nose, hearing my mountain-dry sinuses crackle. "We shouldn't call her crazy. Women suffer all kinds of things we should be empathetic about—pregnancy, childbirth, abuse. We owe it to one another to be generous to all other women." Cicca was giving me a perplexed look. "Even women like Vannina. We should try to remember we don't know their whole story."

"I know Vannina's whole story. She's cuckoo."

I gave up. "Are you family?"

"Vannina's mother was my goddaughter. I tried to help raise her after her mother died. *Bbu!*" Cicca blew one of her vicious raspberries. "She was out of control. She would go walking down by the cemetery when she was only twelve years old!"

"Down by the . . ." I didn't press for details.

"With whoever she wanted—even *married men*. She was very, very beautiful, Vannina," she warned me. "And so, so jealous of Mico."

"Did Mico go with other women?"

Cicca snorted. "Mico's the type who never stops trying, you know?" My chaperone took a sip of her coffee soda. "Good, no?"

"Delicious."

"Delicious." Validated in her good taste, she leaned into my ear again. "Mico Scordo got his key into the lock of my cousin Giuseppe's wife. Petrunilla Romeo," she whispered, and before I could react, she added, "Poor missing Leo's sister."

I was grateful the proprietress arrived with our sandwiches, because I needed a moment to connect all the family threads. When she was gone again, I said, "Wait, so Mico Scordo had an affair with Leo Romeo's sister?"

"With my *cousin's wife*," Cicca corrected, the more important detail. "They were stupid—shameless. Vannina was pregnant and she got so jealous she threatened to throw herself in the ravine. She followed Mico to the tavern and screamed at him, didn't care who was listening."

"Poor Vannina," I said out loud.

Cicca removed the bread from the cheese as if she weren't familiar with the concept of a sandwich. "Maybe if she hadn't been so crazy she wouldn't have driven Mico away."

But what about that heavy box of love letters? I had seen that Vannina and Mico's marriage wasn't all bad times.

"Cicca, you've got to have some sympathy. It sounds like people have been using Vannina—preying upon her—since she was just a girl. Of course she's got problems."

"You don't know the things she's said to me."

"Well, even if you think Vannina should be punished for her mistakes, her children shouldn't be. It's not right for her husband to abandon her with six children he made while he was enjoying her body. If people aren't more generous with their sympathy, they are going to let Mico Scordo ruin six innocent lives."

"The poor children," Cicca said glumly to the table.

"Anyway . . . It's very strange when Mico Scordo disappeared. August 1952, right before Don Tito rebuilt the post office. And . . . I heard a rumor that Mico had gotten involved with Ninedda Lico. That's Don Tito's daughter, right? Did Mico, erm, try to use his key in that lock, too?"

Cicca's eyes glinted with the intensity of her excitement. She leaned forward again, cupping the sandwich alongside her mouth for discretion. "The Wolf locked Ninedda in her room for a *month* to punish her. Her mother had to pass her food through a hole in the door. He only let her out when she agreed to marry Bruno Scopelliti."

I tried to picture such brutality enacted by the soft-spoken man I had only ever seen sitting silently by the *puticha* window. My own affable, distracted father never remembered to lock any door, never mind one with his daughter imprisoned behind it.

"Okay, but also, Dante Nazzareno had no emigration records for Mico Scordo. You saw how organized that man was. Maybe someone stole the file to hide its evidence."

"Why would they do that?" Cicca said dismissively. "It's not like his file would prove that he'd been murdered. Masciu Nazzareno closed his office in 1950, and Mico didn't disappear until 1952."

That was so smartly put that I was shocked into silence. Nothing in the three months I had spent with Cicca had prepared me to think of the uneducated, ham-fistedly machinating old woman as an analytical partner.

"You're seeing conspiracy theories everywhere," Cicca reproached.

"You're right. But . . . if *the post office man* isn't Mico Scordo, then who is it?"

"The post office man." Cicca repeated the epithet thoughtfully. "You don't think it's Leo Romeo?"

"You just saw his papers! You saw he went to America!"

"Who says he didn't come back?"

"And never tell his own mother? That's outrageous."

"There is something strange about the Romeos." Cicca took a bite, and I waited impatiently while she chewed. "They owed Don Roccuzzu a lot of money for a long time," she said at last, lifting her beady brown gaze to mine. "Natale was a charcoal burner. He worked himself to death up in the mountains, chopping trees and carting the coal down to Bruzzano for a few lire. They make nothing, coal men." Cicca ate some more, then said reflectively, "My father was a charcoal man. It's a hard life. Weeks alone in the mountains until you finish the whole allotment, chopping oak and pine trees—any one of them could kill you during the felling, and there was my father with his bad back, having to chop and chop. And sometimes you have bad luck and the burn doesn't go right, you lose all your wood and you still owe the *padrone* for the timber."

"Why would he keep going back?" I asked, though I knew the answer.

"What else could he do? Leave, like his brothers? Those were the choices. Work yourself to death, or leave your family." Cicca's gaze was faraway. "He was a good man."

"Your father? Or Natale Romeo?"

"Both," she said stoutly.

"But you said there was something strange about the Romeos. Natale couldn't make enough to pay back the debt?"

"No. Emilia had to go work for Don Roccuzzu cleaning his house." Cicca applied herself to lunch, and I followed suit, watching her through the veil of cigarette smoke until she added, "Poor Natale, to have to send his wife to work at the Alvaro house. Don Roccuzzu, he was a serious man. But you know how everyone talked."

I did know, unfortunately. Whenever a woman had to go work in the house of a rich man, the rest of her life her reputation was tainted by a whiff of prostitution. It was a truth universally acknowledged that a man in possession of a good fortune would avail himself of the humble women in his vicinity at his discretion.

A tragic keening behind me, high-pitched and nasal, sliced through the euphony of patrons' murmurs and clinking cups, and I swiveled in time to see the proprietress sink to the floor behind the counter. Alarmed, I leapt to my feet, but the woman was standing again already, a three- or four-month-old infant slung against one shoulder, her thick fingers a calming cage around its head. She must have had it napping under the cash register. The baby blinked its fuzzy dark blue eyes at me, all abruptly well in its world.

My heart freshly tender, I took my seat. Cicca was smirking at me, and I said sheepishly, "I can't believe Leo would come all the way back to Santa Chionia and not see his poor mother, who has been looking for him for forty years."

"Who *says* she has been looking for him for forty years," Cicca returned.

No. The idea that Emilia Volontà had lied was impossible—deeply disturbing. Would she have deliberately embroiled me in what she knew to be a murder investigation?

"Why would you think . . . think Emilia already knows where Leo is?"

Cicca said demurely, "Peppinedda mentioned it."

I looked out the window at the passing sun-painted pedestrians, trying not to laugh.

We still had half an hour before the bank would reopen. Cicca took me on a stroll down to the coast and pointed out the spit of sand where she claimed Giuseppe Garibaldi and his Redshirts had landed.

"What's your opinion of Garibaldi?" I asked her. "Hero of the common Italian or imperial northern villain?"

She shrugged. "I never met him."

Walking back into the *centro* toward the bank, we passed the Melito town hall. Its door was standing open and I could see a telephone terminal on the clerk's desk.

"Cicca! We need to stop in here."

"For what?"

"Some paperwork," I lied.

Cicca sat on the bench by the front door while I counted out eight thousand lire for the *municipio* secretary—who, in his defense, tried to talk me out of placing an international call because it was so expensive. I begged my lucky stars not to let Cicca come over to supervise this process—if she found out how much I was spending, she'd be offended on her own behalf as well as mine.

The connection took twenty nerve-racking seconds, and then I listened to a disheartening number of rings. It was almost two p.m. here—was that six or seven hours earlier back home, damn it? I always forgot.

Luckily it was Alexis herself who answered—no seconds wasted on platitudes with her loquacious father.

"Frank! Are you crazy? What are you calling me for! How are you?!"

"Happy birthday, toots."

"You're a little late."

"Or early." Her birthday was in March.

"So good to hear your voice, you lunatic. But I've got to leave for work!"

"Then talk fast." I found my notes about Mico Scordo, so I'd be ready when it was my turn. "What's this about a boy?"

"Dr. Kelly hasn't left for the office yet," she warned. Her father was within earshot.

"Ugh, you are such a weasel. I'm calling you from six thousand miles away and you can't even—"

"How much is this costing?"

"Never mind." The line crackled, reminding me that nothing gold can stay. "Well, you better write me a much longer letter, then."

"Look who's talking! What's going on with Sandro?"

"No news there. Listen, I have a mission for you. Want to help me out with something?"

"A mission?" Her voice slid into a distrustful lower register. Alexis Kelly could be very literal.

"I'm trying to track down a man named Domenico Scordo, S-C-O-R-D-O. He might go by Mico or Dominic. He was living in South Philly in 1952."

"Who is he?"

"Maybe a runaway husband," I said, enjoying the freedom of rapid English banter. Since no bystander could understand me, I threw in, "Maybe a murder victim."

Precious seconds ticked by as we both considered.

"What are you now, Nancy Drew, girl detective?" Alexis said at last.

"Oh god, what a horrible thought."

"Jealous because you wouldn't be able to drive her convertible?"

"Too much good breeding for me. But how 'bout it, could you just check the tax records or whatever it is you do, see if you can find him?"

"Sure, sure, Sherlock," she said. I heard her teeth click, a happy sound. "S-C-O-R-D-O. Dominic. What was the other name? Mee-co?"

"M-I-C-O," I spelled. "But I'd guess Dominic is your best bet." Mico was a common name in southern Calabria back then, but I'd never once heard it among Italian-Americans, for the most part intent on culturally naturalizing. "I'll send you a letter with more details."

"Where does he live?"

"Not sure." My eyes fixed on Lois Blake's address, and following a hunch, I said, "Last known address is a decade old. But . . . he might have been shacking up with a woman named Lois Blake. Eight seventeen South Eighth, apartment nine."

The clerk was looming toward me; my three minutes were up.

"Gotta go, Lex. Love ya."

"See you at Christmas," she said, and hung up before I could argue with her.

37

I COULDN'T WAIT UNTIL MONDAY TO SEE EMILIA VOLONTÀ AT DON Pantaleone's. On Saturday morning, the lactic acid from the previous evening's climb through the gorge throbbing in my thighs, I hobbled up the streets to the shabby north end of town, a stretch of pre–Great War hovel-houses with molting terra-cotta roofs.

Cicca had told me to look for the house with the green door. There was only one such, so I knocked, apprehension bubbling in my chest as I waited in the breezy, silent lane.

I was about to give up when the door finally opened, and the tiny woman's pointed brown face appeared in the gap. "Teacher," she greeted me, dipping her head. Hoping to erase the status gap she had put between us with her humility, I stooped to kiss her cool cheeks.

The house was a single room with a ladder to the lofted second floor. The air was musty with a smell I didn't recognize, animalian, but with the spice of decomposing plant matter—not the house smells of chickens or goats.

"I'm sorry, *something something something*," Gnura Emilia said to me in Greco, pointing to the ladder.

Perhaps she was apologizing for taking so long to answer the door? "Please don't worry, *gnura*," I said, resorting to Calabrese. "I learned some new information in Melito."

The widow's triangle face was grave. *"Something something something."*

Damn it, my Greco was rusty. I had to start drilling vocabulary with Cicca again.

"I'm sorry," I said, "I don't understand."

"Drink?" she said simply.

"Oh! Thank you. Only if it's no trouble."

Emilia led me by her soft, cold hand to the chestnut table. "No trouble, my dear."

While the old woman was making barley coffee, I took in the spartan room, the packed-dirt floor and drooping pallet bed.

"What a clean house you have, *gnura*. You live here all alone?"

"Just me, now," the widow said, placing a tray on the table and settling on the stool opposite me. She looked so small, even thinner than my first impression of her. "There were ten of us here, back then."

"Ten people." I imagined the ruination of the space, the baby messes and animals, the smells of ten people and their weaknesses.

"My husband's parents, our children. I slept up there"—she indicated the ladder to the loft with a jerk of her pointed chin—"with the babies. Now only the silkworms."

Silkworms—that was the smell. I recalled prissy Edward Lear's pronouncement on that "interesting lepidoptera," which he found too grotesque to sleep in the company of, and which he accused Aspromonte folk of stewing and baking into tarts.

"How hard you've worked, *gnura*," I said.

She lifted her hands, a pantomime of inevitability. "My father-in-law was always ill," she said. "My husband never made enough to pay for the medicines."

I met her worried black gaze across the sap lamplight. What was Emilia still worried about? Her ill father-in-law and her underearning husband were both long dead.

"Listen, *gnura,* I went to Melito yesterday. I managed to track down the *padrone* who arranged Leo's visa."

She watched me unblinkingly, the thin black line of her gaze incessant under the strawberry swell of her eyelids. She was braced for a revelation.

"I don't know where Leo is. But the *padrone* had the paperwork to show that he arrived in New York. Proof that he's not the skeleton from the post office."

The widow scratched at a spot on the table with one fingernail. She was staring vacantly over my shoulder. Shouldn't she have been relieved he wasn't the unidentified corpse? But I had given her no resolution.

"I'm sorry I don't have other news, *gnura*."

"Ah," she said. "What are you gonna do."

The silence between us was sparking with the unsaid, and I felt helpless, useless. I couldn't bear it and stood, pointing to her votive shrine, a doily spread on top of her lone chestnut dresser for a statue of the Virgin. "Do you mind if I look?" I asked. I hoped to have another look at Leo's face, but there were only two photos, and neither was the precious, scared boy in Dante Nazzareno's visa. It was easy to identify her late husband, a skinny, large-nosed man in his middle years sitting in the sun on the steps of San Silvestro. The other photo was a glossy-haired teenage girl standing unsmilingly in front of the saint stone on via Sant'Orsola, hands gripping the handle of a bucket. I remembered what Cicca had told me about Emilia's daughter who had died of a "broken heart."

"Is this Rosa? What a pretty girl she was."

"My youngest daughter." The old woman had followed me to the family altar. "The other two are good girls but Rosa was the beautiful one."

I shouldn't have said anything, but I did. "She died during the war? Was it the cholera?"

"No, it was an accident." Emilia lifted Rosa's photo in its heavy pewter frame. The pad of her thumb against the metal was white with pressure, and the wrinkles on her face had contracted to swallow her primordial black eyes.

"An accident . . . ?"

By great force of will I let the silence hang and she finally said, "Her fiancé was sent away to Russia, and when . . . when she found out she would never . . . marry him, her heart began to bleed and she died."

I yearned for postmortem clarity—her heart began to bleed?—but restrained myself. This old woman had had everything she loved stripped away from her. What made her carry on in such gentle good humor?

"These are excellent photos," I said instead. It was not a platitude—the angles were interesting, the light on the subjects' faces forcing a stirring immediacy into moments captured twenty years earlier. "Is there a photographer here in Santa Chionia?"

"It was Donna Richelina. Don Roccuzzu's daughter, the youngest one." The widow placed the frame carefully back on its crocheted doily. "She had a camera from Germany." She said more, presumably about the camera, but what exactly I'll never know, and thus neither will you. "Donna Richelina was always very kind to me when I was working up at the Alvaro house. She made me these prints."

Richelina Alvaro—Isodiana Legato's mother. A thought flared in my mind: perhaps Donna Richelina had also taken the other rather artistic photos I had seen around town—like the one of Vannina Favasuli and Mico Scordo on their wedding day. Or the *municipio* photos that had disappeared "for cleaning." The suspicion that had nagged me before was back, but I still couldn't imagine a reason for Pino to lie to me about the photos. I'd never figure it out if I couldn't see them—which was probably the point.

"Did Donna Richelina ever take a photo of Leo, *gnura*?"

"Oh no, Donna Richelina was just a girl when Leo left," Emilia said.

I felt that dreadful twist in my heart. "You have no photo of Leo at all?"

"I—I thought there should have been one of his passport photos here, but . . . I could never find it." Her ear-high shrug. "Sometimes I still look, but . . ."

For forty years this mother had had no photo of her missing son to remember his face. Meanwhile in the shuttered office of the Melito *padrone* one such photo had been moldering in a file cabinet. I wished it had occurred to me to try to bring the file back.

"I do have Leo's box." She jimmied the top drawer of the dresser, dragging it open after some resistance. "I was saving it for him."

It was the sort of keepsake box I had seen for sale at street vendors' tables. I pulled my stool near Emilia's so we could go through it together. There was a tin saint pin, San Antonio. "I pinned this under his shirt every day when he was a little boy," Emilia said, and from the way she fondled the pin I understood the forensics of its tarnish. There were eight painted postcards: landscapes with castles or livestock, a man in a cape strumming a mandolin. "He collected these cards," Emilia explained, lining them up along the table. "When he was a little boy. They made him happy."

And finally, one unexplained piece of paper the size of my hand, thick and yellow with age. The writing on it was executed in analphabetic discomfort, the A's resembling 2s.

Castle Gate
Carbon County
84 Utah

She had had an address all along.

My stupid heart had begun to pound. I didn't recall Sam Spade's or Philip Marlowe's heart pounding every time they stumbled on a clue.

Certainly not Nancy Drew's. I struggled to keep my voice level. "*Gnura,* what is this?"

"I don't know," Emilia said. "My husband saved it."

"Where did he get it?"

Her black eyes blinked as slowly as a cat's. "Maybe he saw it somewhere and copied it down."

Well, whatever she was hiding didn't really matter. "Could Castle Gate be the city where Leo was living, or the company he was working for?"

The widow pointed to the words "Castle Gate." "Someone told me this means prison."

She'd thought her son was in jail for the last forty years. Suddenly I understood her caginess. "This is a postal address, *gnura*. Shall I write them a letter and see if they know anything about Leo?"

She looked up at me with the piercing hope of a child. "Please?"

38

CICCA MADE POLENTA AND SOW-THISTLE FOR DINNER, AND I milked her for Greco words as we ate. "Okay, what does this mean?" I tried to decipher the phonetic notes I had written down after my conversation with Emilia Volontà. "'Her heart bled'?"

Cicca was denuding an onion with a thumb-length knife. "Sounds not very good."

"Is it the same as 'brokenhearted'? An idiom?"

Cicca's knife paused in the onion flesh. "Who is this about?"

"Emilia Volontà told me her daughter Rosa died because her heart was bleeding."

Cicca snorted like a horse. "It wasn't her heart that was bleeding."

That was almost enough clarification, but I can never pull myself up short. "Did she kill herself?"

"No, poor thing." Cicca kept me waiting as she cut the onion into wedges, the way someone else might cut an orange. "Rosa Romeo," she said finally. "Only bad things come of being too beautiful." I had heard that sentiment many times from my mother. "She was engaged, but all the men in the village wanted her. Then her fiancé got called away to war.

When he was gone, many men bothered her." She knocked an onion wedge off her knife and onto my polenta. "She told them no, no, no, she wouldn't marry anyone else. But there was one man who wouldn't take no for an answer. So one day she was going down to get water and he and his friends abducted her."

Abducted—I knew what that meant. My stomach contracted—in pain for the beautiful girl in the photo, in revulsion at this too-recent reality.

Cicca clucked her tongue, mournful, resigned. "Afterward, well, Rosa had to break off her engagement, didn't she? She didn't want to marry that guy who trapped her, but everyone was saying she was pregnant. But then the day before the wedding she died—just never got out of bed in the morning. Only sixteen years old." Cicca pointed confidingly toward her lap to help me understand. "She had blood like if she was having a baby."

A rape, a forced marriage, and then to die of what sounded like an ectopic pregnancy. *My* heart was bleeding just thinking about it.

"Eat the onion," Cicca said. "Winter is coming. If you eat raw onion you'll never catch cold, like me."

I obediently took a bite. "Who was the man?"

"Turi Laganà."

My stomach turned yet again—how many times a day did I walk by the man while he sat in front of the tavern? "Was he punished?"

"Punished, for what? He did the right thing, he was going to marry her."

I was so angry I didn't trust myself to speak. I chewed masochistically until I had mastered myself. "An 'abduction' can't ever be made right," I said, fighting for measured word choice. "It is a crime, a violent crime, and criminals should be held responsible."

"Held responsible, of course!"

"I don't mean by marriage. Reparative marriage isn't real. You cannot *repair* the violence that was done to a woman. Forcing her to marry her attacker is like putting her through the violence again, for the rest of her life." My voice had begun to rise at the end.

"What do you want?" Cicca raised her hands, including the knife, defensively. "That's how things used to be."

Not sure if I meant it, just to have some way to cap the conversation, I said, "At least Rosa's poor dead fiancé never had to learn about the awful thing that happened to her."

"What dead fiancé?" Cicca said. "He didn't die. He came home. And when he found out what happened"—she mimed an overhand thrust with her paring knife—"*then* the police came and took him away to jail."

I remembered the scar down Turi's neck. "Where is he now? The fiancé? Do I know him?"

"Do you know him?" Cicca snorted. "You invited him over to dinner."

"Bestiano Massara," I said, disbelieving. Limitri the shingle maker had told me the communist had been to jail for attempted murder.

How many times had I walked through the piazza between Rosa Romeo's killer and her lost love?

"He became a communist in prison," Cicca said. "His cellmate taught him how to read so they could discuss Marx." She failed to entirely disguise her pride.

"You told me you never had *fuitina* here."

"Never! Only that one time!" She crunched through the last of the onion and admitted, "Well, maybe one other time."

In 1956, only four years before my arrival, in Sant'Agata d'Aspromonte, a *paese* three hours' walk from our lofty motte, the mayor of the town and seven of his friends had kidnapped the twenty-two-year-old schoolteacher and sequestered her in a hut in the mountains. Despite what happened to her in that hut over the next seven days, the schoolteacher refused to agree to marry her suitor—today, we would call him her rapist—and so his henchmen accordingly refused to release her.

Sant'Agata was a small *comune,* under two thousand people; there was no mystery about the teacher's whereabouts or who had kidnapped her. The only mystery—to the abductors, at least—was why the victim held out so stubbornly. As the days dragged on, the villagers wrung their hands, and the schoolteacher's family retaliated.

"Her father and an uncle tried to rescue her," Cicca told me. "But the mayor had too many men. There was a big fight." In the end, the stalemate was only broken up when the *carabinieri* trooped up into the mountains and arrested the men.

"It's not our tradition here to involve the police in our problems," Cicca told me.

Not our tradition.

"But this situation—it was too much. The teacher's family decided they had to break the rules, even though it meant there would be big trouble."

Even after she was released, the teacher refused to marry the mayor, despite being pressured from almost all sides. Her bravery cannot be overstated. The Italian penal code defined rape not as a violent crime but as a "crime against public morality"; article 544 allowed a rapist to nullify his crime if he "rehabilitated" his "dishonored" victim. There was no loophole, though, if "rehabilitation" plans fell through.

This was 1956, you must remember, an entirely different frame of reference: a decade before Franca Viola would go to court to fight for her right not to marry her rapist, forty years before Italian law was finally changed in 1996 to redefine rape as a violent crime.

In Sant'Agata, no one had anticipated this situation. That "stubborn" schoolteacher had to fight the Sant'Agata town council, who wanted their mayor released from jail; she had to fight the district court that tried to order her to just do as she was expected. She had to weather the bad opinion of every person in Sant'Agata who thought she had broken a sacred code by involving the police. She had to oppose her priest, who told her she was defiled in the eyes of God unless she submitted to spiritual repair.

"You don't believe that, though, do you, Cicca?" I asked. "You don't think God would expect her to endure a miserable lifetime with a man who had hurt her just because she wasn't a virgin anymore."

"That's how it is supposed to go," Cicca said, but she was not making eye contact. "I wouldn't have wanted to marry that guy either. But it was a lot of trouble for Don Pandalemu."

"Don Pandalemu? What does it have to do with him?"

"He was the one who tried to fix the marriage."

Without any exaggeration, I tasted bile as Cicca described the priest's activities. At the request of the mayor's parents, "good friends" of Don Pantaleone, who had performed their other son's marriage, the Santa Chionia priest had traveled to Sant'Agata and spent a week "in confession" with the victim, trying to convince her of the necessity of capitulation.

Don Pantaleone, with his supposedly anarchic struggle for reform—I would never be able to look at him the same way again.

Because the schoolteacher rejected the "reparative" marriage, her rapist's sentence couldn't be commuted. The now-ex mayor of Sant'Agata was still in jail, four years into an eight-year sentence.

The world was changing. A woman was still vulnerable to sexual violence, but she could decide she was worth more than her hymen and fight back.

On the other hand, a mafia thug could still get himself elected mayor.

"Is—is she okay?" I asked Cicca. "The schoolteacher?"

Cicca rolled her eyes helplessly. "She's not married. She lives a quiet life."

Another mind-breaking dichotomy: this isolated mountain civilization was a world where it was taken for granted that a woman's worth was so small that her family would transfer her into the keeping of a man who had been willing to hurt her. But it was also a world where that assumption was *so wrong* it could upend an entire town—a world where a father loved his daughter so fiercely he risked his life to protect her, to support her unwaveringly as she fought back against systems that had been in place for a thousand years. It was a world of the very worst kind of men, but also the very best.

I wrote feverishly until late into the night. The full moon was so bright outside my window I didn't even light my lamp.

The first thing I did was draft and then copy out a letter to Castle Gate. It was hard, begging an unknown entity for information about a third party's whereabouts when I wasn't sure if I was writing to an agency or a residence or something else entirely. Whether the forty-year-old address was defunct, or whether anyone there would have information to help me, or whether they would bother to pay the return postage— well, those were three reasons I might never find out if my letter had reached its destination. But I had a hunch I would be lucky. A change had come over me since I had seen the address on Emilia Volontà's yellowed scrap of paper. The dreadful despondency that had filled me when I'd set eyes on Leo Romeo's tragic passport photo had begun to dissipate.

Next, I wrote a long letter to Alexis, filling in the gaps of our too-short phone call, laying out everything I knew about Mico Scordo: his supposed emigration to Philadelphia, his rakish reputation, his wife's colorful but vague conspiracy theory about how he had been murdered, the rumors that he'd owed the local don money and had tried to seduce the guy's daughter. On the off chance it was still a path worth exploring, I threw out the name Vincenzo "Ceciu" Legato, who might be an inroad to a Santa Chionia immigrant network in Philly. To keep Alexis engaged, I might have spun out a few allusive paragraphs about a brawny mountain man who had seemed to want to imperil my virtue but then turned out to be far too aloof. I embroidered at my own expense. It wasn't as if Ugo was a real candidate, so it didn't hurt to make things up.

In the electrifying blaze of moonlight, my arteries pulsed with the restless excitement of hope. I was going to find them. Leo Romeo and Mico Scordo—I would find them both. Maybe with the truth I could unbreak their broken women's hearts.

39

ON DECEMBER 5, I WOKE UP WITH THAT BRIGHT MONDAY FEELING endemic among morning people, like *this* was the week I might take over the world. I had suffered through Isodiana's Ginzburg novel, paging with queasy determination through the visceral reminders of my own trauma as the book's heroine watched her baby daughter die. Someone else would have just put it aside and spared their own sanity, but back when I was twenty-seven my sense of self-worth was still Catholic inflected enough for me to believe there was some forging, purifying benefit to enduring pain. I'm afraid I'm still very much a person who chews punitively on their chapped lip.

In any case, I was itching to cash in my points with Isodiana Legato. Potenziana the Wolfess and her stupid threats be damned—her niece had shared her favorite book with me, and if that wasn't an invitation into a friendship, then my whole nerd life had been a lie. I took coffee with Cicca, accepted a few dried pears to put in my jacket pocket, then set out with fizzing anticipation for the Arcudi house.

The eight o'clock sun was still a dawnish molten silver, slippery mercury over the mountain crests, and I savored the chilly panorama. Hunters' rifles boomed in the valley below and hawks screeched in protest, their respective ruckuses rebounding off the cliff faces in the windless morning.

It took a long time for anyone to answer the Arcudi door. While I waited, my confidence and enthusiasm began to falter. The door finally opened, only far enough to showcase Isodiana Legato's voluptuously willowy silhouette.

"What do you want, *maestra*?" The musicality of her voice belied the hostility of her word choice.

"To—to talk to you." Tongue-tied by the directness of the question, I felt heat rising up my neck. "About your book. I finished." I fumbled the volume out of my bag.

She stepped forward, revealing the baby on her left hip, to take the book from me. I noticed the curve in her lower abdomen where the baby's leg molded her dress against her—she might have been pregnant. I felt unaccountable dismay.

"I brought something for you," I blabbered. "I thought—I would lend you a favorite book of mine. It's . . ." I awkwardly groped a second book out of my bag, a novel by an Abruzzi writer, Laudomia Bonanni. Isodiana, blank-faced, took it from me and retreated into the door's shadow.

"Wait!" I yelped, a spark of desperation short-circuiting my etiquette. "I wanted to—can I come in?" I had prepared so many smart things to say about her favorite book—I'd read about a dead baby for her, goddamn it.

"I can't." When Isodiana looked up, there was fear in her eyes. The woman wasn't being cold or snobby; she was scared of me.

I thought of what Potenziana had said, that her niece was childlike and nervous. "I'm sorry to disturb you," I said, ashamed. I turned to leave.

"Wait, *maestra*," she said. "I needed to tell you that—that we have decided we won't send Lucia to the nursery school. Please remove our application so the position will go to another child."

"What?" I was off guard, uncensored. "Why?"

Isodiana dipped her chin toward her chest, hiding her face, while her tiny boy watched me. "My husband decided it's better for Lucia to stay home until she is old enough to enroll in Don Pandalemu's Association."

"But—" A terrible blow—the most educated family in town pulling out of the nursery—what kind of message would it send? "I hope you will reconsider. It's—"

"You'll have to talk to my husband," Isodiana interrupted. The whites of her eyes were red with tears. "I cannot help you."

"Isodiana! Are you all right?"

"It's nothing, I just—" The baby, who had been staring open-mouthed at me, whipped around and grabbed his mother's nose. "Ai! Nino!"

"Here, let me take him," I said, closing the distance between us. She did not resist; she was gulping back sobs. As I wrapped my arms around the baby, my right hand brushed against Isodiana's breast, which yielded, weighty and implacable as goose down, against my knuckles. I jerked away self-consciously.

Nino put one little hand on my collarbone as we watched his mother with alarm. The baby's belly and diaper were warm, his chest clammy under his drool-wet gown.

"Tell me what's the matter." I whispered, in case there was someone waiting for her at the top of the stairs.

"There's nothing wrong," Isodiana said, and for a frightful interim I listened to her swallow sobs. Abruptly she looked up, her dark eyes fierce in her pale face. "It's just the sparkle," she said, and I recognized the local euphemism for hormones. "I can't get control of myself today."

"That's miserable." I tried to hide my doubt. "Can I do anything for you? Help with any of your housework so you can put your feet up?"

"No," Isodiana said quickly. "Just—if you have any other questions, you should ask my husband."

I bit my lip. A fine mist had started to fall—I could feel it invisibly catching in my hair. The baby pressed his little face into my collar and involuntarily I held him tighter. "I understand."

Isodiana swallowed again. I watched her goiter bob as the swallow traveled down her slender neck and disappeared into the old-fashioned frill of her dress collar. That was when I spotted the discolored oval on her neck. The hopelessness I had been feeling since I arrived changed flavor.

"Isodiana, whatever you decide about Lucia and the school, I hope you think of me as a friend." As I passed Nino back, I peered at her neck for confirmation I had not imagined the bruise. "Anything you ever told me would remain between us."

Isodiana, clutching the squirming baby, eyed me warily. "I have told you nothing."

"No, nothing at all," I said, conscious of the implications. "I just want you to know that my job here is to help women like you."

"In that case, *maestra,* you would help me the most by leaving." The words were stinging but I saw mirth in her tear-pinked eyes. "I have many things to do."

I gave her a wide, warm smile to make her believe my feelings were not hurt. This woman did not want to deepen our connection, and I was a pest.

It was too late, though, what she had been trying to avoid came to pass: the door swung all the way open, framing a tall man and a rather short younger one. "We're going to get that timber out," the tall one said to Isodiana. "Good morning," he said, noticing me.

"Santo. This is the teacher from America."

"Maestra—Francesca, isn't it." Isodiana's husband held his hat in both hands in a way that looked somehow especially polite. "A pleasure."

"A pleasure," I echoed, trying to guess if he beat his wife. Santo Arcudi was significantly older than Isodiana, perhaps forty. He was thin, his brown hair a horseshoe ringing his bald pate. He reminded me of one of my father's colleagues in the Bryn Mawr history faculty—everything about Santo Arcudi seemed bookish.

Thanks to that thought, I placed him—he was the man I'd seen in the piazza wearing wire-framed glasses. The sixth man in the photo I'd borrowed from Vannina.

The younger man—he was no more than twenty—said jovially, "You're the bitch who's been spying on everyone."

"Excuse me?" I was taken aback by the open hostility from a total stranger.

"Watch your mouth," Santo Arcudi said. His voice was neutral; he didn't turn around to address the boy, whose face was the spitting image of Isodiana's.

"But she's—"

"There's never need for foul language, Nicola." Santo was still regarding me. "Apologize."

"Pardon me, *signorina,*" Nicola sneered. "All due respect."

It was not lost on me that, apology or not, everyone present felt that I was, in fact, a spying bitch.

My mind was swirling with contradictory thoughts. Was Isodiana a victim of battery, and if she was, was my reaching out putting her in greater danger? Or was this just a private, conservative family whose goodwill I had trampled with my prying?

"It's nothing," I said finally. "I would rather people told me what they thought of me to my face." Isodiana had the baby tightly ensconced in both arms, her face turned to the ground again. "Anyway, Masciu Arcudi, I'm glad to meet you in person so I can invite you to reach out to me or the mayor at any time if we can answer any questions about the school."

"Thank you," Santo Arcudi said. His face betrayed no particular impression at the mention of the mayor. What worked on Cicca could not work on everyone.

40

I REMEMBER NOTHING ABOUT MY LEAVE-TAKING EXCEPT THE SUL-len grin on Isodiana's kid brother's face as the door slammed shut. Was it just the Arcudis who harbored such animosity toward me? I climbed up the packed dirt of via Zaleuco nauseated by my shock.

I had to back off. There was no choice. But if Isodiana was being abused . . .

In my turmoil, I was not expecting Vannina Favasuli to latch onto my arm as I turned onto via Sant'Orsola. My already pounding heart came to a complete stop.

"You're avoiding me." Hanks of wet hair were molded to Vannina's neck and the dark circles under her fever-bright eyes were as black as January olives.

"Vannina!" Fighting to catch my breath, I hugged my briefcase. The rain was picking up and I felt it trickling down my scalp. "I'm not avoiding—it's—"

"Come," Vannina said, pulling me as if I were a recalcitrant goat. I caught a fusty odor coming from her, a soft homeless stink. Vannina was a woman in constant crisis. Maybe *she* was the person I should be trying to make a difference for. With that thought motivating me almost as much as the rain, I let myself be pulled.

The inside of Vannina's cottage was even more putrid in the damp. Still no sign of the children she claimed to have. She puttered around her cooking area, railing about how someone had stolen her lamp, until she presented me with a familiar cup of sour wine.

"It's not even nine in the morning."

Vannina sat down hard on her decaying mattress. "I don't know what to do." Her tongue flicked between the gaps of her teeth like a lizard's.

"About what?"

"My son. Niceforo. The oldest." Vannina pushed her soggy hair off her face with one dirty palm, revealing the exquisite angle of her jaw. She looked like Sophia Loren, if Sophia Loren were about to film a scene about a drink-addled prostitute. "He is getting married and I have nothing for the bride gift."

She began to cry, as she had on every other occasion we had ever interacted, but this time the tears were modest and sincere-seeming. I'd been wrong, she wasn't drunk. It was something else with Vannina—an internal persecution, a demon she sometimes controlled and who sometimes controlled her.

We find it hardest to show compassion to those who need it most. There was a small way I could make the world better here today, after perhaps having made it worse elsewhere. I crossed the stinky space and sat on the flea-infested bed, putting a hand on her shoulder. "Tell me about the wedding," I said. "But while you talk may I fix your hair?"

Vannina talked nonstop about Niceforo's romance with a *campagna* girl, Agathi, who by rights should receive gold wedding jewelry from her new mother-in-law. So Niceforo had convinced Giuseppe Petrulli to accept his suit—I felt pleased for him, based only on the courage I'd seen him exhibit in the piazza. Meanwhile I worked through the rat's nest of Vannina's hair. Listening to the minutiae of the other woman's disorganized worries, I detangled a strand at a time. I deloused her scalp, rubbed it with a nub of olive oil soap, and made her rinse in her laundry basin, which I myself lugged through the drizzle to the east end of via Leonzio Pilato to fill for her at the Attinà cataract, still surging from the autumn floods. At the conclusion of my ministrations, Vannina appeared human and sane, just a bit shabby in a ripped but clean dress, which I had forced her to change into by "accidentally" soaking the awful dress she'd been wearing. Above all she did not smell like an itinerant anymore, and I satisfied myself that a little dignity had been restored.

I'd been holding on to my news about Mico. On the one hand I wanted credit for the hours I'd spent pounding the pavement, but the information I'd collected was more unsettling than it was helpful. What was I going to tell her, that I knew about debts and infidelities she hadn't disclosed? That Mico's immigration file was mysteriously missing from the *padrone*'s office, just like his visa had been missing from the Santa Chionia town hall? That not a single person had anything nice to say about her beloved husband?

But I was not to escape—as I was washing my hands in the last of the water she asked querulously, "What about Mico?"

I shot straight. "Well, the situation is strange."

Vannina frowned. "Strange how?"

"Your brother-in-law thought Mico might have taken a loan from Tito Lico—"

"*The Wolf!*" she shrieked, startling me. "That son of a goat and a whore!" She leapt up, kicking the water bucket with a scabbed bare foot. "*Look what he's done to me!*" Vannina's scream was so loud it echoed in the rain-muffled alley outside. "They've trapped me in this shithole! No money to buy clothes to cover my body!" Her fingers clawed at her dress in a way I didn't think the tattered linen could withstand.

The soul-restoring aspects of the visit had faded. "Vannina, I—"

She seized me by the shoulders. "Can you understand that? They've ruined me so that my *own children* won't kiss me in the street!"

"Vannina! Stop! You—"

"They took everything from me *because they could* and no one will help me!" Vannina's fingers dug into my shoulder sockets, and I was caught in the vise of her strange gold gaze. "Not even you, you lying, self-righteous cow!"

"*I told you to stop!*" And without any conscious thought I pulled my right arm out of Vannina's grip and slapped the woman—hard—across the face.

We stared at each other in mutual shock and appraisal. I took a step back, my violence rippling through the thick skin of my palm. I had never slapped anyone before, and yet my hand had known just what to do.

"Do not accost me," I said sternly, fighting to maintain my façade of confidence. "I am leaving. I wish you the best, *signora,* but you are not very smart about making friends."

They were Officer Vadalà's words in my mouth. As I heard them ring through the dank cave of Vannina's sad house, I felt myself flush. *The second goal of activism is don't recapitulate the power structures we seek to challenge.*

But I could not back down.

Out in the alley, I heard Vannina's sash bang open behind me. "Forgive me, *maestra,* forgive me!" the woman called. I didn't turn around.

Although it was still drizzling, the ancient neighbor was on her stool again with a spindle and a basket of wool. At her feet, as if hoping to be mistaken for her friend, was the squat tawny dog whose petrified black tongue draped out of its mouth.

"*Kalimèra,*" I made myself say.

The woman gave a grave nod, her spindle bobbing between her hands. I wondered what became of yarn that was spun in the rain, if the fetidness of this squalid street would be forever twisted into its fibers.

What had I done? I'd physically assaulted a woman in her own house. Vannina Favasuli brought out the absolute worst in me, even when I'd been trying to do her a kindness. Would she report me? Could I lose my job?

After my awful visits with Isodiana Legato and Vannina Favasuli, I was in no frame of mind to have lunch with Don Pantaleone, especially in light of what I'd learned about his intercession in the kidnapping of the schoolteacher. Instead I spent the day atoning with hard work. My candidate interviews were distracted, my thoughts a choking mud of guilt, anger, and embarrassment. It was one of those days when I thought many times of Sandro, aching for the consolation of his embrace and for his articulate, thoughtful company. For the ease of my Roman life with him, in which I'd never imagined a workplace scenario that escalated to physical violence or where I'd behaved in a manner that could cost me my job.

As the bells of San Silvestro were tolling the call to evening mass, I made a decision. I had to apologize to Vannina.

My script playing in my mind—humble, brief—I turned onto

Leonzio Pilato and stopped short. At Vannina's stoop a man was, well, stooping. He was lanky with a hay pile of gray hair from whose depths protruded ears as voluminous as the popped collar of a peacoat. Turi Laganà. I heard Vannina's words in my head: *The goat-fucking swine.*

As I stood frozen, hardly concealed from suspicious view by the crumbling wall, Vannina leaned against her door frame, her arms crossed tightly over her abdomen, boosting her breasts so they bobbed like buoys. Negotiations were short. Vannina disappeared into her dark doorway, and Turi after her, looking a little goofy as he ducked.

41

THE RAIN STARTED ON MONDAY NIGHT—A TORRENTIAL DOWN-pour that seemed as unrelenting as the October flood rains. "It's not going to flood," Cicca told me wearily. "Peppinedda said this is just a one-night sprinkle."

Peppinedda. Always pulling her tricks.

"I've seen the damage and there's no choice, *maestra,*" Mayor Stelitano told me on Tuesday afternoon. "We will have to delay the opening of the nursery until after Easter."

Although the rest of Santa Chionia seemed to have escaped the heavy rain unscathed, the nursery's north wall had taken a bad hit. When I unlocked the door that morning, standing water had spilled over the stoop, soaking my shoes. An enormous shaft of holm oak—an old roof beam from some dilapidated house farther up the mountain—was lying like an abandoned battering ram in a mini avalanche of wet-dark busted wall. I didn't understand the physics of it, or the miserable bad luck. My newly installed electricity had sparkled and exploded when I tried to turn on the light.

"Mayor, with all due respect, I disagree. I have plenty of time—four weeks."

"You're going to get all this fixed in four weeks? It's impossible." He was wearing a flashy yellow gabardine jacket, but its color did nothing to raise my spirits. "Why rush?"

Stamina, Francesca, I reminded myself. Take the hits; get the work done. Pride is nothing. Intention is nothing. Results are everything.

"I have a prospectus to follow and frankly no evidence that I can't meet my organization's goal to open in January. The Chionoti are counting on us."

"It's not going to happen, Franca." Mayor Stelitano crossed his arms, giving me a stern little frown. I trembled, trying to think of what to say to change his mind. "Everyone is worried about much bigger problems. This is the second catastrophic flood we've had in two months and I am under new pressure to order transferment down to the marina—"

"Transferment?" I said, incredulous. "Come on, this was hardly catastrophic."

"Franca." He gave me a pitying, belittling look. "I am sure you've noticed that your project has generated hostile feelings. It would behoove you to let them simmer down."

Was he saying that no one liked me? Not that I was here to be liked; that wasn't the point. But—

A thought occurred to me for the first time: had someone sabotaged the nursery?

"Take a rest for the holidays," the mayor said. "Soften up a bit. You have to start making more friends."

I clenched the sweat-sticky leather of my briefcase handle. "Mayor Stelitano, tell me plainly. Are you removing your blessing from the Child Rescue nursery school?"

"No, no no," he said quickly. "I am very invested. But you must be patient. Here in Calabria we have been left behind for many centuries so it takes us a little longer to catch up to your northern timetables. If your organization cannot accommodate that, well. Maybe they do not really want to help us so much after all."

I studied his finely tailored jacket and waistcoat, his lustrous chestnut desk, his leather chair and porcelain lamp, and the questions Ugo had raised ran through my mind afresh. To whom did the mayor owe his allegiance?

What politician ever simply wanted what was best for his people? The only ones I could think of were assassination victims.

"I understand," I said.

"Good."

I stormed out of the town hall. At the *puticha,* proprietor Saverio Legato was standing in the door. Beside him were Turi Laganà, the dog-eared predator, and his constant companion Pascali Morabito. Bestiano Massara, the communist, was sitting in his eye-catching red cap in front of the disconsolate post office, his stack of pamphlets held down by a rock. All the men watched me stalk across the piazza, and I didn't care. I was going to show them all.

I had lots of cleaning to do.

I was crouching in a scum of stagnant water when Potenziana the Wolfess strutted into my mucky lair. She did not mince words.

"Why were you bothering my niece Isodiana? She told you to leave her alone."

"*Buongiorno,* Donna Lico," I said, rising so at least we were eye level. I batted away the residue of my conversation with Mayor Stelitano. *Nobody likes you.* "Isodiana did *not* tell me to leave her alone. In fact she lent me a book and I was returning it."

The woman's glossy black hair was pinned into a perfect, bulbous chignon. Her eyes, equally glossy, flashed with malice. "I have begun to wonder if you don't have an unhealthy fixation on my niece."

"Excuse me?" A sizzle shot up my neck.

Potenziana folded her arms so her graceful hands tucked into the pillowing fabric at her elbows. "I've heard about the barbaric ways American university girls behave. No one here in Santa Chionia wants any of that. We're modest, pious Christians."

"I cannot even guess what you're trying to imply." My face stung with heat. "Now if you'll excuse me, I have work to—"

"What did Vannina Favasuli want with you? She has no children of nursery age."

"She thinks your daughter tried to steal her husband," I replied before I could think better of it, which would have been right away if I had any control whatsoever over my goddamn temper.

"That's what she told you, eh?" Potenziana's hard mouth turned up at one corner wryly. "Not that her husband chased after my daughter—half his age!—like a billy goat?"

The veins in my temples were pulsing with anger. "You asked me what Vannina wanted, and I told you."

"You did." I tried not to squirm under the Wolfess's ongoing inspection. If her husband, Tito the Wolf, had murdered Mico Scordo like Vannina claimed he had, then Potenziana knew all about it, I would bet my mother's gold earrings. If I only had the courage to ask her, Potenziana Legato might settle all my inquiries right then and there.

But courage was an oblique concept in my suspended reality, a Jell-O world where it was equally inevitable and categorically impossible that this woman's husband had murdered a neighbor in cold blood. Where both incompatible realities might, in fact, be equally true: Mico Scordo was both dead and alive; Tito Lico was both an illiterate yokel and a genialoid strategos; Potenziana Legato was both a lioness and a hyena. And everyone and no one in the village knew the truth.

After a long silence, Potenziana asked, "What about Emilia Volontà? What is your business with her?"

"She asked me to help her track down her son in America." Why didn't I lie? I don't know. I think because my knee-jerk reaction to rich bitches was to level them with candor.

"Her son. Leo?"

"Yes."

"Leo Romeo," Potenziana said thoughtfully. "What a long time it's been since I've thought of him. We were babies together. So did you find him?"

"No," I said. "His visa is missing from the *municipio.*" I stopped myself short of revealing what I'd learned from Dante Nazzareno.

"Leo Romeo's visa was missing," the Wolfess mused. "Now whyever would that be? Do you have a theory, *maestra*?"

"I'm working on one."

Potenziana picked elegantly through the debris on the tile floor, the hard heels of her leather pumps clicking softly. "You answer questions so readily." She reached across the desk and patted my cheek. "Here in the Aspromonte we survive the harsh climate and hard times by protecting one another. What we don't need is help from someone who doesn't understand what that means."

With that unmistakable threat, my intimidation frothed into ire. "Look around you. Santa Chionia needs all the help it can get." Before she could strike back, I barreled on. "I do think that if anyone knew where Leo Romeo ended up, it might be your brother Ceciu. I wish I could ask him."

The Wolfess's nostrils flared. "My brother?" I watched some emotion that looked like anger crowd her dark features. "Whatever could you mean?"

My chest cramped as my terrified little heart accelerated. *Don't be a goose, Frank.* "Ceciu was Don Roccuzzu Alvaro's secretary, wasn't he? Read letters for the unalphabeted and wrote replies for their emigrant men abroad?"

We stared at each other in sticky silence. Although I did not mean to move my foot, my shoe slid suddenly across Limitri Palermiti's glossy tile as a particle of brick crumbled beneath my weight.

Jolted, I persevered. "I was just thinking, he might have a record of those old addresses. Do you know how I can be in touch with your brother?"

Never have I, fragile flower, felt more literally the "withering" power of a woman's glare. "My brother Ceciu is a weak-willed wastrel. Ran off to America after he gambled away the family's savings. There's nothing he can help you with."

"Gambled?" I repeated. There was hardly a casino or racetrack scene up here in the Aspromonte.

Potenziana crossed her arms aggressively. "Ruined my sister-in-law's life."

This contradicted what Don Pantaleone had told me, that Ceciu Legato had left Santa Chionia to escape the heartbreak of losing his son. Had the priest been sugarcoating? Was Isodiana willfully ignorant about her loving, scholarly father?

Or—for once, the universe granted me a flash of logical thinking—was Potenziana Legato lying?

A Calabrian woman never says anything bad about a family member to an outsider. At least, not if it's true.

My skin prickling, I said as dully as I could, "So you don't think he'll be home to see his family for Christmas?"

"Unlikely." I saw the tremble in her frown, though, the shiver in the hint of the double chin that was the only indication of the winters her golden-brown face had weathered.

For the first time since the Wolfess had entered my nursery, I felt like I had the power to clear the air. "Well, *gnura,* if you have any ideas about Leo Romeo, I would be most grateful for your advice. It's a tragedy to think that a Santa Chionia boy was lost forever. I just can't believe there's no way to track him down."

Her black eyes fixed on me again. "I will think about it." Then, without any socially correct parting platitudes, she departed, leaving me with the distinct impression she had been trying to keep me from believing that her brother Ceciu was dead.

Part Three

WHERE
IS
CECIU
LEGATO?

42

THE WEEK WAS LOST TO CLEANING, FIXING, REGROUPING. ON Wednesday morning I gave Oddo a fat stack of letters, hoping, as ever, that in light of my faithful palm-greasing he would see fit to deliver them to federal postal channels without opening or rerouting them. This stack included the letters I had written to Castle Gate and to Alexis Kelly, as well as an update to Sabrina in which I relayed the news about the flood damage but omitted mention of Mayor Stelitano's decision to delay opening the nursery. I wasn't ready to admit defeat.

December 8 was the festival of the Immaculate Conception. The feast Cicca prepared—tagliatelle, cured peppers, *caprino* and fresh ricotta—was a bright spot in my psychological darkness. Another was when Maria Scordo, the teenage daughter of Francesca Scordo, the Alvaros' maid, came to talk to me about a position as nursery instructor. She seemed sweet-tempered and patient, and I was as happy to think of getting her out of her scullery situation in the creepy Alvaro mansion as I was to cross an item off my to-do list.

So it was that I felt like I had my feet back under me on Monday morning when Don Pantaleone Bianco stopped by the nursery.

"Maestra Franca. I missed you last week."

"I had some setbacks here." I was as cold and salty as a basement prosciutto.

The priest didn't know what I had learned since I'd last seen him. He was an emotionally intelligent man, though. "If you have time to come by for lunch today, Teodoro is back in town. You wouldn't want to make the poor man pass the afternoon with me alone?" Don Pantaleone said, his bland expression quivering with mischief.

Despite myself, I felt enthusiasm at the proposition of jolly Dottor Iiriti's company.

I found myself trying not to smile. "Certainly not."

"I'll see you at one o'clock."

I had time for one house visit first. My list was shrinking—only eleven left.

I set out along sun-beaten via Odisseo, past the noisy game of Brig-and King that had annexed the piazza. The wintry wind eddied around my legs, tickling as it plucked at the taut fibers of my stockings. I was headed to the house of a *SCOPELLITI, ANTONIA*. If I had followed all the snarled threads of Chionesi familial relationships, I was walking into hostile territory. Three-year-old Antonia's mother was Ninedda Lico, daughter of Potenziana, my nemesis, and Don Tito the Wolf. I braced myself for a slammed door or worse.

I did not, however, entertain the idea of skipping this undoubtedly fruitless meeting. How could I possibly pass up the chance to see for myself the woman who had, perhaps, gotten Mico Scordo killed?

It was a man who answered my knock, thirty-something, with a newsboy cap of shining black hair.

"Masciu Bruno Scopelliti," I guessed.

"Maestra Franca," he replied. "Come in."

Having coached myself to weather antagonism, I followed him to his living room in a pleasant daze. Like the Arcudi and Legato homes, the Scopelliti residence presented a modest façade to the street and revealed its pricey comforts only within. I recognized the velvet-cushioned sofa and the crystal chandelier.

"Nina!" Bruno Scopelliti called toward the stairwell. "We have a guest! Bring Tota down and make some coffee."

"Who is it?" Heredity was evident in Ninedda's voice, which was exactly the Wolfess's, from cadence to timbre to edge, although I could not imagine Potenziana shouting down the stairs.

"The American teacher! Hurry up."

His wife came bursting into the living room, a red-faced girl clutched against her full bosom. Ninedda Lico lacked Potenziana's refinement— her hair was a messy black braid with a flyaway halo that indicated it had been slept in, and she had not been as successful as her middle-aged mother in maintaining a girlish figure.

Nor did Ninedda feel any inclination toward subtle intimidation. "I can't believe you let her in the house," she spat at her husband, then turned her rage on me. "*You* can cross Tota's name right off your list. We will have nothing to do with your corruption and bad influence."

I felt almost satisfied by the accusation, and interested to hear the specifics of the slandering that must be happening behind my back. I said nothing, though, as a concrete silence had engulfed the room. Husband and wife were staring at each other, the former with blank eyes and a set jaw, the latter with furious contempt.

Nestled against Ninedda Lico's shoulder, the little girl's face cracked open in the most heart-melting of smiles. An instinctive response to the tension between her parents? I felt a lump in my throat. If Sandro and I had raised a child together, would we have been able to do better than this? Or would we have let our three-year-old feel responsible for fixing what was wrong between us? I wanted to take little Tota in my own arms, into my safe haven of corruption and bad influence.

Bruno broke the freeze by speaking to me. "My wife has been advised that we should withdraw Tota's application, but I am not a sheep who lets others make decisions for him." Without looking at his wife, he said, "Nina, I told you to fix coffee for our guest."

Ninedda Lico was apparently unconcerned about my bad influence in this particular moment, because she dumped Tota on the floor by me and stormed to the stove. The poor child. I took a Zuzu out of my case and held it out to the girl.

"This is my friend Zuzu," I said. "Do you know what Zuzu is?"

Tota shook her black head.

"Yes you do," Bruno told her. "Yes she does. It's a monkey, Tota. Monkey."

I conducted my interview with the child and the father, pretending nothing awkward had happened. Bruno Scopelliti described his profession as bookkeeper. Whoever it was he kept books for in this uncommercial village, they paid him well.

When Ninedda returned, glaring, with a coffee, I beamed at her like Dorothy Dandridge would have if they'd given her that Oscar. Could

Mico Scordo have gotten himself killed over this woman? The idea tested credulity.

I stayed only as long as it took me to drink the coffee, which was especially bitter—Ninedda Lico's version of a subtle message. Bruno walked me to the foyer and stopped in the close quarters before unlocking the door. "Who else has withdrawn?" he asked in a voice so low I almost couldn't hear.

"I can't speak about any applicants for privacy reasons."

"Nina's cousins? What about the Arcudis?"

I pursed my lips at him, and he lifted his hands.

"Excuse us, *maestra*. I'll let you know if we decide we want Tota attending."

I was fifteen minutes early at the rectory. Don Pantaleone was alone, as I'd hoped.

"I want to know about what happened in Sant'Agata, with the schoolteacher," I said as soon as he'd shown me to a seat. I needed to offer him an opportunity to justify what he'd done. "I don't need a play-by-play of the crime. I just want to know why you got involved and tried to force that poor woman to marry her attacker."

"Aha." The priest looked only mildly surprised by this onslaught. "I knew something was bothering you." He settled in the chair next to me. "I don't follow your train of logic, though. Can you explain what is upsetting you?"

"It is upsetting me that you took the attacker's side." Two weeks of pent-up disappointment coursed through me. "That you exerted your authority as a man of God to strongarm a vulnerable woman into a life of servitude to a criminal."

His calm brown eyes met mine with earnest concern. "I was trying to help the poor girl, Franca. You are seeing the situation from a very narrow American lens. In the Aspromonte we must look at problems from three hundred sixty degrees."

"I don't see a perspective from which a forced marriage wouldn't have been ruining that woman's life."

"Franca, the *paese* is one organism, a living thing. The life of any individual must always come second to, and in service of, the *paese*. This is for the sake of our *survival.*" He spread his hands so I could see his callused palms. "There, now you know our secret. In the Aspromonte we are all communists."

What a card. What kind of priest had callused palms? He'd probably been out in the forest chopping firewood for crippled widows. Goddamn him.

"Wouldn't the best service to the *paese* be the eradication of that awful behavior?"

"Of *course,*" the priest said, as if I'd suggested the opposite. "But the damage was done, and there were many other factors to be taken into account. There was the poor girl's reputation, as well as the suitor's family, all of whose lives would be ruined if there couldn't be peace. Think of the vendettas and the suffering."

"The *suitor*? Maybe you mean the *rapist*?"

"There was the political setback of the *paese* losing its mayor," Don Pantaleone went on. "And the general concern for public morality if the case were allowed to stand."

"Surely the best thing for public morality would be for violent offenders to go to jail."

Don Pantaleone held up a finger, silencing me despite myself. "Here is the hardest part of all, Franca. The cost of involving law enforcement is—very high. When you call the police in, they begin to look. And where they look they find trouble. Innocent little things that are necessary to our difficult way of life up here in the mountains—well, when you invite the law in, they find fault everywhere, and many hardworking Christians go to jail."

"Innocent little things like what?" I said, incredulous.

The priest shrugged expansively. "For example, our hunting rifles. We need them to defend our flocks against the wolves. We need them to end the suffering of a sheep that has broken its back in the ravine. We need them to protect our families if the brigands come in the night. Would you really take them away?" He was shaking his head. "Of course you would not. But when the police raid our houses, those lifesaving tools suddenly become *illegal firearms,* and then innocent shepherds go to jail, and their children are left with nothing to eat. It happens *every time.* That is why the jail cells of Bova are filled with Chionoti men. That is why we *never* call the police in." He rested his forearms on the table between us. "Do you understand, Franca? The only Christians who think the police are their friends are the ones who are born so wealthy they can buy the police force for themselves."

Something about what he said rang true—his accusation of privilege.

Don Pantaleone was watching me silently, the soft set of his mouth telling me he was confident I would come around to his way of thinking.

"Surely the *paese* could have come up with another solution for moving forward without forcing a marriage," I said at last.

"I agree with you," he said, and for a moment I thought we could bridge our disagreement. "Forced marriage is not ideal. But that is how things are done here. Historically, reparative marriage has been a positive force in the community. Marriage is, you'll remember, an economic liaison. Your romantic notions about it are a symptom of your origin, *maestra*. But reparative marriages have helped end vendettas and maintain property among families. In many cases women end up making more intelligent marriages than they would have if they had chosen their partners themselves."

"*More intelligent*—are you joking?" I stood up, banging my thighs against the table. "You are so backward. I don't have the stamina to argue with you anymore." I bent to pick up my case off the floor and in the process gouged my hip against the table's corner.

The priest stood, much more gracefully. "Franca, there is no point in storming off!"

Smarting in three different places, I extricated myself from the heavy chair and headed to the door. "I am sorry to miss the doctor," I said. Quivering with disgust, I stomped down via Sant'Orsola to try to salvage my nursery.

43

ON TUESDAY, DECEMBER 13, I HAD NOT HEARD BACK FROM Orlando the electrician. I was sitting at my desk despairing of my January deadline when a forty-something man, completely clean-shaven from chin to pate, stepped through my open door with showy diffidence. "*Buongiorno,* Maestra Francesca. I'm here about the *festa*."

"The *festa*?"

"San Silvestro."

The village's patron saint festival. "I'm sorry," I said to him. "We've never been introduced." I still knew who he was—it was Pascali Morabito, who had proctored the election and who was so often sitting at the *puticha* in the company of Turi Laganà. One of Don Tito Lico's men, I would hazard you might call him.

"Morabito," he said, ingratiating, removing his cap—but his manner was at least sixty percent facetious. "Would you like to put something in the collection?"

"Certainly." What would they expect from a well-heeled American spinster type? Would a thousand be too much, offensive, or eyebrow-raising? Or should I be laying out even bigger? I pretended to be rummaging through my case while I panicked through this decision. "When is it?"

"The thirty-first," he said. "New Year's Eve."

No one ever was seriously resented for generosity, were they? Hearts and minds. I gave him everything I had.

That night, as Cicca bullied me to mass to celebrate Santa Lucia, the waning moon was so close—with a crumbling bite taken out of its bottom and the craters so darkly discernible—that it reminded me of a chocolate chip cookie, which I nostalgically calculated I had not had in four years, not since my last trip home to Pennsylvania, that second Christmas after Sandro and I were married.

"Whatsa matter with him, he's not here?" my aunt Phyllis, and everyone else, had wanted to know. "That's no good. He should be eating Christmas dinner with your family!"

I'd been amused and defensive. "Come on, Auntie Phyllis. He had to go to his family. His widowed dad and sister would be all alone. If anything *I* should be *there*."

"What are you talking about, you should be there?" Phyllis's outrage was corroborated by "eh"s and "tsk"s from down the jam-packed table. "*They* should be here, too!"

At the time, in that overstuffed dining room, with one elbow in Uncle Mario's belly and the other in Uncle Ilio's mashed potatoes, I'd thought the whole conversation was a funny joke about Italo-Americans. In retrospect, I think Auntie Phyllis was right.

After the traditional Santa Lucia dinner of boiled wheat, I indulged in a bout of homesickness as I admired the crystal clarity of the thick-smeared stars. Not all stars, I remembered—some of them planets. This place was unfathomable, difficult to believe in even as I stood on its stone piles. I was fortunate to be here, to witness things that most humans could never imagine—the ingenuity, the grit, the squalor, the grandeur, the legend.

Maybe when the nursery was up and running, though, I would go home to my parents for a while. What was I waiting for? For Sandro? For the past to unscar my heart?

In the placid moonlight, the chartreuse blooms on my euphorbia plant glowed yellow. They were tight and geometric, like blossoms of quilled paper art rather than a nature-made weed. I ran a finger over a waxy leaf.

That was when I saw the round residue stain on the concrete windowsill. Like the waning moon—the perfect circle disappeared under the cactus's bottom. My first thought was that I should have put a dish under the pot; would the stain wipe off?

My second thought was: I had not moved the cactus. Why was the pot not still sitting on its stain?

A chill raced up my spine. Someone besides me had been in my room.

Cicca—certainly Cicca. Fiddling and snooping, no matter how many times she'd promised me she wouldn't.

When I lay down, though, my mind was running through other hypotheses: could someone climb into my window from the garden below?

I got up and latched the wooden bar across the shutters.

44

WEDNESDAY MORNING, ODDO THE LETTER CARRIER STOPPED BY the nursery. "I found you!" he crowed. "Always so much mail for you."

There was a letter from the Child Rescue international headquarters in London, the usual envelope from Sabrina, and the weekly blue aerogram from my parents. And there was a letter from Alexis Kelly. Unbelievably, the postmark was only a week and a half old.

I opened Alexis's first. Four pages of juicy gossip, but she hadn't buried the lede:

> *I've found your Dominic Scordo—easy as pie, right there in the death records at City Archives. Died August 28, 1952. I even went and looked up his obit in the Inquirer for you—had to go into the microfilm, you know how much I love that stuff. Survived by a wife and six kids, donations to be made to St. Paul's. Now I gotta know—does that mean he was murdered? Or does that mean he was not murdered? You better write me back about this tonight! I want all the details!*

I sat numbly, holding the letter. So Mico was dead, as Vannina suspected—although he had not been murdered by Tito Lico.

I flipped through my datebook to the notes I'd made while talking with Vannina. Mico must have died only days after he'd left Santa Chionia. The *municipio*'s missing visa must have been just a clerical error, Nazzareno's missing file a coincidence.

How anticlimactic. I must have been hoping in some grotesque chamber of my heart that poor old Mico Scordo had been murdered.

But also: if Tito the Wolf hadn't had Mico murdered for seducing the boss's teenage daughter, then whose bones had been dumped in the foundation of the post office?

I opened the Child Rescue letter next. The letter, dated Friday, December 2, made no sense on first read; it was only on the second, as my cold dread was already setting in, that I internalized the words.

> *Dear Miss Loftfield,*
>
> *We are writing to assure you that we are aware of your situation and that Child Rescue stands by you through this current adversity. We are in the process of finding an agent to send to Santa Chionia to assist you. In the meantime, please do not hesitate to let us know*

if there is anything else we can do to help bring the project to smooth
completion.
   Best,
   Lucy St. John–Jones
   Secretary, International Fund and European Initiatives
   Child Rescue

Child Rescue was sending in another agent. They were demoting me
from my own project.

What "adversity" was this Lucy St. John–Jones alluding to? Someone must have filed a report directly with the London headquarters. A
complaint.

Sabrina, head of Italian operations, would have told me if she'd been
aware. Wouldn't she? Sabrina would never have gone to her British
bosses about me, not without conferring with me first. Would she? Had
I written something that made her think I was in over my head? The lag
in correspondence made it so difficult to put together pieces.

I tore open Sabrina's letter and scanned her pointy handwriting
for the news that I had lost her faith. Nothing—it was a typical chatty
update: her plans to spend Christmas in Rome with her baroness aunt;
a scheme she was working on for a network of mobile libraries in rural
villages. No, of course Sabrina hadn't been the one to tell the English
overladies that I'd fallen short.

I reread Lucy St. John–Jones's letter once more, then closed my eyes,
feeling the cool wood of the desk under my wrists. A complaint must
have been lodged by someone here in Santa Chionia. But who?

Potenziana the Lichena hated me enough. She didn't strike me as a
letter-writer, though, nor the type to ferret out the address of the international headquarters of an obscure charity. Which meant it was someone I thought of as a friend. Don Pantaleone, who had petitioned to
have me brought here in the first place? Or Mayor Stelitano—maybe
that was why he was being so cold with me?

I leapt to my feet, rattled and restless. I had to fix this, right away.

I tried Pino Pangallo and his imperfect friendship first. "I need to
make an international call."

"The phone line is out."

"Still? For how long?"

Pino shook his head.

My chest tight, I rushed back to the nursery and laid out stationery to compose a letter. But I didn't know what accusations had been leveled against me; how could I know what to defend? When would a letter even reach the London office?

I stared out at the dismal gray piazza. I had to make a phone call. Today. I'd have to try the Roghudi town hall.

At least I'd worn my penny loafers.

Skidding down the mountain, I nodded distractedly to the women sunning their laundry in the Attinà bed, crossed over the flood-licked stepping stones, then began a fevered hour-long climb to Santa Chionia's closest neighbor.

Roghudi was as shocking a sight as Santa Chionia, the tight interlocking buildings draping over a crest of mountain shaped like the spine of a fish. On a less awful day, I would have been speechless with marvel. At the *municipio,* the secretary, a short, sixty-something man with a bit of gray stubble, was friendly, but his news was bad. "The phone lines are out all along the mountains."

My feet already hurt from my climb. "So I have to go to Roccaforte?"

"Roccaforte is out, as well. Chorio, Santa Maria, Santa Chionia. You can try Bagaladi, but your best bet is to catch the bus to Melito from Roccaforte."

I couldn't bear the thought.

"You're almost there," the man said kindly. He nodded at the clock. "There's a bus in an hour. Hurry, *signora.*"

I did it—I stumped down the mountain and back up to altitudinous Roccaforte, barely caught the bus, then spent two and a half hours bumping down the Amendolea gorge. When I arrived in Melito at two thirty, I was overexerted and hungry, angry at my wasted day, afraid for my future.

I'd also had the wending bus ride to consider things like: how was I going to get home tonight? Even if I caught the four o'clock bus back up to Roccaforte, I would be blundering home in the dark. *You must never go out walking except in broad daylight, and never alone.* But there were no friends with whom I could stay the night. If I took a room in Melito—

would there be a hostel that would even have me, a lone woman?—I had no way of communicating to Cicca that I wouldn't be home. She would assume I had died, or worse.

I would have to worry about that after I took care of the first problem.

The Melito *municipio* secretary remembered me, and was thusly un-amazed by the idea that I wanted to drop thousands of lire on an international phone call. The line crackled and the voice on the other end was barely audible.

"Child Rescue, how may I help you?"

I shouted uncomfortably over the static: "May I please speak to Lucy St. John–Jones?"

The female voice on the other end said something I could not make out.

"I'm sorry," I said after an embarrassing pause. "I couldn't hear you. May I please speak to Lucy St. John–Jones?"

"Speaking."

"This is Francesca Loftfield, from the Italy office. I am the one in Santa Chionia in Calabria—I received your letter today."

"The line is not very good, I'm afraid," Miss St. John–Jones said.

Feeling like a stupid child, I stuttered through my self-introduction again. This time the woman's response was lost in the transom except the words "So happy to hear from you," which I held out no hope were genuine.

"I was just—" How did I not already know what to say, when I'd had all day to think about it? "Could you tell me what kind of problem was reported to you? I wasn't sure what you were referring to."

"Darling, what can you mean?" For once the line was clear. "We received a letter describing a flood and the discovery of a human corpse."

My racing heart slowed down for the first time all day—I could actually feel my tired heart muscle loosen in relief. "Is that all? That has nothing to do with me. That was a building across the street, and it was sorted out weeks ago."

Perhaps the line had cut out again because the Englishwoman spoke over me. "You must be feeling quite overwhelmed, poor thing. We're trying to find someone who can come down and help you get things back on schedule."

The *municipio* secretary made no pretense of giving me any privacy, standing there with his arms folded around his vest-clad cylindrical torso.

"Who sent the letter?"

"The sender was, let's see . . ." A pause, but a disconcertingly brief one. "A Mr. Giovanni Stilo." She mispronounced the last name "style-oh."

After several long seconds of silence, I made myself say, "Well, don't worry about sending someone else. All the problems you mentioned have already been resolved."

Lucy St. John–Jones spoke as the line cut in and out. I tried to concentrate, but I was distracted by a grayly indistinct sense of danger, by the strangling beat of my heart.

"As the project runs late, budget becomes a concern," the Child Rescue administrator was saying. "We need to make sure we are sticking to a tight timetable."

"We're barely behind," I interrupted. "A miracle considering the flood."

"Yes, it's—" The line cut out for so long I thought it was severed entirely. Just as I was holding out the receiver to the nosy secretary I heard, "—open in January."

"Yes," I said, snatching the phone back. "January. Everything is ready to go."

When I'd hung up, I trudged back to the piazza to wait for the bus. Why had I lied? Why not just take the offered help?

I had to make the January date.

I wished I knew what the letter said in its entirety.

And who the devil was Giovanni Stilo.

45

FIFTEEN PEOPLE BOARDED THE LAST BUS UP TO THE MOUNTAIN hamlets, twelve men and three women. Without Cicca to act as my Doberman I sat alone in a window seat, clutching a cardboard box. I'd spent the nervous half hour waiting at the bar by the bus stop, where I ate three different Christmas pastries. Knowing I'd regret having to carry the box on my long walk home, I went on to order a whole assortment for Cicca.

I tried to stay philosophical as the sputtering bus turned its back on the Ionian Sea. The journey up into the mountains was shorter than the descent since we weren't picking anyone up. We reached San Lorenzo, the second-to-last stop, in forty minutes. I let myself feel optimism that we might arrive in Roccaforte, a two-hour walk to Santa Chionia, before dusk.

A few miles past San Lorenzo, though, the driver, a short man with gray hair that draped like roof tiles over his ears, pulled off the road into a bank of scrub. He scrambled down the steps and disappeared in front of the carriage. There was a metallic thwacking, and I felt a dull sense of hopelessness. Of course the bus would break down.

For ten minutes or so, while I anxiously watched the sun turning a fierier orange, there was an intermittent banging from the front of the bus. The passengers did not say anything to one another; some appeared to be dozing. But then a man got up out of his seat and joined the driver at the front of the bus. The banging ceased and a long conversation ensued. At one point, it seemed to get contentious; the passenger moved to the side of the bus, gesticulating.

I watched their heads bobbing at the bottom of the windshield. Most of the passengers stared at their laps; one woman was rubbing the bridge of her nose.

At last, the driver climbed back up. "Ten minutes," he told the passengers.

"Whatsa matter?" a man called from a seat behind me.

"Ten minutes." The driver tromped back down the stairs, his skinny shoulders hunched like a sow's.

The passenger who had been arguing with the driver, I noted, had not returned.

The bus was absolutely still for perhaps a minute, then one of the male passengers grumbled something and stood. He was followed immediately by two of the others. All three disembarked, two men continuing on foot up the dirt road and the other plunging into the forest where a thin goat path had been cut.

What should I do—get out and walk like the men? It was still another two or three miles to Roccaforte, I guessed, and the sun was sinking rapidly. If it was really going to be ten minutes, or even twenty, I was better off waiting.

Ten minutes, of course, came and went. The other passengers, who had been steadfastly ignoring one another, began to exchange murmurs. No one said anything to me or made eye contact. Then as if by some consensus they stood and filed off the bus.

Alone among the vinyl, I hesitated. The shadows of the trees lay thick on the road now. What a terrible day this had been, beginning to end—misguided and unlucky.

I gathered my case and my pastry box and moved toward the front of the bus. The driver was standing by the engine smoking a cigarette—he was not repairing anything.

Stepping carefully down to the uneven road, I said, "*Masciu,* what's going on? Are you about to leave?"

"There's a part that's broken. We gotta wait for the next bus that comes up."

"Weren't you driving the last bus for the day?"

"No." The man squinted through deeply sun-wrinkled eye sockets. "Not a bus. My friend is coming up this way and he'll have the right part."

That made no sense—was it a bus or his friend? I opened my mouth but my survival instinct was sharper than my brain because the words stuck wisely in my throat.

The winter wind surged down the empty mountain road, sounding off the wet rocks. When it died, the air was so still I could hear the burble of a waterfall from the faraway pocket of forest.

Where had all the other passengers gone? Hadn't they only just dis-embarked? Had I been frozen in some kind of Rip van Winkle spell?

I swallowed the lump and sighed ostentatiously. "If we wait for your friend we'll miss evening mass," I reproved, putting on my thickest Ca-labrese accent. This was not the moment to be identified as a wealthy American.

"No evening mass." He took a drag and regarded me from the side of his eye. "It's the Novena."

The more I talked the more I exposed myself as an outsider. My heart pounding, I turned purposefully on my heel and set off up the tilting road. My hands were shaking, my fingers cramping on the pastry box.

"My friend will be here soon, miss," the bus driver called. "You should wait just a little while longer."

Suddenly there was nothing in my life I had been more sure of than that I did not want to be alone on this mountain road when this man's friend arrived to help him with his mysterious problem. Putting no more energy into role-playing nonchalance, I pumped my legs. My breath was heaving by the time I rounded the first hairpin curve. Still I saw none of the disembarked passengers—the forest was as empty as if no one had ever lived here.

What the hell was going on?

My terror spurred me forward. I rounded a second corner, not allowing myself to slow although the cold mountain air was tearing through my alveoli and I could taste blood at the back of my throat. The long straight passage of road looked so endless I was demoralized, accepted that this would probably be where I died, and slowed my stride, eyes fixed on the stone-pocked ground beneath my feet as I clung to the forest's edge.

How long did I stumble upward in the dusk? It felt like hours before my wheezing lungs remastered the art of inflation. What would have happened if I had stayed on the bus? Would I have been held for ransom in a cave where shepherd-brigands had stashed their quarry for two centuries? Or perhaps just raped and murdered, disappeared into the impenetrable forests of the Aspromonte? My parents would never know what became of me.

The world had lost all color with the dusk, and the road glowed gray under a branch-shadow patina of every shade of black. Faintly through the trees I heard the tolling of church bells, a steady *dong dong dong dong*. Was it six o'clock? I was straining so hard to guess how far away they might be that I didn't hear the engine behind me until it was almost too late.

It was the bus, no longer broken down, roaring up the road toward Roccaforte, its headlights swinging around the bend like searchlights. The driver was hunched all the way over the steering wheel, peering into the darkness.

Wildly I dove into the brush at the side of the road, so distracted by my torture fantasy of what I would suffer at the hands of the bus driver that I forgot that the road hugged the cliff face, that the tree line was nothing more than green trim on a free fall of hundreds of meters to a rocky dismemberment.

As I burst through the shrub, the empty night air tore at my face and my chest filled with hot dismay. This was it. This was how I would die, casting my own damn self over a cliff. It wouldn't be brigands or rapists or angry mobs who did me in; it would be my imagination.

For no good reason at all, my luck held. The fall ended as abruptly as falls always do, concluding the notion that I was going to die a certain death and replacing it with a matrix of lesser discomforts ranging from a twisted ankle to a uselessly belated sense of panic.

I had landed on a ledge barely broader than the distance between my elbows and my knees. The darkness that anonymized the gorge or whatever else lay below did nothing to assuage my vertigo. Shaking, I wondered how far I'd fallen, whether my shredded knees and hands would be able to pull me up the distance to the road. But the darkness began, by some miracle, to rescind itself, smears of blackness to coalesce into the shapes of trees, rocks—and a path.

La luce dell'Aspromonte. The stars so bright that they cut through the nighttime like shards of glass.

Limping on my throbbing ankle, grateful for the rising half-moon, I followed the goat path back up to the main road. There sat the pastry box, which had weathered the evening's hijinks with better grace than I.

My mother must *never* hear about this.

Only after the bus was long gone did it occur to me that the driver might have been looking for me to offer me a ride, not to murder me.

I would never learn if I had been unfairly distrustful.

It was a high-strung trek through the mountains along the decrepit dirt road that would take me as far as Roccaforte, after which I'd be muddling pathlessly down and then back up the gorge in the wolf-infested dark. I jumped at every rustling branch, and swung around to look over my shoulder again and again. Once there was a sharp snap of wings so close to my face I yelped and stupidly lifted my briefcase over my head, as if it could protect me. It was just a bat, and soon there were many more clicking in the night.

This was the state of mind I was in—the adrenaline that had kept me focused frayed and blowing loose in the cutting wind—when my eyes caught a movement by the bend in the road, a flash of a shadow that merged with the shadows around it almost immediately, but I was certain it was a man.

My heart was instantly thundering again. There were no houses nearby, no innocent reasons a man might be ducking out of sight behind a bush here. I stepped—cautiously this time—to the side of the road, tucking into the folds of a mimosa bush.

How many times had they told me never to go out after dusk? Never to walk alone at night? *How many times?*

Crouching on bleeding knees in the brush, I fought to silence the wheezing of my tested lungs. *It might be teenagers trying to tryst,* I told myself. *They don't want to see you any more than you want to see them.* In case it was not, I ran my fingers over the dark ground for a makeshift weapon. They closed around a promising stick that crumpled upon pressure—nothing but bark. Its snapping made my heart jump.

The minutes stretched on, interminable, my thighs burning as I listened to the treacherous rasping of my breathing. The road ahead of me was utterly silent—even the wind had ceased. There was nothing but the relentlessness of the stars above.

What could I do? I had started to question my judgment—my sanity. And yet—I sensed a presence. The stillness of the air was *too* still, as if the normal currents had been interrupted by something else that was not supposed to be there. It was the reason my heart would not stop pounding.

It was the reason that when the hand closed around my wrist the scream was already out of my mouth, vibrating in the winter-bare oak branches even after it had been crushed.

46

I LASHED OUT WITH ALL MY MIGHT, THROWING MY BODY WEIGHT into my elbows to catch him off guard as my feet scrambled for purchase in the dust. It was no good—the man was a giant, his force inexorable. In this moment of greatest helplessness my fear vanished. I stopped struggling beneath his hands, my mind cleanly, quickly taking stock. *Stay alive.*

All at once the hands released me. "Holy Mary Mother of God." The man was gasping in laughter. "Francesca." He pounded his chest with his palm. "You scared me half to death."

Now the moonlight gave him shape. Even so, I almost didn't recognize him thanks to the thick stubble coating his cheeks. "Ugo Squillaci? I scared *you*!" I shouted, my relief manifesting as indignance. "A woman alone in the dark who you . . . you . . . *accost*!"

"*Accost* you?" He spoke between his own relieved bursts of laughter. "I see someone skulking in the bushes brandishing a knife, what am I supposed to think?"

"This is my knife," I said, offering him the broken bark, and suddenly I was giggling uncontrollably.

"What *are* you doing alone in the dark, acting like a maniac? Did your mother never teach you anything at all?"

"Oh, *please* don't bring my mother into this." I was overwhelmed by the purest joy that he was Ugo. All the loneliness and danger had inverted itself. "What were *you* doing?"

"I was walking my aunt home. She lives in Santa Maria."

"Why didn't I see you on the road?"

"I was taking a goat path." He pointed into a patch of brush indistinguishable from all the others. "There's always a shortcut, Francesca."

"Is there?"

The pause stretched pregnantly as we examined each other in the starlight. Then Ugo extended that same huge hand and cupped my shoulder. "Here, I will walk you home."

His touch, even through my jacket, was a warm patch of summer spreading across my scapula and down my spine.

As we started up the road at a much more comfortable pace, I told him of my misadventures. I kept my voice low but spared no detail, not asking myself if I trusted Ugo or why. When I realized he was offering me no advice, only murmurs of sympathy, the thought crossed my mind that I could fall in love with him. I really hated advice.

"Do you know someone named Giovanni Stilo?" I asked.

"That's a common name in this zone," he said after a moment. "But no Stilos in Santa Chionia."

I had been pretty sure of that from the town records. The stooge could be anyone.

Ugo did not take me down the gorge past Roghudi, but on a shepherd's shortcut through the forest. "How do you know these if you're not a shepherd?" I teased.

"We're all shepherds at heart, *maestra.*"

He did not, if you were wondering, use the cloak of night to put a move on me.

I had the presence of mind, finally, to ask him how he and his mother were coping.

"So many visitors. I'm grateful to them for distracting Mamma," he said. "But I had to get out of that house."

When we arrived in Santa Chionia, the streets were empty, shutters drawn. It was eerie—it could not have been later than eight. Cicca's house was completely dark.

"She's probably out looking for me," I said, feeling dreadful.

"She was going over to my mom's for dinner," Ugo said. "I don't think you should worry. She'll be home soon for the Novena."

I felt lucky for the starlight as I fumbled with my house key, my fingers quaking with nerves that were not left over from the bus encounter.

"Good night, *maestra,*" Ugo said as the lock tumbled loudly. He pulled his cap down over his curls. "Perhaps I'll see you again soon."

"I'm sure Cicca would love to see you. You could come in and wait until she's home."

Or he could just go home to his own house, where she already was, which would make a lot more sense. I felt my neck begin to burn instantly.

The pause that hung in the frosty air went on so long that when Ugo finally said, "I could," I felt a relief greater than I had felt after surviving my topple down the mountain.

Neither of us said anything as I led him to the kitchen, where I had the audacity to turn on Cicca's lightbulb. We looked at each other across its halo, but neither of us found the right words to break the silence. I set the pastry box on the table and opened it.

"Have one," I said. My voice was unfamiliar—embarrassingly high. "There's this one with pistachio and fig. I can't remember what the guy said they were called—*pretali*?"

"*Petrali,*" Ugo corrected. "We call them *sammartini* up here, though."

"They're good. You should have one."

"Thank you," he said, but instead of taking the sweet he stepped toward me and gripped my face between his hands. I was both shocked by and expecting the kiss—it had seemed both impossible and inevitable a moment earlier—but I was not ready for the clean, sparkling chemistry of his obstinate lips. I lost touch with myself—the kitchen, the pastry, the sin of the lightbulb—as completely as if I had blacked out, which had happened to me once, freshman year, fainted in the shower and had to be revived by the RA—anyway it was that comprehensive, my disorientation, and when I had finally reclaimed myself I realized I had dropped my briefcase on the tile floor, where it landed with a leathery *splat*.

"Hurry," I said as he knelt to pick it up, and that was the last thing either of us said for a very long time.

47

I WOKE UP FROM WHAT FELT LIKE THE MOST INTENSE SLEEP OF MY life because Cicca was pounding on my door.

"Franca! Franca! It's time for the Novena! Franca!"

"Oh shit," I said aloud, in English.

"I don't know what that means," Ugo said, and I clapped a hand over his mouth.

"What's wrong?" I called to Cicca. "It's the middle of the night!"

"Mass starts at three o'clock!" she shouted back. "Hurry up, get dressed!"

"Three in the *morning*?"

"Right now! In ten minutes!"

"Uh." I scrambled out of bed, feeling around me for anything to cover myself with. My room was unhelpfully pitch-black. "Okay, give me a minute. I'll be right out."

I stumbled to the window and cracked open the shutter so at least there was some starlight to see by. Ugo's eyes were glittering mirthfully from my bed. He was enormous without any clothes on, even bigger, somehow—with hulking triceps that leapt from the sides of his arms and with breasts like Paul Newman's.

How the hell had this happened to me?

It was hilarious—I wanted to laugh out loud. I wanted to brag to Cicca.

I also wanted to live, though, so.

I bent over the creaking bed on my skinned knee and whispered,

"You're going to have to go out the window. Unless you want to hide under the bed until we're gone."

I could see nothing except the flash of his eyes. His hand wrapped around my rib cage, bracing me, and I felt the other slide down my stomach, where it lingered long enough to cause intemperate activity.

"Ugo!" I had to get him out of my bedroom before I accidentally had sex with him. It had taken all my stamina and creativity to prevent such an occurrence all night long. "Cicca's right outside the door!" I barely mouthed the words. It wasn't like he didn't know.

"Just tell her you don't want to go to mass," he murmured into my hair. He smelled like olive oil soap and pine ash and sweat.

"Stop, you have to stop." I was already regretting everything that would not happen.

"We have time. Relax." And with the smoothest maneuver he flipped me onto my back and shifted himself so he was suspended over me, his weight balanced on his hands, those enormous triceps bulging in the starlight. I had never in my life seen triceps muscles as developed as his.

How could it possibly hurt, to let him in? I had just finished my period—it was so unlikely I could get pregnant, even if he hadn't mastered the Catholic fine art of withdrawal. Was I really going to—

Regardless of anything else, you always say no the first time.

"Out! Now!"

"You're right, you don't want to miss the Novena," he said, rolling himself up to pull on his trousers. "It's really something special." He gave me an adorable smirk and I tried to guess how many girls like me he had perfected that smirk on. Not that I cared—yes I did. Yes I cared, I didn't want to think of myself standing among flocks of better-feathered competition. But my heart was sore with longing and I would have given in to him even if I'd known I was just one distraction among many.

"Show me something truly special and let me see you climb out this window."

The chickens, who had never been my particular friends, made such a racket that I feared for Ugo's safety as he made his way among them. I closed the sash, put my euphorbia back on the windowsill, and lay back in bed for thirty seconds of revisitation and reprisal, feeling the thumping in my carotid artery. Then I pulled on panties, which itched punitively with cactus prickers, and thick stockings, a skirt and a blouse and a jacket and a scarf, as if many layers of clothing now would protect me from the truth of how naked I had been only moments earlier.

Then I opened the door to try to lie to Cicca, who was standing there with deeply suspicious patience, holding two pine torches as long as her forearm—Hecate incarnate.

"What is the Novena, exactly?" I asked plaintively. "Why do we have to get up at three in the morning?"

"Nine days before Christmas," she said. "We go to mass now. It's beautiful."

"You do this every year?"

"Every day!" She steered me into the street. "Every day until Christmas!"

The rooftops below us glowed, and the stony streets echoed a faint thread of melody—children's voices, a deceptively simple tune, no accompaniment. The memory of my first sight of Santa Chionia, the women's voices rising from the valley below, shuddered through me like a distracted ghost.

Bewitched, I followed Cicca down via Boemondo toward the church, stepping into a steady flow of Chionoti carrying torches. My ears fought for purchase on the children's sweet-sounding words.

> Light, light of the lovely star
> Follow the Galilee road
> The little angels are departing
> Oh, the Messiah arrives

The church piazza was populated with an astonishing nativity made entirely out of branches and moss. It was surreally lifelike, the angels' eyeless faces whittled from shards of holm oak, and shining ilex ornamenting Mary and Joseph's pine-brush cloaks. I can't imagine who made the effigies—if it was a group effort, or the genius of a single artist—but they could have been an exhibition in a museum.

In the middle of the piazza, an extremely tidy bonfire had been stacked. With children's voices rising in eerie choir from all sides, people poured in from east, south, and west, pausing to lay their torches on the fire before filing into the church. The stars glared garish and too close, and the mortared walls of the ancient city trembled and tinkled with the unearthly sound.

The pews and aisles were packed—no one sat. Long after there was no room left, people were still arriving. I did everything within my power not to spot Ugo Squillaci among the faces, and to my frustration, I succeeded. Smoking pine resin lamps lent the whole ecstasy a spicy, combustible whiff of esoteric danger.

Cicca had described what we were attending as "mass," but I can't imagine the Catholic church ascribing that word to the ritual I observed. The ambient choir of children came to the end of their verses and the dais was subsumed by a band—two bagpipes, an accordion, a mouth harp, and a tambourine. Rafter-shaking incantatory ruckus ensued.

It was euphoria—I felt like I was on drugs. Was it the exhaustion, the altitude, or some collective hysteria? For an hour I heard myself shouting with joy that the baby was coming. I think I even meant it.

"Last night you left a pastry on the table," Cicca said as we were walking home at dawn, after hallucinatory visits to six—seven?—friends' houses, where we'd roasted chestnuts and drunk cordials and sung ancient songs I inexplicably knew the words to.

Cicca didn't mention the abomination of the lightbulb that had been left on despite the fact that there had been no one in the room to bask in its magnificence. This more than anything else made me suspect I had not gotten away with my escapade.

"Maybe we can have the pastry for breakfast," I said bleakly.

The smell of Ugo still filled my nostrils. I was desperate to bathe. I hadn't gone down to the cataract to fill my pitcher the day before—it had been busy—and I only had an icy quart to scrub myself. But scrub I did, sitting on the stool by my bed, dripping onto my linen floor towel. It was an act of penance as much as ablution. I was a *married woman.* Regardless of whether I believed in the institution or not, I had *made promises.* Here I was behaving as if I weren't risking hurting myself *and* others by pretending I had never made those vows. Had I no honor? No respect for either of those men? Even as all varieties of body part vibrated with the lushly recent memory of partial indulgence, I felt awful, committed to never, ever letting it happen again.

This battle of impulses and convictions was lost on all fronts as I gradually became aware of a separate and unplaceable sense of dread. As I had last night, I felt that intense, nearly supernatural sense that I was not alone. That I was prey.

I jumped up and pressed my back against the door to study the room. Something *looked* wrong—yes, my datebook, which I always lined up flush with the side of the desk, was askew. Maybe Ugo had kicked it as he was climbing out the window.

Trust, but verify.

I picked up the datebook and thumbed through it.

Vannina's photo was missing.

I flipped through it again. All my other odds and ends—scraps of paper bearing addresses or aphorisms, an ancient love note written on an *aperitivo* napkin—seemed to be there, but the photo of the six men and the little bagpiper was gone.

Frantic, I reached for my briefcase to see if it had fallen out inside. Only then did I realize how light the case was. It contained my wallet, three ballpoint pens, and a Zuzu. It did not contain my file of student applications.

Dread and dismay took away my balance and I sat on the edge of the bed. I forced myself to run through possible scenarios—could I have dropped the file when I fell down the mountain? But the case had been securely latched.

Could I have left it at the Melito *municipio*? I was certain I'd taken only my datebook and wallet out. My unfocused eyes fixed on the leaves of my euphorbia as they bobbed gently in the breeze.

The breeze.

The window was open three inches. Had I failed to latch it after I let Ugo out?

Or . . . was it possible someone else had been in my room?

My heart was pounding again, pounding so forcefully my chest hurt. With an involuntary squeal I dropped to the floor—no one was under my bed.

I pulled my cranberry A-line on over my rubbery, still-damp skin and ran barefoot down the hall and into the yard. The hard-packed dirt was cold enough to sting my feet. I stared at the chickens roosting on the bar under my window, and they made reproachful remarks to each other. Could the birds be more worked up than usual this morning? I tried to identify footprints in the poop splatter.

Cicca was coming down the alley now, a water bucket in each hand and a third balanced on a rag coronet on her head. "What's wrong, *pedimmu?*"

"I think someone was in my room, *cummàri.* Some of my things are missing." My throat stuck at hearing the thought out loud.

Cicca was instantly defensive. "I took nothing of yours!"

"No, no, not you, of course. I . . ." Swallowing, I pointed to my window. "I don't want to worry you, but I was wondering if someone might have climbed into my bedroom."

"No one could climb that." She rubbed her nubby cleft chin. "I think if anyone was in your room you must have let them in there yourself."

"Hmm," I said, conceding nothing. The window did look too narrow and high to admit someone. Although I had seen Ugo squeeze out, so.

Ugo.

I heard my father's tired lecturing voice. *The correct answer is usually the simplest one, Francesca.*

Feeling violated and increasingly angry, I headed back inside, wiped off my feet, and buckled on my shoes. When had he gone through my things? While I was sleeping? Could he have read my letters, too? Made heads or tails of my journal?

It was all my own damn fault for trusting him. The worst part was he hadn't broken into the garden, literally or metaphorically; I had dragged him in myself.

But why? Was he an agent—some kind of nephew—of Potenziana Legato? Of course he was, they all were—if not biological nephews, then organizational ones. *Friends and cousins,* his own words. Well, Potenziana would have all she needed; the gossip that I had let him into my bed would be particularly useful in helping the village decide this loose-moraled woman must never, ever be allowed near their children.

I pushed tears out of my eyes with the heel of my hand. I couldn't believe Ugo, with his archetypally southern sun-ruddy laconism, would tell anyone about anything he did in private. Even if this had all been a setup—even if he hated me.

It was only after I had knocked on the Squillaci door that I remembered everyone was probably sleeping off the early-morning religious ecstasies. Before I had a chance to be ashamed of myself, the door opened and he was standing there.

"Is everything all right?" He glanced behind him, then said, "Do you want to come in? My mother is fixing coffee."

"You took my papers," I blurted. They weren't the right words, they weren't strategic.

I saw him hesitate before he said, "What? What papers?"

"My—my—" Suddenly I was wary of revealing how much I needed what had been stolen. "You went through the things on my desk, didn't you? There are—papers and pictures missing." I tried to sound firm, authoritative. Meanwhile there was the inescapable truth that he had seen me naked.

"I? Go through your things?" His eyebrows dropped and his jaw clenched. "I am your friend, Francesca," he said after a moment. "I know you are under a great deal of pressure, but don't lash out at the wrong people." He stared at me, the morning light shrinking his pupils so that the cloudy bronze of his irises was nearly uninterrupted. "I need to go to my uncle's. Perhaps I'll see you later."

He closed the door gently in my face.

Shaking, I turned down via Sant'Orsola. Could my gut instinct about someone be so wrong? If he had taken my papers, he was a master manipulator. If he hadn't, I had just said something so offensive he would never forgive me.

Dismally I unlocked the nursery. There—my application folder, sitting on my desk, exactly where I had forgotten it yesterday when I rushed off to Roghudi.

I burst into tears and sobbed at my desk for a full five minutes before cutting myself off. I took my compact out of my briefcase and spread a layer of powder over my dark under-eyes, then opened the folder and riffled through. Nothing appeared to be missing. I riffled through a second time, then through my briefcase and the notebook within, then opened and closed every drawer of my desk.

The application folder was here, but Vannina's photo wasn't.

48

ODDO THE POSTMAN MADE ONE MORE TRIP OVER THE BEAM bridge from Bova before Christmas. On Wednesday, December 21, Cicca and I were having a late lunch—nettles and potatoes—when he dropped off a letter from Alexis Kelly.

I'm sending this to you in Italy instead of telling you in person because I know what a stooge you are, Frank. You're not coming for Christmas. Get your act together soon though or how am I supposed to get your opinion on this John Matthews character.

Anyway. In case you can't tell I'm a bit bored these days, with only the full-time job and then this new application for my MRS and Christmas shopping and whatnot. But after I sent you off that last letter about Dominic Scordo I got to thinking: if this really is a murder mystery, I've shown a wretched lack of curiosity about it, haven't I? You said you were going to send me more details but they haven't come. What with the Italian postal service I assume I'll get them just in time to share with Mr. Matthews over our golden anniversary cake.

So I thought, what the heck, South 8th is only a couple blocks from the bus stop, why not sniff around? See if this dame you said he was "shacking up" with got him killed or something? Seemed like an exciting story to have to tell over cocktails. John's a salesman. They like excitement.

Listen to this, Frank, you'll be proud of me. I walked right up and knocked on that door, and wouldn't you know Lois Blake herself answered it. I wore a trench coat for verisimilitude and I told her that I was a private detective hired by Dominic Scordo's wife to find him. I guess I could have gotten a kick in the pants but she didn't bat an eye, just let me right in. Wasn't what I expected at all—no floozy or moll or anything like that. No, alas. She was an uptight sort of nervous type, more of a Miss Stetson

—that was our high school civics teacher—

than a Rita Hayworth. I felt bad about lying to her, to be honest, because she was so serious, so I acted real professional, took notes in my legal pad and wrote down my number for her if she had any follow-up information. Ha!

Maybe you already know all this, I guess I'll find out when I get your letter in fifty years. But in the meantime, here's what she told me, when I hinted that Dominic Scordo might be dead. She said, quoth, "I wouldn't be surprised. Nick"—she called him Nick—"was mixed up in something way over his head." I asked her what. She said she really didn't know, but she had a bad feeling even before she found out about his wife. There was a problem with money—he owed someone a lot, or was paying someone off for something, because he was working a real good plumbing job but he was always flat broke. She didn't say this cuz she's a circumspect type, I'm putting words in her mouth, but it sounded to me like good old-fashioned mafia stuff.

Does this help you? I don't care! This is about me now—I want to know more! Make your letter get here faster!

I turned over the idea that Mico Scordo had been a victim of a Philly mafia hit. Did Vannina know her husband was a gangster? Or was he just the Americanized version of a "goatherd"? Maybe he'd come home that summer of 1952 to escape a Philly syndicate problem, then gotten himself in trouble with Ninedda Lico and had to choose what kind of gangster he was more afraid of.

But he'd also owed Tito Lico money. For what?

It wasn't possible that Tito the Wolf had put out a hit on Mico Scordo in Philadelphia. Was it? That would suggest an international organized crime network as sophisticated as what the Sicilians were running in New York. There was no way. Not based here, in this blighted, malnourished village. I had no reason to believe Tito Lico even knew how to read.

Cicca had hawkishly watched my eyes scan the stationery and pounced the moment they disconnected. "What does it say?"

I wrinkled my nose. "I have to go talk to poor Vannina Favasuli."

I was still boggy with remorse about our last encounter. And now I was coming with the news that her husband was dead and there was no hope for restitution.

As a peace offering, I brought the remainder of the pastry I had purchased in Melito. Cicca railed at me for wasting good pastry on That Woman, but she'd been eating them so sparingly it wasn't clear if she even liked them, and they were almost a week old at this point. I took out a sweet potato dumpling and left it on Cicca's table. "There. You eat that one. You want to come with me?"

After some mulling, Cicca's hatred of Vannina was overruled by her busybodyness. We trooped through the overcast afternoon down via Lilio, a shortcut I'd never known about that took us to Vannina's alley in a few minutes.

When she answered her door, Vannina seemed to bear me no ill will. "*Maestra!*" She grasped my shoulder to kiss me on both cheeks. "Cummàri Cicca! Happy Novena! Come in!"—as if we were there on a completely habitual social call.

"Humph!" Cicca said, accepting her kisses with a stony scowl. Vannina was unfazed. I wondered, sadly, if she was used to being spurned and slapped. If lavishing artificial affection on people who were mean to her was just her survival technique.

We sat on the anxiety-inducing furniture; I presented the stale pastry to great exultation. I babbled some festive platitudes while Vannina flittered around her smelly grotto trying to find us undesired beverages and Cicca glowered, arms crossed.

"Did you bring my photo back, *maestra*?" Vannina asked sweetly.

"No, sorry, next time," I said, avoiding Cicca's eye. "Vannina, I have some hard news for you. It's about Mico."

She squatted in front of me, her tattered skirt puddling around her thighs and her sand-colored eyes avid. "He's dead."

"I had my friend in Philadelphia trace him in municipal records. I'm afraid he died in August 1952." I nodded to her letter box on its shelf of honor. "Just when you stopped receiving letters from him."

"I knew it." She squeezed my knees, gazing up at me like a penitent. Her bosoms were typically unavoidable, and it occurred to me that she might be awaiting some afternoon commerce. "He was murdered."

"No, he—" I didn't know how he died; I shouldn't make any promises. "Well, he died in Philadelphia. So he is not the body under the post office."

Vannina gave me a sad, gap-toothed smile. "No, *maestra,* your friend is wrong."

"She's not wrong. She's a lawyer, she's very smart and doesn't make mistakes. She found his obituary in the newspaper."

"I know *for a fact* he did not die in Philadelphia," Vannina said fiercely.

"Vannina, is it possible Mico was involved with a . . . a gang?"

Her delicate brows descended in picturesque confusion. "A gang?"

"I mean . . . the mafia?"

"The mafia." She repeated the word like she had never heard it before. "The American mafia?"

"Well—" No, there was no point. "My friend in Philly—she went to see that . . . that landlord, the one who returned your letter." I fibbed my way through some masculine pronouns. "And the . . . he thought that Mico was in trouble with a syndicate. That he owed someone a lot of money."

For the first time, ever, I saw fear on Vannina's face—her eyes widened and her mouth drooped. It appeared to be genuine human emotion, not a theatrical presentation.

What was she afraid of? Why would finding out her husband might have been killed far away by an American crime syndicate scare her when she had assumed he had been killed by her neighbors?

"That can't be right," she mumbled. "What's the point in killing someone if they owe you money? Then you'll never get it back."

"Whoever you think murdered Mico here in Santa Chionia had a better reason than money?" My words were so gummy with sarcasm that even Vannina couldn't miss it. Her gaze skittered from me to Cicca and back again. "What exactly would be a good reason for getting murdered here, Vannina?"

Vannina lurched to her feet, her feminine assets responding to the alteration of personal geography with splendid vellications. "The only reason a murder ever happens is because it *can*," she said. She poured herself a grimy cup of wine. "The state leaves us to our autochthonous justice."

"Autochthonous?" I heard myself repeating incredulously. I hadn't had Vannina pinned for a vocabularian.

Cicca, waggling her eyebrows, caught my eye behind Vannina's turned back. She nodded in the direction of the trunk in the corner. I stared at the trunk, but couldn't figure out what she meant.

"What?" I mouthed.

Cicca scowled and nodded to the trunk again. I spread my hands, trying to communicate that I didn't understand. Vannina almost caught me out when she whirled around.

"Okay, *maestra*," Vannina said. "You need to tell your lawyer friend to—"

"Vannina! No. I found Mico for you," I said. "I have to draw a line. I am sorry for your loss, but perhaps this can help you move on."

"Will you show me your chickens?" Cicca piped up all of a sudden.

Vannina was as surprised as I was. "What, *cummàri*?"

"Your chickens."

"My chickens?" Vannina echoed, nonplussed, but she put her cup down. "They're outside."

Cicca snorted at me meaningfully before she followed our hostess out the door.

I took the cue and tiptoed over to the chest, the belongings Vannina had told me Mico abandoned when he disappeared. A scenario flashed through my mind: Vannina had murdered her own husband, his body had been in a trunk by their bed the whole time! That would explain his lack of visa, her conviction that he wasn't in the States—

My heart was pounding in anticipation. Hoping it didn't make a loud noise, I pulled the heavy lid open.

There was no decaying body in the trunk. Only a single lumpy burlap sack. Which, yes, I fumbled open.

Inside were at least twenty pistols, their black carbon steel magazines gleaming dully.

49

CICCA HUDDLED AGAINST MY ELBOW AS WE BUMBLED UP THE mountain in the seething wind.

"How did you know?" I whispered.

"Know what?"

"What was in the trunk!"

"I don't know what's in the trunk!" she said, affronted. "It's none of *my* business. I thought *you* would want to know what's in the trunk."

I digested that, trying to guess how much she already knew and why. Anyway we shouldn't be talking in public about this.

"Where are all Vannina's children?" I asked instead. "I've never seen any of them at her house."

"Her sister took them away. Vannina wasn't raising them right."

Poor Vannina, I thought for the hundredth time.

We warmed up by Cicca's hearth with half a sweet potato dumpling each.

Why did Vannina Favasuli have a stockpile of weapons?

Why had the implication that her husband had been killed by the "American" mafia bother her?

Was there any chance Alexis's information was wrong, like Vannina insisted? Could someone have faked Dominic Scordo's *Inquirer* obituary? Why would anyone do that?

"What do you think happened to Mico Scordo?" I asked Cicca.

"Your friend said he died in Philadelphia."

"But what do *you* think?"

Cicca shrugged. "What's to think?"

"Do you think Mico Scordo was involved with a gang here in Santa Chionia?"

"A gang?" she repeated, exactly as Vannina had.

I tamped down my impatience. "A clan. The mafia."

"We don't have mafia here," Cicca said. "The only time is when boys get involved in the mafia in America and try to bring it back to the *paese,* but we don't want any part of it."

"Right."

She pretended to be bewildered by my sarcasm.

"What about Sicily?" I said. "They have mafia in Sicily, don't they?"

"Oh, a big problem over there." Cicca's eyes flared judgmentally. "The Sicilians—they're sneaky. You've got to be careful."

"Okay. I'll be careful of Sicilians." I tried a different tack. "Do you think—before he left Santa Chionia, is it possible Mico Scordo had problems with . . . maybe blackmail? Or a blood vendetta? Maybe someone was extorting him?"

"What does it mean, 'extorting'?"

"Like . . . like blackmail. Holding property or information hostage to make him pay to protect it."

"Hostage?" Cicca echoed, brows crimping. "You mean like kidnapping?"

"No, I mean . . . For example, threatening to hurt your family if you don't pay, or to cut down your orchard, or reveal a secret?"

Cicca shook her head, her lip sticking out. "I don't know about anything like that."

"Okay," I said, giving up. I didn't really care about Mico Scordo anymore. I was much more worried about the cache of handguns in a madwoman's house, and whether it was my job to tell someone about it.

"What about hijacking?" Cicca said innocently.

"What?!"

"Well, I mean, Mico got into a little trouble with that hijacking on the Cardeto road."

"What hijacking?" My dumb heart, right on cue, *pound pound pounding* with the thrill of the chase.

"It was a terrible thing that happened. It was after the big flood."

"You mean the flood of 1951?"

"The hijacking happened the summer *after*," Cicca said, pausing to stare at me baldly until she was sure I'd followed her gist. Oh, I followed—she was telling me about 1952, the summer Mico Scordo had disappeared. "So much misery back then. People were living in caves because their houses were knocked down. The *bambini* were so hungry their mammas were feeding them boiled grass. The government was supposed to be sending us money to rebuild, but did we ever see it? *Pfft.* Who was going to believe any hope was coming? Some *ragazzi* decided they would take the government's money for themselves." From the singsong of her phrasing it was hard to tell if Cicca disapproved or if this was what *she* might have called autochthonous justice. "They planned to hijack a pension coach on the Cardeto road."

"A pension coach?" I said, incredulous. "You mean, the *armed caravan* they use to drop off money at the post offices for disbursement? The ones accompanied by *federal police* carrying *Beretta machine guns*?" Cicca was sucking scoldedly on her lower lip. "That's insane. How were shepherds with knives going to go up against machine guns?"

"Not such a good idea," Cicca allowed. "Maybe the *ragazzi* thought they had some arrangement with one of the *carabinieri* who were supposed to be escorting the coach. Give him a cut if he let them tie him up. Who can say, I don't know anything about it."

I bet she didn't. "Surely that plan didn't work out."

"Something went wrong. One of the *ragazzi* was killed, and one of the officers."

Fragments of information were jingling against one another in my mind. Ceciu Legato's dead son, the one Don Pantaleone had told me was killed in a road accident—the photo of the young man on Isodiana's votive shrine. "Francesco," I remembered. "Francesco Legato."

Cicca's head jerked up, and I watched her alarmed expression soften into resignation. "Yes. Little Francesco got shot. The others got away, but so did one of the *carabinieri* officers. The police came up to Santa Chionia to look for the stolen money." Cicca prodded at the banked coals with her wooden poker. "They arrested a bunch of Christians, tried to get them to say who had been behind the scheme. Mico Scordo, he was one of the *ragazzi* who got in trouble then. He went back to America right after."

Had he? Or was "America" a euphemism?

In my lap, my frigid hands tremored. I crossed my arms, clamping my fingers under my armpits. A hijacking heist, only eight years ago. Right here, in the mountains I'd been walking alone through last week, convinced I was about to be the victim of a hijacking heist.

Mico Scordo was involved in a crime that had gone horribly, predictably wrong; then, coincidentally, Mico had never been seen again. Could he have been one of the casualties that day? Then why the cover-up?

Or—accounting for Alexis's microfilmery—had Mico escaped to Philadelphia to avoid arrest, only to have retribution follow him? That seemed far-fetched. Besides, it didn't answer the question of who the damn skeleton under the post office was.

But the timing was too suggestive to dismiss.

Why would Mico come home for a vacation, only to get mixed up in a patently ill-advised violent crime scheme? Money, surely—he'd owed Don Tito for something no one was willing to talk about. Or—my excitable heart stuttered—maybe the whole thing had been a hit. Mico Scordo was rumored to have seduced Don Tito's daughter, Ninedda— had the Wolf, the town boss, organized an impossible crime to set up a stage for punishing the cad?

No, no no. Outrageous, Francesca! That wouldn't even happen in a noir movie. These were real people, soft-spoken shepherds doing their best to make ends meet.

Except when they weren't.

"Does this happen often?" I asked. "Armed robbery?"

"After the war there were Christians so desperate they were trying all kinds of things to get by," Cicca said after a moment. "So many Christians went to jail, thefts and stabbings. Hard times. Women started to *sell their bodies.* In Santa Chionia, even."

"Hard times," I managed.

"But this was before Don Pandalemu was transferred here. Once Santa Chionia had a priest again, when the *ragazzi* had someone to look up to, they stopped being so stupid."

How true could that be? Fear of God inspired various men to correspondingly various extents. I was skeptical that guys like Tito Lico had any real apprehension about eternal damnation.

"Who were the other men involved in the hijacking?"

"Oh, I don't know." Cicca flapped her hand, dissipating the noxious question.

It's not our tradition.

I thought of Vannina's missing photo, taken in August 1952— probably within days of this debacle. *These are the men who killed Mico,* Vannina had told me. *Tito the Wolf. Turi Laganà, the goat-fucking swine. And Pascali Morabito.*

"Tito Lico?" I tried. "Did he organize it?"

"He's too clever to get his hands dirty these days."

These days. The words stuck for a moment in the air between us.

Who wasn't too clever, then? "Turi Laganà?" I guessed, knowing what I did about his past crimes. I pictured him brazenly ducking through Vannina's door in broad daylight. He was used to taking what he wanted with impunity. Utter lack of fear of consequences has always been a monetizable trait in a soldier. "Or Pascali Morabito?"

"Those old goats? They're too senile to do anything but drink in Saverio's tavern."

I knew this not to be true, but I took her point—armed robbery was an impetuous young man's game, wasn't it? Someone for whom ambitions of lucre overruled fear of death. Either that, or someone who was desperate enough to risk it all. Maybe someone like Mico Scordo.

I went back to Vannina's picture. *These are the men* . . . No way was I going to believe malarial Pino Pangallo would hold up an armored vehicle. But what about . . . "Santo Arcudi," I breathed. I remembered the oval bruise on Isodiana's neck. Her bookish-looking husband wasn't without violent tendencies.

"Who knows," Cicca said. She wasn't making eye contact.

"Santo Arcudi," I mused, letting the pieces come together as I spoke them out loud. "Trying to show some initiative. Too bad his grandfather Don Roccuzzu and uncle Gianni were dead, or he might have been in charge of—"

"I never told you Gianni Alvaro was dead."

"You said he was gone," I protested.

"Gone to prison! This is what I'm talking about."

"What is what you're talking about?!"

"This! This is when it happened. After the robbery, the *carabinieri* were tearing Santa Chionia apart trying to find the money, nail someone for killing the officer on the Cardeto road. They were terrorizing us, locking everyone up. You know they force-feed you salt water to make you confess?" Cicca tilted her head back in a disturbing bug-eyed pantomime of interrogation torture. "Don Gianni confessed to shooting the officer during the hijacking to make them leave us alone. He sacrificed himself. Now he's going to be in prison until he dies."

"But it was a false confession? It wasn't him?"

"He wasn't even there!" Cicca waved angrily northwest, to the cliff face above which the Alvaro mansion bletted. "What would he rob a coach for? He has all the money in the world!"

I considered who a man like Don Gianni Alvaro would take the fall for. His weaselly son, Rocco, would have been eighteen or nineteen at the time—a harebrained heist scheme might have appealed to him. I tried to picture the maliciously flirtatious young man firing a gun at a police officer and found my imagination perfectly capable.

"Rocco Alvaro," I said out loud. So four men I knew of had been involved in the heist: Francesco Legato, Mico Scordo, Santo Arcudi, and Rocco Alvaro. The first was dead, the second suspiciously missing, while two grandsons of the old boss Don Roccuzzu seemed to have escaped scot-free. "What happened to the money?"

Cicca was shaking her head silently, staring at the fire. She wasn't going to tell me. She would gossip for hours, reveal the most sordid of family sagas of people I'd never met—but nothing that would hold up in court.

Tito Lico had commissioned the building of the new post office in 1952. What were the odds the unidentified skeleton was unconnected to this town-upending crime?

Out of obstinance more than any hope of further information, I named the last man in the *municipio* photo. "What about Isodiana's father? The mayor, Ceciu Legato? He stepped down right after Francesco died, didn't he?"

This time Cicca met my eye. "Ceciu didn't handle things so well when the *carabinieri* came. He made mistakes."

A chill traveled up my back. This particular epiphany was coming over me slowly, the light of the Aspromonte seeping into my cracking naivete. The votive candle Isodiana burned mournfully for her father in Philadelphia; the half-baked lie Potenziana had told me about Ceciu's gambling away his family's savings.

"What kinds of mistakes?"

Cicca looked down at her hands, massaging her knuckles before she answered. "Maybe some Christians blamed Ceciu's family for why so many Christians got arrested."

"A rat," I said. *We can't tolerate even one in a town like this.*

Cicca's eyes flicked back up to mine. "That was when Ceciu emigrated to America. He's never come home to Santa Chionia since."

The next morning, I cascaded down the donkey path to the cemetery to do some snooping I wouldn't need Cicca to corroborate. Since it was my second visit, I had an idea where to look.

The graves were a poignant reflection of the penury in which the vast majority of Chionoti lived and died, anonymous wooden crosses pegged at evocative intervals. Not all were so humble, though. Miniature marble castles clustered at the enclosure's center, where the "better" families maintained their endogamy in death. The largest, predictably, was ALVARO, where the remains of ROCCO, 1875–1943, awaited his ADELINA, 1890–. I cataloged this masonry confirmation of *paese* elite: LAGANÀ, ARCUDI, MORABITO, LICO.

At LEGATO I lingered: there was SAVERIO, 1870–1940, the grandsire for whom the *puticha* proprietor was named. Cicca had told me this antecedent entrepreneur had been a goatherd who savvily acquired a wine license, thereby opening the tavern his namesake now ran. Another door on the Legato mausoleum was engraved VINCENZO, 1903– and RICHELINA, 1906–, Isodiana's parents. Neither, I suspected, would ever be buried here. I wondered, too fleetingly, where Donna Richelina, that onetime princess of Santa Chionia, was, if her husband had not emigrated to Philadelphia but been silenced for his bad faith and buried under the post office.

Whatever Don Pantaleone Bianco said, I doubted Ceciu Legato was coming home for Christmas. I had a feeling if I were to check the archives, it would turn out his visa was missing, just like Leo Romeo's and Mico Scordo's. But I would never be allowed to check.

The Chionoti were all lying about Ceciu Legato, whether they realized it or not.

50

WELL, WHAT WOULD YOU HAVE DONE, IF YOU FOUND A MENTALLY imbalanced woman to be in possession of a cache of firearms?

Staring out my bedroom window at the winter-green bulk of Montalampi, I made one intelligent deduction: Vannina had not bought those guns herself. She didn't have any money. Someone else had stashed them in her house. Turi Laganà was a good candidate, sure, but it might have been any of her customers. Who might easily include every fella in town.

What was my responsibility at this point? The local traffic cop, Vadalà, was hardly an agent of law and justice, as I'd learned from his attempts to corrupt *me*. If I reported the stash to the *carabinieri* in Bova, Vannina would get in trouble—she might go to jail. There was no guarantee the person the guns belonged to would be held accountable.

Furthermore, I would have made myself persona non grata in Santa Chionia forever.

"There are always going to be difficult calls you'll have to make," Sabrina had coached me, back in the early days. "Sometimes you have to be braver than your own judgment. When you are asking the question of whether to do what you think is right, you need to imagine the damage that might be done by doing the right thing."

The overall guiding principle: if I interfere, is there an immediately obvious path for making the situation better for the majority of involved parties?

"It is painful but necessary to remember," Sabrina had told me. "Just because a situation looks very bad does not mean there is hope for improvement."

Instead of reporting to the *carabinieri,* I went to confession.

"Maestra Franca," Don Pantaleone said through the grill. "Of all the people I did not expect to see here."

I fidgeted on the hard confessional bench, which was six inches too close to the ground to be anything but a trial for someone of my height. I imagined the residual shame soaked into the booth's flimsy pine panels, the unnecessary humbling of already humble lives. I hadn't overcome my disappointment in the priest for his involvement in the case of the Sant'Agata virgin, not to mention I had new doubts about whether he'd been truthful with me about Ceciu Legato. But here I was, forced to come in supplication to him, the only authority figure in a position to help me in this hour of need.

Nothing could have brought home more poignantly the predicament of the citizens in an isolated village.

"I'm sorry to bother you here, Father," I began.

"You're not supposed to apologize to me, you're supposed to apologize to God."

"I'm not here to confess," I said defensively, and he chuckled.

"It was a joke. Don't fret, my dear, I never mistook you for a Catholic. What is it you're here to talk about?"

"You can never repeat anything I tell you here, right?"

"Come, Franca, spit it out, or there will be a long line. Confession is always busy during the Advent."

I still didn't feel good about it. But what were my choices? "I wanted advice about what you would recommend someone do if they found out . . . someone in Santa Chionia was in possession of something they shouldn't have."

"What kind of item?"

"Firearms. A lot of them."

"Who?" His voice through the screen was sharp and urgent.

I leaned close and said as softly as I could, "Vannina Favasuli."

"That poor woman. She is going to get herself killed. Franca, thank you for telling me. I will talk to her."

"Talk to her? What if—what if she's in trouble?"

"She's always in trouble. She's probably hiding contraband for some mountain hooligans. It's the problem with a lifestyle like hers—you take money for one thing, why not take it for something else." He slid back the privacy screen, revealing a reassuring tile of clean-shaven jaw. "Don't worry. I'll make sure the pistols are disposed of safely."

"Thank you," I said. My chest was heavy with misgiving. Could a man who argued blithely for the validity of reparative marriage really be counted on to protect a woman like Vannina?

At least I wasn't the only person in Santa Chionia who knew she was stockpiling deadly weapons.

As I lurched out of the miserable booth, he called after me, "Ten Hail Marys and three Our Fathers!"

Cicca was cooking like a madwoman for Christmas, skinning chickpeas and frying sweet crescent-moon dumplings, *bufféddi*. She huffed down and up the mountain to and from the communal oven, where a line of Chionote women waited for their turn in various attitudes of resignation or conviviality.

Cicca had determined I was a liability in the kitchen, so I spent the Friday before Christmas down in the nursery. From my desk I could see Bestiano Massara sitting on his bench, his stack of yellowed literature beside him. I respected his stamina.

The other thing I saw, oh so clearly, was Officer Vadalà leading Vannina Favasuli, barefoot and stumbling, across the piazza by a rope bound around her wrists. I felt sick to my stomach as they disappeared into the *municipio*. Surely the rope hadn't been necessary—the woman wasn't a goat.

Had that been my doing?

I mean, was there any possibility that it was *not*?

I felt awful. I hated Vadalà, and I hated to have made poor pathetic

Vannina's life worse. What would the dirty cop do with the confiscated guns? Probably sell them for his own profit, I thought glumly. But if the officer was involved, at least the weapons weren't in the hands of a madwoman. At least she wouldn't hurt herself, or someone else.

I just had to hope that no one else would hurt *her* for losing them. Or find out I had been the one to spill her beans.

Sometime after four, when the sun was at its tramontane warmest, the chatter in the piazza was loud enough to distract me from my work. Men had been stopping in front of the ruined post office to talk to Bestiano Massara all day. Now there were maybe twenty people, many I recognized, more arriving as I watched. Something was happening.

I packed my notes and eased into the crowd, curious.

"Put your names on the petition!" Bestiano Massara was bellowing, then he climbed up to stand on the bench. "I'm going to start from the beginning for the new arrivals! Your mayoral election was compromised. Fortunato Stelitano won the election by a margin of eleven votes— a total of six hundred sixty-seven. Meanwhile I"—he held aloft the Italian Communist Party pamphlet—"received six hundred fifty-six. Who here is good at math?"

"One thousand three hundred twenty-three!" a man shouted. Niceforo Scordo, Vannina's black-haired son.

"One thousand three hundred twenty-three!" Massara repeated. "There are one thousand three hundred thirty-one registered voters. You are not fools! Can anyone here believe that only eight Christians in the whole of Santa Chionia abstained or wrote in other candidates?"

"There were no other candidates!" Pascali Morabito called over another cry of "Who were the other candidates?"

Bestiano Massara punched the air with his rumpled literature. "Too many Christians voted in your election!"

Young women with barrels of water on their heads had stopped to listen; old women in black wool dresses clumped at the piazza's periphery.

"Whether you want me for your mayor or not, you are entitled to an honest election. Not just entitled—you *must fight for it!* It is your obligation as citizens to fight back! Otherwise you are choosing to dismantle your own democracy! If you fail to stand up and resist now, how are you going to stop them from taking away all your rights? How will you stop Stelitano from forcing transferment *against your will* for his own profit?"

"Sign the petition!" a young man yelled.

The crowd noise expanded around me, men debating what they believed, whether they knew people who hadn't voted, whether Massara forgot to count the provincial nuns who were registered in Santa Chionia, whether the nuns *were* registered in Santa Chionia, whether Massara himself had faked ballots, otherwise he never would have gotten so close.

Now I felt even guiltier for the votes I might have earned the mayor.

I surveyed the faces around me, hoping to find someone I knew well enough to ask for their thoughts. My eye caught on the striding form of Santo Arcudi, trailed by his leering teenage sidekick, Isodiana's little brother, Nicola Legato, as they broke away from the crowd and disappeared into the *puticha*.

"Who did you vote for?" I asked Cicca at dinner—leftover boiled sweet potatoes she hadn't used for *bufféddi* filling, plus some unpreventable lentils.

"Your friend the mayor, of course!" she said, wide-eyed. "I'm a Christian."

I said casually, "Christians can vote for communists, too, can't they?"

"Sure." Cicca dropped another lump of potato onto my plate. "Actually it's possible that some Christians decided not to vote, because they couldn't decide who to vote for."

"It's possible," I agreed. "Do you know anyone like that?"

"Who, me? No, no."

51

I WISH YOU COULD EXPERIENCE THE ASPROMONTE CHRISTMAS yourself. It does not exist anymore and bears no replication. But the magical relentlessness of the celebrations—from the nine days of Novena, our predawn hazes of cooking and visiting and singing, to the twelve days of Christmas—would have silenced the doubts of the hardest-hearted northern politician asking *why would anyone bother to live there.*

. . .

Saturday, December 31, was the festival of San Silvestro, the patron saint of Santa Chionia. Cicca rustled me exultantly down the mountain after breakfast. "The saint is about to make his journey!"

I'd been to enough Italian festivals to guess the "saint" in question was the marble statue of San Silvestro that usually lived on the dais in the church. "Where is he going?"

"Home. He has been visiting the hermitage," she added anthropomorphically.

The chapel dedicated to the virgin martyr Santa Chionia was deep in the wild woods, somewhere suitably inaccessible, I supposed, to pray to a saint who had spent her last days on earth hiding in a forest. The path was already dense with celebrants, every woman but me barefoot in fulfillment of penitent vows. As we descended into ever-denser forest, the white winter sun illuminated the pine needles like bottle-green stained glass between the mullions of the thickening boughs.

The hermitage turned out to be a seven-foot grotto only ever intended for one monk to meditate in, now accommodating many dozens of nonmonks. "The chapel is very old, older than Our Lord Jesus," Cicca confided as we joined the crowd waiting their turn to salute the saint. "That's why it's so small. Christians were much smaller back then."

Just as I was feeling wistful about being an outsider among true initiates at this ancient rite, I heard my name cutting through the chilly breeze. "Maestra Franca! *Buone feste!*" It was Isodiana Legato, holding her sylph daughter Olimpia's arm. "*Kalé arghie,* Cummàri Cicca!"

"Happy holidays," I repeated, in joyful shock as Isodiana and Cicca exchanged kisses.

Cicca petted Olimpia's cheek with a toil-bloated palm. "Where are the other babies?"

"With my mother-in-law. So Olimpia and I get to see Papà escort the saint." Isodiana nodded to the holly-decked wooden litter waiting by the chapel, where it was propped on four knee-high rounds of tree trunk. "I'm glad you stayed for Christmas, *maestra,*" she said to me with a soft smile. "Aspromonte Christmas is too beautiful to miss, don't you think?"

"I do," I replied truthfully. My heart was pumping with frantic hope at her kindness.

"I read your book."

"Oh!"

"I thought it was very sad. But interesting. I'll have to give it back to you."

"Oh, don't—"

Isodiana's black eyes pulled away from me, and I smarted in the deficiency until I realized Ugo Squillaci was beside us, bowing to kiss his aunt's ruddy cheek. I hadn't seen him since I'd accused him of stealing from me. My heart pumping even harder, I watched him tip his cap to Olimpia, then lean across her to kiss her mother. It was a sterile Christmas greeting, but its very lack of fanfare was what ignited in my imagination an idea of what other, less sterile kisses Isodiana and Ugo might have exchanged.

I did battle against my own face as Ugo gave me a maddeningly neutral nod. "Maestra Franca."

"You must excuse us," Isodiana said, dipping her charming chin first at Ugo, then at me and Cicca. "We have to go find a place where we can see the saint, don't we, Olimpia?"

I watched Isodiana slide through the crowd, her little daughter a close study behind her. My heart was cramping with two different kinds of jealousy, an actual physical discomfort so acute I wanted to rub my chest to relieve it. I thought of Vannina Favasuli and her tactical chest-rubbing and restrained myself.

Ugo's mourning beard had developed an adolescently spacious curl, and he was dressed entirely in black: a black wool jacket over a black turtleneck that lay snug enough against his personal architecture to fire up my memory. A black cap held his ringlets tamely behind his ears. I suspect I don't need to write down here that I was seized by a feverish, buckling need to ascertain whether everything was over between us, but I am a completist, so I shall.

"Poor thing, you must be missing your dad," Cicca said.

"Ehh, it's all right, here we are." Ugo squinted off into the middle distance as though imagining his father's shade there, checking to see if his son was acting like a man. I easily read all this between the lines, and wondered how much of it was performative, what the *cummàris* wanted to see.

"Where's your ma? I need to talk to her," Cicca said, and, with remarkable dexterity for a seventy-year-old woman, vanished.

"She's subtle," I said.

"One of her many gifts." I felt Ugo's eyes on me, easily reading between *my* lines.

I coached myself to meet his gaze. Did he hate me for what I'd said to him?

I was almost mindless with longing.

What was I going to do with myself?

The saint chose that moment to begin his journey, and his litter was borne aloft by six men sporting embroidered bands around their left biceps. Leading the procession, the prow of San Silvestro's litter balanced heavily on his right shoulder, was a man wearing a wooden crown— Santo Arcudi, his thinning hairline obscured by his imperial headgear.

Ugo, who was standing at my right shoulder, murmured, "This is what's going to happen. They're going to march the float across the mountain. The band is going to play. Everyone will follow all the way to the church bonfire and they'll roast a bunch of goats. There will be music and dancing until midnight, and fireworks."

"How lovely!"

"You feel like you need to see it, now that you've heard about it?"

I turned to look at him, unsure what he meant. "It sounds really special."

"It's just a *festa*. I can show you something much more special."

And in front of the entire town, while anyone or no one might have been paying attention, he grabbed my hand and pulled me into the woods.

We had several hours' climb to get to Ugo's "special something," and the trail was not for beginners. "Walking this path is a better observance of San Silvestro than a *festa*," Ugo told me. "The saint spent much time in the Aspromonte. It was here that he cured Emperor Constantine of leprosy by pouring holy water on him."

"You don't really believe that."

Ugo gave me a vaudeville shrug. "What's so bad about a little faith?"

"You warned me to have faith in no one!" My words brought back the gravity of my accusation on the first night of the Novena, and my dishonor at having made it. I bit the bullet before I could lose my nerve. "I had no faith in you. I don't know"—I had to clear my throat—"how you can forgive me."

Ugo stopped climbing to face me. "There is nothing to forgive." The facetiousness was gone. "You can have faith in me, Francesca. No matter what."

The intensity of his words—their simple seriousness—was too much. They were the same words an innocent country boy might use to pledge his lifelong love, or that a smooth-talking cat might use to subdue his conquest du jour. Which one was Ugo? Why couldn't I tell? Maybe because it didn't matter, and I would have taken the bait either way.

The mountain trail became steeper, and I felt the warm weight of his unspoken promises swaddling me like a quilt, or a straitjacket. When had I ever so badly wanted something right within my reach?

One other time. Although Sandro had made me fight for him.

I knew better than to fall for the mirage of straightforward love. I knew better than to let down my guard.

But what was I going to do? Say no?

The cave was barely discernible from below, just big enough for a monk to sit at the lip and meditate on the series of waterfalls. The pool beneath us, glinting teal and magenta like a kitchen window prism, was glass-still despite the rampage of water at its north end. Glowing gold rock monsters piled depthlessly under its transparency. At its south end, the water plummeted in white ruffles into another deadly clear pool, which in turn plummeted into another. My heartbeat bulged in my throat, choking me with vertigo, awe, expectation.

Ugo came to stand behind me to survey this rock-water bowl of feral magic. He was so close that my left shoulder throbbed with received body heat. "That's the Amendolea cataract. The source of the *fiumara*." His voice in my ear was softer than the shimmering pine needles, humble and insidious as the indiscernible footprints of the spiders I had to believe were scaling these secret walls. "This is the life of our civilization, this cataract. Her fast-moving waters brought fertility to our soil. She was the reason our ancestors stopped here, so deep in the mountains, thousands of years ago."

I fought through my concupiscent fog to try to find some undistracted, intellectual response. "She? You sound like a pagan speaking of his goddess."

"We are all pagans here, Francesca. Pagans and Christians at once. Our goddess predates our god." His breath on my bare neck eased under my collar and trickled its sympathetic suggestions down my spine. "Any real Chionoto man will tell you proudly that he subjects himself to the goddess. Only the weak ones pretend we are not a matriarchy."

I felt him move away from me, though his feet made no sound. My heart prototypically pounding, I stepped into the metallic darkness, the winter-sharp air sifting through the wool fibers of my coat and rustling the blood in my capillaries.

Past the entrance, the cave was deceptively spacious. "If I had a torch you could see there's Armenian writing on the walls." He pointed to the rock above us, as if I had any means of ascertaining that he wasn't just inventing. "It's been there a thousand years."

"Armenian?!"

"Sure. A lot of Basilian monks were Armenian. And back here . . ." I followed him into a connecting chamber, one so dim I could see almost nothing. "During the war, when the Americans were bombing, people hid up here. My family lived in this cave for a week."

"It wasn't just Americans," I said defensively.

I watched his shadow remove his jacket and spread it on the cave floor. Then his shadow was part of me, and his hot palm was lying on my breastbone, the pad of his thumb sliding the button at my collar through its eye slit with hair-raising aptitude. "When the sun gets a bit higher, you'll be able to appreciate the runes."

"I hope it doesn't get *too* light in here," I said.

"Don't worry."

52

OBVIOUSLY UGO SQUILLACI WASN'T THE ONLY CHIONOTO TO GO necking in the Basilian grottos. Just everyone else was probably a teenager.

For example, two teenagers who were definitely on their way to do just that caught us, giddy and suffused with fast-moving blood, as we were coming down the path later.

I stumbled into Ugo's back and froze like a deer in the azaleas. Ugo, gallant as ever—where the hell did he come from?—braced me with his left arm and tapped his nose with his right index finger. *"Buone feste."*

"Buone feste," the black-haired boy said. It was Niceforo Scordo, following his mother's example, it seemed, in premarital romantic excursions in semipublic places. He touched his own nose, and the couple passed us by.

The black-haired girl met my eye for half a second—she looked terrified—before turning her face to the ground.

My heart was pounding with adrenaline, but the resemblance was enough to distract me. "Is that his fiancée?" I whispered to Ugo.

"Yes. Agathi Petrulli."

"They looked like brother and sister!"

"You're not the first person to say so." Ugo extended a warm, thick hand and helped me down an awkward rock. "Funny how that happens, isn't it."

We walked back to Santa Chionia through a tunnel of trees I would never have found my way out of alone. Ugo clamped his hand around mine like a mitten, and I could feel my heartbeat in my palm. Blood rushed up and down my limbs, rendering my extremities clumsy. I had no clue what I was doing but I wanted to do it more.

"I have to tell you something," I told Ugo as the sun glowed milk-bright through the pine needles. "I'm married."

"Married?" he repeated. Then, while I was still clawing around for the right words, he said, "Not annulled?"

Cicca had already spoken with him about me—the word "annulled" could only have come from her.

"Not exactly," I said. "I mean—no, not annulled. We've been separated for years, but . . ."

Ugo didn't say anything as he led me through the trees.

"Are you angry?"

"Angry? Me? No. I just think it's interesting that you didn't mention it before, that you were married." His mourning beard was thick enough to disguise any hint of facial expression. Was he offended, or teasing me?

I took a chance. "It didn't seem like it mattered to you at the time."

"What makes you think it matters to me now?"

Ugo's forest path took us to via Occhiali, where he released my hand and nodded wordlessly to the left. I stepped out alone, feeling like a fallen woman. The cool damp of the forest air had settled in my lonely skin, peeled away the warm gauze of satisfaction, and stripped me down to my windblown nerves.

Making my self-conscious way south to the church piazza, I wished there had been some other conclusion to our rendezvous, a Hollywood-style cheek stroke or some other masculine expression of tenderness—anything to make me a little less convinced, suddenly, that I wasn't a total fool. He was a beautiful man; he could sleep with anyone he wanted. Why would he pick me, except because he'd savvily identified a path of least resistance—a liberated, unvirginal American college girl—and fewest repercussions? He had made me no promises, because he hadn't needed to.

But why—*let us interrogate this, Francesca*—should I care?

The procession was only just arriving at the upper piazza. I stumbled past barefoot black-clad women making the pilgrimage on their hands and knees, their meditative progress suspended periodically so they could kiss or lick the ground. Most of them were Cicca's age. Their backs were bent from buckling against the weight of their fetuses and from hauling water barrels up a vertical mile for six or seven decades. Through their resilience and creativity, they had survived the cruelty of the twentieth century. What stories each must have to tell—how brave, how crafty, how stoic each must have been to live to get down on her hands and knees here today. What were they privately atoning for?

The statue of dead Pope Sylvester was standing on his bedecked float in front of the church, where he loomed over the mossy nativity (now complete with a heathery baby Jesus). I found Cicca chatting with evil Mela and black-clad Tuzza. When I slunk up to their group, too twitterpated to panic successfully about how to excuse my absence, Cicca, the *strega,* said archly, "What, you didn't find the preserved eggplant?"

"I—"

"Ai, Mother Mary, protect me!" Cicca scowled commiseratingly at Mela. "I'll get it myself when we go home."

"Are we going home now?" I asked, ever stupid.

"Not now!" Mela chirped. "Shh!"

"Do you see?" Cicca pointed to the emaciated woman prostrating herself before the saint's litter, a black lace shawl shrouding her flax-ball of white hair. "Donna Adelina. Don Roccuzzu Alvaro's widow."

I would not have recognized her as the woman I'd seen at the Alvaro house if Cicca hadn't pointed her out. She was obscure in black except for her leather-brown feet, no features worth remembering on her expressionless face.

"A very religious lady," Tuzza remarked. "She does the whole pilgrimage on her knees."

"There's nothing she wouldn't do to protect her family," evil Mela said darkly. I caught her eye as she was crossing herself and she gave me a remorseful grimace.

"God forgive her," Tuzza and Cicca murmured in resigned unison.

A chill traveled up my back. I might have puzzled over the fervor of the other penitents, but I could easily believe Donna Adelina had atonement to seek. All that was left to my imagination was what specific role this woman had played in her husband's business empire. Maybe turning a blind eye and praying for Don Roccuzzu's soul from the comforts of her palace on the hill. Or maybe much more—knowing what I did of Philly gangsters' wives, I might guess her duties included moving dirty money under her veneer of godly respectability, brokering political marriages for her daughters, ruthlessly rearing her children to put their dad's prosperity above all other concerns, and embroidering their opportunism with a Christian-sounding axiom: *Family before everything.*

Every functional partnership has a unique division of labor.

"A very fine lady," Cicca concluded. "Look at all that lace." There was no admiration in her voice.

By some signal I missed, the crowd fell into quivering silence. Among the thousand faces I spotted the mayor and his wife, not far from the communist and his. Don Pantaleone, stalwart arms crossed, stood under the pigeons spectating from the church eaves.

The cry began at the south end of the piazza, a man's voice, starting deep and rising, rising in a most feminine of ululations, like the formal keening of a widow at her husband's vigil. "O—!"

The wind, for once, was respectful, and the cry rang across the mountainside.

"O—!"

The crowd sank back, and there was the singer, Don Tito the Wolf, alone in the bared piazza. He raised his arms above his head, and then, after a heartbeat of breathless suspense, brought them down violently, clawing at his hair like a professional mourner.

"O—!"

The agony of the cry made my pulse pump. I had never imagined I would see the proud, subtle Don Tito in such a melodramatic spectacle.

When the fourth cry went up, Don Tito was not alone—a chorus of voices, all male, rose from the crowd. "O—! *Chrono!*"

Nine men now formed a ring in the piazza, all of them graying, tearing at their hair or clothes—the most theatrical display of grief I'd ever seen in my life, and I have attended many Italian funerals. The only singer I recognized besides Tito was Turi Laganà.

O chrono epèthane asce nicta!

Their eerie harmony rumbled through the piazza, an unaccompanied dirge. In the circle around us women wept silently. I gave myself over to the ghostly song, feeling the men's voices reverberating in the stones under my feet, trembling in the chilling marrow of my bones. I fought to catch any Greco words that might be a clue as to whom we were mourning.

Ce àfike tèssere miszìthre!

The only one I understood was . . .

"Cicca," I bent down to whisper, "are they singing about . . . cheese?"

"Shh!"

Dio alatimène, dio anàlatese
jà tu ppòveru carceràtu!

I listened as the last notes died away into the stillness of the evening. I
felt the tension coursing through the women on either side of me, the
winter air thick and twitching with repressed emotion. Then a tall black-
clad man stepped forward to join the ring of singers. It was Santo Arcudi,
denuded of his pageant crown. His voice shocked me as it cut across the
mountain: "O—!"

At this signal the perimeter of the crowd loosened, the older men fad-
ing into the spectators and eight younger men stepping forward. "O—!"
they cried in return, and they grabbed in anguish at their hair, their faces.
"O—!" It was the same haunting harmony, but then they began to sing in
Calabrese, and this time I understood all the words:

The year dies at midnight
Bring forth the four cheeses
Two fresh, two salted
For the poor incarcerated

It took me the duration of the song to realize I recognized several of
this younger generation: toothy Rocco Alvaro, the late Don Roccuzzu's
bratty heir; Nicola Legato, Isodiana's horrible teenage brother. I watched
as four boys filed into the piazza, each bearing a molded ricotta, and laid
the offerings at the feet of San Silvestro.

"What incarcerated?" I dared to ask Cicca.

"Shh!" she said, then, "Our boys down in the Bova jail. We can't forget their sacrifice."

"Sacrifice?" I considered the implications. "How many boys are in
jail? For what?"

"Oh, this and that," evil Mela answered, revealing my indiscretion.
"Nothing serious. All the shepherds end up in jail at some point."

"*Ciao*, Mamma. Aunt Cicca. Aunt Mela. *Maestra*."

The *stregas* and I all turned, and there was Ugo, golden and brown
in the setting sun, so nonchalant that it occurred to me *he* might be a
gangster.

"*Ciao,* Ugo," I said carelessly. He was here, and not any of the other places he might have gone now that his lust had been satisfied. I wondered how I could arrange to satisfy it again.

That was when the tarantella began, and we watched until night had descended, the full moon gloating on the slope of Montalampi. The tarantella in the Aspromonte is not a dance, it is a duel between men, each of its rounds a performance of strength arbitrated by the dance master. In Santa Chionia, this was the *puticha* proprietor Saverio Legato, who wore a cape and wielded a wicked-looking carved swagger stick to oust the defeated and usher in the next contender.

"You don't dance?" I teased Ugo.

"Not me."

I didn't really care to see him dance the tarantella, not as much as I wished I could dance cheek to cheek with him to some Billie Holiday in a dimly lit club. Our respective native concepts of "dancing," I realized, were each completely culturally inappropriate to the other. We were the proverbial fish and bird, situationally impossible partners.

As we stood shoulder to shoulder watching, I imagined I could catch the secret smell of his skin, dry as cotton and twinkling like pepper. I asked, "Have you ever gone to jail?"

"Of course not."

The fireworks began at eleven thirty p.m. and lasted until the tolling of the church bell at midnight, when we would all head to Cicca's for dinner: goat meatballs in tomato sauce, pasta, cured eggplant, and—you guessed it—lentils. Ugo, his brother Mimmo, Tuzza, Cicca, and I watched as sparks showered down from the Saracen Tower.

"That's a lot of fireworks," I commented at what turned out to be only the halfway point.

"Wait until the *festa* of Santa Chionia in April," Cicca said.

The schoolmarm in me couldn't help but say, "With no fire department or running water up here it seems like fireworks are pretty dangerous."

"Huhn," Cicca said. No one else responded as we watched a blue boom bloom across the moon.

"What do you do if something goes wrong with the fireworks?"

"Pray," Cicca said, and Ugo said, "Run."

53

APPARENTLY OTHER PEOPLE WENT TO MASS ON JANUARY 1 FOR the Solemnity of Mary, but obviously I lay in bed all day. I relished the fiery churning in my gut and wrote coded messages to myself in my journal. Looking back, I've always wondered about that—why I was so shy about putting my thoughts and deeds into words no one else would ever see. We used to be more circumspect back then, it's true. It felt like a disaster if people knew things about you. I lived through this shift in the American character; I watched my own character shift in reflection. Now I am only annoyed at myself for being afraid to say what might have made a difference at the time.

I did go to church on January 2, though—to reconcile myself with Don Pantaleone.

"Teodoro is here!" he said, cheerful as a child, as he let me into the rectory.

There, indeed, the chubby doctor was sitting by the space heater with a book open on his lap. He lurched up and gave me two ticklish kisses.

"Franca! I get to see you before I head back to Rome!"

Emilia Volontà, silent and fawning, served us parsley-fragrant chickling vetch soup.

"*Cheràmine, gnura,*" I said when she put a bowl in front of me. "No news from Utah yet," I whispered. She nodded in acknowledgment, then hid herself in the kitchen.

The doctor spoke of his upcoming cardiology seminar, and the priest of his diploma candidates who would be graduating in a few months. Don Pantaleone put some pressure on Dottor Iiriti to help him suss out university opportunities for them; I could tell it was not the first time they'd had some version of this conversation.

When I dared get a word in edgewise, I asked Don Pantaleone, "By the way, what happened to Vannina Favasuli?"

"Vannina?" I had the doctor's attention. "What do you mean, what happened to her?"

"I saw Officer Vadalà . . . uh, escorting her to the *municipio* before Christmas, and I haven't seen her since."

"Vannina was unfortunately bragging about hiding some firearms for a *friend* of hers," the priest explained. "Vadalà had to pretend to raid her house and lock her up for her own safety."

This sounded like good news. Maybe I had done the right thing after all. "She's—she's out now? She's safe?"

"She'll be fine," the priest said, turning his warm eyes on me.

Teodoro Iiriti blew his mustache. "That poor woman. If it's not one thing with her, it's another."

"What about—the friend? Vannina's not—in danger from him?"

"The man—a lowlife from Sant'Agata—the *carabinieri* had already caught him for trying to arrange a sale."

I moved my beans around with my spoon, then decided to go ahead and ask, "Do you have problems like this a lot?"

"Problems like what?" the doctor and the priest said in unison, from either side of the table, wearing nearly matching expressions of perplexed consternation.

I looked from one man to the other—these classy, polished men, educated, pillars of their professions. They weren't the products of a culture of mountain brigandage.

Except they were, was the thing.

The charade emboldened me. "Mafia." I said it, I said the word. "Organized crime."

There was a shocked silence, and then both men broke into laughter. I felt silly sitting there watching them laugh—I felt an almost uncontrollable urge to join them and obligingly lessen the tension. I made myself fight it.

"My dear, you have been reading all the propaganda," Dottor Iiriti said eventually. "I thought you would know better." He stretched his arms as if to take in the whole of the *paese*. "How could this place have mafia? What would they traffic? Goats? Ricotta cheese? To whom? Peasants with no money for shoes?"

I turned to Don Pantaleone. "But you told me yourself the Chionoti do not cooperate with law enforcement. What's to stop a syndicate from taking advantage of that and seizing control of the whole village?" I met his intimidating gaze. "Like what happened in Sant'Agata with the . . . the kidnapping mayor."

"No, no, no," the priest was saying, and the doctor spoke over him. "What happened in Sant'Agata *proves* this point. A stupid man was elected mayor and he thought he could make his own rules. A smarter man would have known the crime wasn't feasible."

"Well, the mayor of Sant'Agata was elected by the people, so he had *some* power over them," I started.

"Sometimes people elect stupid leaders," the doctor admitted. "That is a problem."

"But the mafia—no, the mafia is not a problem," Don Pantaleone said.

Dottor Iiriti slapped the table with his palm. "Absolutely not."

"Look," Don Pantaleone said, leaning his forearms on the table and clasping his hands, as if he was about to confide something. "Santa Chionia once had a problem with these kinds of . . . rough men. A *long* time ago. When was the pig problem, Teo?"

"Eighteen ninety-three," the doctor said.

"Eighteen ninety-three. So there you go, seventy years ago, no one is alive who even remembers it."

"What happened?"

"It was an ugly thing."

"Ugly," Dottor Iiriti agreed.

"There were some delinquents stealing the village animals and taking them over the mountains to sell in the markets at the big towns, Melito and Oppido and Bruzzano." The priest rubbed at his cheek. "Everyone had their pig stolen. But this is the problem with delinquents, they are idiots. You cannot steal every animal in the *paese,* or the victims will stop participating. The *paesani* stopped raising animals, and there was nothing left to steal, and the knuckleheads killed their own industry. So we had no sausage for a few years, but then the problem went away."

"There's no quick money around here, because there's no money," the doctor said, shaking his cupped fingers at me in that most Italian of gestures. "What is the point of crime when Christians have nothing? Idiots."

I wondered if he believed himself.

"This is the truth," the priest declared, "which I will tell you from my thirty years' experience hearing the darkest of man's deeds in the confessional. Crime is the product of stupid, lazy people thinking there is a shortcut to a comfortable life."

I wasn't in the mood to let him off the hook today. Maybe, after our fight, I never would be again. "What about your *noble brigand history*? What about your mythologies about the gentleman outlaw who stood up to the Bourbon imperialists and who outsmarts the evil Italian state? You're not going to try to tell me that there's no romantic cult built up around gangster culture."

"Absolutely not."

"For crying out loud, the children are playing a game of Brigand King Musolino right outside your door!"

"*Maestra,* listen to yourself." Don Pantaleone chuckled softly. "Children also play Queen of Fairyland, and that is just as relevant to our reality."

How dry his voice was. I heard Ugo's words in my head: *A completely dry response*—that was the only way to protect yourself.

Don Pantaleone locked me in his thoughtful brown gaze. "Listen, *maestra*. We are civilized people here, despite everything we have been through. We all have the same resentment against the state—"

"More or less," the doctor interjected.

"More or less. But resentment is no incentive to embark upon a life of crime for any reasonable person. Anyone in Santa Chionia would tell you that. We can protest the system, as we have for a thousand years, anarchists and antifeudalists that we are. But only stupid people become delinquents."

I thought of Donna Adelina and her black lace, of her dead husband's mahogany desk and the elegant extortion letters written by his missing secretary, Ceciu Legato—the future mayor. "Only stupid people get *caught*," I muttered, with some Aspromonte rebelliousness of my own. "The criminal masterminds make sure there are plenty of stupid people to get caught."

"Oh, my dear," Don Pantaleone said. "Now *you* are the one indulging in romantic fantasy. If there is one thing thirty years in the cassock have taught me, it is that there is no such thing as a criminal mastermind."

We were interrupted by a second course, a roast chicken—the first cooked chicken I had seen in Santa Chionia. A special feast for the doctor. As Emilia Volontà laid the plates, I remembered my conversation with Potenziana the Lichena—I had told the woman I was looking for Leo, which Emilia had explicitly asked me not to share. My appetite was soaked up by remorse.

Dottor Iiriti cut the lunch short, because he had house calls to make before his long walk back to Roccaforte to pick up his car. "Listen, Franca," the doctor said as he kissed me goodbye, "when the bridge is back up you must go to Bova and visit my poor wife. She can't join me in Rome until March because she's helping her niece with a newborn."

"I will," I promised.

"You *must*!"

"I *will*!"

"Bova is just exquisite," the doctor said. "What a city! One of a kind. There's nothing more beautiful."

"Well, there *is* Santa Chionia, doctor," I said, smiling through my unsettled thoughts. "I can't imagine anything more exquisite than right here."

The priest nodded with great solemnity. "The *maestra* makes a fair point."

54

AS I WALKED HOME THAT NIGHT, I SHAMELESSLY CONSIDERED whether I could drift down via Erodoto and see if I bumped into Ugo—of course I couldn't; you had to be way cleverer in a village. But then I stepped into Cicca's kitchen and found him sitting there having a glass of wine as she scutched hemp.

"*Kalispèra.*" Ugo's sap-lit golden-brown eyes were especially stupefactive tonight.

"Sit," Cicca said, because I had stopped short in the doorway.

Ugo was here to visit—a chaperoned, proper visit. It was—it was like courting.

For an hour, Cicca sawed away at her hemp bundles and asked Ugo alternating nagging and boastful questions—torn as she was between tricking him into moving home to Santa Chionia and tricking me into marrying him by painting his life in the most glittering possible light. His voice only just carried over the squeal and clump of the machine.

I did not talk much—I couldn't find words. It was that cleaving kind of moment in the early days of a liaison where you want to spend every hour with a person, where every hour apart is a trial. If this were New

York, or Oxford, or Venice, I would have just taken him home. But that wasn't what happened in a village.

Did I love Santa Chionia enough to hitch my cart up to a recovering shepherd's and commit to this place, in some capacity, for the rest of my life?

I wasn't looking for *another* husband. I hadn't even figured out what I wanted to do with the husband I had.

I remembered—could not stop myself from remembering—a conversation I had had with Sandro two and a half years earlier, in July 1958. I was almost seven months pregnant; we were lying in the airy heat of our Trastevere loft, Sandro's shaggy head bearing into my breastbone, me half-twisted to the side so my lost little girl kicked liquidly against the pillow pressing into her bowl. I was at the moment in my pregnancy when I most took her for granted, complacently admiring the force of her little limbs. It is this detail, the feeling of her tiny knee, that makes this memory stick in my craw as it does, I think, not what Sandro said.

"Will you talk to me about what you remember from our early days together?" I had asked him. The pink light of smoky midmorning blotted the window. Seconds dragged by as I stroked his forehead and he didn't answer; I could tell he was annoyed by the question. I battled on. "I'm asking because I was going through my diaries yesterday and I realized I didn't keep any kind of journal that fall. I hate the idea that I might forget how it went."

"I remember your moldy room on that tiny canal. I remember our orange tree." He meant the one the neighbor on the other side of the *calle* had kept on her balcony, just out of arm's reach of my bedroom.

"I mean specific memories. Things we did, or conversations." I didn't tell him I'd been trying to remind myself what it had felt like to fall in love with him—that I needed help in willfully turning a blind eye on the wreckage of the last six months. We had not fought in several days, and I was hopefully reworking my narrative about us. "Things like—I remember the toast you fixed the morning after I first stayed over at your apartment. You didn't have any jam but you crushed tomatoes and sprinkled salt—do you recall?"

Sandro had chuckled, pleased with himself. After a trembling silence, he said, "I remember that night after the student union. When we went to Harry's."

"Harry's!" It was funny to think about either of us ever patronizing such a tourist trap. We hadn't known each other then, hadn't known our mutual proclivities.

"I remember the whole group, Carlo and Nelia and the rest of them, crammed in that little booth," Sandro was saying. "And there was . . . this sense of inevitability."

I remember the pain in my chest as I tried to sound amused. "What a romantic you are. I'm asking you about falling in love and you don't talk about attraction or desire or even curiosity. You talk about inevitability!"

"That *is* romantic," he returned, because Sandro would always return. "I'm saying I knew right then something was going to happen between us."

"So I was something you let happen to you."

"Something I let happen for the rest of my life."

I remembered hearing the smile in his voice. He was purblind to how fatally disappointing his answer was. Could he have saved us if he'd just named one thing, just one single thing, he admired about me, or *had* admired about me at one time? Offered me one happy memory as a toll to walk through the open gate of my sore heart?

But he could never bear to give me something I asked for so specifically. He couldn't help himself; even when doing so hurt him, he had to take every opportunity to remind me of my place.

As I sat at Cicca's dinner table two and a half years later, half listening to her and Ugo argue about whether there was real risk of transferment, I sympathized with Sandro's perspective for the first time. The idea of two people being so suited that they were inevitable together—it was an unlovely turn of phrase, but not an uncompelling one.

There was nothing inevitable about Ugo. He was the opposite of inevitable: he was impossible. We were the poorest of fits. Our romantic résumés aligned in no relevant points: not background or breeding, not mother tongues or dispositions, not circles of exposure or experience. I was graceless and he was artless. I had none of the charms valued in a southern Italian wife—I couldn't cook or clean; my one attempt at childbearing had gone ruinously awry. I had instead spent my energies in the world's most selective institutions refining my knowledge of histories, foreign languages, social philosophy. Ugo had never set foot inside a classroom. We would do nothing but be ashamed of each other in our respective sets.

Ugo stayed and chatted until and then through dinner. Then we played *briscola,* Cicca sharkishly swiping hand after hand. Eventually he got up and said good night.

Back home even a bad date would have ended with a kiss on the cheek.

"He's a very nice boy," Cicca scolded me when Ugo left.

"Is he? Are you sure?" I could see she was ratcheting up to explode. "He hasn't settled down, even though he's thirty."

"He could get whatever he wanted," Cicca said stuffily. "But he doesn't. Because he's a nice boy."

I was aware of at least one recent occasion when he'd gotten what I assumed Cicca assumed he wanted.

"You know, one time a teacher from Sicily came to Casalinuovo," Cicca said. "She fell in love with a Casalinuovo man and they got married and then she just stayed instead of going back to Sicily."

"So you're saying only once in the history of time did someone come to the Aspromonte from some other place and marry a local?"

"I'm saying if it happened once there's no reason it can't happen again!"

"Cicca," I asked, because why not, "was Ugo ever engaged to Isodiana Legato?"

"Of course not! He's never been engaged to anyone."

"Really? At his age? How is that even possible?"

Cicca wrinkled her nose and rubbed her spikes vigorously with her right palm. I was testing her loyalty. "Maybe he was in love with Isodiana a long time ago, but her marriage was already arranged when she was young."

I let this thought turn over, mucked through the jealousy.

Of course Ugo had been in love with Isodiana. She was teeming with feminine perfection. I was sick thinking of her, of the sloping cinch of her waist, of the runcible shiver of her breasts under her incitingly high-necked dresses, of the furtive innocence in her evasive black eyes. I felt ashamed that I had offered myself up to him for comparison, my galumphing Scandinavian breadth, my unpinnable hair of unnameable color, the lumping inadequacies of my warped husk.

And how could Isodiana not have returned Ugo's affection? Each was the Aspromonte platonic ideal of their sex. They would have spent their childhoods playing together, their puberties noticing each other. Every Chionese must have at some point considered what a handsome couple they would have made.

Instead of strapping, glistening Ugo Squillaci, though, Isodiana had been betrothed to Santo Arcudi, twice her age and, from my limited experience, not particularly nice.

"You don't think Ugo has been hung up on Isodiana all this time?"

"Ugo, how could it be? No way." Cicca pushed herself up from the table and took down her bottle of anisette. "Here, we have to drink more in the winter to keep warm."

There was no update from Child Rescue in the mail Oddo the postman brought on Wednesday, January 4. Instead, there was a completely different kind of soul-crusher. In an innocent-looking envelope from Sabrina was a letter Sandro had sent me care of her.

The letter was dated December 10, postmarked from Lonato del Garda.

> Dearest Francesca,
>
> Your letter is the most magnificent Christmas gift. You have tested me by leaving no return address but I will prevail upon Sabrina, who has always had a soft spot for me.
>
> I think of you every day. Write again and tell me where you are, and I will come to you. I have so many things to tell you, and I want to hear all your things.
>
> My father and sister wish you happy holidays, with much love.
>
> Sandro

I was all but hyperventilating, gulping back joy and fury. With only a few words he could still upend me.

We had been apart now almost as long as we had been together. How long was "moving on" supposed to take?

What if it never happened for me?

I did not sleep that night. My corrupted carcass was lousy with guilt.

Why had I sent that damn letter? I had ruined everything. As long as Sandro had no way of being in touch, I could pretend we had never been. Maybe someday our marriage would have faded away entirely. I never had a very clear idea what that would look like from a legal perspective— neither of us would ever be able to remarry in a church, which meant nothing to me, but he desperately wanted a family. I had too, once, for one heartbeat of my life. I'd wanted a family with him.

I had been the one who couldn't hack our marriage, who had walked away when the going got tough. I was the one who had abandoned my husband during our mutual grief. He was still sticking by his vows, despite everything I'd said to him, all the bridges I'd tried to burn.

55

MAYBE IT WAS BECAUSE I WAS SLEEP-DEPRIVED ON THURSDAY that it seemed like a good idea to stop by Isodiana Legato's house to pick up my book. I'd vowed I'd do everything in my admittedly feeble powers to stop myself from fishing for information about Ugo Squillaci. This vow was never tested because Isodiana answered her door with a crying baby and a blood-laced black eye. "Maestra Franca. Oh, your book. Let me go get it."

"Isodiana! What happened?"

"Just—Santo. You know." Her neck looked especially fragile in its tall collar. The pregnancy bulge in her silhouette was too present to ignore. "It's not as bad as it looks."

"Your husband did that?" I said before I could think better of it. "Isodiana!"

"It's not that bad," she said again, jouncing the shrilling, raisin-faced Nino on her elbow. She flopped him over her shoulder like a carpet sales-man would have a rolled-up area rug and he immediately stopped crying. "He was drinking at the *festa*," she said in a much lower voice. "You know how they get." She had moved back and was easing the door closed. "Listen, I have to—"

I shoved my shoe into the gap. "Is he here?" I whispered.

She pressed her lips together, then finally nodded. The busted capillaries in her right eye had turned even pinker—she was on the verge of tears.

I had to leave. "Isodiana. Please come to me if you ever need anything, okay? Anything. I will find a way to help you. No one has to know."

"The book's just up in the salon," she said with loud, fake cheer. "Wait here."

I nodded—it was the best either of us could do—and stepped back so she could shut the door. I heard her bolt the door from the inside. In the past I would have thought that was overkill. Finally I was beginning to understand.

When the door opened again, it was too-skinny Olimpia, who handed me the Bonanni novel. She looked up at me with her thin little face and said in a thin little voice, "Please don't come here anymore, *maestra*. You get my mamma in trouble every time."

Morning solitude thickened the air as I wobbled down via Odisseo. A moment earlier, my blood spiking with adrenaline, I had been ready to go to war against Santo Arcudi, to bundle Isodiana up in my Viking arms and haul her off to safety. Now the momentum had dissipated, leaving me in a daze of misgivings.

My psyche was still tender from Sandro's letter. I couldn't help but wonder at the dramatic irony of our respective fortunes: Isodiana—the embodiment of feminine perfection—locked obediently in an arranged marriage to a middle-aged man who physically abused her; me, Pandora's sloshing box of second-sex shortcomings, with a handsome, well-bred, and devoted husband I'd never felt I deserved in the first place and whom I'd abandoned the moment the going got rough. Isodiana had followed all the rules, even the ones she must have dreaded. And this was her reward? A prisoner in her own house, helplessly offering up her body to her violent husband's bad moods, her chain of pregnancies binding her ever tighter into his thrall?

At the west end of the piazza, children had already started to gather around their long-suffering rag ball for their morning exertions. I stood in a cold shadow watching them, soot-blackened bare feet flickering across the January pavers like tawny butterflies. How many of them had fathers who beat their mothers? How was it possible for such violence to exist in a place like this, where future spouses played around the same hearth fires, where cousins were friends and everyone's aunt kept an eye on everyone's son?

The mountain morning was dry and humming with the chirring of insects, and Santa Chionia was the most peaceful place I had ever been.

I wondered at my own naivete.

Only a year earlier, when I'd been living with Sabrina in Cosenza, a woman named Elda Cacciola had come into the baby clinic for powdered milk. It was a difficult time because the Crati River had flooded in November, damaging huge stretches of the ancient city. Elda's man was out of work and going crazy stuck at home. Apparently he'd convinced himself that Elda was having an affair.

I can't honestly claim I got to know her very well in the two months between the day I met her and the day she was murdered. But her death affected me profoundly. She was warm and funny; she told me a joke about a squirrel and a rabbit I have repeated hundreds of times to other women's children since.

What most binds Elda to my memory is the cliché but unshakable idea that if I had done something differently she might still be alive. I knew things were not happy at home. The second-to-last time I saw her, there was a banana-yellow contusion on her face, a bloody scab standing at the peak of her cheek. "That asshole, hope he hurt his hand," she'd told me with dismissive irony.

"There is nothing we *can* do, Francesca," Sabrina had told me. The law allowed a husband to "discipline" a wife as he saw fit; for Child Rescue to interfere in the private aspects of a marriage was forbidden in our code of conduct, and bad judgment, besides, as it would likely only cause trouble for the victim and drive her out of reach of our influence. All of this was true, and I knew it—but would it still have been true if we had known the case would end in Elda's death?

In relief work, you have two choices: you either accept that you will make mistakes that cause harm, or you remove yourself entirely from the work and accept that it may never be done. You put a price on the damage you will do with your good intentions, and you weigh that against the human cost to the people you are trying to help if no one ever dares to go in and risk making mistakes. It is why activists live shorter lives.

If I could go back, would I make different choices? Bet your bottom dollar.

Was this my chance to do better? Or to get everything fatally wrong again?

As the children in the piazza shrieked by me, the shutters directly above me creaked open and a woman I didn't recognize popped her head out to appraise me. Numbly I moved away from the cold wall, displacing the mustard-gold cat that had settled by my feet.

What was I supposed to do about Isodiana Legato?

Santa Chionia was so isolated it would make it all the more difficult to get her help, if she wanted it, but it was that very isolation that might make that help all the more necessary. What the hell were my choices?

I had to tell Sabrina, was my first thought. I couldn't do anything without her advice. I hurried down the length of the piazza and into the *municipio*.

Pino Pangallo regarded me with chilly reserve. "No phone," he said before I could even ask. "You'll have to try Roghudi."

Right. That had worked out so well last time.

My despair was welling in my throat, so I left without bidding him goodbye.

56

I WAS SITTING AT MY DESK TRYING TO DECIDE WHAT TO DO ABOUT Isodiana Legato when Don Pantaleone Bianco breezed in. "Maestra Franca. Have you heard back about the funding?"

"Funding?" I honestly did not know what the priest was referring to.

"Your organization was going to send funding for the new science course."

"Oh. Right." My mind was dull with worry, and I should have taken more time to choose my words. "I was supposed to write and see." I pinched the bridge of my nose, feeling my sinuses click. "Even if I do, Don Pandalemu, there is almost no chance they will have any surplus."

"Don't tell me that, *maestra*." The priest folded his arms.

"Don't tell you what? The truth?"

"Don't tell me that something is not going to work out when you haven't even tried."

"Well—" I felt myself flushing defensively. I hadn't tried, it was true. "I will try, Don Pandalemu, but it is a waste of both my time and yours. There are many projects clamoring for precious budget allocations and Child Rescue won't see a private upper school's science program as directly related to their core philosophy of early childhood health and hygiene."

"How they see it depends entirely on how you present it to them, *maestra*." The priest had come to stand directly in front of my desk, and I was aware of his physicality in a way I never had been before: his arboreous build, the martial unyielding in the canyon of his gaze. What was dawning on me was—what was this feeling? Intimidation? "Perhaps you should be thinking harder about what you're going to write."

In this downtrodden moment, my chest aching and my concentration scattered, I found myself quailing under his censure. "I'll see what I can do," I said, knowing I didn't want to do him any favors, already not sure if I'd be crafty enough to figure out how not to.

The priest heard the crack in my voice, because his expression shifted into concern. "Franca, what's wrong?"

I bit the inside of my lip, trying to force myself to think intelligently. I needed advice about what I should do now that I knew Isodiana Legato was being abused by her husband. If I didn't tell anyone, if the information stopped at me, then it was possible no one in the world was protecting or helping her.

"Franca. You must get whatever it is off your chest." With subdued grace he crossed the tiles and clicked the door shut. "Go on. Otherwise how can I help you."

I made myself say the words. "Isodiana Legato. I'm worried—I'm worried that her husband hurts her."

The priest's face fell. "That is truly a shame. What makes you think so?"

"I know so," I said, sturdier. "She told me."

Don Bianco studied me, disbelieving. "She *told* you?"

For Isodiana to have confessed such a thing to me would have been horrifically taboo, I realized too late. Rattled, I tried to cover. "I meant to say—I noticed the bruises."

"There might be any number of explanations."

I wasn't going to allow denialism space in the conversation. "Santo has beaten her very badly at least once that I know of, but I suspect it happens often."

"That is difficult news." The priest's bow tie lips disappeared into his beard as he pressed them together, grimacing at the window, through which I saw the communist Bestiano Massara in his old red cap waiting patiently on his bench. "I will pray for them."

That was not what I'd been hoping he'd say. "An abusive husband will never stop abusing. The situation will only escalate."

The priest nodded gravely. "Marriage is a sacramental responsibility in which men must find their own paths to godliness. But I will try to see if I can't help Santo get closer."

"With all due respect, that is not adequate." I struggled to speak evenly; I did not need him deciding I was irrationally emotional. "Santo could do any amount of damage while we give them the privacy to sort things out." I made it this far without letting my voice break, but no further. "I know women who have died in situations like this."

"You don't need to fear that kind of abuse of power here in Santa Chionia, Franca. The family net does not allow it. *Capisci tu?* This is how Santa Chionia stays safe and peaceful in a savage world. But it means the family structure is sacred above all other things." His eyes darted apologetically heavenward. "*All* things."

But Isodiana had no parents whose respect Santo needed to curry or wrath he needed to fear. Who protected her? Her tricky uncle Tito the Wolf, who sent his wife to spy and drive me away when it seemed like I was getting too close?

During Don Pantaleone's speech, I had cooled down enough to find my voice again. "If family is so sacred, how can you tolerate a man abusing it like Santo is?"

"Oh, Franca." The priest wrapped his long fingers over the chair back so I had an unavoidable view of his thick gold ring. "Here's what you need to think about right now. Interfering in Isodiana's life can cost you everything you have. You are alone here; you don't have allies." He leaned forward to force me to look him in the eye. "Is helping one woman really worth the cost of all the other good things you are trying to do?"

"I—if her life is at stake, then—"

"What if *your* life was at stake?"

I scoffed. "I'm not afraid. No one here would ever do me violence."

"Now you show your ignorance." The winter air between us vibrated with his threat. "Gentle men do ungentle things if you endanger their family. An Aspromonte mother will take a knife to anyone she thinks is trying to hurt her boy. *Anyone.*"

I felt my heart tightening like the bladder of a bagpipe. I wasn't trying to hurt anyone's boy. Did some Aspromonte mother think I was? Or was she a metaphor I was failing to parse?

Don Pantaleone let the discomfort hang between us, watching me brace for his closing argument. "We have an adage here: *Il tempo è galantuomo.* Time is a gentleman. He heals all wounds. He will heal Isodiana's." As he opened the nursery door to let himself out, he turned back. "The laws of chivalry exist for a reason, Franca. Without them, our world isn't safe. If you respect the people with power, they become men of honor. If you don't, they become villains."

Confused and scared, I sat staring at the dreary horizon. I hadn't gotten around to lighting my gas stove, and the chill poured through the crack under the door.

Don Pantaleone had a flair for the dramatic—I already knew that. But a warning like the one he had just issued—would he make something like that up? Was my life actually in danger?

Was Santo Arcudi, with his professor glasses, so scary that no one was willing to tell him to stop beating his wife?

Even Don Pantaleone Bianco, with his holy untouchability, was only willing to *pray for them.* For pity's sake, was that the best anyone had to offer Isodiana Legato?

Across the piazza in front of the destroyed post office, Bestiano Massara put down the arm-length piece of oak he was whittling—how could he move his fingers in this cold?—to stand and kiss Emilia Volontà on her brown cheek. I watched her present a cloth-wrapped bundle to her ex–future son-in-law; he opened it and removed a piece of cheese as she continued toward the cataract with her water barrel. I thought the picture of him chewing there in front of the wreck of stones was unbearably forlorn.

I locked up the nursery and headed up the mountain.

If Cicca was surprised to see me home, she didn't let on. She had a pot of beans simmering on her hearth and was sorting through a knee-high pile of hemp fiber. "Here, you can help me," she said, and handed me a paddle of rusting nails.

I passed a fretful hour carding with her, hoping I wouldn't clumsily puncture myself and end up dying of textile-related gangrene. Meanwhile I told her about Isodiana. "Don Pandalemu said there's nothing to be done about it. Basically that I should mind my own business."

There was such a long pause that I risked self-harm to look up from my carding. Cicca's eyes were fixed on her own fast work. "You told Don Pandalemu?" she said at last.

I felt stupid admitting I'd thought the man would help me. "He asked me specifically what I was upset about. You can't lie to a priest, can you?"

That was intended to pander to my audience, but Cicca just hummed.

"What can we do, *cummàri*?"

Cicca shook her head, intent on her work. "Nothing, *pedìmmu*. You cannot interfere."

Several minutes passed with only the *fft-fft* of the hemp combing to fill the stuffy kitchen before I could make myself ask her, "What about you, *cummàri*? When your husband was cruel to you, was there anything that anyone could have done to help you?"

"What could anyone have done?"

I tried again. "Is there anything you ever *wished* someone would have done?"

Cicca had not made eye contact this whole time. "A man has to be allowed to run his own household, Francesca. Usually a wife can control her husband by doing you-know-what. It makes him be nice to her. In my case . . ." She shrugged. "Pietro was, you know. Sick. So I couldn't use that trick. So he was always angry."

"So your advice to Isodiana would be to have sex with her husband more." I did not subscribe to this method as universally applicable; Sandro and I had had vicious fights while we were naked.

"Doesn't work for everyone," Cicca conceded. "Sometimes the better solution is when the man emigrates. Sometimes when husband and wife don't have to live together the marriage is very good."

Now, there—she had hit upon something.

I spent the early afternoon laboring over a letter to Sabrina.

I am concerned that a woman's life may be in danger from her husband, and I need your advice on how I should proceed. What help can I offer her?

Santo Arcudi was a danger to his wife. They had been married a decade and she had survived so far, but in one short month, I had noticed two examples of escalating injury; where would this lead next? And what was Isodiana going to do, with no money, no legal right to leave her marriage, and no one she could go to for help? The law was against her. Not that Isodiana would ever invoke any law; that would be seen as a betrayal to her whole community.

She has four children and one more on the way, I wrote. *The children may also be in physical danger.*

What other relevant facts could I include? Maybe:

The husband spends his time with violent companions and is connected to some kind of organized crime syndicate. He stops her from associating with anyone and from seeking education for her children, who are not allowed to attend public schools. Is she a prisoner?

But probably not:

She has no familial protection in the village since the mysterious disappearance of her father. I have compelling reason to believe he was murdered.

Trying to find the words to explain Isodiana's family to Sabrina, I discovered I was pretty sure I knew who the skeleton under the post office belonged to.

57

I COULD NOT LEAVE THIS LETTER A WHOLE WEEK FOR ODDO THE postman.

Ugo's mother, Tuzza, answered the Squillaci door. "*Cara mia.* What's the matter?"

"I have to send some urgent mail," I told her. "Do you think Ugo could escort me to Roccaforte?"

We took his shortcut through the mountains. Our physical history filled the air between us, tacky as pine sap. He was a circumspect man, Ugo. He did not mention my awkwardness for the entire journey. It was only as we were on our way home, when he knew we would only have a limited time to spend together in the repercussion of his words, that he said, "Franca, I was thinking maybe you might come to Milan."

The phalanxes of white pines were dense around us, the needled silence that absorbed our footfalls thick and predatory. "You mean—to visit you."

"Yes. To visit." His eyes searched the woods, probably unnecessarily. His nose was a sharp, clean arrow in profile, a grace note on his brawn. "To stay."

Ugo had no idea I was carrying Sandro's letter in my briefcase, or of the turmoil it unleashed every time I unfolded it. I felt sick to my stomach. Instead of answering, I said, "Are you going back soon?"

"Next week."

Much ground had been covered before I made myself ask, "What do you . . . Are you . . . Will you live in Milan forever? Or do you want to come back here someday?"

He took a long time to answer. "I think there is a good chance there will be no Santa Chionia to come back to."

"You mean . . . transferment? The Chionoti are totally against it." As I spoke, I heard my own doubt.

His voice was grim. "Mark my words, they'll do as they're told and follow their corrupt leaders down to the sea. It will unfold for Santa Chionia exactly as it did for Africo, for Casalinuovo. The Chionoti will live in temporary housing for however many years it takes the state to find some swampland on which to build the new *paese.* In the meantime, the old folks will die of diseases they never encountered in the mountains and the young men will emigrate because there are no jobs and the middle-aged men will wither in shame because they won't be able to feed their families because all they know is mountain herding. In one way or another, many souls will be lost."

"You think my nursery is worthless," I accused.

"I think the nursery is very worthy. I think that unfortunately no one is going to have the chance to use it."

If Ugo, my supposed friend, was saying it to my face, what were people saying behind my back? If he didn't believe in me, who did?

To get back at him, I said, "What's the real story with you and Isodiana Legato?"

Nearly without breaking his stride, Ugo bent to snatch up a pine branch off the path. He snapped it at its fork and chucked the smaller arm into the woods, worrying off chips of bark from the remainder as we walked. This procrastinatory technique, the Very Important Stick, was familiar to me from that summer I spent as junior coordinator at the Cradle of Liberty Boy Scout day camp. As the ten-year-olds had taught me to do, I waited him out.

"What do you mean?" he said at last. "There is no story."

"Did she break your heart?"

"Teenage boys don't get their hearts broken, Francesca. All disappointment occurs in a different part of their anatomy."

"That's not true at all," I said. "Don't be unfair to your sex."

He stopped walking and looked me in the eye. "What is it you want me to say?"

To be honest, I didn't know. "I . . . want to understand you."

"How does it help you understand me if I talk about Isodiana Legato?"

"Every tiny piece fits into the puzzle somewhere."

"Am I the puzzle?"

I didn't answer; my gut was roaring with sorrow and longing but I couldn't for the life of me figure out what I wanted to have happen. Instead I waited, again. I tried to savor this interlude when I could stare without impropriety at the cinnamon-crystal of his eyes. Some woman would bear his children and there would be a fifty percent chance they'd inherit that eye color. It wasn't my personal responsibility to prevent it from going extinct.

A hawk called angrily across the hillside, two short barks.

"Isodiana." Ugo turned away to toss the stick into the brush. "I had a crush on her when we were children. That was before I realized what she would become."

"What do you mean, what she would become?"

"A sheep." He scanned the trees. "It's not her fault. She couldn't help it."

"I thought you Aspromonte boys loved your sheep," I tried to tease.

"We love our *goats*," he corrected. "Sheep are too stupid to respect. They'll follow one another over a cliff." His gaze was back on mine, full and golden. "Are you jealous of Isodiana Legato?"

"How could I not be?"

"Don't be. There is nothing in her life to be jealous of."

We walked for many minutes in silence while I wrestled with whether to voice my worries. "Actually, I—I think Santo beats her."

"Santo Arcudi is not a nice man," Ugo said shortly.

"I—I think she needs help. Isodiana and the children. I think they are in danger."

"You can't help her, Francesca. You should not try." He surprised me by seizing my shoulder, bringing us both to a halt. "You must take my word on this."

"Okay," I said, frightened by his intensity.

"Okay," he said after an excruciating wait. His hand slid away. "I wish we had more time. I could take you to see the Aposcipo waterfall. It's almost as beautiful as the Amendolea."

"Maybe if you come back in the summer," I said.

He squinted at me, his mouth rueful. "Maybe," he said.

We both realized I had just turned him down.

58

MY MELANCHOLY MADE ME INSENSITIVE TO ATMOSPHERIC CLUES that Cicca had company before I stumbled right into the party. There at her kitchen table, eating the beans she'd been boiling all day, were Bestiano Massara, the communist; Ligòri Scordo, Mico's younger brother; and evil Mela from next door.

Was this political canvassing? Or just another iteration of "friends and cousins"?

Ligòri Scordo leapt up to offer me his stool. "We're having a feast for the last day of Christmas. Have some ricotta."

Cicca picked up the conversation they'd apparently been having before I arrived. "Francesca was asking me, why is there so much violence in our *paese*? What caused this cultural decay?"

"I didn't ask that," I hurried to say, but who cared?

"These hoodlums running through the mountains with their guns and cutting down your trees if you don't pay them protection." Ligòri snorted. "They call themselves men of honor like our poor brave fathers—"

"God bless their good souls," Mela murmured.

"—but they have no honor."

I accepted a bowl of beans from Cicca, my heart accelerating in my chest. I was pretty certain no one was supposed to say the words "men of honor" in front of me.

"Our fathers did what they did because they had to protect their families. That's what honor is, putting your *own* life on the line to protect other people's freedom. These lowlife scum only want *you* to honor *them.*"

"Now, be careful," Bestiano Massara said. "Nostalgia is the root of fascism, don't forget. The idea that things were once better than they are now is preposterous. Our parents starved and watched their children die unbaptized. Our grandparents were reaped by their masters like zucchini, lived in thrall, and worked for no pay. Things get better every generation. Our current unhappiness springs from the fact that we are learning to ask better questions." He stepped away from the table and pried the fire stick out of Cicca's hands. "Cummàri Cicca, let me do that. You've been on your feet all day."

"But, Bestianeddu," Mela said, "you cannot pretend there isn't more violence now. It has gone beyond our control."

"We *know* of more violence now," the communist corrected. "That doesn't mean it wasn't always there, the strong taking advantage of the weak. Those with power to exercise over other people will always do so—

this is axiomatic. There is no need to romanticize our past. The brigands of a hundred years ago were as despicable as these delinquents today."

"A hundred years ago they carried knives, not guns," Ligòri said. "How can one simple man fight back anymore, no matter how brave he is?"

Cicca, who was laying slices of cheese meaningfully in front of her guests, murmured, "Hunger turns the wolf into a monster."

It sounded like she was quoting a proverb, but all I could think of was Don Tito the Wolf. Had hunger made him a monster? Or had he always been one?

A hush had fallen over the table. Ligòri, who was still standing, poured himself a cup of wine, then crossed the room to sit on Cicca's scutching bench, Rumpelstiltskin among the unspun balls of hemp.

My mind was sparkling with fear. I wanted to ask about the men of honor—about this escalation of violence they alluded to. I wanted to know if every other person in that room knew who the skeleton under the post office was, and also who had murdered him.

"The Wolf—" I started.

They were all looking at me, their eyes blank and bright. The ancient taboo that bound their tongues had gripped me, as well. Maybe I was not quite an outsider anymore.

"The wolf," I said instead. "There are so many stories about the Aspromonte wolf, but I have never seen one."

"You won't," Bestiano Massara said. "The wolves are long gone."

"Nineteen forty-seven was the last sighting," Mela said. "A wolf came down from the upper massif and it slaughtered fifty lambs. Carcasses all over the mountainside."

"What did you do?" I asked. My voice felt rusty in my throat. "Did you hunt it down?"

"All the shepherds of Santa Chionia." Ligòri's eyes were wet with reverie. "We slit its throat like a goat's. And then we roasted it over the fire and we ate it."

"I would never eat the flesh of a wolf." Mela shuddered. "How could you eat a wolf?"

"It was as sweet as candy."

· · ·

It was nearly dawn before the party broke up. I could barely keep my eyes open when I heeled off my muddy boots, finally, and trundled into my bedroom. The air was chilly, and I saw the shutter was open. Angry with myself that I would have to shiver to sleep, I set my lamp down on the sill. There—this time I was not imagining it—the euphorbia was knocked akilter, its sea-green arms bobbing in the sinister ice-breeze.

My hands shaking, I bolted the sash, all but collapsed on the floor to check under my bed, swooped through the papers on my desk, trying to find something amiss. Barefoot, I scuttled across the cold foyer and up the too-shallow treads of the concrete staircase to Cicca's bedroom. I pounded on the door until she opened it, her hair poking up greasily as if she had already been mashing it into her burlap pillow.

"Someone's been in my room." I was breathless with fear. "I am sure."

Cicca blinked worriedly in my sap lamp, the only light between us. "When?"

"I don't know. I was gone all day, remember?"

Cicca led me back down the stairs, checking the locks as we passed the front door. I wondered if she felt the same danger that I did about the conversation she had hosted tonight. Or maybe meetings like that happened every night in private kitchens.

As she examined my room, prodding soft surfaces and running her hands over flat ones, I could see she was unhappy. She unbarred the window and leaned out over the chickens as January air swarmed into the room. "There's no way," she said to herself. "It's too high."

"No, you're right." Now that I saw she was afraid, my instinct was to pooh-pooh the whole thing. "I think I didn't lock it before I left and the wind must have blown it open."

We rebarred the window and Cicca chided me to get to sleep. I tried, I really did, but the wind scraping the dry leaves across the paving stones sounded so much like human footfalls that I got up to peer out the window four different times in the hour before dawn.

On Friday, January 6, I was awoken by a shriek. My head pounding from wine and scant sleep, I went running to the foyer, where Cicca was crouching at the open door.

"What is that?" I drew closer to make out the object she was staring at in the dawn shadows. "Are those . . . is that a pile of coal?"

"The Befana came." The Epiphany witch. "It means someone who lives here has been very bad."

59

ON MONDAY MORNING, THE MAYOR'S SECRETARY WAS WAITING for me at the nursery door. "Mayor Stelitano would like you to come to his office."

"Right now?" My nerves were frayed after a weekend of huddling in Cicca's kitchen wondering who had left the coal, such a terrifyingly childish threat, and which specific transgression it was punishing us for.

"Do you have something more important to do?" he said, his manner woundingly mild.

I followed him across the piazza like a whipped spaniel—like Vannina had followed Officer Vadalà. In front of the *puticha,* Pascali Morabito was talking to Santo Arcudi and his sidekick, Nicola Legato. I accidentally met Santo's hawk eye and looked away. Had one of those men left the coal? Had I put Cicca in danger by annoying Isodiana's husband?

Or her aunt, Potenziana?

Or by clumsily snooping around about the past criminal activities of those ever-present tavern patrons on behalf of Vannina Favasuli, the universally disrespected town working girl, who thought they had murdered her husband?

Or maybe by impinging on the town's sexual morality by engaging in extramarital physical congress with Santa Chionia's most eligible bachelor?

The fact that there were so many possibilities didn't do much credit to my hearts-and-minds campaign.

On the other side of the piazza, smiling Bestiano Massara doffed his red cap as we passed. *"Buongiorno, maestra!"*

It had crossed my mind that the coal had been political, not personal— that some shameless contingent of the town's right wing was harassing Cicca for hosting Bestiano Massara and his leftist friends. Ashamed—of my current circumstances, but also of my fear of being seen to be friendly with him—I could barely bring myself to return the communist's greeting with a nod.

"Fight back against corruption!" Bestiano Massara called optimistically to our backs.

. . .

Mayor Stelitano was as dapperly mustachioed as ever. "Listen, Maestra Franca. The council and I must put a pause to the nursery project. A referendum on transferment has been requested."

"Transferment?" I swallowed. I wasn't sure why everything was going wrong at once. "But—"

"There's nothing I can do now. I have to let them vote on it." The mayor leaned on his elbow and cradled his forehead in his hand, the picture of a manly man laid low by distress. "It's been a hard winter, with the two floods. The Christians are tired."

Ugo had called it. "Who requested the referendum?"

"The *paesani* did." The mayor spread his hands helplessly. "I promised to represent them." He stood, gesturing toward the door. "In any case, the nursery will have to wait."

I stood, too, but didn't leave. "Until when?"

"After the referendum. Perhaps you will want to go home to Rome for the interval."

Was he trying to get rid of me? "When will that be?"

"I cannot tell you what I do not know, *maestra*." Impatient, he inclined his head toward the door.

My self-righteous frustration had blotted out my anxieties. Of course he knew. It would be his sole discretion to hold such a referendum. It might happen tomorrow to catch the opponents off guard, or it might happen in six months to maximize the fiscal benefits of foot-dragging vis-à-vis state-sponsored disaster relief largesse.

In the meantime, why shouldn't children be learning?

"I've promised my organization that I will open the nursery," I told him. "They already disbursed the sums. So, mayor, I'll move forward, and we can reconvene any time you want to be involved again."

His mustache twitched at each tip to accommodate his frown. "How about we discuss it at Easter," he said.

My dread of my January promise to Child Rescue was coagulating, a thrumming pressure in the back of my cranium. "Fine."

Which problem did I try to fix first?

None of the expected ones—I spent the rest of Monday on via

Steisicoro at the Zavettieri house, where two children, Melina, six, and Mimmo, four, were suffering from diarrhea. My medical supplies hadn't been replenished since September, and I didn't even have any saline tablets to offer. Their mother, Nilledda, was terrorized by the idea that the cholera had returned. I scoured her kitchen while she nursed them, made trips to the cataract for water to boil into herbal infusions.

I had missed lunch at the rectory, which I only regretted because Don Pantaleone might have given me some insight into the withdrawal of mayoral support for the nursery. I no longer trusted him; nevertheless, he was a fixer when it suited him to be.

On Tuesday morning I drifted by the rectory to see if I could catch the priest, but he was already in session with his Association for the Future students. I listened glumly outside the open window to the chanting of what I eventually recognized as the quadratic formula. I tried to guess whether I'd been older or younger than these kids when I'd first memorized it to the tune of "Pop Goes the Weasel." What would these shepherds' children do with the quadratic formula? Would they fly on its wings to universities in Naples or Milan, use it as an excuse to leave the mountain home of their ancestors forever? I doubted they would solve quadratic equations with it—no one I knew had ever gone on to do that.

Tuesday dragged by in a lonely, nail-bitten haze. I wished Ugo would stop by, or that I had the courage to go to his house and see him, but I had closed that door for both of us.

Vannina Favasuli shuffled dirty-footed over my doorstep in the early afternoon. "Any news for me, Maestra Franca?" Her upper gum, which I remembered as containing one front tooth, was now entirely bare.

"Your husband who died in 1952 is still dead," I might have said, but instead I said, "No. No news."

"Do you have my photo?"

The photo. I'd forgotten about it. "Not with me, Vannina."

"All right. You'll let me know," she lisped, and went mercifully away.

When I was sure she was gone, I went through all my papers yet again. How had I lost her photo?

Someone had gone to great pains to remove the same photo from the *municipio;* Pino Pangallo had tried to scare me out of tracking it down. Had the same someone stolen Vannina's copy from me, as well?

What was so dangerous about that photo?

I thought of the pile of coal the Befana had left on Cicca's front step. Was I safe?

Storm clouds had banked the afternoon sun like a drowsy hearth fire. My head hurt from squinting in the ashy light. I put down my pen and looked out the window.

Were they not rebuilding the post office because they knew they wouldn't be here to use it?

"Hope is not a strategy," my father would have told me. "Make a list of problems. Be completist, even if it feels silly. The best solutions are so simple they seem silly. When you look at all the factors together, they cancel one another out."

I opened my datebook to find a clean page, turning past my notes about Leo Romeo and my notes about Mico Scordo. I wrote

PROBLEMS
headache

and stared out the window a little longer, my mind dead with malaise.

I persevered.

possible transferment
London office January deadline
student roster—send acceptance letters
Potenziana boycott—how to end?
one more teacher
replacement supply shipment—how to get it from Bova?
Association science funds?
Sandro letter

For some reason, I couldn't make myself write Ugo's name.

Isodiana and children in danger
Vannina photo, nagging, etc.
where is Leo Romeo?

Last of all, embarrassedly, I wrote

welfare of infants of Santa Chionia

Poor things.

Proceed rationally, my father would have advised. In terms of items canceling one another out, my list seemed quite neat. All I had to do was admit defeat and walk away from Santa Chionia, which might not exist soon, anyway. It could be argued that no other course of action made any sense.

But the Fund's money was already spent—not recoupable. Other children in other needy villages had not received that money. Didn't I owe it to *those* children to keep trying until I was certain I could do no more?

I was staring at the list when I had my next visitor. An unusually popular day for an unusually unpopular gal.

It took me a moment to recognize his shiny black hair that looked like a hat. I had, after all, interviewed seventy village parents in the last three months.

"Masciu Bruno Scopelliti." I was pleased with myself when I came up with his name—a tiny victory; I was not entirely without human touch. I recalled his sweet dark-eyed daughter, Tota. Then I recalled his hostile wife, Ninedda Lico, the only child of Don Tito Lico and Potenziana the Wolfess, and I recalled the fact that Bruno had told me he would follow up about withdrawing Tota's application. My briefly cheered heart tumbled back where it belonged.

"I wanted to see how you are doing," he said, settling into the visitor chair. I was so dispirited I couldn't come up with an appropriate platitude, and his expression registered alarm. "What is wrong, *maestra*? Is it funds? We could put together a collection—"

"No," I cut in. "Funds are not the problem." I felt a knee-jerk swell of emotion. Bruno Scopelliti genuinely wanted to help me. "It's just that—" *No, Francesca. Never confess your weaknesses.* People wanted to be part of projects that seemed successful. "Do you think Santa Chionia is going to vote for transferment?"

"Never," he said without a moment's hesitation. "We all saw what happened in Africo. Who would be stupid enough to fall for a transferment proposal?"

"Why is the mayor worried people want to leave?"

"Worried people want to leave!" Bruno shook his cupped fingers at me. "Worried about the election, is more like it! Trying to distract Christians so they don't force a recount. Listen, *maestra,* with politics, you can never take anything at face value. You always have to ask yourself, *Cui bono?* Who does it benefit? Every single thing you hear—who does it benefit for me to believe that?"

I thought it was a rhetorical question, but he was looking at me expectantly. *Cui bono?* Who would transferment benefit? "Someone who stands to make money." *When all else fails, follow the cash.*

"*Brava.* Think about *that, maestra,* and you will figure out who is really your friend."

I was as fortified by his straightforwardness as by his optimism. "Thank you," I said, so sincerely we were both startled.

"For what?"

"You helped me. I was struggling with how to proceed when the question of transferment is still open. But you've reminded me it doesn't really matter. Santa Chionia will live on either way, and children will need a nursery school."

"Absolutely." Bruno Scopelliti stood up. "At your service, *maestra.*"

"What about your mother-in-law? Potenziana the Lichena?" I couldn't resist.

"What about her?"

"Has she changed her mind about the nursery?"

"Changed her mind?" He looked at me blankly. "Not at all. She's thrilled about it. She's the one who sent me here to ask you if you needed anything."

All the way home I thought about what Bruno had said.

Was it true, the Wolfess did not hate me? Had I invented that all? Was I as paranoid and delusional as Vannina? Or was Bruno misled, or misleading me? Could he also be misleading me, intentionally or not, about transferment?

Cui bono?

Who would make money if the Chionoti signed away their rights to their hereditary land? Politicians, certainly—politicians far away in

Rome, where the utter travesty of the Calabrese postfeudal land reforms had been a national embarrassment for fifteen years. Forget spending all that money to carve up the old iniquitous holdings and distributing them to the poor people who labored away on them nearly uncompensated—instead, just move the people away and make their land illegal. Pay off the effete ex-lords to stay quiet. A great opportunity for some artful kickbacks. Further down the line there would be contracts to exploit—someone would have to be in charge of building the new municipality.

If I had to hazard a guess at who would be in a position to make a bunch of money off a transfer, it would be the same guy who'd managed to make a bunch of money off the 1908 earthquake. Of course it would be Bruno's father-in-law, Tito Lico.

Part Four

WHERE
IS
SANTA
CHIONIA?

60

ON WEDNESDAY, JANUARY 11, ODDO THE POSTMAN BROUGHT NO
letter from Sabrina, just an obviously American white business envelope.
The return address was a corporate one, *Utah Fuel Company*. My fingers
tingled as I tore it open. Leo Romeo. I'd found him.

Dear Miss Loftfield:

We wished to lose no time in replying to your inquiry of Decem-
ber 9th. We regret to inform you that Leo Romeo, who was employed at
the Utah Fuel Company Castle Gate #2 mine beginning in 1921, lost his
life in the explosion on March 8, 1924. We send our sincere condolences,
and our sincerest regrets that the news is reaching you only now. Our cor-
poration made every effort to contact victims' families in a timely fashion.

Regarding workman's compensation after this tragic accident, in due
accordance with Utah State law Leo Romeo's next of kin, one Saverina
Rizzuto of Pizzo, VV, Italy, listed as the deceased's mother, was informed
immediately. The Utah State Workman's Compensation Board issued
$5,000 in relief funds to Saverina Rizzuto over six years, ending on Sep-
tember 14, 1930. In addition, our files indicate a disbursement from the
governor's Castle Gate Relief Fund was made to Mrs. Rizzuto in 1926.
The disbursement of the governor's funds is a matter of public record.

If the funds did not reach their intended recipient or some other
information in this letter does not seem correct to you, we suggest you
contact the Utah Workman's Compensation Board.

Sincerely,

Hyrum Rigby

Secretary, Utah Fuel Company

. . .

I realized I was crying only when Cicca put her arm around me. I hadn't understood how much I had been hoping I would find Leo Romeo alive. To learn he had been killed so long ago, in such an awful way—I felt grief, as if Leo were mine to grieve over.

Doubly so, because someone had swindled Emilia Volontà not only out of knowledge of her son's fate but out of at least five thousand dollars. She could have lived like a queen; she could have built the road to Bova herself, or the school she never had a chance to go to. Instead she had spent forty years cleaning people's houses and paying back an extortionist.

Her husband had worked himself to death making coal here in his native mountains; her son had left in search of a brighter future, only to lose his life to a different kind of coal thousands of miles from everyone who loved him. How could fate be any crueler?

"Tell me, *pedìmmu*," Cicca said, and when I could, I did.

"Some con artist in Pizzo stole Gnura Emilia's money," I concluded. "A lot of money."

"How much?"

I couldn't begin to guess the period exchange rate, or what any of that would mean to a woman who had never held even a single coin until she was thirty years old. "Millions," I said. "Millions and millions."

I had fixed my lipstick and powder and was unlatching Cicca's front door when Ugo Squillaci knocked.

"I'm leaving tomorrow," he said, while I stood there in shock. "Come with me."

"Aren't you supposed to leave a pile of sticks on the doorstep or something?" As soon as the words were out of my mouth, I felt my neck flame. He had never said he wanted to marry me; I would never have made that joke in English.

His mouth twisted wryly. "I'm not a brave enough man to be rejected by Cummàri Cicca in the church piazza. Good morning, Cummàri Cicca," he added, because Herself was resolutely at my elbow. "I will be on the eleven forty-five train to Napoli tomorrow. Why don't you come with me?"

"That's not—"

"Just for a while. You can come back when you can get things done again."

He was steady, implacable, a cliché of a romantic hero. For several heartbeats I was afraid I would say yes.

"Ugo." I looked him in his water-clear eyes, which glinted like Lithuanian amber. I was out of his league, and he was far, far out of mine. "I will not go to Milan with you." His lips parted—he was going to try again. "But I will take the train with you as far as Pizzo."

"Pizzo?"

"Pizzo." It was an impulse, but I was certain it was the right one. I turned to Cicca. "Do you want to come?"

"Come, me? No!" she answered immediately, but I saw her brows quirk as she second-guessed herself. She had never in her life left her province; the idea was outrageous. But we both wanted to know who Saverina Rizzuto was, who had been impersonating Leo Romeo's mother. I watched the annoying calculations contort her face; she frowned at me and then Ugo and then me again. She landed on the side of giving me one last chance to come to my senses about her boy. "No, I'll stay right here."

Packing was difficult; I only intended to be gone two nights, but I had to look like a million bucks. Cicca "helped" me refold everything into my overnight valise.

"You won't go in alone," she begged.

"Of course not. I'll make Ugo come with me." Both statements were lies.

I was still awake at dawn when Ugo rapped on the door to take me to the station.

He insisted on carrying my suitcase the whole hike to Roccaforte, which made me feel even more awful about what I was about to do. But I had made myself a promise. I had to try again.

The bus dropped us off at the Melito piazza at 11:25, from which it was a half-mile walk to the station. I was jumping with nerves—I have always had a phobia of missing a train, although it never turns out to be as big a deal as what I put myself through to make sure I get to the platform far too early.

I stuck to my guns.

"I have to stop at the *municipio*," I told Ugo. "I hope it will be a fast errand but you should go to the station without me."

The corners of his eyes tensed. "I will come with you."

He was not making it easier. "Will you do me the favor of waiting outside?"

The *municipio* secretary, blessedly unoccupied, seemed pleased that for once I was placing a domestic call, even if it was a long-distance one, to a bank office in Rome. The connection was absolutely terrible.

He answered before the second ring. "Sandro Cenedella."

I listened to the static, thinking of the approaching train I should have been rushing to, and still I let precious seconds pass before I got myself to speak. "It's me."

"Franca. Franca! Are you all right?" That voice—that clear, throbbing voice. It cut across two years and made my chest tighten so that I had to gulp for air. "Where are you?"

The line crackled so loudly in my ear I jerked the phone away reflexively. "Listen." Quick, before I lost my nerve. "I'm on my way to Pizzo—"

He spoke over me. "Where are you, Franca?"

Feeling hopeless, I tried again, shouting: "I'm going to Pizzo. Pizzo, Calabria." The desire to see him, which had been fermenting since I received the letter, had swollen intolerably at the sound of his voice. "If you want you can—you can meet me. Ten o'clock tomorrow morning in the piazza."

I was shouting into a dead phone. I noticed the dull silence on the other end half a second before the blaring dial tone.

The secretary, exceedingly amused—of all the conversations to have in front of him in Italian instead of English!—said, "The line got cut. Do you want to try again?"

The frustration and mortification welled up in my throat and I wanted to throw myself on the ground in tears, like Vannina would have, if for no other reason than that someone might have pitied me for a moment.

Wretched, I snatched my change off the counter. "I have no time."

. . .

Melito station was duly hustled to, the train duly caught.

The first leg of the journey was an hour on a rickety, goat-filled local, and we were both mostly silent. I was conscious that everyone who saw us must think we were a married couple, because what else could we be?

Once we'd changed trains at Reggio, Ugo spoke so circumspectly I almost couldn't hear him over the juddering of the axles. "What's in Pizzo?"

"An errand," I said, then, feeling stingy, I added, "I will tell you what it is, but you have to promise not to try to talk me out of it."

I described the saga of Leo Romeo: the missing boy, the mine explosion, the embezzled workman's comp. He took the letter from me, scanning it as if he could read the English. "You're just going to walk into a con artist's house?"

"We don't know the facts," I said. "There might be an innocent explanation—a way to get Gnura Emilia her money."

"You are not this naive. This is a bad person, a criminal."

"From everything I've heard, you don't have criminals in Calabria, only misunderstandings."

Ugo didn't take the bait. "I'll go with you."

My pulse picked up. "You're not invited."

"You cannot go in alone."

"I won't."

He wanted to argue with me, but instead he pressed his lips together. Had he guessed about Sandro? Overheard my humiliating attempt at a phone call?

Seething with two different kinds of regret, I looked out at the unrealistic turquoise of the sea as we passed the shimmering strait where three thousand years ago wily Odysseus had chosen between Scylla and Charybdis. A world apart from Santa Chionia, only a few miles away as the crow flies. A world apart and almost as beautiful—almost.

This was not my real life. I was a tourist here—a barely tolerated outsider.

I wanted the man beside me so badly, and at the same time I saw all that I would ruin if I made the impossible attempt.

"I'm sorry we had so little time to get to know each other," I said out loud.

"It was more than enough to make a decision." His tone was flippant. It was the first time I had ever believed him to be smarting at anything.

"Obviously it is not enough time." My sorrow was pulsing in my throat, tremoring in my hands. "I thought it was enough, once. That's why I married Sandro, and that's why things went so terribly wrong."

I had never said Sandro's name to him before. Ugo said nothing. I had been so careful up until now, but what was the point? We were about to say goodbye forever. "What went wrong between me and Sandro—it's a bruise." I touched my chest, purely for dramatic effect, but I felt it, the purple-black of my tenderized heart sore under my fingertip. "I'm not ready to go through that again."

"Francesca."

I met his gaze, and it was hard.

"If it had been the right thing for you, you would have felt ready. That's how this works. You have the feeling, or you don't."

"No!" I surprised myself with my urgency. "I . . ." I felt my face burning. There was no one else in our booth; no one in the whole carriage seemed to take any notice of us. But my lack of discretion was what made me American. "I have the feeling. It's just—I'm much older than I was when I met my husband. Maybe I'm too old. I'm not willing to drop everything for someone anymore."

The silence stretched. Things he did not say, which he could have said if he'd wanted to, included *What if someone dropped everything for you?*

The trail of the sun was growing long on the sea. I took out the meal Cicca had packed for us, winter pears and chestnuts and cheese.

In the quiet hour that remained of our journey together, I almost broke down oh how many times—rescinded my proscriptions, invited him to disembark with me in Pizzo. But no. Why drag out the inevitable?

And what if Sandro had decoded my phone call and actually showed up? Wouldn't that just be the screwball comedy of the year.

At Pizzo, Ugo lifted my suitcase and walked me down to the platform. He was an old-fashioned gentleman—a village boy, with his codes of rustic chivalry. But Sandro had turned out to be old-fashioned, too. Maybe they all did. Maybe that was the trouble with marriage between a man and a woman. It was never really going to work, because it never really had.

He lingered on the platform in front of me long enough to make me nervous the train would leave without him. He clasped my upper arms and kissed me on each cheek.

"We are friends, are we not?"

"Forever," I said. It was the kind of thing you know you don't mean when you say it, but which, once you've told the lie, has to become true.

Blind with confusion, I turned my back on Ugo Squillaci and walked away.

61

LEFT SHOULDER TO THE SETTING SUN, I TRUDGED FROM THE PIZZO station to the center of town. I had walked many miles already today, but none of them had felt this demoralized.

It was January, the dark nadir of the offseason, and I could realistically have shown up, an indecorous woman alone, and found nary a place to sleep. But luck was with me, in that one specific sense. Not caring much for my personal safety, I asked for hotel recommendations at a deli, then followed the directions to a hostel with no fleas in evidence. Disconsolate and fearful, I lay down on the mattress, which was stuffed with something much softer than the dried broom leaves I had grown accustomed to.

I woke up in unidentifiable darkness. I turned on the lamp—electric!— and set about whiling away the hours until dawn.

I could look for a telephone somewhere in Pizzo—*You're not in the Aspromonte anymore, Dorothy*—and call Sandro again. But why should I do that? If he'd understood my first message and decided to come, he'd already be on his way here. If he'd understood and decided *not* to come, I'd have to listen to his eminently reasonable excuses—well, that didn't bear thinking about.

If he hadn't gotten my message—did I even want him to come? I had yearned for him, yes—his letter had electrified me, his voice on the phone reignited my hope. But now that I'd said goodbye to him forever, I could think about nothing but Ugo. The chemistry, for shame—but also his courtesy, his strength, his implacability, his simplicity. Our lives would never match up. What was wrong with me that now that it was too late I wanted them to?

I lay in bed and waited for the sun, for the earliest tolling of the cathedral bells, for the hours to pass until ten o'clock. I'd find out at ten, and I'd be done with it.

Sandro. Sandro Sandro Sandro.

I put on my cornflower dress and my Brunos, which I had forgiven again, perforce. I applied mascara for the first time in six months, which made me ask myself what I was doing. Against all odds, I pinned my hair into something I approved of on only the first try. Then I stalked up the flagstone streets of this exquisite medieval town with the sea wind rosing my cheeks and thunder in my mind.

Sandro! My Sandro.

If I had lived my life correctly, I would not have jammed myself into this problem.

The charm of Pizzo was unignorable, even in January drab—the encastellated piazza, shaped like a teardrop, overlooking the royal blue of the Tyrrhenian; the gallant ghosts patrolling the ramparts. Almost all the cafés were shut. I found an exception and sat by the window, where I had a nearly satisfactory view of the piazza. I took out my Mary Renault novel as if I was going to be able to concentrate, and then my journal as if notetaking would help, and I ordered a coffee. It was a real coffee, not barley or chicory, and the vivid bitterness spiked the deranged hope coursing through my arteries.

I had not been an espresso drinker before I met Sandro. My turning point had been that first rainy afternoon I'd spent with him wandering the streets of San Polo. He'd hustled me under his jacket into a dingy bridge-side café across from the Frari basilica and when he said, "Would you like a coffee?," instead of saying "I don't drink coffee" or "I'll have a hot chocolate" or just "No, thank you," I said yes. We sat by the window and watched October rain pellets crash into the algae-slimed banks of the canal and offend the curmudgeonly pigeons, and he spoke to me of the importance of an expanded workers' rights movement, his hands fluttering and furling in Italian punctuation so that my eye was drawn to the mysterious furrows cut into the fingertips, which I would later be undone to learn were the product of his abandoned training as a violinist. I drank the coffee in wondering silence, and because Sandro appreciated it I realized it was magnificent.

I'd consumed a thousand espressos since, but I am an associationalist of the worst order, and this perfect cup of bitterness tasted like six years of triumph, struggle, and craving. I ordered another coffee and a cornetto, then a cappuccino, then was a wreck of nerves and ordered a cognac, which the barista brought me without looking askance, and then when I asked if they had anything to eat besides the cornetto (imagining something not mostly made of sugar) he presented the specialty of the house, a ball of chocolate-covered ice cream that turned out to have more liquid chocolate in the middle. What was I going to do, not eat it? And then—how could it be?—it was ten of ten.

My stomach and head were a mess, all the blood pumping in the wrong directions. I jitteringly requested my bill, regretting the moments I had to turn away from the window to assure the waiter yes, I wanted him to keep the change—Americans tip, and I was American, after all. A big messy American with a big messy life she kept dragging other people into, and if the poor man didn't get out of the way he was going to be one of them.

Every minute until ten o'clock stretched longer than the previous. Finally the cathedral bells began to intone. Then, very quickly, it was 10:10, then 10:30, then 11:00, and the waiter was back at my table asking if he could help with anything else, and I don't know what it was, the caffeine or the alcohol or the sugar or the grief or—I scuttled by him to the water closet and vomited it all away.

Still sick to my stomach, but now also mortified, I leaked out the door and down the concourse toward the sea. I sat watching the purple waves crash on the walls of the castle where Napoleon's general Murat had conducted his own execution by firing squad.

There was only one thing left for me to do.

I returned to the café, ordered another espresso, and said to the tactful waiter, "I'm looking for Saverina Rizzuto."

. . .

It was a pinkish two-story box of a building, the door standing open, offering a glimpse of a shadowy hallway. A woman opened a balcony window across the alley to shake a tablecloth, glanced my way, then went back inside. I had no witnesses.

Whoever had taken Emilia Volontà's money had done it thirty years earlier. Even if they were not dead, there was no reason to assume they still lived here, or ever had.

But: there was the chance I was walking into the den of a syndicate, or the house of a professional scammer. Someone who was happy to rip off old ladies wouldn't have misgivings about sticking a knife in a troublesome girl-investigator type, would they?

I had promised Cicca and Ugo I wouldn't go in alone. I had assumed that Sandro would be here with me.

No, I hadn't—I had never pictured Sandro by my side for this. I couldn't imagine doing this any way but by myself.

I followed my gut. I walked right in.

62

A LEMON-SCENTED CLEANING SOLUTION CLOTTED THE MILDEWY darkness. The hallway offered me two choices of egress: a staircase to an upper story or a doorway obscured by a peach-colored linen curtain. The whole house was silent.

"*Salve?*" I called. The January sea air rushed up the alley and ruffled the curtain. I felt fear creeping into my chest. How many film sequences had I seen in which a too-quiet door stands open, leading inevitably to a brutalized corpse?

I lifted the curtain and trespassed through an unlit kitchen and salon. Nancy Drew would have noted the frugal nonuse of electricity and deduced that whoever lived here was a woman of about Cicca's age.

Emboldened, I returned to the hallway and tried the staircase. "*Salve?*"

Still no answer, but on the other side of a dark bedroom a floor-to-ceiling double shutter stood open, creating a tunnel of light. "*Salve?* Is anyone there?"

Beyond the shutter was a rooftop garden no bigger than a bedsheet. On a stool under a trellis of winter-naked grapevines sat a woman with a paisley bandana tied around her white hair.

"*Salve,*" I said again.

"*Salve,*" she said, as if it weren't strange that a foreign woman had just walked through her bedroom.

"I'm looking for Leo Romeo."

I watched my words take hold of her. "Leo Romeo," she said. "Leo. Leo." She dropped her chin into her chest and pushed one finger into the inner corner of her eye. "I had given up," she said at last. "How far you must have come." She extended a hand and I helped her stand. "Come downstairs. Do you want some *pastina*?"

"It was March eighth, 1924. There were three explosions—boom boom boom, like that." Saverina Rizzuto rubbed her eye again with one baggy finger. "I pray to God they didn't suffer. That's what they said—they said the men died right away, there was methane in the air and the coal dust caught fire and it was just a flash of death, zap, like lightning." After a moment, she said again, "I pray to God it was fast."

I couldn't stop seeing little Leo Romeo's dark-eyed passport photo, the scared expression he wore as he sailed off to his death. "You lost your husband, too?"

"Thirty-five years old." Wooden spoon still in hand, Saverina reached up to touch the gold St. Barbara medal she wore on a chain. "The bodies were so badly burned they couldn't bury them for a week—women were still trying to identify their husbands. They made us go to a dance hall—they lined up all the coffins like this"—she made a chopping motion, conjuring an invisible parade of corpses—"and we walked up and down, trying to say, oh, this one is Luigi, this one is Leo."

I couldn't speak. I couldn't stand that this was the end of Leo's story.

The table between us was covered with a pink cloth with camellias printed on it. She served me a bowl of *pastina,* set a place for herself across from me. During all this she never turned on the light.

"I loved him like a son. He was full of goodness, Leo."

"How did Leo end up in Utah, do you know? He was supposed to be in Chicago."

Saverina did know. In March of 1920, she and her late husband, Luigi, had been living in a Chicago rooming house next door to Annunziato Volontà, Emilia's brother. Only three days after Leo arrived with his uncle, Annunziato had been killed by a streetcar. There was Leo all alone without a dime to pay for the room. "He was fifteen, but he looked nine or ten," Saverina remembered. "A starving country child. And he only spoke their Greek, not a word of English, or Italian. In the middle of Chicago, can you imagine, this poor boy who had lived his entire life among sheep."

"And goats."

"Exactly."

The Rizzutos had no children—"We were still hoping back then"—and took Leo in. He slept on their floor, mute and obsequious. "He peeled carrots, scrubbed the sink, took the clothes to the laundry—anything I asked. He was afraid to take our food. He ate like this." Saverina modeled a tiny portion with her work-warped index fingers.

Luigi Rizzuto hated the grueling brutality of the meat market, and a mining company agent recruited him and several friends to relocate to Utah. Leo went with them—what else was he going to do? "He was desperate to send money home to his mamma," Saverina said. They got on a train and went west to Carbon County.

For three years, Leo lived with the Rizzutos; he was a son to them. Leo worked hard in the mines—he grew up. He picked up English and taught himself to read and write. "He was attending night school," Saverina told me. "He had to ride a bicycle ten miles each way—he went almost every evening, though, even after a whole day in the mines."

I accepted Saverina's information with a teaspoon of salt. She had been the one to collect at least five grand of Leo's workman's comp.

"Why did he never write home? His mother never knew if he was alive or dead."

Saverina squinted at me. "He sent home money every month. Before he could write letters himself, he had Luigi do it for him so he never missed a payment. He was tortured by this debt his mother owed—something very bad had happened back at home, and she owed someone a lot of money. Leo was obsessed with paying it off."

Something very bad had happened. Had Leo been lied to and extorted? Or had Emilia Volontà left out part of her side of the story?

"His mother never received anything," I said.

Saverina regarded me with age-grayed eyes. "I was afraid of that. Maybe that's why . . . Wait a minute." From a shelf in her sideboard she removed a yellowed envelope. "This is Leo's last letter. He never had a chance to mail it." She turned it over in her hands several times before handing it to me. "I meant to mail it to his mother. But I think—I knew it would never get to her. Something about the whole arrangement wasn't right."

"What do you mean, the whole arrangement?"

Saverina sat down heavily on the other stool. "When—when it happened—the explosion—it was . . . I was not thinking so clearly, you know? But I sent a letter to Signora Romeo. My Leo's other mother. I didn't hear back from her, but I knew she couldn't write."

"Tell me about the money."

"The workman's comp?"

"All that. You filed for it. You listed yourself as his mother. What did you do with it?"

"This is what I'm trying to tell you. This is when I started to think there was something fishy. I applied for the workman's comp and the governor's relief, and sent a letter to Santa Chionia to tell Signora Romeo I was collecting the money on her behalf. I asked her how she wanted me to send it to her. Utah Fuel would pay sixteen dollars every week for six years, five thousand dollars total, for each victim. Luigi only made sixty cents for removing a ton of coal, so that was—" Several seconds passed before she continued. "It was more than they thought he was worth when he was alive."

"Did Emilia write back?" I was going to make her explain where the money was no matter what.

"A man did. He said he handled money for the Romeo family. He said there were no banks in Santa Chionia and they couldn't receive American funds. He told me to send the money in cash lire. So I did, for a few years." Saverina looked down at her lap. "But it was not nice, living there in the mine town, after what happened. I had no family, no *paesani*. So I came home. I thought I would lose the rest of the workman's comp, because how could they send it to Italy? But there was a lady from the union, I think, or the governor, I can't remember—she visited me and she told me her group would arrange it so I would get the rest. Not every week, but they sent money four times a year until it was done."

"And you kept sending Leo's money on to Signora Romeo?" I said disbelievingly.

"Every time."

Someone had been playing all the Romeos—extorting Emilia for repayment on Leo's passage loan, extorting Leo for some debt his mother owed. Someone had intercepted all the correspondence and lied to them both.

Either that, or Emilia Volontà had lied to me.

Or Saverina Rizzuto was lying right now.

"How did you send it?"

"In the mail. In a letter."

"But addressed to whom?"

"The man, that one who handled Signora Romeo's money."

"What was his name?"

She shook her head. "This was thirty years ago. Vincenzo something."

Vincenzo Legato. Ceciu. I would put money on it.

"Do you have that letter, by any chance?"

Saverina Rizzuto shook her head again. Why would she? "But this letter, here—this one for his mother. You can give it to her?"

I nodded. My throat had tightened again.

"I didn't even tell you the saddest part." She looked down at her lap again. I thought she might be blinking tears into her apron. "Leo should not have been in the mine that day of the explosion. The mine was running out of coal. Just the week before, the Castle Gate company had laid off all the unmarried men—anyone who wasn't responsible for supporting a family. Leo lied and said he was married so that he wouldn't lose the paycheck. He was so worried about his mother—about the debt she owed." She rubbed her eye with the full length of her index finger again, rubbed and rubbed. "They squeezed him to death."

63

I LEFT SAVERINA RIZZUTO'S APARTMENT IN A HAZE OF HEART-break for a man—a boy—I had never met, who had died before I was born. I thought about the cheapness of immigrant lives, of the people

who were so ready to take advantage of the vulnerable at every juncture.
I thought about a mother whose child had been stolen from her—by
poverty, avarice, and a casual disregard for human life.

Leo Romeo, who had risen above his humble roots to try to make
something of himself with bootstrap resourcefulness, was supposed to
be the American dream. Instead he had disappeared, one more invisible
man. He'd been bled dry for his labor, exploited for his loyalty. His death
might have been caused by a mining accident, but that didn't mean it
hadn't been cold-blooded murder.

My tired heart was aching after thirty-six hours of nonstop drama. I
tilted down the ramping concourse back to the Bar Dante and ordered a
hot chocolate. I had hoped, in vain, that the same waiter would be there
so I could undo any offense he might have taken from my unfortunate
behavior this morning.

The hot chocolate was restorative; the damp chill of the January sea
breeze had leaked into my bones. I had tonight to myself to clear my
head, then the morning train back.

How was I going to break this news to Emilia?

Across the piazza, I caught sight of a man smoking a cigarette by a
lamppost. He was dashing enough for me to look twice, even in silhouette against the weak silver sun—the way his jacket clung to his torso, the
casual confidence of his springy stance.

As if he felt me looking, he turned around and dropped the cigarette.

It was Sandro.

"The train stopped at Eboli for four hours!" he protested before I could
yell at him.

But I didn't want to yell at him. He was my first love. He was my
daughter's father. Nothing could ever change either of those facts, and
everything else was negotiable. I fell on his chest, sobbing.

"*Cara mia,* please don't cry," he said. His long arms were a brace
against the winter wind, against public opinion or the vicissitudes of my
personal biology. "Any reason for crying is so far behind us."

I'm not proud of it, but the first thing we did was go back to my hostel.

I hope I remembered to pay for the hot chocolate.

This was the addiction of Sandro—that after six years and six hundred fights, I wanted him so badly that in those hours, at least, I didn't feel any Catholic school residuals. Tumbling down the shortcuts to tandem gratification we knew so well, I felt only the mind-blanking, nerve-racking heat of desire.

As I lay in his warmth, his palm on my abdomen where our little daughter had once pressed back against him, my yearning subsided into wistful contentment. She was gone and this twist in my heart would never be, but under his hand my belly thrummed with the idea that all hope for us was not lost. *This* was the man I was inextricably linked to— we had been through too many things we could never share with anyone else. He pushed all my buttons, it was true, but only because he knew me so well that he *could*. I never wanted to show my buttons to anyone else.

I was not over him, because I never would be.

I had so many things to tell him I couldn't speak quickly enough, Santa Chionia and Cicca and the cactus prickers and Greco and the flood and the Novena and lentils and above all the road-to-Bova situation, an endless jumble of stories, until hours later, when we pulled our clothes back on, barely in time to catch dinner. Because Sandro was there, all the restaurants were open, glowing with romantic candlelight rather than shut up for the winter.

"So how are you going to break this bad news to your friend the little old Greek lady?" he asked as he refilled our short glasses from the carafe of wine. His brown eyes lifted deliberately to hold mine. "The passing of the years hardly makes this kind of thing easier."

The sparkling halo of our conversation nearly collapsed under the weight of his implication. We stared at each other across the table, and I remembered a time when our perfect little world had contained only the two of us.

"It's always better to know the truth, isn't it?" I said after a choked moment. I tried to joke, "Too bad I never went to detective school. I bet they make you pass a course on how to deliver bad news."

"Certainly," Sandro said. "And another course on how to get paid up front. So, Signora Holmes, you didn't solve the mystery of the bones."

"No, but I solved two other mysteries." The waiter brought us our *fileja* pasta, and I told Sandro about Mico Scordo. "This poor woman Vannina won't accept that her husband wasn't murdered. She fixates on this story she made up when she should be worrying about other things, like the fact that her son might be about to marry his half sister—"

"Franca." Sandro's humor had faded. "You need to watch yourself. You can't just go meddling like this. Don't you know how dangerous that is? Especially down in darkest Calabria among the brigands."

"Darkest Calabria? Really, Sandro?"

"Don't tell me Calabrians welcome strangers interfering in their private lives."

"I mean . . . ," I fudged. "Two poor old ladies asked me for help, so I helped." I was starting to wish I'd been more selective about which details I'd shared with him.

"You're a saint, everyone knows. But listen, in this one town of a thousand people—"

"Eighteen hundred."

"—there are two women who assume their men met violent ends? Does that not seem like a high proportion to you?"

I obviously didn't mention I knew of at least one more such woman. "Things were very hard during the war years," I said loftily.

"Oh please! It's not like they had Germans flushing out partisans by razing their churches and bayonetting old women." He said this very matter-of-factly as he bayonetted himself a forkful of pasta. "The war in Calabria was nothing like the war in the north."

"The partisan war was awful, I would never claim otherwise! But that doesn't mean that what happened in Santa Chionia wasn't brutal. The young men who were massacred in Greece and Russia, and there was an epidemic—"

"Every *paese* lost men in Greece and Russia and Africa." He wiped his mouth, and his sensible black eyebrows lifted delicately. "Why does Santa Chionia warrant special consideration?"

"Sandro!" Five years ago we had been on the same side of this argument. "Santa Chionia needs attention because for hundreds of years they have been neglected and preyed upon. They are victims of colonial imperialism."

"Don't quote Lenin at me. Lenin would have said it is the responsibility of the Santa Chionesi to rise up, not for people like you to try to save them."

"Chionoti," I corrected, willfully ignoring his wrongheaded interpretation of socialist philosophy.

"What?"

"Their demonym. They call themselves Chionoti."

"Oh, that's cute," he said. "Must be from the Greek?"

"Yes, but—"

"My point is, Franca, there's absolutely no grounds to go blaming other people for their backwardness." He blinked placidly. "It's up to a people to move on and rise above their circumstances. If they choose not to, well, why is that anyone else's problem?"

If I'd been an even-keeled, levelheaded kind of arguer, I might have calmly, slayingly quoted Mazzini on the nationalistic necessity of improvement of the quality of life wheresoever a fellow creature suffers in pursuit of happiness for the greatest possible number. But I have never been even-keeled or levelheaded, and I was on the verge of furious tears. "You cannot *imagine* the hardships these people have been through. How *dare* you say they don't deserve things like roads and running water!"

"Don't get excited," he said, which of course had the opposite effect. "This is the weakness of the liberal left—you count on being able to break people's hearts with sob stories, but everyone has their own worries." He was cool as a cucumber, dabbing bread in his onion sauce. "You need to rely on facts. You'll get much further." He fixed his deep-set eyes on me. "I'm just helping you figure out how to have this conversation more effectively."

My fury was bubbling out of my pores. I stared at his narrow, resolute face, his adorable nose, and the bend of his collarbone just visible under his open top shirt button. Beautiful Sandro, whom I had fought so hard for—laid down everything on the line of scrimmage. This was the prize I had won.

There was no point in arguing with him, or defending myself. He would never lose; he would keep going until he had reduced me to nothing. If I capitulated, he would forget the conversation had ever happened. I would remember every word.

In my mind's eye I was seeing Ugo Squillaci standing in front of me on the train platform. Ugo had never once infuriated me, or reduced me to tears. Then again, I reminded myself, he hadn't really had the chance.

"You're not people, Sandro," I said finally. "I'm not here to practice conversations with you."

"Neither am I. Thank you for reminding me." He somehow summoned the waiter without perceptibly turning his head. "Let's have more wine."

After dinner we walked through a gauze of fleecy sleet along the pebbly beach, past the famous grotto where the Virgin had saved shipwrecked sailors. When this surf-flecked slice of romance became too cold, we climbed the cobblestone *corso* to my hostel.

Back in my room, we behaved as a married couple again. This time, though, I don't know what it was—the wine, maybe? Except I felt more sober than I had before, when I'd been sober. There was something about the way he cupped the flabby lip of my belly—the skin that didn't used to be there before my pregnancy—that gave me the willies for a long enough moment that I could not reconnect my desire to my body. I could only think about the baby.

I didn't say anything; I continued through the motions. He did not notice. Or worse, he noticed and didn't let on. Sandro was only innocently ignorant when he chose to be.

At some point we both dozed. My body was no longer used to him next to me; the way he slept with his left arm across my back and his left leg heavy over my right was both physical contact I craved and claustrophobic.

I lay in the buzzing darkness and breathed his familiar soft sweat scent—a little bit acidic, like an unripe lemon. In my gut there was a gloppy guilt, rising like sourdough, the icky knowledge that I had shared my body with two men in a short space of time. I was never good at that. My intellect rejected the slings and arrows of feminine subjugation but my faithless backwater body wanted to be dominated by only one man.

He was dressing in the gray dawn and I was trying to cram everything back into my suitcase when he said, "Franca, there is one thing I must tell you. So that we can start fresh."

"Start fresh." I hadn't agreed to that—not in our millions of words.

"When you come back to Rome. We cannot keep secrets from each other—I would never even try, you know that." He was looking at me so earnestly, his large brown eyes engaged in that intense Italian way. "So I have to tell you that it is over now, but I had a *fidanzata* last year."

I didn't mean to be dramatic, but the suitcase tumbled out of my hand. "Excuse me?"

"Her name is Caterina. It lasted about six months. I met her when I was—"

"No." I crouched to reassemble the suitcase. *Fidanzata*—meaning it had been quite serious between them. My anger almost blotted out the jealous hurt of this revelation. "I don't want any other information." And for the only such instance in my life, I didn't—I meant what I said.

"All right, no more, I just didn't want to—"

I forced myself to look up at him, to remind myself of everything I hated about his smug, selfish face. "How could you, Sandro? That poor girl. You're *married*."

"Franca, you can hardly criticize me for giving up on you," he said, ever so reasonably. "You've been gone for two and a half years. You haven't returned my letters."

"Enough." I'd caught the side of my hand in the suitcase clasp as I fumbled to snap it closed—I actually broke the skin. Mostly I was mad because I knew I had no right to be. It wasn't as if I hadn't been rolling in my own yellow hay.

Telling me, though—that was nothing but selfish.

"I don't know why you would spoil our weekend like this," I spat, even though saying anything at all only opened the door for him to refute me.

"Because it's for the best to clear it up now." He took me by the shoulders. "If I'd concealed it, it would have been much worse if—when—you found out later."

My skin boiled under his touch, and I extracted myself.

"I have a train to catch."

"You can't leave angry." His voice was *so neutral*. He was *smiling* at me.

Insufferable, closed-minded Sandro, with his arrogance and his certainty he always knew best. It all came rushing back—every bad thought I'd ever had, all meticulously indexed in my grudge catalog. I don't know why my brain has done this, erased so thoroughly all the tender, scintillating moments from our early liaison that made me fall so wildly in love with him, but left behind such a comprehensive record of every sin. We are tragically too busy to keep diaries when we are falling in love, and tragically too introspective not to when we are falling out.

I stood in the doorway, clenching the handle of my suitcase, trying to channel all my frustration and malaise into the wood.

"I'm not angry," I said at last. "Goodbye, Sandro."

I kissed his cheek with a stale mouth and left him there.

Ugo, I couldn't help but think, would have walked to the station with me.

64

THE WHOLE TRAIN RIDE BACK I STARED OUT THE WINDOW AT THE Tyrrhenian Sea, my insides writhing with remorse and confusion. There was the transfer at Reggio, the bus from Melito, the goddamned walk from Roccaforte. I was not going to attempt Ugo's shortcut through the woods alone, so it was down into the Roghudi gorge for me, lugging my valise, two and a half hours of trudging through the semidarkness.

By the time I was in Santa Chionia, it was dark and bitterly cold. When I stepped into Cicca's kitchen, I couldn't stop shaking—she brought me a burlap blanket to wrap my shoulders, and that was when I realized I had chills that were not to do with the weather. I'm not sure how much incoherent time passed, whether I succeeded in explaining what had happened with Saverina Rizzuto, before I dizzily pulled myself up and lurched to bed.

My next memory is Cicca making me drink grape must vinegar. As it squeezed down my fiery throat I almost asked her if she had any favorite pessaries, just for safety's sake. Someone up here must. Otherwise why hadn't I encountered families with fifteen children?

I was sick for three days. My whole body ached too much to sleep, so I lay miserably half-awake and worried unconstructively. Cicca brought me more vinegar and chamomile tea and performed a smoke-spreading ritual that was surely to do with the evil eye. She force-fed me roasted eggs to reduce my fever. She massaged behind my earlobes to relieve my headache.

I don't remember a lot about those days, but I remember telling her, "I'm sorry you didn't get to be a mom."

"I did," she said.

65

THE SNOW STARTED TUESDAY AFTERNOON. ON WEDNESDAY, WHEN I was feeling well enough to get out of bed, I sock-footed to the dark, cold kitchen, where the air was unnaturally muffled, the shutters snowed closed. The electricity might have been out, but we never tested it by turning on the forbidden bulb.

"Lucky we have plenty of lentils," Cicca said. Lucky us. "Mela says there was an avalanche over the path to Roghudi."

In other words Santa Chionia was completely cut off.

I wiped my dripping nose on my handkerchief, enduring the fabulous burn of contact on my abraded nostrils. "What great timing for more extreme weather, right while everyone's arguing about transferment."

"*I* don't think it's great timing at all," Cicca said starchily.

Good old Oddo the postman squeezed in one last letter-drop before the sky fell down on us. There was still no letter from Sabrina. Three weeks had passed since I'd seen Isodiana's horrendous bruises. In the interim her husband might have killed her and I had done nothing at all to change the course of anyone's fate. If I was supposed to.

But there was a letter from Alexis Kelly, and going back to bed after breakfast had to be delayed because Cicca made me open it and translate it verbatim.

The date on the envelope was December 21.

Obviously there was something wrong, wasn't there—finding the obituary that easy. I should have figured it out myself, if not right away then when I met that Lois—the Dominic Scordo who died in August 1951 was 74 years old, way too old to be your guy.

But listen to this, Nancy Drew—I should get my own girl detective badge for this. I looked him up, Dominic Scordo, in the 1950 South Philly phone book—we got all the old ones at the office. Two Dominic Scordos, easy as pie, two addresses, one on Marvine, one on 11th. I check the 1961 phone book they just delivered this week and what do you know, the Dominic Scordo who lived on Marvine Street in 1950 was still listed.

"No way," I said out loud in English.

"What?!"

"It's the same darn address Vannina had in the first place."

So you don't have a corpse after all, sorry to say. Nick Scordo is as alive as they come, on the fat side, in fact, living with his American wife in South Philly.

Obviously this was too juicy for me not to get to the bottom of. I bought a German butter cake at the Market and waltzed right over there after work and rang that doorbell.

Wouldn't you know it, he answered the door himself. He's a big bastard, Frank, tall and a big belly, like the linemen from the Penn team who all went into bank jobs and let themselves go. Anyway I figured he'd be no use to me, so I asked if his wife was home, told him I'd just moved to the neighborhood. He gave me the old up-and-down—that could have gone real wrong for sure. But my particular style didn't bother the wife. She invited me right in and served me my own cake and told me all her secrets. Lonely woman. Then again, aren't we all? Now I'm just afraid I'm gonna get suckered into being her friend for the long term, and I'll have to forge my own whole second life to keep perpetuating my ruse. She thinks we're going to meet up to play bridge after Christmas— BRIDGE, Frank! You'll be the end of me.

Anyway, here's what's the truth about your Dominic Scordo. Helen (that's her name—she's like you, Philly-born Italian) has been married to him since 1940.

"He's had two families this whole time," I said, trying to remember Vannina's convoluted explanations of when Mico had come home for the summer and when he hadn't.

"Fft," Cicca raspberried. "Probably more than two."

Nick and Helen have three sons—the oldest one is in the Marines, then one is a high school senior, I met him, very handsome, another linebacker type, and there's a little one who's nine or ten. Cute kid. Obviously none of that adds up with your gangster-daughter-love-affair problems in Italy, does it, so I tried to fish around more. Helen Scordo is NOT very discreet and told me all about how she kicked him out for a few years, but you know how Italian families are, so they worked it out and now they're "happy."

The Dominic Scordo who died ten years ago was his uncle, in case you were curious. Sounds like he was a nice guy. Owned a pastry shop.

So there you go. And hey, maybe if you ever come home you can meet him for yourself. I might become best friends with Helen now to replace you. I hear she makes a mean lasagna.

"So maybe he didn't owe anyone money after all," I said to Cicca. "Maybe it's just that he was supporting two families that whole time until he decided to cut Vannina off."

"Uncle Domenico was a nice man," Cicca said.

"That's what Alexis said."

"Probably he made Mico do the right thing and send money to his wife. Then he dies and poof, no one to make Mico do the right thing anymore. So he never comes back."

"Okay, listen, Cicca, this is important." I sniffled and she glared at me suspiciously. "So we know for sure Mico had an affair with this American woman, Helen, while he was married to Vannina—in fact he got married to Helen, too."

Cicca made a face like she was about to retch. "Bigamy!"

I blushed away thoughts of my own recent dabbling. "And we know he had an affair with at least one other American woman, Lois Blake."

"And Ninedda Lico," Cicca whispered so loudly I was grateful for the snow muffle on the walls.

"My question is about—Giuseppe Petrulli. Your cousin."

Now she looked wary.

"Mico Scordo—he had an affair with Giuseppe's wife, right?" I had to cough into my hanky for an interval. "Petrunilla Romeo? You told me yourself."

Cicca clopped over to the fire to put a pot on. "You need some more grape must."

"Cicca, did Petrunilla get pregnant by Mico Scordo? It seems like he makes everybody pregnant."

She rounded on me with such energy that her erect hair trembled. "Anyone who is stupid can get pregnant!"

Well, that statement was enough to distract me, and it took me a few scrambled seconds to reassemble my train of thought. "Could Agathi Petrulli be Mico Scordo's natural daughter? Is it possible that Vannina's son Niceforo is engaged to his half sister?"

"No!"

"Cicca. Not possible at all?"

"Absolutely not." She was decanting vinegar into her saucepan with a higher level of violence than is usual for decanting vinegar.

"Come on. They look so much alike—they look like brother and sister."

"*Everyone* looks alike in Santa Chionia," Cicca declared, which was observably false. "We are a mountain race. We don't look like other Christians and other Christians don't look like us."

"If Niceforo Scordo and Agathi Petrulli *are* brother and sister, someone needs to stop the wedding."

"You should never say such a thing to anyone." Cicca held a vinegary finger right under my nose. "Do you hear me? You can ruin those poor children's lives."

"Cicca. If they're siblings, they *can't* get married. Their babies could have all kinds of awful diseases—"

"They *aren't*. Anyone can see the girl looks like her father."

I watched Cicca bang around fruitlessly on her pantry shelf. "I'm curious," I said at last. "Back in the fall we saw Giuseppe Petrulli reject Niceforo's courtship for Agathi, right? But now they're engaged. What made him change his mind?"

A crafty expression came over Cicca's dear, transparent face. "Maybe he thought like you did back then, but then he had some proof that it wasn't true."

"Maybe."

Or maybe Agathi was pregnant. After all, anyone who was stupid could get pregnant.

. . .

I hadn't translated every line of Alexis's letter. I didn't think Cicca would be interested in this sheer volume of granular detail about the résumé and observable habits of one John Matthews. And so I accidentally missed this part at the bottom:

> *By the way, the other guy you asked me about—Vincenzo Legato. I got nothing for ya. No Vincents, Vinnies, Enzos, either, not in the tax or property records or the obituaries. Sure he went to Philly?*

66

ON THURSDAY, JANUARY 19, MY NOSE WAS STILL CHAPPED, BUT I was a human being again, thanks to Cicca's witchcraft.

"I'm going to see Emilia Volontà," I told her after lunch. "I have to tell her about—about everything. Do you want to come?"

For Holmes was no one without Watson.

Which was I in this scenario, though?

Cicca grappled with the pain of turning me down. "She asked you not to tell anyone."

"That ship sailed a long time ago."

"You should at least try to pretend."

The *paese* was silent in the snow blanket, the sloping streets a pernicious mix of mud and ice. Except for smoke trailing from chimneys, there was no indication of any life.

Emilia Volontà appeared unsurprised to see me at her door. She kissed me on each cheek and led me by one persuasive hand to her humble table. The stale, mossy smell I had noticed last time was much stronger today.

"I'm so sorry, *gnura*." I didn't know where else to start.

"Sorry? For what."

"I—for many things. I have bad news. About Leo."

I tried my best to explain to her in my clumsy Greco. How awful to break such delicate, ruinous news in a language you have limited command of. Cicca had helped me prepare a necessary vocabulary list, but I couldn't fake the culturally correct platitudes for telling a woman her son was dead.

Emilia Volontà listened impassively as I fumbled for words. She made no reaction: not to the news that Leo had been killed in a mine explosion in Utah, that her brother had been killed by a streetcar in Chicago, that letters had been intercepted and this information maliciously withheld.

"Leo left you this." I laid the envelope Saverina had given me on the table. At last the widow moved: one tentative finger extended, like the curving claw of a hermit crab seeking bashfully in the surf, and traced the handwritten address. "That's his script, *gnura*," I said. "He had taught himself to read and write. He almost earned a high school diploma."

Her nasal voice was so high that her words were lost in the singsong of her breath. "A diploma?"

"Do you want me to read you what he wrote?" She didn't answer, but I understood that she might not have been able to. Uncertain, unworthy, I took the envelope from under her fingers. I unfolded the stationery and rearranged her trembling hand so that she was propping it open while I sounded out the words, transliterated Greco that Leo had written down in an adorable pidgin of imposed English phonetics. I only understood a quarter of it, more than enough to break a much less susceptible heart. I imagined the hours and ink the bone-tired boy must have poured into crafting letters like these at the end of a twelve-hour day in the mines, the precious dimes he had wasted on international postage to mail them. All his effort destroyed before his mother could ever take any solace from it.

I did not cry while I was reading. It was my job not to cry. But my job required lots of gasping pauses.

Emilia Volontà did not cry, either. She sat as still as a saint stone, listening. The stagnant air in the snow-cloaked hovel vibrated with thick trapped energy.

I had to tell her the rest. "*Gnura*, someone stole a lot of money from you. Millions of lire. The mine—they gave the families a . . ." I resorted to Italian. "Compensation. For lost lives. They sent five thousand dollars to Leo's mother—that should have come to you. Someone here in Santa Chionia took your money."

Her totemic face was as emotive as Don Tito's carved walking stick.

"Is there anything I can do for you, *gnura*?"

"For me? No, it is too late."

"The money?"

"Leo is gone. Money would not bring him back." Emilia pulled herself up and shuffled to her keepsake drawer. She stood there for a long time, fiddling with something I couldn't see. "Money would not bring him back," she murmured again.

"But maybe—maybe you know who has it? Maybe I can try to—"

"No, my dear," she said, her back to me. "You would only make trouble for yourself. Someone who would do something this heartless is someone who should not be bothered."

She returned to the table, the mossy stink very strong now.

Even if she refused to be outraged, I still was. "They've taken so much from you! How can you let them get away with it?"

"My life is over. There is nothing left to ruin." Her walnut fingers scattered, and on the table where they'd been I saw a dark wooden pipe. She held a splinter of wood to the flame of the smoldering sap lamp between us.

"Why did you ask me to find him in the first place, *gnura*? If you weren't going to do anything about it?"

"So I know who I'll see in hell."

In stunned silence, I watched as she lit her pipe, inhaling invisibly. The green nugget in its well flared.

It was weed. She was smoking weed.

"Here, my dear. Have some of this."

Flabbergasted, I took the pipe from her. No one had offered me weed since university.

"I—I'm sick," I remembered.

"Don't worry. It burns all the infection away."

I was fairly sure that wasn't true. But was it crueler to leave her alone in her grief?

"Thank you, *gnura*," I said, feeling meek—the wrong woman to be sharing this terrible episode of mourning.

It was only after taking a hit that I realized we'd been speaking Italian, not Greco.

Gnura Emilia's marijuana was strong. Never had the stone alleys of Santa Chionia seemed more like a warren, tilting caves looming incoherently. The strip of sky above me twirled like a majorette's baton and the ground beneath me slid constantly sideways.

Cicca dusted me off like an old lamp. "Eh, what happened to you?"

"Drugs," I coughed, and followed her to the hard kitchen stool.

"Drugs?!"

"Marijuana," I said, expecting, I think, that she would not recognize the word.

"Marijuana *and* drugs?!" she said, alarmed.

"No, just marijuana. The widow, she made me smoke—"

"That's good. You'll sleep well tonight."

"I—" Reality was an accordion, compressing and expanding in that way it does when you're stoned. "Do *you* have marijuana, too?"

"I don't think you need any more right now," she chided. "What did Emilia say?"

"That she knew who she'd meet in hell."

"Who?"

The world was swirling, but the truth was clear.

"Ceciu Legato."

67

"I KNOW WHAT HAPPENED," I TOLD CICCA.

"What?"

"First you have to answer some questions. Were Tito Lico and Ceciu Legato friends?"

"Don Tito is married to Ceciu's sister."

"Yes, but . . ."

"Friends, what. Everyone is friends."

"Did they get along as children?"

"Never."

"Don Roccuzzu Alvaro—which one did he like better?"

"It's not the same. Tito was just a poor mountain boy. Ceciu was like a son to Don Roccuzzu."

"How?"

"The don paid for him to go to school with the priests in Bova."

". . . Then brought him home to marry his daughter Richelina and take over all the secretarial work for his extortion business. Didn't he?"

"Well."

"Okay. So back in the twenties, when he's just starting to work for Don Roccuzzu, Ceciu Legato intercepts every letter Leo Romeo sent his mother. There was money in every one. And then after Leo died, there was even *more* money—millions of lire. Meanwhile, Ceciu told Gnura Emilia that Leo had never paid off his passage debt, which compounded—she and her late husband, what was his name?"

"Natale, good soul."

"Natale—they worked and worked for years to pay it back. Ceciu never told them that Leo was dead, because it would have been the end of a great arrangement."

"God rest his soul."

"The Romeos probably weren't the only ones Don Roccuzzu took advantage of, were they? How many families couldn't read and write? I mean, Don Roccuzzu had to get a little bit lucky—if the immigrant came back there would have to be some reconciliations. But Leo Romeo wasn't the only immigrant who never came back."

"God rest his soul."

"Ceciu Legato was . . . that wasn't the only way he helped out Don Roccuzzu, was it?"

"He was very smart."

"Ceciu Legato helped Don Roccuzzu embezzle all the earthquake recovery money from the *comune,* didn't he? They controlled all the money that came into and left the *paese.* Don Roccuzzu and his men were the reason Santa Chionia never rebuilt damaged houses or had the money to build a school, or a road or a bridge. Am I right?"

"No one would tell you anything like that."

"Where was Tito Lico during all this? During the 1930s?"

"Tito had to go to jail. For maybe eight years."

"For what?"

". . ."

"All the shepherds go to jail."

"All the shepherds go to jail."

"Maybe Tito the Wolf got arrested for some work he was doing for Don Roccuzzu? Maybe . . . hiding stolen goods up in the mountains? Using the goat paths to ferry contraband? Is that something the shepherds do?"

"Shepherds take care of sheep."

"And goats."

"And goats."

"Intimidation?"

"I don't know what that means."

"Yes, you do. Vendetta? Blackmail?"

" . . . "

"Assassination?"

" . . . "

"Never mind. So Tito is in jail. And then Don Roccuzzu died in the cholera epidemic, and so did his pet policemen—the ones who used to work out of my barracks. So Ceciu is left in charge of . . . all Don Roccuzzu's business opportunities after the war? Maybe Ceciu arranged some kickbacks to keep the *carabinieri* out of Santa Chionia so he could rule his own little empire here. Does that sound right to you?"

" . . . "

"Then Tito Lico came home from jail, and when he got here maybe there's some problems between Tito and Ceciu. Maybe Tito feels like he made a sacrifice for Don Roccuzzu and Ceciu reaped all the rewards."

"This is just storytelling."

"Fair. Okay, but then Tito Lico 'found' all the earthquake recovery money that had been missing for twenty years. Then *he* built things like the *municipio* and the communal oven and the post office and the bridge, when Ceciu Legato, the mayor, had failed to. Seems like Don Tito was trying to make some kind of point."

"The point was, Santa Chionia needed those things."

"Right. And then at that exact same time, isn't it a coincidence? There's a ridiculous hijacking heist, which was completely doomed to go wrong from the start; Ceciu Legato's son is killed; and Ceciu disappears off the face of the earth."

"Ceciu emigrated."

"Right. Or maybe Ceciu was so angry or grief-stricken he decided to break taboo and testify to the *carabinieri* about the hijacking."

"Ceciu would never have gone to the *carabinieri,* not even if his son was murdered."

"Maybe he thought his position as mayor would protect him."

"Ceciu wasn't that stupid."

"He *wasn't,* eh?"

"..."

"Where do you think Ceciu Legato is these days?"

"America?"

"I don't think he's in America."

That's what I said to her. Or something like that. I don't remember, I was stoned.

68

SNOW WAS FALLING WHEN CICCA WOKE ME UP IN THE MIDDLE OF the night. "Put your boots on," she whispered.

I sat up with some dizziness. "What? Why?"

"Peppinedda came to me." Cicca was pulling my coat around my shoulders. "She's going to show us."

I followed her because my policy was to just do what Cicca said.

Santa Chionia was a moonstone mausoleum in the suffused light of the waxing crescent, a swarf of rhodium hanging low on Montalampi's eastern slope. Fresh snow rounded the walls and the brightness of the nighttime tweaked my bleary eyes.

"Peppinedda walks with the saint," Cicca whispered, clutching my arm as we trundled past the crouching church.

"Okay," I said, wondering if I was still stoned.

We made our phosphorescent way, *piano piano,* down the granite waterfall of via Sant'Orsola. Above us the stars were gold and blue and pink, the abyss surrounding us anthracite black. I thought of shepherd astronomers and acceleration due to gravity.

"See," Cicca whispered as we rounded the corner.

There stood the saint stone, eerily bald in the snow. From its base, human footprints led down the steps, as if the pillar had taken itself for a walk.

My whole body trembled in the cold, and the psychological chill that crawled up my spine was amplified. I felt its reverberations in my clammy cheeks and my tingling toes.

The mouths of the alleys were undisturbed drifts of snow.

Cicca's brawny hands tightened on my elbow. We started to move again, following the footprints down the snowy mountain, disturbing

the powder far more than our predecessor. Certain thoughts chased each
other along the faraway skyscape of my mind—that it was wrong of us to
ruin these footprints, that it was disrespectful or dangerous to catch up
with whoever had made them.

Down via Sant'Orsola we trailed a mysterious someone, past the may-
or's dark house and the dead eyes of the nursery's battened windows. The
footprints continued resolutely across the moonlit piazza and directly to
the ruins of the post office.

It was not possible that the most-likely-imaginary Santa Chionia had
stepped out of a stone pillar and guided us to the erstwhile resting place
of the murdered Ceciu Legato. That—that didn't even make sense.

"I don't believe it," I whispered back.

"It doesn't matter if you believe."

We slid down the last steps of Sant'Orsola and followed the filling
footprints east, toward the torrent. They continued around the curve of
via Odisseo and ended at the niche in the *paese* wall where the communal
oven was built.

All at once—fatally late—my body was racked with fear. The dead-
ness of the silence encased us like pitiful pork sausages curing in the January air.

"Where are they?" I barely breathed.

"Who?"

"Whoever they are. They must be right here."

The seconds seemed too short for the volume of obscuring snowflakes collecting in the footprints.

"There's no one here," Cicca said flatly.

"How can there be no one." I was shaking, my teeth chattering. I was
going to die.

"The saint has given us the answer to our question."

"What question?"

"What happened to Ceciu Legato."

The fickle wind awoke from its nap and plundered past us, scattering
the top-lying snow dust and knocking a drift off of the tiles above the
puticha.

"Why do the footprints stop at the oven?" In the racing wind, I barely
heard my own voice.

Cicca drew me even closer, stretching her short neck so her hot breath thawed my earlobe. "We'll never know until the oven's been knocked down, too."

We drank grappa by Cicca's hearth to warm up. I felt like we were the only living souls in the cold, silent village.

"Are you telling me Tito Lico killed Ceciu Legato?" I asked her.

"Me tell you that! How could I tell you that?" Cicca's eyes glinted blackly in the fire. "Maybe the *saint* was telling you that."

"Do you *think* Tito Lico killed Ceciu Legato?"

"I don't know anything about that." She took a slurp of grappa. "Although Tito *did* kill my brother Pepe."

"There were a bunch of young men at the *puticha* one evening, drinking wine and playing cards and the usual. Then there was a brawl that started, two *ragazzi* fighting over a woman, drunken stupidness, and someone blew out the lamps. You know that trick."

"And Pepe was killed?"

"He was only twenty-five. They said it was an accident."

They.

"But you don't think it was an accident."

"It was a knife in the neck," Cicca said.

I remembered Vannina Favasuli's second smiling mouth. "When was this?" The residue of the cannabis and the creeping burn of the alcohol in my brain began, unbidden, to harvest my subconscious thoughts, uprooting them like turnips for rinsing and dicing.

"Nineteen twenty-eight," Cicca said. "The mountainsides were crawling with *carabinieri*." Mussolini's crackdown on organized crime. "Normally they didn't bother us here, they understood us and left us alone." She meant, of course, that Don Alvaro paid them off. "But there was that bad time when the Fascists were arresting everyone. They arrested Pepe, locked him up in the jail in Bova for two weeks."

"What for?"

"For nothing!" Cicca waved angrily. "For stealing animals, they said. There were some delinquents hiding in the forests, and they would attack shepherds coming along the goat paths to graze. They'd tie them up, rob them, take their animals. But Pepe was never involved in any of that."

Of course he wasn't. "So the *carabinieri* arrested Pepe."

"They took him to Bova, and the magistrate said, 'O, Pepe, you're either guilty because you did it or you're guilty because you're hiding the person who did it. If you tell us who the real thieves are we'll let you go.'" She shrugged. There were tears in her eyes. "He never learned how to choke down a grudge. He thought, *I'll testify against Tito Lico and it will serve him right.*" She tapped her head with her index finger so hard I heard it thrum like a ripe melon. "A fool, my little Pepe."

"So the fight in the tavern was a sham, it was just so Tito could get revenge."

"Not revenge. It was a reminder. About what happens when we don't stick together."

The kitchen was quivering with the cold of dawn. My grappa glass was empty. "No wonder you hate Tito Lico."

"Eh." Cicca waved this puerile articulation away.

"It was so important to send that reminder that he was willing to take a life," I said wonderingly. "To go to jail for all that time."

"That's not what the Wolf went to jail for. That was years later, some trouble he got in in Africo. Back when Pepe died, no one was ever arrested. Tito had to pay a fine for stealing because of Pepe's testimony, but he was never punished for killing Pepe."

Autochthonous justice.

Ceciu Legato had had Aspromonte justice invoked for him. I wondered what secrets he hadn't kept, or what tribal loyalties he'd misapprehended.

69

ON FRIDAY, JANUARY 20, THE SUN WAS BLINDING ON THE SNOW-drifts. I felt foggy-headed from our nocturnal adventures, my knees sore from bracing myself on the ice in the dark. I decided that the best thing I could possibly do was get back to work.

I wished that Ugo Squillaci were still there to advise me about his enigmatic and sometimes infuriating *paesani*. It was a yearning of such intensity that I almost wrote *him* a letter. But look what had happened last time.

My spiritual stew of defiance and misgivings had been simmering over low heat all night. Now I gave it a masochistic stir by pulling on my coat and crossing the snowy piazza to the *putìca*. I wanted to look a killer in the eye—see if that could help me figure out what I believed. Help me figure out what to do.

Tito Lico was sitting on his sun-shadowed stool by the window, a glass of unmixed milk on the table in front of him. Saverio Legato was polishing the counter.

"Just wanted to see if you had any newspapers."

Saverio looked at me sidelong, then grudgingly pulled out a three-week-old *Tempo*. It wasn't my ideal reading material but at least it wasn't one of the far-right weeklies. As I placed my money on the counter, Tito Lico caught me peering at him. He lifted his cap, showing me the salt in his pepper.

I tried to picture a twenty-something version of him brawling with Cicca's brother right here in this very room, Saverio's grandfather standing behind the counter, Saverio's father, Ceciu—another future victim—witness or accomplice.

The Chionoti generations were as tangled as the hemp fibers Cicca spun every night, an Archimedean spiral of marriages, kinships, and debts. There was no way to clip or extract a single strand. The Chionoti had to absorb their own violence, swallow it down—otherwise their whole society would be rent apart.

How can there be progress when people have been trained to swallow and swallow their own violence?

Where did I fit in?

"Good morning, Don Lico," I said bleakly as I took my purchase.

It only took the time I spent crossing the piazza for my hopelessness to combust like firedamp, leaving behind angry determination.

Eight years earlier Tito Lico or one of his henchpeople had buried a murder victim under the post office. But eight years was a lifetime. The world had changed so extremely since 1952—rock and roll, the Cold War, social movements for desegregation and land reform agitating governments from South Africa to South Korea to South Dakota. Even here in Santa Chionia young people like Ugo were breaking the power chains and making their own channels to prosperity. Parents like Ligòri and Teresedda Scordo—and so many others—wanted better for their children and were ready to sacrifice for it. Fear of the old brigand regime was dying out.

So they'd vandalized my nursery; I fixed what they'd ruined. So they'd tried to frighten me by breaking into my room. They wouldn't actually hurt me, not with my net of connections. If someone tried to hurt me, Sabrina would make sure they went to jail. She would go down fighting. So would my dad. So would my mom.

None of them was here, true. No harm in sleeping with a knife under my pillow.

Whether or not Tito Lico was a murderous old wolf, I wasn't going to let his machinations derail me further. It was 1961; it was time to make life better for everyone from the ground up. The era of gangster politics was over.

The snow had melted off the well-trodden alleys and crusted over with a glittering film of ice on the less-trodden. My hands were numb and it took me longer than usual to get the nursery's potbellied gas stove to light.

I would never make the Child Rescue deadline: there were only ten days left in January. But if I sent the student acceptance letters and announced an opening date, I would give myself half credit. The other problems would be forced to resolve themselves.

I sat down and started to write.

I closed up at four; the gloomy afternoon had already begun to darken into dusk. A crowd of men stood in front of the *puticha,* and another sizable group milled near Bestiano Massara's bench. Children ran between the clusters of grown-ups, not letting the human obstructions slow down their game of King in the Middle. I had to cut through to get to the steps of Sant'Orsola, and the ball went sailing toward my head. Instead of ducking, I took a chance and headbutted it, hoping my middle school soccer training wouldn't fail me. The ball rebounded satisfyingly, arcing over shouts of outrage and appreciation.

A black-haired twelve-year-old boy went skittering by in pursuit, quick as a fire salamander. It was Danilo Brancati, whom I'd hired to whitewash the nursery last fall.

"Danilo!" I called.

He subdued the ball and came jogging back. "Yes, *maestra*?"

"I have a job for you if you want to make a couple lire. Deliver a bunch of letters for me?"

His leaf-green eyes were bright in the overcast. "To the *posta*? The road is snowed out."

"No, just around Santa Chionia."

He looked at me like this was a crazy idea—I guess paying someone to walk around Santa Chionia when I could walk around Santa Chionia myself did seem crazy. But there was no reason not to accept money from crazy ladies. "I can do it. Right now?"

"Why not?"

"Why not," he agreed, and kicked the ball toward his protesting teammates. I pulled the packet of letters and he accepted a hundred-lire bill with stalwart reverence.

"Say hello to your mother for me!" I shouted as he bounded away up the marble steps of via Sant'Orsola.

"I will," he lied over his shoulder.

My heart beat with nervous excitement as I walked home. As I passed via Leonzio Pilato, a woman called out, *"Ciao, maestra!"*

I shielded my eyes from the bright setting sun to see who it was: Saverio Legato's wife, Sinedda, waving from her balcony, where she was hanging linens. The last time I had spoken to her had been the day her aunt Potenziana the Wolfess had commandeered my home visit and told me the Chionoti would never trust me with their children.

Sinedda set her hands on the railing, smiling. "Have you eaten, *maestra*?"

I waved back, my throat filling with the sting of hope. "On my way home to Cummàri Cicca right now."

Saverio Legato's wife did not hate me. Her little son Vincenzo—the grandson and namesake of the disappeared ex-mayor, Ceciu Legato—would receive his acceptance letter today, and his mother would be happy about it.

Through education we could shine a light to cut through the bleakest darkness. Through education could the grandchildren of killers and the grandchildren of their victims be lifted above their parents' misery, the sins and scars of their forebears washed away from their innocent little personalities.

No one was beyond redemption.

Not even me.

As I lay down that night, a great weight had been lifted off my chest. My nursery school was opening; I was only two weeks behind Child Rescue's schedule.

My only real problem was Isodiana Legato, and how I could help her. My last thought before I fell asleep was annoyance that Sabrina still hadn't responded to my urgent letter.

70

ON MONDAY, JANUARY 23, I SPENT THE MORNING TRAINING MARIA Scordo in Child Rescue pedagogical philosophy. She was bashful but had plenty of common sense. We filled out her employment paperwork to mail to the bureaucratic Brits. I let her go at quarter of one with a salary advance, then started toward the rectory per my standing Monday invitation. Bestiano Massara called to my back, "Don't let Mayor Stelitano force transferment!"

I flashed him a smile over my shoulder. "From each according to her ability!"

Don Pantaleone's door was answered by Mica Mafrici, the mother of my future pupil Salvino, who was lining up wooden spoons on the priest's floor.

"*Maestra!* Nursery's opening soon, isn't it? Salvino is counting down the days. Aren't you?"

The little boy looked up at me very seriously. "I'm all ready," he said.

Warmth spread through my chest. "I'm so glad, Salvino."

"Hello, *maestra!*" Don Pantaleone was only just arriving at the rectory himself. "Apologies, Mica, I forgot to warn you the *maestra* joins me for lunch on Mondays—is there enough?"

"Plenty." Mica tucked a cleaning rag into her apron at her slender waist. "I'll go get it now. Come with me to the kitchen, Salvino."

"Where's Gnura Emilia?" I asked when they were gone.

"She quit last week." The priest gave me a sad expression. "She told me she's too old and the work makes her tired. I hope she's not unwell."

"Me too," I said. Guilt frayed the edges of my newfound optimism. I've never believed in coincidences.

Talkative Mica had made a *bucatini* with sauteed fennel dressed with raw olive oil. The flavors were bitter and bright.

"In April, I will make you my wild artichokes." Mica tapped her cheek—*delicious.* "With olives and mushrooms—chili pepper if you can take the heat."

"Wait till you see them, the Aspromonte artichoke," Don Pantaleone said. "Bright purple flowers, spiny as a hedgehog."

"I can't wait." April—springtime—seemed just around the wash-riverbend.

Salvino wanted to sit on my lap and let me play dormouse with him (a surprisingly violent game—the dormice were to be smashed under trap stones and roasted). I had meant to discuss some of my concerns with Don Pantaleone over lunch, but instead I found myself spending most of my time on the floor pursuing make-believe rodents.

This was the moment, while I was tucked at least partially out of sight among the priest's lower-lying furniture, when there was a knock on the door. Mica admitted a dark-haired young man. "Don Pantaleone, good afternoon." He stepped past the housekeeper without acknowledging her but doffed his cap for the priest. "I'm sorry to bother you."

I did not recognize him because his expression—respectful solicitude—bent his features in a completely unfamiliar direction. Only when the priest said, "*Ciao,* Nicola, what's the matter?" did I realize it was Isodiana's disgusting little brother.

Nicola paid me no mind, or didn't see me on the floor. "They want to see the lien."

Don Pantaleone was still finishing his pasta and took the time to chew and swallow an unperturbed bite before replying, "Tell them the lien is all in order."

"They insist. They need to see it themselves."

"I'm not going all the way to Paracorio in the middle of a snowstorm to show them a piece of paper."

"Of course not, Don Pandalemu. Rocco can take it."

"Why should he have to? My word is enough for them to proceed." The priest gave his lips a decorous pat with his linen napkin and said to Mica, who was still hovering by the drafty door, "Thank you for that lunch, Mica. Just like my mother used to make."

Nicola Legato shifted in his snow-splotched boots, of which I had a peculiar vantage. I was about to stand when Salvino backed up and lowered his warm little bottom into my lap.

"They said they couldn't move forward without proof in writing," Nicola said. "They won't take no for an answer."

Don Pantaleone set the napkin on the table, regarded Nicola for a long enough interval that the horrible boy fidgeted. Then the priest stood and drifted to the shelves behind the lecture space and took down a leather-bound binder.

"Here. Feast your eyes." The priest's irony made his words ferric with implication. "It is the lien Don Roccuzzu was awarded by the Ruffo family. Now you have seen it and have no further need to test yourself with faith." He snapped the binder closed and put it back on its shelf. "But I don't know our friends in Paracorio well enough to give them the benefit of the doubt. Let them demonstrate their faith in me by requiring no further validation." The priest clasped the younger man's shoulder. "I'm sure they're counting on you to help them not offend me."

Insolent Nicola was visibly at war with himself, resenting the priest's refusal. "What do I tell them?"

"Tell them that I thank those who grant me the favor of their respect. But equally do I thank those who struggle against me. God gives me the gift of such adversaries, for they help me clarify my own path and ensure that I do not stall."

Mica shot me a scandalized glance. There was a tortured breath of static, and then Nicola was murmuring his angry thanks and stomping back out into the snow.

I had been savoring the warm weight of Salvino's little bum on my thighs, but he popped up the moment the door was closed. "The dormouse!" he cried. "It's getting away!"

"Where did it go?" I said, trying to reflect his distress, though I was distracted by the priest's threat still hanging in the air.

"It ran in here," he said, patting the oak storage trunk against the wall, and before it occurred to me to prevent him he was pushing the top open.

"Stop, Salvino, we mustn't go through other people's things." I reached out to grab the underside of the lid, which was too heavy for him, so that it wouldn't come smashing down on his little hand. My eye, naturally, caught what was inside the trunk.

I admit my troubling experience with Vannina Favasuli's storage trunk perhaps predisposed my mind, but for a terrifying moment it appeared to me that the trunk was packed with thousands of tiny muskets, stacked like Cicca's kindling.

Don Pantaleone was leaning over us, hooking the child in his elbow as he eased the trunk closed. "Ah ah, Salvino, those are not toys."

No, indeed, not toys. They were fireworks.

"Salvino!" Mica cried, belated. "Don Pandalemu, I'm so sorry—"

"It's nothing." The agile priest put the little boy down on the floor, where he crouched in humiliation. "Now, don't cry. No harm was done."

"Why do you have those?" I exclaimed. The hitherto mostly innocuous presence of the gas-canister space heater had suddenly become alarming.

Don Pantaleone didn't seem remotely embarrassed to have been discovered with the illegal and dangerous equipment. "For the Santa Chionia festival, in April."

"You keep them here, in the rectory?" It was on the tip of my tongue to ask him if he realized how unsafe it was—the idiocy!—but my wiser angel for once prevailed. It would do me no favors to undermine the priest's authority in front of a parishioner.

"Where else, *maestra*? They must stay dry, and under my supervision they can't be pilfered by teenage boys trying to show off for one another." The priest tucked a silver curl behind his ear, and in this foolish moment the vanity annoyed me. "Mica, I have some things I have to take care of at the church. *Maestra,* come with me, please."

It wasn't exactly a request, which I did not like, but I didn't realize that until it was too late for me not to accede. At least we would have a chance to talk alone.

The sanctuary was cold, and the priest didn't turn on the lights. We sat in the last pew. "Don Pandalemu, I am—"

"Have the arrangements for the money been made?"

"What?"

"The money for the Association's science program."

My throat stuck and I had to clear it. "I have had no reply." I had not, of course, actually written a letter that could be replied to. I didn't *want* to ask Child Rescue for money for Don Pantaleone's private project; I didn't believe it was appropriate. But I felt caught—he had backed me into a promise.

I was sure he saw the truth in my face. "Perhaps you will hear this week."

"Perhaps," I agreed.

"It's in everyone's interests, Franca," he said soberly.

He was a priest—of course he was adept at pressuring people into charity. But this request of his was discomfiting. It disfigured what I'd once thought of as a friendship between colleagues on matching missions. "The chances of their accepting such a petition are extremely small."

"They would send the money if they understood it was to support your success and welfare." He said it mildly, but his word choice caught my attention. A sour current curdled the air in the sanctuary.

The priest set his hands on his knees to stand, and I realized he was done with me. "Wait. I wanted to ask you—"

"Yes?"

I had his attention, but was no longer sure what to say. In light of his nagging for funds, I couldn't ask him for any favors—I couldn't afford to be perceived as in his debt.

There was one matter that involved no intercession on my behalf. "Agathi Petrulli."

"What about her?"

"I am afraid she may be engaged to marry her half brother."

The priest's frank, handsome face contracted. "Niceforo? What are you saying?"

"It's just that—that—" I stammered. "I was—Vannina Favasuli asked me to try to find her husband for her, and—"

"Did you?" he interrupted.

"Not exactly," I said slowly. I couldn't tell the priest what I had not yet told Vannina. "But I found—evidence that Mico had extramarital relations. Including—with Agathi's mother. And I believe—there is a possibility that Agathi and Niceforo are half siblings."

"Franca. You must be very careful. Cuckolding is taken very seriously here. These are words we never, ever say."

"Even if they're true?" I protested. "You would let a brother and sister marry?"

"Of course not. But even the *specter* of this thought must not be raised unless there is no shadow of a doubt. Do you understand me?"

My neck was heating up quickly and I tried to remind myself that I was *doing the right thing.* "Don Pantaleone, I am telling *you* now so I never have to tell anyone else. I thought that if there *was* a problem, you might be able to fix it in the most discreet way."

"I see." He was silent for a moment. I couldn't interpret his expression. "I will see what is to be done."

71

THERE WAS A FRESH BLANKET OF SNOW ON TUESDAY MORNING, and its white brightness filled me with resilient energy. That lasted until I got down the slippery hill to the nursery, where Mayor Stelitano's secretary was waiting for me.

"Mayor Stelitano needs to see you. Right now."

The mayor did not invite me to sit down.

"What could you have been thinking, *signorina*?"

"I don't know what you mean," I said, although I had an inkling.

"Why did you send out an opening announcement? All those letters!"

"You told me you weren't going to be involved anymore," I stammered. "I had to—"

"I told you I would let you know after Easter if we would be opening the nursery."

"That's not what you said! You asked me not to bother you, so I moved ahead." That goddamn flush on my neck. Goddamn it.

Stelitano rubbed his face in artistic dismay, allowing his hand to come to rest on his mouth as he shook his head disbelievingly. "You are pathological, *signorina*. You do things because they are on your list of things to do, not because you've used any common sense about whether they really need to be done."

I couldn't find the words to defend myself—maybe because I knew he was not wrong.

"You have a lot of awkward conversations to have now," Mayor Stelitano said. "You may leave. Your problems have nothing to do with me anymore."

My exit from the *municipio* was blocked by none other than the traffic cop Vadalà.

"My office, *signorina*." He gestured to the door on his left, and I stepped through it because I couldn't see any choice. I was quaking with dread. My eye went directly to the barred cell in the corner. Was that where they had locked up Vannina?

Vadalà closed the door behind us, which caused me to assume I was about to die. He sat at his desk and looked up at me condescendingly.

"*Signorina,* you've upset many Christians with your foreign assumptions. Morality is taken seriously in Calabria."

My racing heartbeat was slowing as I realized he was not going to kill me, at least not yet. "I know that," I said. What could he be alluding to?

"It's not like how you do things in America, where women sleep with whatever man they want and husbands raise other men's children."

Of course he knew about Ugo. Everyone in the village probably knew.

"I know," I said again, but my words were barely a breath.

"Then you should know better than to interfere with any Christian's marriage. You could tear a family apart for no reason."

My gut twisted. That didn't sound like it was about my adulterousness. What could he be referring to? What I'd uncovered about Mico Scordo's son Niceforo and his fiancée, Agathi Petrulli? Or was this about Isodiana Legato and wifebeater Santo Arcudi?

"I understand," I said. "I'll never interfere."

"Good." I suffered his greasy gaze for a long minute. "Remember that."

I was dismissed.

· · ·

Outside the nursery window the piazza was gradually filling, as it had every day since the referendum had been announced, with laconic shepherds and snowbound farmers. Against the winter-dismal wreck of the post office, their poverty was more starkly visible than ever: shabby wool sweaters hung with holes, feet clad in nothing but leather-strap laces, despite the wet snow.

The mayor wasn't my boss—he couldn't tell me what to do. Anyway, why was he so hell-bent on stopping the nursery from opening when it had been part of his campaign promise?

Because he was no longer committed to modernizing. He was trying to shift everyone's energy to transferment.

Someone had purchased the mayor—or more likely, the person who had always owned the mayor had decided Santa Chionia would be moved down to the marina. Some gangster who was intending to make a chunk off the dissolution of a millennia-old mountain culture thought I was going to roll over and let him.

I would not be intimidated. It was my choice not to be.

I marched back across the crowded slushy piazza and into the mayor's office, where I sat right down. He frowned at me, and I smiled back.

Be classy, Frank.

"I've had a chance to think," I told him. "I understand your predicament."

"My predicament?"

"I wanted you to know I am sympathetic. You have *so* many things to worry about." I looked him steadily in the eye. "The nursery must not be one of them. Leave all that to me. *Even if* the town ends up transferring to the marina, I will make sure the children have a nursery school to attend. I will not give up on them, and neither will my organization."

I hope he heard my determination, my independence, and my threat. We stared at each other.

"This community is special," I added, because I can never just leave things where I should. "It's worth every sacrifice necessary to preserve."

Mayor Stelitano's disbelief twitched in his walrus mustache, and I met his sad blue gaze. "All right. I understand what you're saying." He nodded to the door. "Good day, *signorina*."

. . .

As I petit-pointed my soaked-shoe path across the cobblestones, a woman's voice scattered the idle shepherds behind me. "You! American teacher!"

I turned around. I was face-to-face with Vannina Favasuli.

My chest clenched with that mild dread she always evoked. "Hello, Vannina."

"This woman is a monster!" Vannina screeched, thrusting her black-nailed finger in my face. "She is a *false teacher*! She is a *rat*! She will be the death of our *paese*!"

The crowd around us was forming an amphitheatrical semicircle. Hugging my briefcase, I looked past her at the battalion of familiar and unfamiliar faces. My heart was jumping with adrenaline. We were part of a pageant, I realized—this was like the proposal rejection, a drama to be played out for the information and entertainment of the citizenry at large.

No. I was not going to be a part of it.

I put my head down and walked past Vannina, feeling my face flaming.

Not quickly enough. She clawed at the neck of my dress. The collar sliced into my throat as she whirled me around with her gorilla strength.

"This woman!" Vannina shrieked as I coughed and rubbed my neck. "She comes into your homes and collects your secrets and steals your precious belongings! She has tried to *destroy* my family—she is probably trying to *destroy yours*!"

This had always been the eventuality of trying to help the town crazy woman. Not even the bleedingest of hearts can come out of such a blunder unremorseful.

"Vannina," I tried to say, and coughed again. "Vannina. Let's talk in private."

"*No!*" Her big dirty bare toes spread fiercely over the icy flagstones. "I will never speak to you in private again!" She turned back to the crowd, her wild curls flouncing picturesquely, her liberated breasts, as ever, magnificent. "This *rat* has been spreading *vile rumors* about my *beloved late husband,* who was *murdered*—"

"Vannina!" This time it was I who shrieked. She fell silent immediately. No one reacted to her accusation of murder, which probably shouldn't have come as a surprise. Everyone was looking at me expectantly. It was my turn to perform my soliloquy.

"Mico wasn't murdered." I spoke in a normal voice. My pity was genuine, even if it didn't look it.

"Lies!"

"He's alive," I said.

Vannina's face spasmed. "Prove it! *Rat!*"

"Okay," I said, and even though the woman had already suffered enough, some wretched part of me wanted the vindication. I opened my case and handed her Alexis's letter. "It's all in here," I told her, and the audience. "He's been living in Philadelphia this whole time. My friend tracked him down and had dinner at his house with his other wife."

The letter fell from her fingers, and I bent over to rescue it from the glistening pavers.

"Sorry to disappoint you, but he's not dead," I said. "He's just a bum."

I pushed through the crowd and hurried up Sant'Orsola.

I was rounding the bend by via Teano, breathing heavily as always, when I realized I wasn't alone. I turned and saw Rocco Alvaro a few paces behind me. My heart jumped. I soldiered upward—it wasn't my job to acknowledge him.

When Rocco spoke, his voice came from less distance than I would have hoped. "You have some curious friends, *maestra*."

I didn't reply, but my morning barley milk was churning to ricotta in my gut.

"You spend a lot of time with Vannina Favasuli?" He was at my elbow. "Vannina's an interesting lady." His words had that half-flirtatious, half-malicious energy behind them. "Not the person a schoolteacher would usually be expected to be friends with."

We were soon to summit the church piazza—he wouldn't be able to bother me much longer.

"Vannina knows lots of card games. You like to play cards, too?"

He had made his meaning too clear for me to pretend to miss. I glared at him, hoping I was hiding my fear. "I don't play cards with anyone."

"That's not what I hear."

A long beat of windy silence stretched as I thought frantically of how to react.

"I hear you're quite a card sharp," Rocco said at last. "Cummàri Cicca says we should all watch out for you and your American tricks."

The *thwack-thwack* of my heartbeat stumbled in hope. He had not said Ugo's name. He was only guessing. "I could never in my life beat Cummàri Cicca at cards."

I turned and walked briskly down via Boemondo, kicking unavoidable slush with my saddle shoes as I passed the closed-up church.

Rocco Alvaro was at my elbow again. "So if you don't play cards with Vannina, what *do* you do with her?"

I made myself stop. Most harassers trickle away when confronted, I reminded myself. "You seem to be lost." I pointed past the church piazza. "Your house is that way."

"I thought I'd walk you home." He showed me his sharp eyeteeth. On my right, the rectory was locked up, the windows dark behind the iron bars. Where was Don Pantaleone when I needed him? "After all, I'm a gentleman. And you seem like the kind of girl who is always looking for friends."

I tasted bile. "I'm not looking for friends."

"Maybe you should be."

I felt the menace of his physicality, although he was no bigger than I was. It occurred to me that this was not casual sexual harassment.

"Francesca!"

It was Cicca, appearing at the mouth of via Lilio with an oblong barrel of water balanced on her head.

"What are you doing, Francesca?" I heard the high tension in her voice.

Rocco Alvaro smirked and sardonically touched the rim of his hat. He strolled away across the empty church piazza.

72

I SAT AT THE KITCHEN TABLE WHILE CICCA STEWED LENTILS.

"Why was Rocco following you home, *pedimmu*?"

"I wish I knew." I was embarrassed to describe the scene in the piazza. I didn't want to be scolded yet again for getting mixed up with Vannina in the first place.

Vannina had called me a rat, I realized. I remembered the bottle of hydrochloric acid Rocco Alvaro had shown me in Don Roccuzzu's gleaming library.

That's what we use for killing rats.

A coincidence of word choice. Right?

Cicca tapped her wooden spoon on the rim of the pan and took a seat at her scutcher. "Ugo is much better looking than Rocco," she said with some bitterness.

"Oh god, please, Cicca. I was not flirting with Rocco Alvaro." I shuddered so as to leave no doubt. "Does Rocco Alvaro, uh, work for Tito Lico?"

"Rocco doesn't work." Cicca sneered at the floss in her lap. "The lord's son. Lazy chump."

"Yes, he does." Wariness sparkled in my marrow. In the rectory the day before, Nicola Legato had mentioned a Rocco involved in the deal he'd needed the lien for. "Rocco works for Santo Arcudi, doesn't he?"

Cicca's face was a moue of disapprobation.

Had Santo Arcudi sicced Rocco Alvaro on me? Why? To scare me into minding my own business? Or had Rocco just been picking on me for his skeezy entertainment?

"What exactly does Santo Arcudi do?" I asked Cicca. "He's a forester of some kind?"

"Forester, no, absolutely not. It's illegal to cut or sell any wood in our territory."

"What? It is?" I had been under the impression Santa Chionia had a thriving timber industry.

"Yes, since the Fascists." Cicca blew an angry raspberry. "They changed the law thirty years ago, for environmental preservation, they said. They made three-quarters of our forest into a restricted military zone. No more cutting down any trees of any kind on Montalampi. All the charcoal burners like my father had to find some other kind of work. Well, my father was dead already, so he didn't have to."

Environmental legislation destroying heritage livelihood for an already impoverished people—yet another incidental cruelty by the callous state. "That rezoning—was that the same time they started fining shepherds for their goats?"

"Same new law." Cicca lifted her face so I could see the totality of her disdain. "Now it's illegal for shepherds to graze their goats on our own land! What are Christians supposed to do?"

What exactly did the Italian government think would happen if an entire people suddenly had no legal means of making money? The state had turned every Aspromonte goatherd into a brigand. If you've already been painted with that brush, well—why not make a buck?

Could it be any wonder the Chionoti saw the state as their enemy?

Could it be any surprise that unscrupulous men stepped up to fill the power void?

I listened to the *shuck-shuck* of the hemp cards between Cicca's arthritic hands. Santa Chionia was an aerie of a human prison—no road in or out; no economy except the illegal ones; no law except its syndicate.

I felt like I had been staring at an object in the dark, coming closer and closer to try to make out exactly what it was, and now, too late, I realized that it was the velvet black nose of a wolf.

I had stood up to the mayor today, oh so bravely. But who else had I been standing up to without realizing it? Stelitano was only the wolf's nose.

So—what? Was I helpless, alone, deluded?

No, I wasn't helpless. There was one thing I had not yet done to help myself.

My limbs were weighted down with the sluggishness of misgiving as I removed a page of stationery from my briefcase and clicked open my pen. The noise drew Cicca's interrogating gaze, and guilt spread through my terror.

Dear Miss St. John–Jones, I began, *A need has arisen for an additional tranche of money—*

How could I word the request for funds for the Association for the Future science program that wouldn't cause Child Rescue to reject it outright? I would have to commit fraud—invent a need of my own and then manufacture a paper trail. If the petition was granted, I would basically be embezzling money from children in some other village.

The transactionality of this made me feel especially disgusted. Clientelism was the antithesis of progress. But expedience for the greater good could sometimes be a moral choice. Was it now? Much money had already been spent on the Santa Chionia nursery. If my project failed, all that overhead would be unrecoupable. For the price of a little quid pro quo, I could buy Don Pantaleone's support—and thereby God's, I thought sourly.

—to repair structural damage sustained during a flood that occurred on December 5, 1960. The onset of winter weather has revealed a need for professional attention—

There were no lies here. I could have written to Child Rescue in December asking for money for flood repairs, I reasoned. This was money they might have allotted me if they had known the predicament. Maybe I wasn't stealing money from other children; I was just borrowing it from myself.

To justify that, I would be paying "myself" back for years. My conscience might never recover. I knew that already, and there I was, still writing that damn letter.

I grunted my anger as I concluded the letter—certainly I wanted Cicca to ask me what was wrong. When she didn't, I had to volunteer the topic myself. "What do you think about Don Pandalemu's school?"

"The Association?" Cicca peered at me, trying to trace the chain of my thoughts. "It's very good. When I was a girl, there was no school. *Analfabeti,* all of us. A beautiful labor your friend the priest has made for the *paese.*"

A pay-to-play diploma factory, Ligòri Scordo had called it. "My friend the priest," I repeated. I watched Cicca *shuck-shuck* away at her fiber pile. She might not be sure where my loyalties lay. She had spoken worshipfully of the mayor as long as she'd thought he was my friend; only after she'd realized he wasn't had she invited her communist friends over for dinner.

"Tell me truly, *cummàri,*" I said. "Do you like Don Pandalemu?"

"Like him?" Her head popped up, her eyes globes of alarm. "He is such a holy man! So accomplished and blessed!"

"I know," I soothed.

"Don Pandalemu is the savior of Santa Chionia!" Cicca threw down her carding. "He has lifted our children out of the dark ages! When we were starving during the war, he carried sacks of dried pasta on his own back past the American blockade! He heals the suffering Christians with his hands!"

"I know!" I yelped.

Cowering under Cicca's suspicious gaze, I moved my writing aside and accepted a bowl of lentils.

The Association for the Future was still in session. I stood outside in the muddy snow, watching the sun disappear behind the mountains, before the door finally opened.

"How can I help you, Franca?" Don Pantaleone asked as the teenagers filed out. They were all boys, and touched their caps as they passed me.

"May I come in?"

"Not now. I have a meeting this evening."

The sting of his rejection was not entirely softened by his ever-dulcet voice.

"I just—I wanted you to know I sent the funds request to Child Rescue—"

"You sent it?" the priest said sharply.

"Yes, I—"

"How? Did you walk all the way to Roghudi in this snow?"

The last two teenage boys were leaving the rectory, notebooks under their arms, and their cap-doffing had an affect of shrewd curiosity. I wet my lips anxiously. "No, but I wrote a letter and when Oddo the postman comes—"

"So you didn't send it," Don Pantaleone corrected. "You *wrote* it. Let us not misrepresent the progress, *maestra*."

I have always crumbled under reprimands, even when I later kick myself for it. "I'm sorry. But I—"

"You made me a promise, Franca." Standing before each other like this, eye to eye at our full heights, I felt the power of the priest as adversary, the angelic ferocity of his charisma. "I will consider it honored when it has been completed."

"I understand." I felt the pressure of my fear behind my breastbone. I needed to protect myself from the evolving wrath of the mayor, of the men behind the mayor. I needed God on my side, just for a moment. "I was hoping we could talk about—"

"Not now," Don Pantaleone said. "I'll come down to the nursery and see you tomorrow afternoon, all right?"

He turned, and I realized that on the other side of the open rectory door, sitting in the armchair by the hearth, Santo Arcudi was studying me through his professor glasses.

"All right," I said. Don Pantaleone was already closing the door.

73

THE NEXT DAY, ODDO THE POSTMAN DROPPED BY THE NURSERY AT midmorning. "*Maestra,* there you are. I left four letters for you with Gnura Cicca."

"Oddo! How did you even get here?"

"I stayed in Roghudi last night so I could deliver to the interior *paesi* today," he bragged. His trousers were dark with snowmelt from trekking the goat paths.

"That's above and beyond," I said dutifully.

"Neither rain nor snow nor gloom of night." He gave me a twinkling blue-eyed wink. "Gnura Cicca said you had a letter you wanted me to take to Bova?"

I furrowed my brow at him. "I don't think so."

"You sure? The shepherds are saying more snow is coming. I might not make it back next week."

"I'm sure." The letter requesting funds from Child Rescue was burning a hole through my briefcase and surely scorching my desk. "I wonder what Cicca was thinking of."

"All right." He tipped his hat. "Keep warm, *maestra.*"

If I'd known that would be the last time I'd ever see the middle-aged delivery boy, I would have given him an American hug.

A little shaky from my impulsivity, I decided to go home. Cicca was out, the house dim and stale in its wintry wrap. I shut myself up in my room to read the stack of letters.

There was an aerogram from my parents and a letter from Sandro, which I opened first, out of addictive habit, and scanned with unfamiliar impatience—Sandro-esque exuberances about Pizzo; promises about our life together when I returned to Rome, in his mind a foregone conclusion; vexing admonitions about risk-taking behaviors I should avoid. Feeling brutalized by its presence, I sequestered it in the back pages of my old diary for later acts of masochism.

My parents' aerogram was from before Christmas. It was mostly in my mother's hand, and its chief content was her neuroses that none of her siblings wanted to drive out to Bryn Mawr for Christmas dinner and resented my mother for insisting on hosting. My father's short postscript announced he was going to attempt a Victorian-style crown roast, which I knew for a fact three-quarters of those people (including his wife) would bypass with confusion or alarm as they sought out the ravioli trays.

I started to smile at the image, but I was overcome. I missed my dad. I wished I had been there to gnaw on some beef bones with him in solidarity. I missed my mom. I wished I had been there to defuse her anxiety by helping her bake six times as many appetizers as could possibly be consumed by the number of guests expected—I was sure my dad had been blithely unsympathetic, maniacally focused on the outcome of his own experiment.

I tucked the aerogram into the sheaf I'd collected for six years—there were more than three hundred. The stack was nearly too thick for the rubber band I used to hold them.

I could always go home. Just—give up on everything here.

Now the tears were spilling down my cheeks. Leave behind Santa Chionia? Cicca? The children? My whole effort shrouded in failure, my overtaxed boss left to pick up the pieces? Who was I? How lazy, how devoid of honor?

Come on, Francesca.

I stopped myself, swallowed. I knew I wasn't lazy. I knew that honor was a multitextured idea.

I knew I shouldn't be feeling this exhausted or this sad. "An activist's life is a short one," my father had warned me when my parents had visited me in Cosenza last summer. "Think of Rosa Luxemburg, José Rizal, Sophie Scholl."

"Ida Wells," I'd retorted. "Mary Jones. Sojourner Truth. Elizabeth Cady Stanton."

"All right. But keeping up the stamina to worry about everyone else takes years off your life. Make sure you give up on all this before it gives up on you."

When people are counting on you, how can you convince yourself to let them down? How much personal cost to yourself is too much? Where can you really draw the line?

The other two letters were from the Child Rescue Calabria headquarters in Cosenza and the Baronessa Mento in Rome—Sabrina's aunt, whom I assumed Sabrina must have asked to drop this letter in the mail for her.

Dreading more bureaucratic rebuking from the former, I opened the *baronessa's* first. It had been four weeks since I'd sent my plea for advice about handling Isodiana Legato's domestic abuse situation, and I felt renewed urgency swelling in my breast as I worked my thumb through the gum on the linen-paper envelope.

Never in my life has the gap between my expectations and reality been crueler.

I read the *baronessa's* letter twice in denial. Then I tore open the other envelope, finding compassionately worded corroboration.

I had received no response to my plea for help because Sabrina Mento had passed away in her sleep on Monday, January 9. The doctors had been able to offer no explanation—she simply hadn't woken up. She was thirty-eight years old.

I should have known.

I should have known, I should have known.

I *did* know.

I mean, I didn't *know*. But I'd known Sabrina was in imperfect health, with her asthma and her poor sleeping habits. When we'd shared a sleeping chamber, there had been nights when she'd woken me up with a choking noise. The first time it had happened, I thought she was going to be sick and I'd leapt out of my bed to help her, only to find she was still asleep. I'd known, too, that she didn't take particular care of herself—she'd never go to a doctor, despite how often she counseled mothers on the necessity of regular checkups for themselves and their children. Why hadn't I pushed her to do the same?

My friend was dead. All the moments I'd imagined sharing with her for the rest of our lives—they had all been forced out of existence. All her secret stones I'd intended to turn over, eventually, when the moment was right, would go forever unturned.

I cried—I sobbed—for the children she'd never had. She'd put her desire to be a mother behind her; she was a true believer, and her notion of God's will had healed her of her loss. A family of her own would have taken her away from the hundreds of other babies she had to coddle. But knowing she had, at one time, wanted nothing more, in combination with my own heartsick desire—for some reason, this stupid grief disarmed me.

I struggle to think what else I can write here of my feelings. In sixty years I have spent many more hours grieving Sabrina than ever we passed together. She has haunted the most mundane moments. I think of her when I am caught by a window near twilight, because for precious months in 1959 I had spent every twilight by a window with her. And I think of her, still, every time I have the privilege of wiping a baby's bottom.

74

I LAY ON MY BED CRYING LIKE A CHILD FOR PERHAPS AN HOUR— long enough to hear Cicca come home, to muggily defer lunch. I remembered, eventually, that Don Pantaleone had made an appointment to stop by the nursery. Why should I not keep it? Crying all afternoon wouldn't bring me any closer to emptying myself of grief and regret.

I slunk down the xylophone steps of via Sant'Orsola. The gray sky was thick and close, the valley below disorientingly flat and colorless in the staling pressure in the atmosphere. More storm was coming.

The piazza was forlorn, the communist Bestiano Massara alone at his bench. He did not appear disheartened. I wondered if he had learned this equanimity in prison.

It was very difficult to concentrate. I listlessly wasted stationery trying to phrase my procedural questions—my boss was dead; to whom did I report now? Maybe I had no Italian boss at all; maybe I reported directly to London. Where, I was forced to remember, the general impression of me was that I had not been handling things well.

It didn't help to know that I had no allies or supporters in thousands of miles—no one with any stake in my success, or survival.

I was alone.

I was kneading my temples with my knuckles when the nursery door thudded open without a courtesy knock. Turi Laganà sauntered across the tiles, his hands hanging by his thumbs from his pockets. He did not bother to remove his cap.

"Maestra Franca."

My fear at being alone with this man hadn't caught up to me yet, although I knew it was coming. "Not applying for the teaching position, I hope. I'm afraid it's been filled."

He laughed more than the sarcasm warranted. "Too bad, too bad." He was watching me with playful warmth in his eyes. We had never spoken to each other before; he had never acknowledged my humanity, and I had abhorred him from afar. "Actually, *maestra*, I came to say you should give up on this idea of a nursery school here and move on to another *paese*."

"Oh, should I?"

"You should." His ridiculous ears gave even this intimidation a veneer of farce.

"Would you care to give me any reasons?"

"Reasons." He tilted his head back to look at the ceiling, an incongruously adolescent posture. I noted the striation of his gullet, the red trail of Bestiano Massara's scar down his clean-shaven neck. "Listen, *maestra*, there are Christians who do not want a foreign-run nursery school in Santa Chionia, and there will always be a struggle no matter what."

There was no further hurt to be sustained today. "You're threatening me."

"You misunderstand me, *maestra*. I am not threatening you. I am warning you."

"What's the difference?" In that moment, I felt only bleakness and disgust.

"The difference? Between a threat and a warning?" His boxy jaw hung low with amusement. "Only in your head, isn't it?"

We stared at each other, the air between us sparking with poisonous jocularity.

"Please give Don Tito my warmest regards." I showed him my teeth.

Turi Laganà doffed his cap, clasped it over the buttons on his waistcoat in two hands, and gave me a little bow. "He'll appreciate that."

Don Pantaleone Bianco never came to see me.

I didn't go see him instead. I was too angry and morose.

How much would have played out differently if I had? How many lives could I have saved that day? Or is it pure hubris to think that anything I could have done would have made any difference?

75

ON THE MORNING OF THURSDAY, JANUARY 26, I KNEW SOMETHING wasn't right before I'd rounded the corner of Sant'Orsola. I saw one of the nursery's shutters hanging open, hinge ripped away, and then I saw the debris in the snow.

I rushed the rest of the way, slipping over the flagstones. The door was ajar. Lying on the floor, among the busted limbs of benches and shards of glass, was the bloodied body of Bestiano Massara, so badly beaten that I recognized him only by his brick-red cap.

Saverio Legato came running from the *puticha* as soon as I shouted.

"What happened?"

"He needs a doctor!" I said, stupidly—there was no doctor. The unconscious communist was breathing raspily. I thought of all the things to be afraid of—concussion, broken ribs, punctured lungs?

"I'll get Don Pandalemu," Saverio said, and was gone.

In these distended minutes, I laid my jacket over the communist's blood-crusted shirt. His skin was the same temperature as my chilled hands. I crouched on the smashed tiles, my body wallowing in dulled inaction, shivering as the January breeze trundled through the broken door.

Bestiano Massara was a brave man—I'd seen him stand up to authority and convention every day for the last five months. How could anyone do him physical harm? Everyone in Santa Chionia was family; everyone knew what he had been through. Everyone had to respect him for continuing to fight the good fight.

Maybe the corner had been turned because he had *too* much respect.

The pieces were finally clicking into place. If my ugly emerging picture of the *paese* was correct—if the right-wing mayor was kept in power by a criminal syndicate overseen by Tito Lico, who needed Stelitano to force transferment to the marina so he could capitalize on whatever illegal contracting or deforesting or banking relationships had made him so wealthy—I had never been anything to Santa Chionia but a pawn to win the election for the Democratic Christians. The nursery project was a joke, doomed from the start. Now I had proven myself to be too much of a problem and they needed to get rid of me. We were tied together, Bestiano Massara and I: he an unexpectedly too-viable left-wing candidate poised to upend seventy years of brigand hegemony, I the unexpected traitor to the genteel status quo.

He'd warned me, I thought helplessly. Tito Lico had sent Turi Laganà to warn me to back off and I had spurned him and now Bestiano Massara had paid the price.

And here I was waiting for the medical intervention of the priest, who in all likelihood was in Tito Lico's pocket just like the rest of them. He'd been the one to bring me here, after all. Maybe he'd known from the beginning his cousin the mayor was going to use me to fix the election. Don Pantaleone Bianco had never been my friend.

I had no friends at all. Only arrogance, and illusions.

"What happened, *maestra*?" Ligòri Scordo was standing in the snowlight at the nursery's vandalized door.

"Masciu Massara is hurt," I said. "We're waiting for the priest."

"Eh, Bestianeddu." Ligòri crouched, gently prodding the communist's neck for a pulse. His jaw was tense with worry. "They left him here like that?"

I nodded. I was expending a lot of effort not to cry. "Why . . . why would anyone do this?"

"It's a message."

"To say what?"

"It doesn't matter what it says," he said shortly. "It matters that we received it."

A hundred years ago they carried knives, not guns, I remembered Ligòri saying. *How can one simple man fight back anymore, no matter how brave he is?*

Ligòri Scordo was removing his jacket to pile under Massara's head as three more men arrived: Limitri Palermiti, the shingle maker; Turi Laganà's companion, Pascali Morabito; a shepherd I didn't know. Pascali turned around and left immediately without even bothering to pretend concern. *The wrong man's creature.* Could there be so much evil in these politics that a man could turn his back on suffering because its victim was on the Other Side?

I was too scared to be offended.

Arms crossed over his chest, Limitri surveyed the damage: furniture dismembered, expensive glass windows broken, profanity knifed into the paint. "Who did this to you?"

"I don't know."

"This isn't right." Limitri was personally aggrieved by the damage to his floor tiles.

I had been unfair to Pascali Morabito; he was already back, and he had a broom and a woman who must be his wife, who was carrying a bucket and some rags.

"This isn't right, *maestra,*" she echoed. She took the broom from her husband and began sweeping the glass.

"We can get this fixed," Pascali said.

"We can get it fixed." Limitri was toeing dejectedly at a broken floor tile.

"*Carina,* what happened?" It was Mica Mafrici and her mother-in-law, who hunched to pick up shards of furniture.

When Don Pantaleone arrived, I was sitting, useless as a *pietà,* with Bestiano Massara's prone body at the eye of a hurricane of Chionoti industriousness. Numb, overwhelmed, I watched the priest feel along the unconscious communist's neck and spine.

"This does not look good. We need to get him to a bed. Eh, boys!"

I watched as the full-grown men—Pascali Morabito, Limitri Palermiti, Ligòri Scordo, the fourth one I didn't know—all obediently stopped what they were doing.

"You—arms and head. You—shoulders. Make sure to support the neck and spine. You—get the legs."

Little men, and big: I watched them carry the sagging communist out the door with dexterity and tenderness.

"Don't worry, *maestra*," Mica said. "The priest and God will take care of him."

"And *we* will take care of this."

Standing in my doorway, silvery sunshine backlighting her like a Renaissance angel, was Isodiana Legato.

"Stupid children." She pulled her cloak off her shoulder, revealing Nino, who was chewing on the dowel of a wooden spoon. "Grown men acting like stupid children. This is an *embarrassment*."

I saw Mica and her mother-in-law exchange a look. "Masciu Bestiano is badly hurt," Mica said.

"An *embarrassment*." Isodiana thrust the baby into my arms. "Keep him out of trouble, *maestra*."

She pushed up her sleeves.

We worked, from each according to her abilities.

I dipped ineffectually, baby on my hip, to pick up one piece of debris at a time, while around me the women swarmed and scrubbed. No one spoke. I tried to think about what this meant for Santa Chionia, violence like this, so splashy and public. I wondered how many of the women in this room knew who was responsible.

It was not long before there was nothing else that could be done without new materials. I had to urge my helpers to go back to their own busy days. Isodiana kissed me on the cheek as she took Nino. "Try not to worry, *maestra*," she'd said, and this terrified me.

When they were all gone, I stepped out onto the piazza. The air was sticky with the promise of springtime, the bright sun clearing wet stone through the snow. The church bell began to toll, a long, redundant clang. I listened mindlessly to the clanging, listened until I realized it had tolled many more than twelve times. The bell wasn't ringing the hour. It was announcing a death.

I left the nursery door standing wide open behind me and walked to Bestiano Massara's bench, whence he had done his best to persuade the Chionoti it was their right to demand more than what they had.

The ruptured wall behind the hole of the post office opened up into a V of breathtaking vertigo, a breach in the thousand-year-old city balustrade. A mile below, the Attinà crashed against the white sand of the ravine. Life in Santa Chionia had always been lived on the edge of the abyss. The beauty of it lulls you to the fact that any step you take might be a fatal one.

I couldn't help Bestiano Massara anymore.

But for the rest of my life I would carry around the unanswered question: had he died for me?

Would Bestiano Massara have won the election if I hadn't come to Santa Chionia?

Would the corrupt local power channels have been disrupted? Would the town not have been forcibly evacuated? Would the people of Santa Chionia still be living in their mountain home, modernized and made safe, instead of scattered into now-vanished ethnic ghettos in inhospitable big cities like Reggio and Milan?

If I had never stood in that piazza and stared out at the unearthly loveliness of the valley, the foothills glinting like the green dorsals of fish tumbling toward the concealed promise of the sea, would there still be a piazza? If I had never thrown myself so blindly into my cause, would there still be a cause? Would this ancient kingdom be more than a choking net of wild raspberries bursting through rubbled stone?

Or would everything have turned out exactly the same as it had?

76

CICCA FORCE-FED ME BEAN AND POTATO SOUP.

"I can't eat this," I'd told her.

"What, my cooking is no good?"

"I feel sick thinking about Masciu Bestiano."

"He is in God's hands. Now eat." Cicca went as far as to lift the spoon to my mouth and nudge my lips open. "It doesn't help him at all if you starve."

Bestiano Massara had been Cicca's friend; I should have been the one comforting *her*. Suppressing my nausea, I accepted a mouthful of beans. "Who would do that to him?"

"Stupid thugs." She slammed the pot down on the table between us. "Stupid thugs who only care about getting their way and nothing else."

I thought of the faces of the men I had met in Santa Chionia. Their gentle eyes, their soft voices, their quick fingers on their hand-whittled musical instruments. I couldn't imagine any of them beating a middle-aged activist to death.

Almost none of them.

Twenty years ago, a young local thug, Turi Laganà, had kidnapped, raped, and caused the death of Bestiano Massara's fiancée, Rosa Romeo. That local thug wasn't young anymore, but he roamed the streets, rehabilitated; he proctored the local elections.

Cicca pulled her stool alongside mine and put her callused palm on my forearm. "What are you going to do about the nursery, *pedìmmu*?"

"I don't even know."

"Think it through. What are your choices?"

It's what my father would have said, too.

"Clean up and keep going." When I had mastered myself, I went on, a little brokenly: "Or take the hint and give up. I can't let anyone else get hurt for me."

Cicca refilled my bowl. I had no appetite.

"Do you think whoever did it will do it again?"

Cicca looked down at her hands. "I don't know."

Exhausted by two days of layered griefs, I retired at nine o'clock. I was combing out my hair when I heard a rapping at my window. My heart stopped, I mean literally stopped—I felt it stutter as it restarted.

The euphorbia's little yellow face beseeched me from the sill. No—no. No one had ever climbed in through my window, prowled through my belongings while I slept. My window was too high up from the ground.

The rapping came again.

I was suffocating, and forced myself to suck in a breath. The men who had attacked my nursery wouldn't knock.

I opened the shutter two inches, just enough to see the top of a woman's kerchiefed head in the indirect light from Cicca's kitchen.

"Maestra Franca," she rasped. "Please."

My panic vanished like a morning mist in the mountain sun. I opened the shutter all the way. "Who is it?"

Her tracks cut through the snow over Cicca's garden wall. She had climbed up onto the roosting beam to reach my window; the faithless chickens slumbered on by her skirts. All this time my bedroom had been much easier to break into than I had been deluding myself.

"Please, *maestra*." I still didn't recognize her voice, hoarse and phlegmy, but Isodiana Legato raised her broken eye to meet mine just as the baby in her arms started crying. "Please hurry."

In the kitchen, I held the crying baby, feeling his angry heartbeat against mine, while Cicca tried to clean Isodiana's face. She had groaned in pain as I'd hauled her up through the window, and I wondered what other injuries her cloak concealed.

"This is too much, *pedimmu*," Cicca told her.

"I know."

What had scared Isodiana enough that she had fled her house was this time Santo had strangled her until she lost consciousness. When she came to, she told us, she had snatched up the crying baby and her feet had carried them here.

Patchy red stripes on the left side of her neck conjured an unmistakable ghost hand over her throat. One eye was as red as a tomato, the white completely blood-flooded by the vessels that had burst.

"He's going to kill me. He'll actually kill me." Isodiana's voice cracked into hyperventilating sobs.

"Don't cry in front of your son," Cicca admonished her, and Isodiana stopped instantly. "What did you do that made him so mad, my dear?" she asked, even though Cicca of all people should have known better.

"It was me," I answered, and Cicca treated me to her most baleful scowl. "Wasn't it, Isodiana? You came to the nursery to help clean up, even though Santo told you never to have anything to do with me." Her head hung and I couldn't see her face. Two more pieces notched together in the jigsaw puzzle I was assembling in my mind. "It was your brother and Santo—they destroyed the nursery, didn't they?"

"Not . . . not Santo," she whispered.

No—Santo was too important. I felt the power map I had been trying to draw in my mind shifting—the organization was still murky to me. All I knew was that all the Chionoti were somehow part of it, either in its employ or in its thrall.

Cicca's ministering hand dropped to her side and she took a step back, knotting the bloody rag among her knuckles. "Nicola? Nicola killed Bestianeddu?"

Isodiana didn't reply. She had turned her face to her lap and was pressing her fingertips into the bruises on her neck.

"Why, Isodiana? What good did it do him to kill our sweet Bestianeddu?"

I clutched the warm packet of Nino, hiccupping silently against my shoulder. The bite in Cicca's voice made me flinch, but I wanted to hear the answer to her question.

"Was it the election?" Cicca demanded. "Bestianeddu had too many people deciding they were ready to be brave again?" A pale pink droplet fell from the rag in her shaking fist to leave a wet blemish on the concrete floor.

"I don't know—" Isodiana broke off and tried again. "If my father had been here . . ."

"He's not here, though, is he? So who is going to be responsible for this bloodshed?" Cicca's anguish was distilling into rage, and there was battered Isodiana, captive to receive it. "This was not an act of honor. This was an act of shame."

"What do you want me to do about it?" Isodiana snapped. "I cannot even protect my own children. I cannot even save my own life."

I wrapped my hand around Cicca's elbow and squeezed, and she leaned her trembling shoulder against me. "I'm sorry this happened," I told Isodiana. "I am so sorry."

Her one dark eye and one red eye flashed up at me, wet with controlled tears. "Nothing has been right since you got here. Santo thinks—he thinks the worst thing about you. He has never trusted one thing I've said since you got here."

I wondered what the "worst thing" was in his mind. That I was some kind of lesbian American seductress? That I had tried to empower his meek housebound wife to make a salary for herself? I guess it didn't matter.

"How can I help you?"

"You can't," Isodiana said bitterly. "I came here because I was afraid he would kill me and now he is going to kill me for coming here. I have no one to go to. My brother Saverio would send me back to Santo to apologize. Nicola would stab me with his own knife." She raised her skirt to her face in two fists. "I don't know what's wrong with me. I am not my mother. What was I thinking? I don't deserve to live."

"You can stay here," I said, before realizing the house wasn't technically mine to offer. "Right, Cicca? She would be welcome, wouldn't she? There's a whole extra bedroom upstairs—you and the children would have plenty of space."

I bounced the baby in the uncomfortable silence. Isodiana was staring at her skirt. Cicca's lips turned halfway up in a little smile I realized was not a happy one.

Of course Isodiana could not stay here. Cicca was afraid of Santo, too. She was a tiny old woman who had survived this long by appeasing priests and cops and rebelling only in the shadows. She would not contradict me now, but only because on some level she was afraid of me, too.

I bit my lip, hard, then harder, until it seemed like it wouldn't hurt as much to make myself say the words. "What if we could get you out?"

The baby on my chest turned his bright eyes on his mother, and my words hung, too loud, in the cold air.

"Out where?" Cicca said.

"I am leaving Santa Chionia. Come with me, Isodiana."

"What?" She looked like she hadn't understood. "Come where?"

"Rome." In my mind, the contingencies clicked together like train tracks, speeding a vision of us toward where all roads lead. "You can live in my apartment. You'll love the city. So many parks and shops. I will find you a job with Child Rescue—it will be perfect for your temperament."

"Leave Santa Chionia?" I might as well have asked Isodiana to believe in dragons.

"Just for a while," I lied soothingly—just the way Ugo had tried to talk me into leaving with him for Milan. "Until things calm down."

"My children—"

"Of course we'll bring them. You can say—you can say I've invited the children on a holiday to Rome. Or—that you need to see a specialist doctor."

"A—specialist doctor?" Isodiana put a hand on her abdomen, which made me optimistic. "Really?" She looked at Cicca, then back at me, with her frightening red eye. "I don't have any money for tickets."

"I have plenty of money." If I succeeded in talking her into this, what would I do? I had no apartment in Rome except the one owned by Sandro—I would have no choice but to return to my marriage, to bottle up the badness and try to make it right. I would have to trade my soul for her life.

Put in those terms, the choice was obvious. I gave Isodiana a resolute smile.

She gulped a thirsty little breath. "What do you think, *cummàri?*"

Cicca took Isodiana's hand in one of hers, then mine in the other. "I will be happy you will be safe." She squeezed my hand hard. "Both of you."

Cicca boiled Isodiana laurel leaf tea and the baby fell asleep on my chest, so beautifully, while I babbled frenetically—about Rome, about opportunities and sights and foods her children would enjoy. Isodiana said barely anything.

"What are you thinking, Isodiana?"

She said softly, "Santo will never let me go."

"He won't know. He doesn't matter." I was electric with my decision—I would abandon Santa Chionia, but it would be a worthy sacrifice if I could save this exquisite woman and her vulnerable children. I just needed her to have faith.

"He'll track me down." Isodiana took a swallow of the tea. "He'll find me and bring me back in a cage if he has to."

"That's not going to happen. It is 1961. Women do not belong to their husbands anymore. He can't make you do anything you don't want him to."

"He can take away my children."

"He wouldn't dare try. My friends in Rome know all the best lawyers." I hoped my voice didn't betray my misgivings on this one. "You will be safe and happy and you will raise your children without any fear that their father will hurt them."

Isodiana's eyelids dropped shut for a long moment. "Every day I have to pray it is only me and not them."

"One day it *will* be them. Only you can stop that day from coming, Isodiana, and it's by doing a difficult thing now." I stared into her eye, and she stared back. "It will be hard, but I will do everything I can to make it easier. Are you ready?"

Isodiana Legato gave me a tight, trembling smile. "I'm ready."

77

SANTO DID NOT COME FOR ISODIANA DURING THE NIGHT. PER-haps he didn't know she was with us. It had seemed unlikely to me, though, that he wouldn't search, and what were the odds that no one knew where she'd gone?

After Cicca sent Isodiana to bed upstairs in the cheese loft, we barred all the windows and sat in the kitchen together. Cicca told me to go to bed, but it was halfhearted—neither of us wanted to be alone. Instead I helped her card hemp, my fingers clumsy with exhaustion and snagging periodically on the nail boards. A little blood was good—it kept me alert, and lethargy was more immediately deadly than tetanus.

Cicca and I sat elbow to elbow, she on her bench, I on a stool, so close I sometimes tapped her knee by accident. At least I could whisper to her and hope Isodiana wouldn't be able to hear through the floor. "What will happen to Nicola? And the others?"

"What can happen," Cicca said after a moment. "It's not like Bestianeddu can testify."

"So—nothing?" I heard my voice rising.

Cicca's face was tight with worry. "If Santo finds out what she told us . . ."

"What she—" I started to ask, but realized what Cicca meant before I finished. Isodiana had violated the sacred wall of silence by giving us any clue that she knew her brother was involved. "I might have gotten Isodiana in terrible danger," I said.

"They cannot find out. They'll say she was a rat, just like her mother."

A rat. "But—"

Cicca began to cough suddenly, turning her face into her shoulder. When she turned back, her eyes were red and watering. "Sometimes it's better for everyone not to know the truth exactly."

"But a man has been murdered. Your *friend*! How can the *paese* not demand justice? He was—he was a pillar of the community!"

Cicca glowered at me, and I wondered if the idiom "pillar of the community" didn't render into Italian. But then she said, "When someone knocks down a pillar, what happens? The roof comes crashing down. So unless you want to get killed, you get out of the way."

I let this sink in. "Even now no one will go to the police?"

"Francesca. What can you be saying." I had never heard Cicca so dismayed with me, even back when she used to hate me and steal my underwear. "Police, police, always with the police. The police answer only to money."

"That's not true or fair. There are police who—"

"*All* of them," she interrupted me. "Yes, there are probably good men who become *carabinieri*. But they follow the orders of bad commanders. Or maybe *those* commanders are good men, too—who can say? Anything is possible. But *they* are kept in their jobs by politicians who care only about filling their own pockets. Don't you understand?"

I felt a rising sense of panic at this utterly bleak vision. If everyone felt as she did—if everyone gave up hope before they even tried—the only possible outcome was the worst-case scenario. "The policing system is nowhere near perfect. But you *have* to report a murder—a line must be drawn at some point."

"There is not a police officer in the entire province who would come after Bestianeddu's killers." Cicca was not emotional about this; this was her reality, facts and circumstances she had been born with. "Oh, they would give us a million reasons—there are no witnesses, the attackers were defending themselves. If there is an arrest, it will be for show, and it might not be the person *you* want to see arrested. And through all this the Chionoti will stay silent, because they are as frightened of being stitched up by cops looking for easy convictions as they are of appearing to have collaborated." She shrugged, her eyes fixed on her work. "We *are not traitors*," she said, and there was a fresh intensity in her voice. "To betray the whole *paese* like that—no Chionoto would do such a thing, or he would expect to pay the price. A mother would kill her own daughter before she would let her collaborate with the police."

This specific hyperbole ignited my fury and my grief. "What a grotesque adage for people to repeat. Of course a mother wouldn't kill her daughter."

Cicca dropped her nail pallet and seized my wrist, squeezing. "You are wrong." Her small black eyes were cinched with anger. "And no one in the world knows that better than Isodiana Legato." After a contusing long moment Cicca released my arm and picked up her carding again. "No police, my dear. We need something different from your idea of justice."

In the chilly silence I tried to guess what Cicca wasn't telling me. When her father went missing, had Isodiana tried to go to the police? Had she had that forsaken notion beaten out of her by her own mother?

What were the odds that Isodiana hadn't known it was her father's body under the post office this whole time? That everyone in Santa Chionia, except maybe Emilia Volontà and Vannina Favasuli, hadn't had an inkling?

That Cicca, my co-investigator, hadn't?

Watching her card, I allowed my hopelessness to subsume me. "Aren't you terrified? Is this the new order in Santa Chionia, bullying and violence, everyone living in fear? Don't you understand that if you don't fight back now it will get harder and harder?"

"I am an old woman," Cicca said.

"I know," I said, ashamed. "I didn't mean—"

"I am an old woman," she said again. "I have nothing to lose. It is up to people like me to fight back, *pedimmu,* isn't it? Because girls like her"—she lifted her chin toward the ceiling, where Isodiana's scuffing feet paced the floor above us—"they have everything to lose. We cannot ask them to fix the mess we have made through our cowardice."

"The old and the young have to fight together." And here I was, leaving her. "I will come back as soon as I get Isodiana and the children safely to Rome, in the care of my friends. I will—"

"No, *pedimmu.*" Cicca shut me down with a hand on my knee. "*You* must fight where you can do your best work, and not waste yourself on the wrong battles."

· · ·

There were so many conversations I still wanted to have with Cicca, so many questions to ask her, and now I was out of time. But that night I couldn't bring myself to talk. The shock of Sabrina's death, the guilty weight of Bestiano Massara's, the violence done in my name to Isodiana—the mélange of failure and fear and disbelief was too much.

Cicca boiled us a third pot of coffee and I was listening to San Silvestro drone six o'clock when Isodiana came downstairs with the baby. She looked awful, the bruises of yesterday newly black and livid, the dried blood rimming the insides of her nostrils giving her a ghoulish skeletal affect.

"Sit down," Cicca said. "Would you like coffee, my dear?"

"I don't—I don't know what to do." Isodiana stood by the table as Nino grabbed at the gold saint medal around her neck. "I have to go home to the children."

Desperation rose in my chest. She couldn't back out on me. "You said Santo would kill you."

"I have to take the chance. My poor girls. I have to get them out of there." She turned her beseeching blood-red eye on me. "*Maestra,* will you walk me?"

"You cannot come to my house," Isodiana whispered as we walked, heads down, past the cistern. We were going the long way to avoid the foot traffic on Sant'Orsola.

"How shall I get in touch with you?"

"We'll meet," she said. The packed road glinted with melting snow. "Dawn tomorrow—that's when I go downstairs to collect the eggs. Wait in the bend in via Zaleuco. We can make a plan then."

"Got it."

"But—we cannot leave tomorrow. The roads will still be closed."

"It's very sunny. If the snow melts we will leave on Sunday. Can you be ready?"

Isodiana shook her head. "There's nothing to get ready. Just the children."

"And will the children be able to walk as far as Roccaforte? From there we can get the bus, but—"

She laughed, a humming chortle. "They are mountain children, Franca. They can walk to Rome if they have to."

The sound of her laugh lifted my heart. I squeezed her arm. "You have such a bright future, Isodiana."

But my optimism was only gold plating over my fear for her. What would happen to her when she got home?

I left her at the end of the road so as not to get her in worse trouble.

I was coming home down via Boemondo when I spotted tiny Emilia Volontà bent over a weighted wheelbarrow of firewood dry-wrapped in burlap. She was toiling to push it around the steep snowy curve up via Occhiali.

"*Kalimèra, gnura,* can I help you?"

The old woman dropped the handlebars, her spine slumping as she took two deep breaths.

"*Gnura!* What are you doing?"

"I have to get this up to the Alvaro house, teacher." She gave me her outsized shrug.

"I'll help you," I said, though I dreaded pushing a wheelbarrow up that isosceles hill.

"No, teacher, this is my job to do." She lifted the handlebars again. "God bless you, teacher."

"God bless you," I repeated.

I watched the skinny ancient woman force her burden up the mountain. I wondered if this could be my fault, too—the fact that she had quit her job working for Don Pantaleone and had had to go back to physical labor at her age.

I wondered, with much-delayed insight, what Don Pantaleone had done to make her quit working for him.

78

IT WOULD HAVE BEEN VERY CONVENIENT IF I COULD HAVE CALLED Sandro to warn him I was coming. But when I stopped at the *municipio* I found, of course, that the Santa Chionia phone line was not working.

For some reason, this fact was a death blow to my crushed spirit, though I couldn't have reasonably expected any other outcome. "When are they going to come fix it?"

Pino Pangallo looked at me almost pityingly. "I don't know if they are."

I walked to the nursery, trying to appear nonchalant—a normal day's work in a vandalized building. I packed everything I wanted to keep into my briefcase, which I was too paranoid to ever let out of my sight. I thought guiltily of the donors' money wasted on furniture that had been broken and electricity wired and rewired to no child's benefit.

Could I really walk away from it?

I thought of the parents like Mica Mafrici, who thought her Salvino would be coming to enjoy this space in two weeks; of Ligòri Scordo, who had seen the nursery as a way of giving his Ninuzzu a better shot. I would be one more northerner who had abandoned them when things seemed complicated.

Things would always seem complicated.

I thought of what my father had said—that it wasn't worth my life.

Whose life was it worth?

The sun had not yet risen when I started down the mountain to meet Isodiana on Saturday morning, but the hillsides were already seething with goldfinches.

A shepherd I didn't know was following a winter-puffed flock of sheep east toward the Bova "bridge" as I crossed the piazza. He removed his hat and gave me a formal half bow. "*Maestra.*" His accent was lilting and Greek.

I turned to watch him go, this respectful stranger, and my heart ached with regret.

I waited in via Zaleuco for what felt like a very long time, watching silvery dawn slide up the dripping moss of the cliff alcove. I was chilled to the bone by the time Isodiana came around the corner.

"How are you?" I whispered.

"Fine." Her scalp was covered by a shawl, which was pulled low over her face.

"The children?"

"All fine. Tell me quickly what you need to, Franca. I cannot stay away."

"We will leave here at dawn tomorrow—all right? As long as we catch the eleven forty-five train from Melito, no one will be able to catch up with us until we're safe in Rome. Cicca is going to walk with us to Roccaforte so we can manage the baggage better, but try to pack light. We can buy anything you need when we get to Rome."

Isodiana was silent. The morning air was so still that if it hadn't been for the ruckus of the finches in the cliffsides I would have wondered if time had stopped.

"What is it, Isodiana?"

"I'm so afraid." Her head tipped down toward the ground and all I could see was her perfect round brow.

I wanted to reach out and squeeze her hand, but I felt a barrier between us I wasn't brave enough to cross. "Change is terrifying. That is natural. Don't be afraid of your fear, Isodiana. It's a sign that you've taken control of your own fate. Yours and your children's. You're giving them a bright new world."

"What if they follow?" she whispered.

They.

"They wouldn't dare," I promised her. "They have other things to worry about right now. Your brother Nicola has just murdered a man. They could hardly want to force you or me into calling in the police and testifying against them."

There was another long silence, so long that I was worried Santo would come out of the house and catch us and it would all be over. Finally she lifted her face. Her left eye was a ball of blood, and I was shocked afresh by the brightness of its red.

"*Maestra.* Did you ever figure out—did you ever figure out who the remains under the post office belonged to?"

"I did," I said slowly. I was not cut out for these two-sided charades of plausible deniability. I had never been able to see no evil, not unless it was a byproduct of my existential nearsightedness.

"Who—who did it belong to, the remains?" The petechiae stippling her left cheek were the ugly brown of an oxidizing slice of eggplant. "Was it that—that Leo Romeo boy?" I was still choosing my words when she rushed to add, "The one who—you were looking for my father's letters about?"

"No." I owed her the truth—if for no other reason than it might ease her decision to leave. "No, Isodiana. It was your father."

"My . . . my father?" I watched her brow come down over her livid right eye. "Do you—do you know what happened?"

"Not exactly. But—I am pretty sure . . . He was killed the summer you got married. When the pension delivery coach was hijacked on the Cardeto road—August 1952? When your brother Francesco was shot by the *carabinieri*?"

Isodiana didn't say anything. She was sucking on her cheeks, and her round face was pinched by shadows and bruises.

"That's around the time your father supposedly emigrated to Pennsylvania, right?" I persevered. "I couldn't figure out why he would emigrate. Why would a middle-aged man like your father—the mayor of a town, well-off, with adoring children and grandchildren—leave everything behind and start over in a foreign country? It doesn't make any sense." I watched her black pupil slide down the cherry-red ball of her visible eye as she broke my gaze. "Your aunt Potenziana tried to make me believe he had gambling debts he was running away from, but that doesn't fit with anything else I've learned about him or your family. His prosperous children could have lent him money. Your brother Saverio runs a bustling shop. Your husband, his son-in-law and nephew, seems to be involved in a lucrative timber business." Which I now knew was illegal—I let that implication hang between us. "Santo *should* have been able to bail him out."

Did I put too much emphasis on "should"? Did she hear the unspoken accusation?

"You don't really believe he emigrated either, do you?"

Isodiana's mismatched eyes beseeched me. "So—you think my father was killed over a gambling debt?"

"No." It was difficult to say this to her face—I felt foolish, convinced that my spelling it out was the most tasteless of taboos. "I don't know what exactly happened, but I think—when Francesco was killed, your father decided that enough was enough. I think he testified when the police came—he told the truth about what he knew about the crime. Maybe he thought his position as mayor would protect him."

Isodiana Legato closed her eyes. Tears scudded down her cheeks.

"He was wrong," I said softly. "He couldn't protect himself. They—they had to use your father as an example of what happens to rats." An image flashed through my mind—the bottle of muriatic acid on the bookshelf in Donna Adelina Alvaro's salon. "The post office was being rebuilt and they dumped his body in the foundation."

Through her parted lips I saw her clenched teeth. "Who do you think They are?" she said finally.

The immortal question. "I think you already know. Don't you?"

Dawn bore mercilessly down on her face, white and purple and bloodless with terror.

"I do." I barely caught her words in the lifting breeze. "I know now."

Those were the last words I ever exchanged with Isodiana Legato.

79

MY SUITCASE WAS SITTING IN THE FOYER—I'D REDUCED MYSELF to just one for the trek through the snowy gorge. After much gnashing of teeth I'd said goodbye to all my books. I'd consoled myself with the thought that they'd live fuller lives in Santa Chionia, where books were so precious.

There was still an hour until Bestiano Massara's funeral mass. "You've got to relax or you'll wear yourself out," Cicca said. "Sit down and we'll have some chamomile."

"Relaxing doesn't work for me," I told her for the eight hundredth time in our acquaintance. "I think—there's one thing I still need to do before I leave. I need to apologize to Vannina Favasuli."

The woman was standing in front of her house, leaning against the decrepit shutters. Next to her, perched worryingly on a too-tall stool, was the bent old grandmother who usually sat sentinel at the mouth of the lane. As I approached, the old woman set her spindle down on her lap so she could take a pipe Vannina proffered. The itching smell of cannabis was unmistakable.

"My friend the teacher." Vannina crossed her arms in a manner, presumably practiced, that gently jostled her décolletage.

"Good morning, Vannina. *Kalimèra, gnura.*"

"What brings you to our humble quarter?" Vannina said. Her hair was combed and two pins above her forehead organized it off her face. She looked pretty today, and sane.

"I wanted to—can I talk to you inside?"

She ushered me to a seat on the bed, and what with feeling guilty I took it without trying to defend myself.

"I came here to apologize."

"Apologize for what, Maestra Franca?"

"For—for saying what I said in the piazza."

"A person doesn't apologize for telling the truth."

"Sometimes they should."

"No, *maestra*. We must live by the truth." Her ethereal hazelnut eyes fixed on me. "The only exceptions are for the weak, and the weak do not deserve exceptions."

This tongue-tied me for a moment. "I still want to apologize for saying those things in front of other people. I—I am humbly sorry I embarrassed you."

"Embarrass me, how?" She sat next to me on the bed and leaned in so close I thought she was going to grasp my chin.

"By—by telling the whole *paese* about—about Mico's infidelity."

"I knew Mico was living in Philadelphia with another wife. I might be crazy but I'm not stupid, *maestra*."

"Really? You knew?" Why push, why not just let her pretend? Because, I suppose, it was *so* hard not to want to put this irritating, hypnotic woman in her place. "Then why did you waste all my time trying to track him down?"

"Because they paid me."

A stretch of silence as her words saturated the putrid air.

"They . . . paid you?"

"Yeah. They paid me to rile you up. Convince you Mico had been murdered."

My mouth had gone dry as the rocky gorge in August. "Who are They?"

"Who do you think?"

". . . Tito Lico?"

Vannina gave me a disappointed closed-mouthed grin. "Come on, *maestra*, with your fancy university degrees. I thought you would be smarter than that. Why would Tito pay me to make you think he murdered Mico? That doesn't even make sense."

I felt my shock and humiliation gathering in my gut. "Who? Tell me."

She was shaking her head.

"Who?" I begged.

"Oh, *maestra*. Think it through for yourself." She bounced to her feet as gaily as a girl and poured herself a cup of water from her pitcher. "I'm parched. Would you like some?"

"Why are you telling me now, Vannina?"

"We ladies have got to stick together, don't we?" She spread her lips in a jack-o'-lantern grin. "And now *you* can thank me. Leave me a present as a gesture of gratitude."

I sucked on my teeth, trying to force my stupid brain to catch up.

"I am very grateful," I said, and the words grated indeed.

I took a thousand lire out of my wallet and left it on her table.

80

I WORE MY BLACK DRESS TO THE FUNERAL MASS—I'D BE WEARING it for at least twenty-four hours, as I had decided to travel in it tomorrow, because why not be superstitious this one time and avert the evil eye? Why not.

I looked furtively for familiar faces in the crowd and spotted many, but not, to my relief and anxiety, Isodiana. Nicola Legato had not been seen since the day Bestiano Massara was killed, but Santo Arcudi was there, in the second row, his arms crossed over his chest and a somber expression on his face. The hypocrisy of his attendance made me sick to my stomach. Next to him was Tito Lico the Wolf, his black head bowed, and his immaculate stone-faced wife, Potenziana the Wolfess.

I wondered if Massara's widow had an inkling of how and why her husband had died. What about Don Pantaleone?

At Filippo Squillaci's funeral in November, the genuine grief of the entire town had moved me. Today, the sobriety of the mourners had a different texture. We stood in the shadow of a horrific crime—an act of violence that seemed to have no repercussions. Every Chionese must have been boiling with their awful choices.

It is your obligation as citizens to fight back, Bestiano Massara had shouted across the piazza, and half the people in this church had stopped everything they were doing to come listen to him say it. *If you fail to stand up and resist now, how are you going to stop them from taking away all your rights?*

The sanctuary was a gas canister of Aspromonte justice, and any number of mourners might be standing there, shoulder to silent shoulder, trying to talk themselves into lighting or not lighting that match.

I cannot tell you what Don Pantaleone spoke of in his eulogy. It must have neither moved nor angered me, the kind of eulogy Bestiano Massara least would have desired. But I was running through the next twenty-four hours in my head—how I would manage if the weather was terrible or if we missed the bus from Roccaforte. Where everyone would sleep when we got to Rome—what I would say to my estranged husband when I showed up with a whole family.

I would just have to take each moment as it came and trust in my ability to problem-solve.

The faithful were receiving the Eucharist as the explosions started. The sound came from outside the church but nearby, and bounced off the walls louder than gunshots.

Pandemonium was instant. It was, I swear, as if everyone had been waiting for it. As the mourners, shouting, pressed toward the church's one exit, I thought with rising panic of the Hartford circus fire and grabbed Cicca's hand. We made it outdoors alive and stood in the piazza among the statue grotto of *paesani* with their faces turned to the mountain above us. There, under the ruins of the Saracen Tower, against the gray duffel of low-hanging clouds, the Alvaro house was gasping black smoke out of its third-story windows. Another boom echoed across the valley, and a hole appeared in the façade, baring a chunk of attic like a doll's-house diorama as plaster came plummeting through the shrubs.

A hair-raising shriek rumbled through the black-clad Chionoti. Old Adelina Alvaro, who had been piously attending the funeral mass, fell to the ground only a few feet from me as we all watched flames crawl along the new opening in the attic wall.

"It's the fireworks that were supposed to be for the Santa Chionia *festa*," Cicca whispered next to me. "Mela told me someone stole them from the rectory yesterday."

It took several moments for my synapses to connect, and then awareness of my complicity caused my heart to thud in my chest. "I never would have thought the old girl had it in her," I said out loud.

Cicca didn't ask me who I meant. "Her husband was a charcoal burner. She used to help him build the timber piles."

At first the strategy wasn't obvious; the little explosions side by side in the attic seemed like topical damage. But as the flames crept up the roof rafters, I realized Emilia Volontà had known exactly what she was doing.

She had decided who she was going to see in hell.

Cicca and I watched yet another explosion as people around us shouted and ran toward the cistern to try to put out the blaze, toward their children to get them out of the way, toward their houses for their valuables.

What do you do if something goes wrong with the fireworks? I'd asked.

Pray.

Run.

81

CICCA AND I JOINED THE ASSEMBLY LINE HAULING BUCKETS OF water from the cistern, and for three futile hours we tried our best. We gave up when the sleet started.

My back ached as we walked home arm in arm; my heart was heavy. The air was full of soot, the whole village caked in dampening flecks of ash. This would be the last time I'd ever walk home to Cicca's, and my memory of our road together would be forever singed by tragedy and bottomless wrath.

At her stoop, Cicca pulled out her brass key, but she did not open the door. Instead she stood as still as the saint stone, the skittering of the crystallizing rain on the cobblestones around us intensifying. Long seconds dragged by and I felt it, too—a disturbance in the storm-thick air. Cicca lifted her face at last, spoke of her wariness with her sad brown eyes, and tumbled the lock open.

The unelectrified foyer was as dark as the Amendolea cascade cave, but a shaft of murky light fell from the door of my bedroom, which was standing open, as I never would have left it. It meant my shutter must have been wide open, as well.

In that moment I wasn't even afraid—I was numb. Part of me had been waiting for the assault for months—waiting for the proof that I hadn't been terrified for nothing.

Cicca closed the door behind us and barred it, then took my arm tightly in hers again. My mattress had been knifed open, its hemp bowels dumped on the floor. My clothing, which I had so recently sorted for Cicca to distribute as she saw fit, was no longer fit for distribution. Perhaps Cicca could use the rags to stuff a new mattress. The euphorbia lay in a brick-red pool of pottery fragments. My trunk had been reduced to splinters.

My books were torn signature from spine in a way that made me heartsick—not as a proprietor who regrets their ruined belongings, not even as a book lover. The thought that sickened me, instead, was that whoever had done this held so little affection or respect for his own *paese* that he would willfully destroy something so precious. He didn't care about the value of a book, how it might change a poor child's life.

"I'm sorry, *pedimmu*." Cicca, looking very old in the storm light, knelt to gather a shredded blouse.

"Stop, *cummàri*, what if he's still here?"

"He's not." She rubbed the ruined cotton between her thick fingers. Poor Cicca had probably never owned anything as soft as that scrap that used to be a blouse. "You're not supposed to know who did this."

"Do you?"

"No," Cicca said, sounding more worried than convincing.

The cold, damp air circulating through the busted window was chunky with ash. We sorted the fragments into rags and kindling, salvaged what we could of the books, and blocked up the window with the broken bed boards. My heart was sore with fear and unclassifiable remorse. Every time a noise carried in from the street, I jumped, convinced a home invader was about to leap through the window, again.

As we listened to the bells of San Silvestro ring ten p.m., Cicca and I sat by her kitchen fire, sharing the same burlap blanket.

"I'll never hear them again," I realized out loud. "The bells of San Silvestro." By six in the morning, when they rang next, we would already be gone.

"I need to make you your favorite lentils one last time," Cicca said.

Then the reality hit me hard, like a fist in the chest. What were the chances I would ever see my sweet, stubborn friend again? "Maybe you'll come and see me in Rome," I said, willing my voice not to break. "Then I will cook for *you*."

Cicca blew me one of her signature raspberries. "You don't know how to cook."

"Or I will take you to meet my parents in Pennsylvania! You'll love my mom." Actually, she might hate her.

Cicca reached up and held her hand flat against my cheek. "I'll tell you what, *pedimmu*. We can meet in our dreams. Peppinedda will show us how to see each other."

Peppinedda never did come to me. In the sixty years that have passed since that day, I have never entirely given up hope that tonight might be the night.

82

IT MUST HAVE BEEN AFTER MIDNIGHT—WE'D FINISHED EATING and were chatting clingily in the cooling kitchen—when we heard the knocking on the door, quiet but clear as a woodpecker.

I saw my own fear plain on Cicca's face. Frozen, we listened to the pattering of the sleet until the rapping came again. Unmistakable.

We crept into the foyer. Cicca gestured for me to hang back, and I, coward, obeyed.

The visitor carried no lamp. In the cloud-banked light of the full moon, he was a terrifying silhouette.

"You!" Cicca said. Her fear had been smothered by anger.

"May I enter?"

Cicca stepped aside, huffing loudly to show her protest, and Don Tito the Wolf moved noiselessly into the foyer. He gripped his ornately carved walking stick in one hand; with the other he carefully closed the door behind him so it did not even click.

"You're leaving, *maestra*," he said to me.

"I—" I'd been caught. "What?" I tried.

"Now. You're leaving now."

Fear raced up my spine. Was this—a hit? Was he dragging me up to the Saracen Tower as he'd dragged the priest forty years earlier?

"I can't," I said, voice breaking. I wasn't ready to die. I'd been bullheaded—I'd made mistakes. None of them were commensurate, though—were they?

"Your plan is not a secret anymore," Tito said. His soft voice was thickly Greco. "You can leave with me or you can wait for unhappy people to come."

"Unhappy people?" In my panic, my mind struggled to piece together what he was saying. "You mean Santo?"

"You can take what you can carry in your arms. Now come quickly."

I looked at Cicca, stout and helpless in the thrall of her lifelong enemy. She had nothing to offer me in this moment—no comfort or guiding interpretation. "I—is Isodiana all right?" I regretted my words immediately—all I had learned of discretion was to hate myself for failing at it.

Tito Lico examined me with what looked like pity. "Isodiana is fine."

If she was fine, I thought, why was he here?

"I can't go with you." I was sweating in my disbelief. I would die and my parents would never know how much I loved them. "I can't."

"*Maestra,* my niece told her husband you were pressuring her into reporting him to the *carabinieri,*" Don Tito said. "That you were preparing fake evidence to get him and other Christians locked up for murder."

"Your niece said—" My whole body had gone cold. "Isodiana? But—Santo—Santo was going to kill her."

"Women who want to stay out of trouble stick by their husbands," Tito Lico said. "My niece knows what's best."

Unlike you.

My vision was liquid and I fought for breath. "But the children—"

"Right now, *maestra,* you should be worried about yourself."

Cicca was cowering beside me, glaring up at Tito Lico, the man she hated so much she would throw away his *salame* uneaten. This man had killed her brother—had thrown a priest off a cliff. Had covered up at least one murder—and that was only what I knew of. He had certainly done any number of unspeakable things I didn't know, done them to his own friends and family in the name of building his empire: subtle intimidation and savage violence, sneaky rule-bending and backroom appropriation.

Was I going to walk away with him into the night?

"What do I do, *cummàri*?" I was crying, despite myself. Don Tito averted his eyes; in Santa Chionia, only women like Vannina cried.

Cicca looked at me uncertainly, the wrinkles of her scowl still etched in her forehead. "You can trust him, *pedìmmu*. He wouldn't lie."

Don Tito raised his woolly bear eyebrows—he didn't care if I trusted him.

"Where?" I said pathetically. "Where are we going?"

"You'll see."

What were my other choices? At least if I followed him, Cicca wouldn't have to watch.

83

THE NIGHT AIR WAS RIFE WITH THE PROMISE OF PRECIPITATION. I followed behind Tito Lico, barely able to keep up with him on the slick pavers.

Slipping and tripping to my own execution.

As we passed the dark mouth of via Erodoto, I thought hopelessly of Ugo Squillaci, far away in Milano. If I screamed now, would his mother come running to help me?

But who else would come running if I screamed—how many of the Wolf's soldiers were lurking in the dark to help control me? How many innocent people would I be endangering by begging for help? I clutched my briefcase to my chest. In it were my journal, my wallet and passport, my pile of letters, a handkerchief Cicca had embroidered, and, pinned in the lining, the gold hoop earrings my mother had given me for my twenty-first birthday. It was the entirety of what I would take with me on the rest of my life after this moment. Maybe I had chosen the few articles I'd be buried with.

Why hadn't I listened to Ugo's warning? Why hadn't he tried harder to convince me to leave with him?

Still trying to blame other people for my bad choices. *Growing up is realizing it doesn't matter whose fault something is,* my father used to tell me. *It matters who has to pay the consequences.*

Don Tito's great back was a gray shadow sliding ahead of me through the moonlit fog. I sagged across the piazza after him, past the wreck of the post office and the gaping wound of the city wall behind it. I thought, hysterically, of taking a running leap into the ravine instead of following him farther.

Sheep are too stupid to respect. They'll follow one another over a cliff.

Abruptly Tito the Wolf stopped and turned to me, waiting expectantly.

"I—" It wasn't what I intended to say, but what came out was, "I regret that I made myself your enemy."

His eyes were as black as his eyebrows, a night deeper than the moonlit night. "I was never your enemy, *maestra*. I am the one who must apologize to you."

He never said for what.

We had arrived at the communal oven, I realized—we were standing in the saint's footprints. My heart began to pound even harder.

"You must be very careful," Tito the Wolf said. "This weather."

"Weather?" I repeated stupidly.

"Get in." He pointed into the oven's upper opening, the brick-floored hole into which village wives would shove their bread dough for baking. Then he touched his nose. Reflexively, I touched my own nose, and he nodded. "Hurry up. All the way in."

Watching us from the abandoned doorway across the street was the doomed stray dog with the too-long tongue. Of the two of us, he'd been better at surviving the odds.

"Come now, *maestra*. In you go."

Barely able to gasp in air through my constricted windpipe, I climbed up into the oven, pushing my case through the opening and ducking awkwardly to fit my body in. Tears streamed down my face. Uselessly, claustrophobia set in—discomfort with small spaces was hardly going to matter. Wasn't being burned alive supposed to be the worst way to die? I sobbed in the darkness, wishing I'd had the courage to take a flying leap into the ravine when I'd had a chance—at least it would have been fast.

"Goodbye, *maestra*." Tito Lico's words echoed at my feet in the mouth of the evil cave. "May you walk with the saint."

84

I WAITED, FRANTIC, SOBBING, FOR THE HEAT TO RISE UNDER MY palms, for the pain, for the awful death I had walked myself into, that I had not lashed out against. I never thought I would be one of the people who didn't fight back.

After all the stupid things I'd done in my life, was this how I was going to die?

If you were wondering what kinds of things you think about when you're about to die, in my case they were: Why had I spent so many hundreds of hours practicing piano when I was a kid? In retrospect they had been useless. I might as well have been playing pinball.

And: What would my mother say?

But the stones below me never grew hot.

How many minutes passed before I understood?

Too many—they took an equivalent number of years off my life, I am certain.

When I had stopped sniveling like a child—making so much noise I couldn't hear anything but my own fool self—I finally caught it: the whistling of the wind, but not at my feet. From ahead of me, in the black at the back of the oven.

Trembling with my new unrealistic hope, I pulled myself forward by my grazed elbows—the oven was not tall enough to let me crawl. I swallowed back the anathema of the small space and made myself keep going, deeper into the stifling blackness, until my case started to slide away from me—the back of the oven sloped into a ramp.

At once I had a new vision: a chute that would spit me out into the gulley, a last free fall against the picturesque backdrop of the Attinà torrent. Pulsing with claustrophobia, I eased down, palms and elbows clinging to stone. My case preceded me, as if valiantly to break the fall, until it slipped from my grasp and with a swoosh was gone, to wherever this adventure ended.

Trying to control the hyperventilation, I gave myself over to gravity—after all, it wasn't like I was going back up. Down I slid, belly to winter-cold stone.

The cave of the oven opened into the night air; the waterfall was crashing only a few feet away. I came to a rest on a plateau barely wider than my briefcase—I could have done with a couple more inches. But beggars can't be etc. With shaking hands, I clambered for my case handle. Fifteen feet above me, the Santa Chionia city wall rose, reassuring and ancient, out of the cliff face, and the beam bridge broached the abyss of the Attinà.

I was alive.

For now.

My ears rang with the sonorous crashing of the waterfall at its winter fullest. The darkness was not even frightening—it was ludicrous. If I fell, I would laugh at myself as I died.

I absorbed little information besides the swirling wet wind on my back, the slick grass under my fumbling feet. I inched across the plateau, briefcase pressed scuffingly against the stone of the cliff as I fought for the patience and mastery not to die. I came so close to the waterfall I felt its spray hit my back.

And then I was past the waterfall. I was—behind it. The plateau became a shelf—a cave, like the thousand-year-old Basilian grottos, more than wide enough for a person to walk. From underneath, the waterfall was a thin rumbling wall of darkness and motion, past which I could see, clear above me in the light of the full moon, the Bova side of the Bova road.

I walked on invisible feet through the thick, wet secret, under the waterfall and out toward the moonlight. The moon, I thought wildly, had always been my friend.

My feet appeared—the darkness was thinning. I was trying not to cry again, in relief and adrenaline. Crying never helped.

And then—because there was just enough light to see her—my eyes caught on the lavender-grays of the cave wall to my left. There she stood, in a storm of painted snowflakes, slender and diminutive—she had never had the chance to grow up—with a long Byzantine face and a pointed nose distinctly reminiscent of Gnura Emilia's: Santa Chionia, her precious book crooked tight in her right elbow, her left hand raised in benediction.

"Thank you," I whispered to her. My words were drowned away by the pounding of the waterfall.

85

THE ORDEAL WAS FAR FROM OVER: THE UNPLEASANTNESS OF Aspromonte roads in the dark; the awkwardness of waking up Dottor Iiriti's poor wife, Ippolita, at four thirty in the morning, shiveringly begging for her succor.

There was a morning wasted in Bova, during which Ippolita insisted I report everything to the *carabinieri* like a rat. I was stewing in unspoken promises. I had been a Chionota—or had tried to be—for five months. Now any of them who had ever had any affection for me would hate me forever.

I reminded myself that I believed in evolution. How could the justice system evolve to become better if it was thwarted and evaded at every step?

Wearing one of Ippolita's dresses, too tight around the bosom, I followed her to the precinct. I did my questionable part; I filed the report. I tried to parse my exhausted confusion and choose the correct facts to relay—my facts, only. My organization's property had been vandalized during a violent attack; a witness was beaten to death.

Could I identify the perpetrators? the *brigadiere capo* asked.

How would you have answered?

"I have no idea, unfortunately," I told Brigadier Captain Sergi.

"Surely you must have some idea, *signorina.*"

"I wish I did. My employers will be very frustrated that there is no one to hold responsible."

I met his eye for a long count of three, my heartbeat accelerating as I wondered frantically how much I had promised Tito Lico by touching my nose. He had saved my life, and I had broken enough oaths already.

"But there's a man named Santo Arcudi," I said. "Probably you are already aware of him from his involvement in the 1952 pension coach hijacking. He has violent tendencies. Also his brother-in-law, Nicola Legato, has threatened me verbally. Although I have no proof, I believe they were responsible for the death of Bestiano Massara."

There. I had made trouble for the ones who most needed trouble. Maybe.

"If arrests are made and this goes before the tribunal, *signorina,* you will be wanted for a witness." Brigadier Captain Sergi passed me his notebook and a pencil—adorable. "Will you write down the address where you can be reached for summons?"

In meticulous block letters I wrote down the address of Child Rescue's clinic in Cosenza, realizing as I did so that no tribunal would ever be gone before, that if I had ever believed there was a possibility for formalized justice I would have needed to commit myself to participating in the trial. Instead I was going to flee to try to protect my own life.

Feeling like a rag that has been washed out so many times it is worthless for anything besides staking tomatoes, I slid the notebook back across his desk. "You'll find me there," I lied.

"Is there anything else you would like to report?" the *capo* asked. "Any other illegal activity in Santa Chionia that we should investigate?"

"Well." I did not mention the arsonist who destroyed a private residence, the trafficking of illegal firearms, the voting fraud. "I have a question, actually."

"Yes?"

"Did you ever identify the body that was dug up in October?"

Brigadier Captain Sergi's dark eyes narrowed in consternation. "Dug up where?"

"In Santa Chionia." My heart knew better than my brain, and my heartbeat was accelerating again. "Under the post office."

The *capo* shook his head, his expression half pitying, half vacant. "I'm afraid I don't know what you're talking about, *signorina*."

86

ONCE THE REPORT WAS FILED, IPPOLITA RACED ME IN THE DOCtor's abandoned Fiat down the hairpin turns of the winter-eroded Bova road. She was a kind woman, and a sharp one, but I found it impossible to follow the thread of her conversation. I was distracted beyond salvation by questions I could not ask her. She got me to Reggio just in time to catch the express to Napoli.

The journey was long and I had plenty of time to consider what I didn't understand.

Was the body never reported, or was the *capo* part of the cover-up?

In either case, was Dottor Teodoro Iiriti involved? What had happened to the medical testimony he was supposed to have furnished? What would he do when his wife told him I had fled Santa Chionia in the middle of the night during a snowstorm?

It should have come as no surprise to me that a police investigation had been suppressed, or had never existed. How naive could I have been? A waste of time to even try to consider who was behind it—there must have been a hundred Chionoti who would have opposed an investigation, for a hundred provocative reasons.

How, how, how could I have been so stupid I thought I could get away with an investigation of my own?

But I had never tried to prove the corpse belonged to Ceciu Legato. All I'd ever done was track down evidence it did *not* belong to Leo Romeo or Mico Scordo. Ceciu's killers had no reason to believe I even knew he'd ever lived.

Who had paid Vannina to distract me?

Someone who didn't want me to find out the truth about Leo Romeo—who wanted me to go chasing geese.

Aching from my head to my stomach to my feet to my conscience, I flipped through my journal—bless my lonely hours of journaling—and checked. Whether or not it was a coincidence, Vannina Favasuli had approached me about finding her husband, Mico, two days after I so indiscreetly spoke to Emilia Volontà in the piazza—announced Leo's visa was missing from the *municipio* archives. I'd noted in my journal that I had been shaken by Gnura Emilia's unfriendliness, but also by the hostile expressions on the faces of the men who'd observed our conversation: besides Tito Lico, there were Turi Laganà, Saverio Legato, and the man in glasses who had turned out to be Santo Arcudi. Had one of those men paid Vannina to trick me into framing Don Tito for the murder of her husband? Was the point for me to report the Wolf and get him in trouble? Get him out of someone's way?

Or was it only to take my eye away from Leo Romeo—away from the five thousand American dollars stolen from his humble mother by the obscuring of his death?

Emilia Volontà had begged me not to tell anyone I was looking for

Leo. Why hadn't I taken her more seriously? I hated myself for under-estimating her.

But the men who had stolen that money from her—Roccuzzu Alvaro, Ceciu Legato—they were both dead. Who would go to such lengths to cover up a toothless old crime?

Someone who stood to lose something.

Follow the cash, maestra.

Not—Isodiana? Protecting her inheritance? Protecting her dead father's reputation?

It seemed—too, too far-fetched. Sweet, intelligent Isodiana.

Who had betrayed me to her murderous husband—who might easily have gotten me killed.

Did you ever figure out who the remains under the post office belonged to? she'd asked me as we'd stood in the ice-crusted moss of her alley my last morning in Santa Chionia. *Do you—do you know what happened?*

Not *What happened?*

Do you know what happened?

The train carriage was terribly cold, and a chill was spreading through my rattled bones. I ran through our last conversation again. She hadn't been terrified to learn that her husband had conspired to murder her father—no, she'd been terrified that *I knew* he had.

Women who want to stay out of trouble stick by their husbands.

I hadn't been protecting Isodiana from her husband; she had been protecting him from me.

I stared blindly out the window, shivering, coursing with rage and betrayal and humiliation as the gray hillsides clattered by.

She is a battered woman, Francesca, I eventually managed to remind myself. I could be mad at her, but I couldn't blame her.

Had Isodiana sabotaged me in other ways? Had she enlisted her aunt Potenziana to discomfit me, not the other way around? I felt sick to my stomach as it occurred to me that Isodiana might have been the one undermining my applicant pool.

But—had Isodiana really paid Vannina to slander her powerful uncle, to frame him for murder? Those ideas didn't fit together—Isodiana stood for *family before everything,* and Tito Lico was family.

What was I missing?

Who else? Who stood to lose the most if the secret of Don Roccuzzu Alvaro's emigrant extortion racket were revealed?

Someone who had inherited the dead don's clientelist network. I'd thought that man was Don Tito the Wolf. It was dawning on me now, thanks to my midnight escape, that it hadn't been Tito who ordered Nicola Legato and his accomplices to vandalize my nursery. He hadn't sanctioned the murder of Bestiano Massara.

To whom did Nicola Legato report, then? Well, obviously—Santo Arcudi. Was Santo Arcudi the real demagogue of Santa Chionia? Could it be simple leadership jockeying, Santo Arcudi using me to try to get Don Tito out of his hair?

Was hiring Vannina Favasuli for a role-playing con Santo's style?

I thought furiously, thumbing through the pages of my journal to see what, exactly, Vannina had said to me about Mico and when.

What about Pino Pangallo's missing emigration files for Mico Scordo? Or the missing files of Dante Nazzareno, the agent in Melito? Was it too much of a conspiracy theory to wonder if someone had had them removed to make me more suspicious that Mico had never left Santa Chionia?

Who had put the idea in my head about trying to find Dante Nazzareno in the first place?

Don Pantaleone Bianco.

Don Pandalemu, my friend who had let me down in my hour of greatest need.

Please, don't tell Don Pandalemu, Emilia Volontà had said to me that first day she ever spoke to me.

Don Pantaleone had told me, when I'd asked him for help finding a record for Leo Romeo, that there were no ecclesiastic records from the 1920s or 1930s. And yet—now my brain finally registered—when Nicola Legato had come to him looking for a property lien, the priest had had binders of records in his office.

Don Pantaleone, the only person I had told about Vannina's gun stash.

Don Pantaleone, who wasn't ashamed to have performed the marriage ceremony of the son of the Sant'Agata mafia don, a close, personal friend.

Don Pantaleone, who had petitioned Child Rescue to send me to

Santa Chionia, where he encouraged me to work closely with his cousin the mayor—until the election, when his investment in my project waned.

Don Pantaleone, entrusted by local government officials to step into the breach to handle money matters for the *paese,* to carry pensions to the old men in the absence of *carabinieri* to guard the post.

Don Pantaleone, who made hundreds of thousands of lire off a private school for Chionoti children while the mayor, his cousin, stymied the opening of any local public school.

Don Pantaleone, who negotiated timber contracts for Mayor Stelitano and for Santo Arcudi. The Aspromonte was protected from deforestation by government edict. How did Don Pantaleone get around that?

Priests aren't supposed to own property in their parish.

Priests aren't supposed to wear jewelry.

You know how much the Association charges for one of Don Pantaleone's meaningless diplomas?

There is no such thing as a criminal mastermind.

I was shivering, staring out the window at the Tyrrhenian, bitterly cold in my horrifying thoughts.

Murder, extortion, intimidation, exploitation—all those dirty facts had slipped away from me with the sour realization of how I had been used. Forget meaningful victories—inspiring hope, vision, and action. I had never interrogated the righteousness of my foreign mission. I had allowed myself to be a weapon of the hegemony itself. Bestiano Massara had been right all along. My own shiny credentials had blinded me.

You are not a battery; you are a wire.

I had been—I had been a wire. I had completed a power circuit that had ended a good man's life, a circuit that might end up destroying a whole town.

I looked at my hands trembling in my lap. I could have hated myself—I would have, at another time; I should have, maybe. But instead I was thinking about Emilia Volontà. Without her, I would have finished my days in Santa Chionia no more dramatically than any other well-meaning bourgeois agent of a failed charitable endeavor. Emilia Volontà had been the catalyst for everything that had fallen apart. And—she had been worth it. With her patient anger, her quiet rebellion, she had saved me from ignorance and misuse. I would never outrun my guilt over the price Bestiano Massara had paid for the fact that I hadn't understood the truth sooner. But if I was going to be a wire, Emilia Volontà was the kind of battery I wanted to hook myself up to.

On that freezing northbound train, I had no idea what was to become of me. In fact the years and decades that followed my escape from Santa Chionia have been generous. I might have hoped but wouldn't have guessed that I would be graced with so many opportunities to atone for my mistakes, to channel my energy into fighting for change as an academic, an educator, a policy advisor. All I knew on that train was that whatever came next, I would be the wire. I was encased in metal and surging with the will to conduct.

At Vibo Valentia a short, elderly woman joined me in my compartment. Without asking, she reached above me and jerked the window closed. What blessed stupidity—I had not even realized the window was open.

The car began to warm up immediately. The bent-backed old woman plopped into the seat across from me. I lifted my hand in a gesture of thanks and squawked in pain as it brushed against my skirt. Disbelieving, I raised my palm to my face so I could see, even in the shadowy corridor, the prickly pear needle sticking out of my skin.

My elderly companion examined me with consternation. I gave her my most American grin.

87

I HAD FIVE HOURS TO WAIT FOR MY CONNECTING TRAIN IN NAPOLI Centrale. I was vibrating with my revelations, and I was not done making them. There was a bank of pay phones in the terminal, and I braved the encirclement of teenage Roma boys to indulge my masochistic curiosity.

It was seven o'clock. I tried Dottor Iiriti at his Rome apartment and his practice before I finally got through to him at his university office.

"Franca! I'm so relieved to hear from you. Ippolita—"

"She's a treasure, doctor. I wish I could have spent more time with her."

"When you come back to Bova, she'll be waiting," he said gallantly. I surmised he knew enough about the situation to recognize I would never be back.

"There's one thing I needed to tell you," I said after I had run as

THE LOST BOY OF SANTA CHIONIA

quickly as I could through the necessary platitudes. "It's the lost boy of Santa Chionia."

"Who?"

"The body under the post office. I figured out who it was—in case anyone is still concerned with the police file," I said leadingly. He said nothing to assuage my curiosity. "Do you know if they identified the corpse?"

"I haven't heard anything of the kind," he said. "I haven't been called to give testimony in court yet."

I tried to parse this. Did he know? Was he one of Them? "I haven't told anyone but you, but . . ."

"Enough suspense, Franca!"

"The body belongs to Vincenzo Legato. Ceciu. He disappeared in 1952, executed, I believe, for testifying to the police—what is it?"

Dottor Iiriti was laughing sadly on the other end of the line.

I waited, annoyed, until he had stopped. "What?"

"My dear, you have gotten yourself all excited. Murder conspiracies and criminal networks—"

"I have proof!" I sputtered.

"You most certainly do not," the doctor said, still lightly. "The lost boy of Santa Chionia. Oh, you have a vibrant imagination. I'm afraid you have been misguided in your little detective project. The skeleton that was exhumed under the post office is obviously that of a female, one who has given birth at least once. So it was a lost *girl* you should have been looking for this whole time."

"A lost girl," I said blankly. This time, I did not ask myself if I believed him. The truth was rushing over me like a tide, battering against the cringing corners of my brain.

Through the din of my thoughts, I made out Dottor Iiriti's waggish words just before the call was cut: "Maybe you can investigate who *she* might be on your next visit."

88

IT WAS A VERY LONG TRAIN RIDE—THE LONGEST I HAD EVER BEEN on, two overnights sleeping upright and breathing diesel exhaust. I finally disembarked on Tuesday afternoon, wearing Ippolita's sweat-rumpled dress and my muddy waterfall shoes, carrying only my battered briefcase. My heart was racing but my head was clear.

I bought an espresso at the train station, then another before I got on the Metro, which was, as always, more difficult to find than one would have expected. I ate a nervous late lunch, a plate of *pappardelle* with mushroom sauce—because when has a plate of pasta made a situation *worse*? Eventually I could not justify killing any more time. I found the apartment building and rang the bell.

Anything could have happened—or nothing.

After a wrecking minute of suspense, Ugo Squillaci opened the door.

"Are you the woman who burned down my town?"

"Not the whole town," I said, though metaphors might not support me. "But how can you possibly know that already?"

"My mother called."

"... Called?"

"On the telephone?" He held his hand mimingly to his ear.

I opened my mouth to protest that there was no phone in Santa Chionia from which she could have called but found I didn't care. I was stinky, and I didn't want to take my eyes off of him.

I could never return to the place he called home—I had burned too many figurative beam bridges. There was no hope for us. And here I was, standing at his door.

"It's hard being homeless." His clear brown eyes were bright with amusement. "I hope you figure out somewhere to stay."

"I am staying with you," I said. "Unless you explicitly tell me not to."

His face cracked into a grin. "I'm not going to tell you that." He held out his enormous brown hand.

NOTABLE RESIDENTS OF SANTA CHIONIA D'ASPROMONTE
IN THE AUTUMN OF 1960,
MORE OR LESS IN ORDER OF APPEARANCE

Francesca Loftfield, American charity worker

Francesca "Cicca" Casile, landlady
Cicca's sister: **Giuseppina "Peppinedda" Casile,** (1896–1916), meteorologist

Carmela "Evil Mela" Nucera, Cicca's evil neighbor

Don Pantaleone "Pandalemu" Bianco, parish priest

Fortunato Stelitano, mayor

Giuseppe "Pino" Pangallo, municipal clerk

Giuseppe Vadalà, traffic cop

Sebastiano "Bestiano" Massara, communist

Saverio Legato, tavern proprietor

Salvatore "Turi" Laganà, loafer, of the German shepherd ears
Pascali Morabito, Turi Laganà's companion

Limitri "Palermito" Palermiti, shingle maker
His wife, **"The Palermita"**

Don Annunziato "Tito" Lico, "the Wolf," goatherd
Don Tito's wife, **Potenziana "the Lichena" Legato, "the Wolfess,"** formidable
Their daughter, **Giovannina "Ninedda,"** mother of **Antonia "Tota"**
Ninedda's husband, **Bruno Scopelliti,** bookkeeper

Domenica "Mica" Mafrici, of the clean fingernails
Her husband, **Corrado,** shepherd
Their children, **Maria, Antonella, Domenico,** and **Salvino**

Emilia Volontà, housekeeper
Her children: seven, including **Leo** and **Petrunilla**

Isodiana Legato, the perfect woman
Santo Arcudi, Isodiana's husband
Their children, **Olimpia, Giovanni, Lucia,** and **Antonino**
Isodiana's brother, **Nicola Legato**
Isodiana's father, **Vincenzo "Ceciu" Legato,** former secretary
Isodiana's mother, **Richelina Alvaro,** onetime princess of Santa Chionia

Vannina Favasuli, madwoman
Vannina's husband, **Domenico "Mico" Scordo,** angel
Their children: six, including **Niceforo,** an honorable boy

Donna Adelina Alvaro, a very holy woman, widow of **Don Roccuzzu Alvaro**
  (1875–1943), mother of seven, including **Olimpia, Rosalba, Richelina,**
  and **Gianni**
Rocco Alvaro, her grandson, son of Gianni; Alvaro heir
Francesca Scordo, Alvaro housemaid; sister of Mico
Francesca's daughter, **Maria,** also a housemaid

Ugo Squillaci, steelworker
Ugo's mother **Ippolita "Tuzza" Criaco**
Ugo's father, **Filippo Squillaci,** nephew of Cicca Casile

Gregorio "Ligòri" Scordo, shepherd, philosopher
His wife, **Teresedda Sergi,** mother of four children, including
  Antonio "Ninuzzu"

Giuseppe Petrulli, farmer
His wife, **Petrunilla Romeo**
Agathi, their daughter

Danilo Brancati, errand boy

NOTABLE NONRESIDENTS OF SANTA CHIONIA

Oddo of Bova, middle-aged delivery boy
Teodoro Iiriti, cardiac surgeons
Santoro Maviglia, Africo communist-anarchist
Giovanni Stilo, unknown

AUTHOR'S NOTE

The average Anglo-Saxon would ask himself:
Are they all brigands, or only some of them?

—NORMAN DOUGLAS, *OLD CALABRIA*

Calabria, where my grandmother was born in 1920, is the most misunderstood region in Italy. Even within Italy, general knowledge of Calabria is limited to its touristic qualities (white sand beaches, chili peppers), its abjectly impoverished recent history, and/or its seemingly unsolvable problems with its native mafia, the 'Ndrangheta. None of this is incorrect, but reducing Calabria to these points is about as accurate as describing the Troubles in Northern Ireland as a religious conflict—the tip of the nose of the wolf in the dark. You can't talk meaningfully about organized crime if you're not also going to talk about immigration, forced population movements, politics, multicultural heritage, colonialism, land reform, economic development, religion, and patriarchy.

Calabria's lack of representation is the product of the marginalization of its citizenry, who have historically been blocked from the resources that would allow them to tell their own stories, as well as a product of deliberate campaigns of disinformation and censorship by bad actors (which is to say, organized criminal syndicates, political entities, and others who benefit from the status quo). Until very recently, almost all published accounts about Calabria have been by dubiously intentioned foreigners. The quotation on the previous page, for example, is from Norman Douglas's *Old Calabria,* a 1915 travelogue that, unfortunately, is still the most widely read English-language piece of nonfiction prose about this part of the world. Douglas was a lonely traveler, embittered and often malicious. Yes, he had an eye for poetic detail, but he saw his human subjects as zoological phenomena, and by the way he was a pedophile. Suffice it to say, I have long felt my grandmother's people deserve less problematic representation.

I wrote *The Lost Boy of Santa Chionia* in part as a response to this dearth and fallibility of primary sources, and with a fiery desire to preserve for posterity a forcibly dismantled way of life. But I also had other axes to grind, and so this is not a pure historical novel. It is important to me that this text not add to confusion about this region that is so precious to me. I want to thank you, dear reader, for your tolerance for my homage, anachronism, and allegory. I have given you the brigands and the spicy salami—I hope you receive them with an enraged little grain of untaxed under-the-counter salt.

Not all the writing about Calabria and the Italian South is as troubled as Douglas's. I owe a debt of inspiration to other, better-intentioned non-natives who bewitched or infuriated me to the point that I set down five years of my life to offer this counterargument. I am similarly indebted to the Calabrian writers who risked their lives to write against the reality of systemic organized criminality. These two groups include Corrado Alvaro, Tommaso Besozzi (with a hat tip to Tino Petrelli), Umberto Zanotti Bianco, Edward Lear, Carlo Levi, Corrado Stajano, and most especially Ann Cornelisen and Saverio Strati. I am also grateful for the groundbreaking modern scholarship of Amber Phillips, on media representations of the 'Ndrangheta; Stavroula Pipyrou, on minority governance among the Grecanici; and John Dickie, on organized criminal syndicates of the Italian South. If you're interested in more fulsome notes on these and other primary and secondary sources, please visit julietgrames.com/further-reading.

My own education about Calabria has been enriched by the incredible generosity of Calabresi. This book's godfather is the writer Gioacchino Criaco, who was a stranger in 2017 when I awkwardly confessed my obsession with his family's ancestral home, the abandoned town of

Africo Vecchio. I am so grateful to him for his friendship over the years, not least for escorting me on my first trip up to the Aspromonte interior and for allowing me the privilege of editing his novel *Black Souls,* which taught me so very much.

As for godmothers, well, this book I wrote to honor formidable women has many such behind it. Chronologically, I will begin with Julia Modern, who saw the volume of Grecanic history on my coffee table and introduced me to her friend Dr. Maria Olimpia Squillaci, the modern face of Greco Calabria. This tireless and huge-hearted individual offered me introductions to fascinating Greco people, including the musician Danilo Pantaleone Brancati, who spent two weeks escorting me through past and present Greco villages and assisting with translation. Under their aegises I was able to interview people from Africo, Africo Vecchio, Amendolea, Bova, Bova Marina, Casalinuovo, Chorio di Roghudi, Gallicianò, Palizzi, Palizzi Superiore, Pentedattilo, and Roghudi. Thanks to Ugo Sergi and Lilo, Mimmo Catanzariti, Giuseppe Massara, Rocco Modafferi and Emilia Cartisano, Anna Maria Delfino and Aurelia Zirilli, Silvana Borrello, Cicciu and Saveria Marcianò, and the late Domenico "Millinari" Nucera and Costantino Criaco. As people like me always say, what I got right is thanks to their help; what I got wrong is entirely my own error. Many of my generous interlocutors have kept in touch and patiently continued to assist me (for years!) with my never-ending investigations. I especially want to thank Salvino Nucera, Tito Squillaci, and my dear friends Antonella Casile and her mother, Maria Volontà, ninety-nine at the time of this writing and an arresting witness to history. They are the true *luce dell'Aspromonte.*

Thanks also to my Italian-American interview subjects who helped me understand Francesca's reality, among them Camilla Trinchieri, B. Amore, Paulette Jenkins, Tina Witek, and Anna Acaputo. Sincere thanks to the activist and writer L. A. Kauffman, the author of *Direct Action,* for allowing me to paraphrase her tenets for activism, and also for sharing the story of her friend the late activist Brad Will, who inspired Sabrina's "be the wire" credo. Thank you to the many people who have allowed me to have a writing career, for whom gratitude never dies, especially Marie Miller and Megan Lynch, but including every bookseller, librarian, rep, and reader I have had the privilege of connecting with.

Thanks to my greater Calabrian family, Margherita Ganeri, Francesca Fragale, Luigi Mascaro, Caterina Gallo, and Rina Scalise, as well as to Jim LaRegina, a newfound cousin whose jaw-dropping genealogy work has rewritten my understanding of my own family's emigration story. Thanks to the greater Cusanos and the greater Loftfields for their inspiration and cheerleading. Thanks to my greater Soho family, especially Bronwen Hruska and Rachel Kowal, who give me the space and support I need to keep the machines running. And thank you, forever, to the late, great Ellen Raskin. In the words of Otis Amber, Boom!

Over the last twenty years I have studied the literary form and philosophy of the crime novel via the act of editing it. I owe many writers my thanks for granting me the great privilege of being their editor, and for everything they have taught me through application, but I dedicate this paragraph to my dear friend Peter Lovesey, Mystery Writers of America Grand Master, my model for how to plot a crime novel, but also for how to live with honor, dignity, and joy.

Thank you to all those who have helped this book on its path to publication. This list will be shamefully noncomprehensive, but here goes. Thank you to my early readers, Andromeda Romano-Lax, Rachel Cantor, Casey Donnelly, Linda Grames (that's my ma), Elissa Sweet, and Camilla Trinchieri (again). To Karen McMurdo, my first companion in Calabria, and Jennifer Ambrose, my protective muse. To the Time Traveling Circus and all the writer friends who have buoyed my work and spirits with their creative reciprocity and sympathy. To my non-writer friends, whose support and tolerance cannot be reciprocated. I appreciate you all the more for that, especially in the cases (the Sextet, Ms. Weiler) where I've blithely pillaged your names for characters. Thank you to my agent, Sarah Burnes, who understands my essence—other writers should be so lucky!—and to the whole team at Gernert, especially Rebecca Gardner and Will Roberts. Thank you to my exquisite editor, Diana Miller, a deep thinker of boundless patience and devilish intellect, and to the whole team at Knopf, including Elora Weil, Ellen Whitaker, Andrea Monagle, Casey Hampton, Jenny Carrow, Lisa Montebello, Beth Meister, Laura Keefe, Erinn Hartman, Anne Achenbaum, Reagan Arthur, Jordan Pavlin, and Zuleima Ugalde.

To my mother, Linda; my mother-in-law, Nancy; and my sister,

Katherine; each of whom trekked through pretty remote parts of the Aspromonte on sometimes dangerous data-collection missions for this text, and each of whom has at least one colorful story to tell about her adventure—we're going to have to save that for another book. Thanks to Katherine Grames (again) for the beautiful mapping of Santa Chionia.

To my mother-in-law, Nancy (again), and my father-in-law, Paul, who dropped everything and moved in during the early pandemic to help out with childcare. Without them this book would be a bag of index cards.

To my mom and dad. Their fingerprints are all over this entire crime scene, so I don't think the detectives need any further clues regarding their involvement.

I reserve this paragraph for Paul, who didn't explicitly tell me not to.

I'm going to close with a paragraph that contains spoilers, so if you don't like them, stop reading here. My grandmother Patricia Ann Loftfield Grames, a great reader, told me after my first novel was published: "You've written about your other grandmother. Next you have to write about me." I have not fulfilled that mandate here, only used her name, but I nevertheless keep finding new evidence of her DNA in *Santa Chionia*. Grandma was my first publisher; back when I was thirteen, in the very early days of the internet, she ran a short story I wrote on her website, Acacia Artisans. She was a woman repeatedly ahead of her time, and also a devotee of the mystery novel. She passed away as this text was going into copy edit. When her children and grandchildren gathered around her hospice bed, we took turns reading her Dorothy Sayers's *Busman's Honeymoon,* at her suggestion. This was how I learned that I was not the first writer to have weaponized a prickly pear cactus in the execution of a murder mystery plot. I am glad I had the chance to share this nugget with her; I am convinced she would also have wanted me to share it with you.

A NOTE ABOUT THE AUTHOR

JULIET GRAMES is the best-selling author of *The Seven or Eight Deaths of Stella Fortuna*. Her essays and short fiction have appeared in *Real Simple, Parade,* and *The Boston Globe,* and she is the recipient of an Ellery Queen Award from the Mystery Writers of America. She is editorial director at Soho Press in New York.